Richard,

I would have put a great scene in the book where two thieves meet, mounted on bike and cars, at railroad tracks. But the Phoenicians didn't have these ~~things~~.

Too bad. Better run me over before I make a sequel!

Best,
Fred

FIRE AND BRONZE

A STORY OF DIDO OF CARTHAGE

FIRE AND BRONZE

A STORY OF DIDO OF CARTHAGE

BY
ROBERT RAYMOND

ibooks
new york

DISTRIBUTED BY PUBLISHERS GROUP WEST

An ibooks, inc. Book

Distributed by Publishers Group West
1700 Fourth Street
Berkeley, California 94710
www.pgw.com

The ibooks website address is:
www.ibooks.net

ISBN: 1-59687-120-2
First ibooks printing October 2005

10 9 8 7 6 5 4 3 2 1

Printed in the U.S.A.

FIRE AND BRONZE

A STORY OF DIDO OF CARTHAGE

The Prologue

The thing on the pyre withered.

Bitias rocked back and forth in the bitter-sweet smoke, held erect by his bronze corslet and the spear butts he'd jammed into the dry Libyan soil. Around him, the other armored figures stood motionless, dazed by what they'd just witnessed.

"Oath-breakers!" Opposite the armored men of Carthage, Hiarbas stood tall upon his four-horsed chariot at the head of his army, javelin horizontal over his head. "Dogs! Defilers of wells!"

The curses echoed off the armored men around Bitias. Crackles from the nearby flames punctuated the silence that followed. Dido was dead. Without her, they were lost, leaderless, unprepared.

In the open ground between the opposing forces, Hiarbas' young gift bearer stood motionless, eyes gazing on the blacked horror atop the pyre, arms laden with the precious carved ivory box and animal skins. A sirocco curled a tendril of smoke around him before lifting it into the bright clear sky.

A loud clatter came from the Libyan column as Hiarbas launched his chariot forward. The team, long pampered by the Libyan chieftain, promptly brought the vehicle to a full gallop. He corrected ever-so-slightly, purposely riding down his own gift bearer who was oblivious to the danger. The ceremonial offerings scattered into the dust.

Hiarbas pulled the team back and fourth, crossing and re-crossing the pulped remains. A scythed wheel jolted over the ivory box, shattering it. His oaths were no longer Canaanite, but his own harsh language.

Behind him, his warriors began to swing out from their road formation like wings of some great carrion bird. Their crane-skinned shields flashed in the sun.

Bitias watched the fire-hardened spears drop into the horizontal as the Libyans formed up. With his own vision limited by his helmet, he looked to the right towards Hêgêsistratus, seeking guidance. The colony's general stood erect, large rounded shield to his side, twin spears upright in his left hand, bronze armor and helmet glimmering.

Bitias waited for Hêgêsistratus to say something, do something that might defuse the situation. Hiarbas' screamings continued. The Libyan ranks dressed up their line with trigonometric precision, clan commanders calling out their readiness.

Then Hêgêsistratus looked over his shoulder. Bitias turned as well to see Scylax the priest on the elevated slope of Bursa Hill, the women and children flanking him, the structures of their *Qrthdsht*, their Carthage, a backdrop. The priest exchanged a nod with the general. Bitias now noticed the bows circulating amongst the women. Bows normally kept stored away yet brought forward this day for the archery competitions that were to follow the wedding celebration. Dido's idea.

We're going to fight. The thought chilled Bitias' back like ice water, but brought little comfort in his sun-heated armor. *Seventy five hoplites, backed by women archers. Against hundreds of Libyan warriors.*

Bitias thought hard, but there was no diplomatic solution; the Libyan line was now advancing at a trot. No retreat—the blue Mediterranean was at their backs.

"*Grn'bn!*" bellowed Hêgêsistratus. *Cornerstone.* He'd anchored himself near the pyre, using it as a barrier against flanking. Bitias' mind recalled the abysmal training and the inability of the Carthaginian citizens to meld into the tight formation required. They were Canaanites, a race of independent merchants and not warriors; their failures in training proved it.

But this was war, not practice.

Bitias found himself stepping up to Hêgêsistratus' left side, touching the man's shoulder to assure him that he was there, and also to get the distance just right. His shield slipped forward to overlap. Then someone patted his shoulder, and he glanced sideways to see Barcas at his side, handsome face set as he peered towards the oncoming line. Shield overlapped shield as the line formed, a continuous clatter. Behind him, he could sense the lightly armed second rank forming. True ranks, Hêgêsistratus had said, should be many rows deep. But you made do with what you had.

Bitias wished for a drink. The bronze armor was roasting him alive. The hoplon shield felt as if it would pull his arm from its socket. He gripped his two spears tighter and used them as props to keep the shield up, the wall intact.

A bead of sweat trickled from beneath the leather cap under his helmet, stinging his eye. He blinked it clear.

"*Nsh'*!" rang the call to ready arms.

As one, the ranks transferred a spear from their left to right hands, raising them over their shoulders. Bitias momentarily feared that he would not get the first two fingers of his throwing hand through the leather loop at mid-shaft. But the line slipped around his fingers easily, the shaft settling into his palm.

The Libyan line had swept up to their king's position and he started his chariot forward, pacing his running men so as not to outstrip them.

Scylax's reedy voice drifted down from behind. "Draw your bows!" There came a creak from a hundred Scythian missile weapons. "Aim left, where their line extends beyond ours." The priest gave the enemy the space of several fluttering heartbeats to shorten the range before giving the order to release.

"*Tpp!*"

Like the locusts of last summer, the arrows hummed overhead. To the left, Libyan shields acquired quivering arrows. Perhaps twenty men faltered and went down, trampled by the following ranks.

If they get around our left flank...

Bitias' thoughts were interrupted by a rhythmic clanging to his side. Hêgêsistratus was rapping his spear shaft against the top of his shield. From the darkness of his helmet rose a chant.

"Dido. Dido. Dido. Dido."

All around him, the other men took up the pulse. The noise grew, a wall of sound radiating from the Carthaginian line. Bitias found himself shouting along with the others, heat and fear forgotten.

"Dido! Dido! Dido! Dido!"

Hiarbas' chariot was to Bitias's left. The chieftain's dark face twisted in rage to have *her* name thrown at him. The woman he'd been promised, now dead atop the pyre. But all through the Libyan host, Bitias detected flashes of doubt and fear. The men of Carthage, with their bronze and noise, must be fearsome to behold.

The attackers swept nearer. Bitias itched to throw his weapon, as if that might end it all. Someone chanted "Hold...hold..." calmingly. The dark men were almost on them.

Over the tulmit came Hêgêsistratus' bellow.

"*Tpp!*"

Bitias grunted as he heaved his spear, the line around his fingers aiding the force of his cast. His target had been a howling warrior, shield bone-white in the sun. He'd aimed at the man's head, hoping for a heroic cast. Low, his iron-tipped spear struck the shield opposite, punching through it and body behind it. All along the Libyan line, men were tumbling into the dust.

Bitias pulled his other spear from his left hand, swinging it up over his shoulder. Something pressed up against his back—the second rank, planting their shields against the forward men, forcing rigidity into the defenders. And then the lines came together with a crash.

Bitias thrust his spear forward, catching a Libyan just below his collarbone, driving deep enough to debilitate but not to foul. Something crashed twice off his own bronze shield. Over the press of colliding formations, he saw another flight of arrows and a chariot wheel spinning up and through the air, bringing a wild laugh to his lips. Then a lance tipped with an antelope's horn skidded over his shield from the left, ringing off his helmet. He sensed more than saw Barcas' thrust, heard a scream, and saw the lance-point quiver upwards.

He saw no men, just shields, spears, screaming maws, hate-filled eyes. His spear rose and fell, sowing carnage. It seemed to go on forever...

THE FIRST BOOK
ENTITLED MELQART

ONE

Elisha leaned far over the palace parapet, stones warm against her belly, trim legs cocked for balance. The falling sun flashed like fire across her gold headband, just visible in the spill of jet-black hair.

She savored the dry evening breeze, so welcome after the winter rains. Around her, the island city of Tyre recovered from its months of pounding storms. After four consecutive days of sunshine, the priests had declared Egersis, the time of rebirth and renewal, to be upon them. The festival had begun.

The marketplace fronting the palace was thronged with people. They moved in strange patterns, congregating here, scattering there. Shouts and merriment lifted past her high perch.

A wooden figure stood in the center of the expanse, the representation of the god Melqart. Its painted face looked west, away from her and her city. Its stillness seemed a form of god-like contemplation.

A pebble tapped against her back.

She ignored it, hoping *he* would go away and leave her to the peace of the distant festival.

Another pebble landed.

"*Y!* Leave me, Pumayyaton."

He shuffled out of his hiding place amid the growth of the palace rooftop garden, leaning against her wall with his perpetually-scabbed elbows. He was a gawky boy of ten, little older then she. His hair was cut in bowl-fashion, his head a ball upon his skinny neck.

"Greetings to you, gentle sister." Formal mockery.

She grunted a reply, watching the people below.

He watched for a while. Growing bored, he spat over the side.

"Don't do that." She tried to make her frown firm, not petulant. She'd been practicing. "Father told you not to."

"Father isn't here." He looked with some interest over the city wall immediately to the south, to the lines of tubby trader vessels lining the quays of the merchant harbor. "He's getting ready for his part in the celebration, the part he does with mother, alone in the royal chambers. Alone but for a dozen high priests of Melqart witnessing." He smirked. "Maybe we will have another sibling soon." The smirk darkened. "That is, if father has the wind for it."

She twisted and lashed out, catching him in the arm. The punch surprised him more than it hurt him, but he stepped back, rubbing his injury.

"*N'*, Elisha, calm yourself. I didn't mean anything. Father just, well, just seems so weak these days."

He's doing it again, she thought. *He's using that tone in his voice, that trick of his. He speaks and owns your heart. His words were evil, yet now I feel sorry for him.*

She turned back towards the distant goings-on. "He's your father, Pumayyaton. He's also our king. You should respect him."

Her brother didn't answer, simply leaning against the wall at her side. Truce.

A rough hymn drifted up, spontaneously rising, a gift from the people to the setting sun. On the roof of the massive Temple of Melqart adjacent to the Palace, lesser priests worked through their complex worships. Elisha's nose wrinkled at the aromatic mixture of brine, barley beer, and incense. Suddenly she felt a great love for the island citadel of Tyre and its thirty thousand inhabitants who swarmed within its ancient walls.

"Let's go down," Pumayyaton suddenly suggested. "To the street."

"Without an escort? Father would never permit it."

"Father is busy. And besides, what he does not know...." He left the remainder unspoken.

She looked back to the celebrants, feeling something drawing her.

"Come." He scudded through the rooftop garden brush, not giving her a chance to argue. She hesitated, then dove after him, calling for him to wait.

As children of the palace, they knew all the back hallways and passages. The royal kitchens were cold and silent, the servants and slaves enjoying the festival. The hall outside the royal bedchamber was teeming with holy men, awaiting confirmation from within. None of the impatient priests noticed the two darting figures. Finally, they reached a small side door, a single guard stationed there.

"Ho, Ib," greeted Pumayyaton. "We wish access to the street."

The young guard hesitated. "Young prince, I cannot permit it. King Mattan would have my head on a stick."

"Princes grow to become kings. Risk now or risk later. Your choice, Ib."

Elisha peeped over her brother's shoulder, watching the young man's discomfort. A moment later, he unbarred the door. It swung open in a spill of pale twilight.

"In Melqart's name, please return quickly, Lord."

Pumayyaton laughed easily, reassuringly patting Ib's linen armor in passing. Then they were through.

The narrow alley ran between the palace and temple. Its eastern end opened on a small private dock for royal skiffs. West beyond the gate rose sounds of merriment.

"We should not..." cautioned Elisha.

"Then do not." He was already strutting towards the gate. She frowned at her lunacy but followed him anyway.

What met her beyond the gate was the most wondrous and terri-fying experience in her young life. A great swarm milled about, laughing, yelling, singing. And she, Elisha, daughter of King Mattan, stood in its swirl without escort. It was beyond her experience. Balking, she nearly lost Pumayyaton in the press. Squeaking his name, she darted after him, grabbing onto his hand with clinging desperation.

The people around them were a cross-section of Canaanite society. Callused deckhands with short linen kilts and stained vests. Princely merchants, jewelry flashing, dark beards immaculately curled. Robed women standing in tight knots exchanging shrill laughter and timeless gossips. And fishermen, reeking of herrings and palm wine, purposely singing off-key.

Small stalls sold trinkets, biscuits and treats. While her people were the shrewdest of traders, the jubilation was removing that edge. As the time of renewal neared, merchants virtually gave their wares away. It was Egersis. The storms had ended. Melqart would be reborn. Life could go on.

Temples bordered the marketplace, houses for Melqart, Astarte, and Baal. Their torchlit interiors glowed in the descending night, their halls thronged with traders. Gifts, news, and information were exchanged. Bargains were struck. Tyre's vast mercantilism network was coming alive after its winter hibernation.

At that moment, a solitary horn shrilled from the palace. It was echoed by a dozen trumpets, screaming into the night air. King Mattan and his queen had performed their duties in accordance with the festival. The crowd gave a lusty, good-natured cheer, and Elisha's ears rang. The noise redoubled when torches flamed the kindling at the wooden effigy's feet. The figure went up in a rush, painting the thrilled crowd in flickering orange.

Unable to see the crowning moment of the event, the children backed up the steps to the temple of Astarte. The priestesses, reeking of an odor as pungent as the fishermen, made room for the two. As they watched, the burning figure collapsed, tumbling off its platform and showering the careless onlookers in sparks. A moment later, a trap door sprang open and a capering figure leapt onto the glowing embers of the platform. Its robes were white and red, swirling like muscles and bones, the embodiment of rebirth. It jumped downwards and dashed through the crowd. People strained to touch it in passing, hopeful for the good fortune it might bring.

The stars were burning steadily in the sky now, and a chill was coming on. There was still dancing and singing, but the celebration was now unstructured, losing momentum. Some people were leaving, making towards the darker avenues and their homes.

Pumayyaton was moving again, taking it all in. Elisha followed, but like the wooden image of Melqart, her excitement was burning low. She thought of her pallet and the sleep that would follow. But there was still confusion and carousal taking place in the square, coarse yelling, crude singing, nothing she wished to face alone. She was thinking of what she could say that might make her brother consider returning home when he suddenly stopped short, causing her to bump into his back. Questioningly, she looked around his side.

They were standing near the canal that bisected the island in two, linking its northern and southern harbors. A broad bank of rough stone steps led to water pungent with sewage and pitch. The torches were distant here, the lighting uncertain. Elisha was about to ask her brother why he'd stopped when she realized that they weren't alone.

Two people reclined on the steps a short distance off. At first, she thought they were wrestling. Then she realized that it was a man and a woman, and what they were engaged in was not any sport she was familiar with. It was confusing, strange, and clumsy.

"What are they doing?" she whispered.

Pumayyaton stood easily, his smirk apparent even in the gloom. "It's how the *'bny*, the lower classes, perform Egersis." He made no attempt to lower his voice.

Elisha squinted into the dark, attempting to see more. This shuddering confusion could not be the same act of divinity that her father and mother performed. She could not imagine how a desperate embrace such as this could somehow lead to the human that she was. Melqart could not have structured things in this way.

Just then, the man craned his head about. Seeing the children, he snarled, "*Lys*! Can I have no peace, no privacy? Be gone!"

Pumayyaton stood quietly for a moment. Then he nodded. "Be gone? Certainly, sir. At once." He started walking again, passing one step up from the couple. Following behind, she almost missed his sudden smooth stoop. The square stone in his bony hands. The downswing. The crack of a head staving in.

Blood spread from the curious concavity atop the man's skull. In death, he shuddered, bringing a moan from his partner, then a horrified scream of realization. Elisha stood frozen, and would have remained rooted for eternity had not Pumayyaton grabbed her hand. Suddenly they were running, dodging through the crowds of the square once again. Neither royalty nor murderers. Just two children mingling in the festival's press.

She could see the roofline of the palace reflecting the torchlight of the square, and suddenly Elisha wanted the security of her pallet more than anything in the world. Tears of confusion welled up in her dark eyes, but she dashed them away, lest Pumayyaton see them.

"Don't worry," he assured her without looking back, "They were only *'bny*."

The throne room took up a large part of the palace's upper floor. Columned openings looked over the island city and the Upper Sea beyond. Rugs and skins covered the floors, gifts from a dozen lands. At the head of the chamber was an ivory settee.

The long day of kingship was nearly at an end. The orange dusk poured through the western opening across King Mattan. It painted his frail white skin and gray hair in false tones of health.

Elisha observed from the concealment of the servant's area, watching her father speak with the man before him. In the haze of sunset, she could not identify the figure. No matter. Their quiet talk was winding down.

Two servants waited respectfully behind the lattice screen with her. They were on duty, ready to assist the king. When she'd slipped from the back stairs into the screened area with them, their conversation ceased, their eyes focused on nothing. In the company of their silence, she wondered about what her brother had said.

Only *'bny*. Only the lower class.

Was it true?

Finally the conversation ended. The broad man facing her father bowed in respect, turning to leave. With dignity suiting to her station, she slipped around the screen and approached the throne, moving to pass the departing man. Seeing her, he stopped with a broad smile.

"Sparrow," he beamed with a voice as deep as the sea. He bowed deeply, white linen robes flowing across his broad form. His head was hairless, shaved in the manner of priests.

"Uncle Arherbas," she felt her own smile blossom. "Were you here on Melqart's behalf?"

"My own, little one." He tousled her thick hair, purposefully dislodging her narrow headband. It was his game with her, annoying and endearing. "Nay, not the business of gods and kings. Just one brother visiting another."

She felt her smile fade. "How is father fairing?"

"Not badly." *But not well,* his dark eyes added.

She could not tarry—the king would be tired after the long day of royal business. She went up on tiptoe and kissed the silky cheek. Arherbas chuckled in response, then drew back into the dignified presence his office demanded, departing.

She continued across the cool floor to the throne. Her uncle had not lied; her father had slipped further. He slumped across the ivory seat, his face drawn. Every movement came at a cost. She'd seen men like this, old men, sitting in the sun, forgotten by every god save Mot, ruler of the underworld. For men who'd enjoyed their full lives, such an ending was natural. On her father, just thirty-one years old, it was obscene.

She pushed the worry from her face, bowing. Mattan's smile unfolded like crumpled papyrus. He gestured to nearby pillows. "Sit, my child. What a blessing family is. First a visit from my brother. Now my daughter." He squinted into the growing shadows. "Pumayyaton did not come with you?"

"After the day's lessons, he trains during the evening's cool. Guardsman Ib tutors him in the military arts."

"Well, there is nothing wrong with that. A king must be prepared."

Elisha flinched at her father's reference to Pumayyaton as king. Such would occur in the time beyond his.

"I have..." she frowned, "questions. Father, I seek your wisdom."

"So serious for one your age. I find it becoming."

She ignored him.

"Father, are people different?"

He sat still in the waning sunlight, and for a moment she'd wondered if he'd dropped into a nap. His words, when they came, were as slow and soft as a summer's breeze.

"My time in this world has been short, but my experience, broad.

I've met many races of men. Aye, they are different. Witness the Egyptians, once a race of conquerors. They exacted tribute from the people of Canaan, our timber and dyes. Yet now they are diluted, constantly bickering about religion and primarily focused on their incessant civil wars.

"The Greeks, to the north, are as different from each other as they are from the rest of the world. Their cities are like pebbles on a gameboard, seeking advantage over one another.

"And then there are the Assyrians." Here her father paused, licking his dry lips, gathering his breath. "Warriors. Their eastern grasslands are vast, and it is as if their armies spring directly from the soil. Two or three years pass and their chariots roll again, crushing the lesser nations." A dry laugh followed. "But their pony carts can't cross the channel to our island. They stand on the shore, screaming their threats, building their skull mounds, demanding tribute, but they cannot take us. Not now. Not ever." He paused again, and when he continued, his voice had a note of regret. "If El saw fit to give me the gift of more years, I might have truly repaid those *ogl-hnorm*, those chariot-boys, just as was done at Qarqar." He smiled at the images in his fading mind.

Elisha remained still for a moment. "Father, I understand that every race in the world has its own gods, and people are cast in their image, explaining the differences between races. But what of the people *of* that race? Are they different from one another?" An image flickered briefly in her mind, a corpse sprawled on stone steps. "Are the *'bny*, the poor, inferior?"

Mattan sat still, the only sign of life the raising of an eyebrow.

"Ah." A wry smile flickered into being. "The princess ponders her place in this world."

"Father, it is not about me..."

"Tell me, daughter. What are donkeys good for?"

She blinked, unsure of the question. His expression was masked in the gloom, his tone by his weariness.

"Donkeys carry great loads."

"And horses?"

"Horses travel quickly. They pull chariots."

"And what of the fishes in the sea?"

"They provide us with subsistence."

"And would you harness a chariot to a fish?"

In spite of her desire to appear adult, Elisha giggled. She shook her head no. Her father continued.

"Every animal performs a certain task well. They carry, they pull, they feed. The master rewards the animal for performing the tasks it is best suited for. But the master should not whip the animal for not doing a task impossible to it.

"The men of Tyre are like domesticated animals. There are those who are suited to building boats. There are those who transform the murex shellfish into purple dye. There are those who guard the city from pirates. There are priests like your Uncle Arherbas, who represent our race to its gods. And there are the *rzn*, the princes, who organize our trading fleets."

He paused again for breath. Elisha tried to not focus on his laboring respiration.

"The efforts of all of these men make our commercial endeavors possible. Without their unified efforts, we would be little more than a backwater island. Instead, we are a race of traders, reaching across the Upper Sea, moving the cargoes of dozens of nations.

"Every man of Tyre is important. All of them perform their jobs well. And none of them deserve the lash *nor* our disdain."

Elisha sat quietly, taking in the lesson. Against Pumayyaton's cynicism, her father's words were a cool balm. But there was one more thing that haunted her, seeded into her consciousness by that night beyond the palace walls.

"Father?"

"Yes?" He blinked himself awake. It *had* been a long day for him. For a moment, she almost didn't ask her final question. Then a frightful image of dirty bodies grinding away in the darkness returned. It disturbed her, more so because of the possibility that one day it might happen to her. Panicked words came out in a rush.

"A man and a woman, how do they have a child? By what manner does this happen?"

Mattan sat silently, his form silhouetted against the red sky. Elisha was glad of the darkness, that her father could not see her blush for being so forward. She took a deep breath and pressed on.

"Yourself and our queen, you must do something in the master bedchamber. Some act or service, something the priests witness and approve." Her father remained still as death. The image came to her of her father and mother as dirty and foul as that common couple, rolling about in that confessed, sweaty embrace. She pushed it away as impossible. "Uncle Arherbas told me that ten years ago, during Egersis, Melqart came and delivered Pumayyaton to the queen. The following year, I was yielded. Did Melqart actually appear in physical form before you? Were you frightened? And what..."

"Silence." Her father's voice was level, terrifying in its tonelessness. She pressed a small hand against her lips, realizing that she had begun to babble.

"Some day," he continued, "you will be given to a man, a gift of Tyre. It might be to a foreign ruler or a merchant prince. But you shall be our gift. I refuse for you to be tarnished with corruptive thought."

His voice had slowly risen. She winced, eyes on the carpet before her. A teardrop marked it.

"At that time, your husband will instruct you as to your wifely duties. Until that event transpires, you will not discuss this with anyone. Do you understand me, Elisha? Not with the queen, your tutors, nor the kitchen slaves. And never dishonor me with such impertinence again. Do you understand me?"

"Yes, father." She sniffled.

His voice remained hard. "Do you understand your king?"

"I understand, my Lord."

Her eyes remained lowered. He allowed her disgrace to root before calling for his servants. There was a whisper of cloth as they crossed to him, gently lifting him to his feet. Bearing most of his weight, they guided him from the room.

She remained kneeling for some time, her face cupped in her hands.

TWO

Elisha twisted in the sweltering air of the inner apartment, her cotton shift snarled around her.

The coolness of spring was gone. Tyre simmered beneath the sun, sweltered under the moon. To escape the closeness of the summer night, the residents of the teaming city moved their pallets to their rooftop gardens, seeking respite in the night breezes.

Sleep had become a random occurrence for her. Her father's harsh words had shamed her deeply. She'd tossed and turned by night, troubled by fears and doubts. Early on, her murmurs and occasional tears had brought an onslaught of concern from the older Syrian governess whose night-station was at the foot of the princess's pallet. Seeking solitude, she'd banished the older woman to the hall. She preferred to fight her demons alone.

Tonight, one of her worst nightmares revisited her. Her father, seeking to placate the Assyrians, had wed her to one of their generals. More beast than man, he showed her the thing she'd glimpsed on Egersis. In full armor, he pressed down atop her, breath hot and foul, lice wiggling in his unkempt beard. And he did *something* to her, something alien and barbaric.

She jolted up on her pallet, eyes blind in the dark, willing away the image. If only she could speak to someone of her fears, but her father had forbidden it, leaving her ignorant and fearful.

In the darkness of the room her hand located the small clay pitcher of water, located in the same spot every night of her nine years. She filled a cup, but found its tepidness unappealing and left it unfinished.

Closed and windowless, her room was a crypt. Suddenly she had to get out, if only to walk the halls or talk to the sleepy kitchen servants. With a rustle of her cotton sleep dress, she crossed the room, her fingers closing automatically on her favored golden headband. Slipping it on, she carefully exited.

The hall was empty, her Syrian governess having fled to the roof's coolness. A single torch burned low, magnifying the orange of the wall stones. The silence was absolute.

She drifted through the halls. In one or two key locations, guards drooped at their spears, struggling to remain awake. She easily circumvented them, knowing well the palace's routine.

The kitchen was quiet, its hearth fire burning low. Two servants somehow slept in the heat. A heavy woman lay atop the butcher block, drooling into her sackcloth pillow. Within the grain bin, a young man snored amongst the kernels. She hesitated to disturb them with her restlessness. It seemed so unfair, bordering on what her father had implied, the respect of nobility for the lower class.

A faint voice drifted over her.

She frowned, turning quietly this way and that, wondering what she'd heard. She was about to dismiss it when she heard it again. Halting, she turned to face its origin.

A narrow flight led upwards to the throne room.

She slipped across to the stone steps worn by a thousand years of hastening servants. The voice that drifted down the steep shaft was high-pitched, childlike, disturbing.

She ascended through absolute blackness towards an opening traced in faint starglow. The words were like threads, ensnaring her, drawing her closer.

"*Stand I...*"

There were few Canaanite poets; the harshness of their language frustrated their efforts. But the hatred that propelled these words sent a shiver down her spine.

"*...before the assembled people...*"

Reaching the top of the flight, she waited just short of the corner, her back to the cool wall. When the words came again, she identified the speaker.

"*...a king of kings, a prince of princes...*"

14

Pumayyaton.

She chanced a peek around the corner. The throne room was hazy in the starlight. She heard something stir from the throne but her vision in that direction was blocked by the latticework screens. Was Pumayyaton here with their father or was he alone? She felt a compelling need to know.

A frown crossed her lips.

In the faint light, her cotton shift would glow like a beacon, even through the screens. With it, she would not be able to get close enough to spy. And it would take too long to go back to her apartment for one of her opulent purple gowns.

A sound drifted through the screen, metal scraping against metal. *What was he doing in there?*

Almost without thinking, she shoved her cotton shift up over her head. Appearing naked before *anyone* would be a great disgrace, which would just add to her current burden. But she had to risk it. It was almost as if she were being forced to witness Pumayyaton's doings.

As the shift passed over her head, it snagged on her headband. A moment, its gold was cool upon her forehead. Then she could hear it tinkling as it tumbled down the stairs into the darkness. She froze, waiting to see if her brother had heard, but he was still speaking to himself with mumbling urgency.

Her shift went into the linens alcove. Now she was bare as the day Astarte had summoned her into the world. Where moments ago the air had been close and hot, it now felt icy. Any moment she expected a cry of horrified discovery. With a dry mouth, she glided across thick rugs to the screen to peer through its minute openings.

Pumayyaton was alone, perched on the throne in gross insubordination to his still-living father. His bearing was one of lordship, his expression forced dignity. He wore his practice armor, and in his hand was his naked bronze sword.

"So the Assyrian's ambassadors will speak with me now, will they?" A chortle. "Not a word for us before, but now that we have tumbled their chariots like market carts and put their armies into flight, they seek mercy? You guards, lay hands upon them and hold them. Safe passage from our city? *'Bl*, I shall grant such passage.

15

Take them to the wall and heave them over. Of course it is high, its base lined with rocks, but they shall be safe while in our hands."

Elisha's dark eyes remained locked on her brother. His play-acting on the throne did not seem like child's play. It bordered on usurpation.

He leaned back, arms crossed in supreme satisfaction at having banished the ages-old occupiers of their lands. Suddenly he looked up at an imagined courtier.

"What is that? You have captured *her*? This is fine news. Yes, bring her forth." He came to his feet, hands at his hips, bronze sword glowing in the starlight. "So you tried to escape to the mainland. Well, bear me no grudge; I only act in the manner of kings. I simply cannot risk my throne to any who might move against me. Not even my own sister."

Elisha's fingers tightened on the screen's canework.

"You beg forgiveness, whoreslut? You seek compassion from me, you who would endanger my rule? As your brother, I shall spare you crucifixion and the agonies it would bring. But your life I shall not spare. Shove her to her knees. Ib, take hold of that thick hair she is so proud of. Yes, that's it. Hold her neck out, just like a beast to be sacrificed." He stepped from the throne, eyes down on his imaginary victim. "Do you hear that, Elisha? I'm sacrificing you to Melqart, the god of the city. It is a more nobler end a usurper has claim to."

He raised his sword and in the dim light, Elisha could see the naked savagery on his face. His features, once comical in their boyishness, now appeared as a distortion of humanity.

With a snarl, he brought the sword down. In his over-exuberance, its blade sparked against the floor.

Elisha recoiled, her foot brushing a small urn. Its scrape was slight.

Pumayyaton froze, blinking into the darkness, looking towards the screen concealing her.

She could see his head tracking back and forth. A moment later, he was gliding in her direction, his weapon a low glitter in the gloom. She watched his approach, frozen in horror, a deer before a lion. In an instant he would be at the screen, able to see her.

She broke free of the lock of fear. Her first instinct was to dash for the stairwell, but there was no time. Against the painted walls he would see her clearly. To the left was the main runway into the throne's presence where supplicants would enter. Pumayyaton would come that way. She fled to the right, following the servants' accessway between screen and wall. Sometimes, at the head of the room, the screen was left open behind the throne so that King Mattan's physicians might comfort him during a sudden bad moment.

With the rugs aiding her silence, she reached the rear wall of the throne room. Through the screen, she could see the cold ivory seat. There was no gap. The panels could not be slid aside without making noise. She was trapped in a cul-de-sac, walls ahead and to the right, screen to the left.

She looked back to see that Pumayyaton had come around the screens and had moved to the kitchen stairs, peering into the darkness of the shaft, seeking spies. She prayed to Melqart, Astarte, and Baal that he would descend and investigate. If he did, she could slip out the main entrance and make her way to her room. She knew the palace well enough to remain undetected.

Pumayyaton stood in consideration, almost as if he were replaying what he'd said and how it could damage him. Eventually he turned, looking up the accessway between screens and wall. His small eyes sought to pierce the darkness. Nothing. The access ended at a large window.

Something moved against the star field.

His own fears rose. Was it a trick of his eyes, or had something really crossed the opening? He remembered his play-acting and how his words could be used against him. If it were a servant, he would kill them. Ib had shown him the ways, and there would be little question concerning a prince killing a nocturnally trespassing commoner in Tyre's palace throne room. Gripping his bronze weapon tighter, he eased along the screen.

The accessway ended at the large bay looking over the sleeping city. To either side sat large urns, used by servants for tossing discarded foodstuffs from the daily afternoon banquet. A slight reek rose from their maws; they would be emptied in the morning.

The prince stepped to the window, left hand touching the cool sill, right hand heated by the hilt of his weapon. The city was laid out before him, his city, Tyre. It glowed in the faint starlight and the phosphorescence of waves playing across the surrounding reefs. Distantly, a dog's bark echoed over the rooftops where thousands slept amid their small gardens. He could feel the dormant energy of the Canaanites resting all around him, a farmer's field radiating hidden vitality.

Soon its armies, navies, and merchant fleets would be his. He would no longer play-act, he would rule.

He had to be more careful, and quietly swore to resist the urge to seek the throne at night, to play out fantasies.

He stepped to the large amphora to his left. Inside was dark, and the smell of rotting food drifting like a corpse's breath. He thought about feeling inside it and frowned. The opening was silent, holding its secrets.

A tight smile came. Bringing his sword into play, he slid it into the opening. It encountered no resistance until the half-way mark when the blade bit into debris. He paused, then jammed the blade deeper, probing about. Nothing.

He thought how he must look; a true 'bny, probing through palace trash. He pulled back, looking towards the second amphora, wondering if he should check it too. Shaking his head silently to himself, he turned to go.

The throne gleamed through the screens at him, representing all his hungers.

He turned on his heel, took two quick strides to the container, and pushed it over. It struck the wall and shattered, its contents spilling, his sword already slashing through it. Nothing but rotting fish, biscuits, bones.

He stepped back, nodding to himself. Now the servants would have something to do besides lulling about behind the screens, gossiping. With a care, he stooped to wipe his blade across the rugs at his feet.

He'd been here long enough. Every moment added to the chance of an uncomfortable discovery. But before leaving, he went back to the window again and looked out at the city. And then he leaned well out, looking around the columns to either side, checking the ledges and the palace face above and below. Nothing.

He cast one more look around the silent area as he sheathed his blade. Without another word or act, he strode out, leaving by the main entrance, as suited a king.

For a long time, the stillness of the room remained unchallenged. Eventually, two rats slipped across the chamber, scudding to the spill of garbage. They ate full and well, yet their whiskers were agitated, their eyes darting. Their instincts whispered that they were not alone.

A moment later, one squeaked a warning and the pair darted into the darkness, back to their distant hole.

Against the adjacent wall, a rug flopped up and Elisha dragged herself out from beneath it. She'd suffered the heat and dust, biting her hand to still her whimperings as her brother had stomped about. Naked, dirty, and shivering, she peered through the screens at the throne. It seemed to glow in the faint light, and she wondered what it was doing to her brother. Pumayyaton was turning into a monster.

Like the rats before her, she scurried from the room, grabbing her shift from the closet before dropping down the stairs into the darkness.

The party stood on the royal landing. In the limited space, Elisha was pressed from all sides; servants, priests, her aging governess, and the goat whose lead she gripped. If only her duty were done.

She raised her hand to her forehead, compulsively feeling beneath her cloth cap for the headband that wasn't there. In the two days since her nocturnal spying, she and her governess had been carefully over every step and corner of the stairwell. She'd repeatedly asked the kitchen staff if any of them had come across it. Nothing. She'd backed her questions with gold and guarantees. Still nothing.

The headband had dropped from the world.

Impulsively, her hand rose to touch her forehead again, jostling those around her.

"Elisha, stop that." Uncle Arherbas frowned down at her. "This is an important service we must perform. We desperately require

Melqart's blessing." He looked north along the city wall. "The boat nears. Make ready."

The approaching vessel seemed to skim the water, propelled by its fifty oars. From the bow above the craft's painted eyes, a beardless young man gauged the distance, calling back to the tillerman.

Elisha noticed the odd figurine mounted on the prow. While many ships had distorted images of gods mounted thus, few were like this. Yam, god of seas and rivers, grinned wickedly over his raised posterior. She carefully placed a hand across her lips to stifle a giggle. Uncle Arherbas frowned.

Still, the craft appeared expertly helmed. The port oarsmen managed to get the craft moving sideways, the starboard team lifted its oars at precisely the right moment, leaving the black craft to nestle against the landing with the smallest of squeals.

"Right," called the young man as he moved from bow to amidships. "We're to pick up a consignment of priests, princesses, and servants." Elisha's animal chose that moment to bleat. "Ah, and a goat. If you would care to come aboard?"

Arherbas stepped over first, ignoring the young man's hand. Turning, he called for Elisha, helping her across the narrow gap, intently watching where she placed her small feet. The trio of attendant priests crossed next, the goat in their midst. As Elisha's three chirping female attendants came aboard, a dour priest passed the goat's lead back to Elisha.

Her governess remained firmly on the quay.

Elisha stood on a broad deck that ran the length of the fighting ship, from steep bow to hooked stern. To either side, the oarsmen were arrayed in two banks, staggered so as not to foul their sweeps. At the stern, a tillerman rested on the beam connecting the vertical rudders. At his side, a tall, bald captain watched the confusion amidships with barely masked contempt.

"All aboard," called out the young man. The captain nodded. The youth then turned to Arherbas. "Your pleasure, Holy Lord?"

"A mile out."

The youth called out, "Due south until we round the harbor! Quarter speed!"

A rower called out in a low chant, taken up by the others. The oars hissed, thrusting the craft into motion. They slid away from the landing, moving authoritatively into the strait between island and mainland.

Arherbas and his priests went aft to extend their complements to the captain. Elisha, alone with her servants, noticed some of the rowers leering on their upstrokes, their eyes traveling along the lines of her young body. Tugging on the goat's lead, she moved forward, taking up a position in the bow. There, the dwarfish figure still looked forward over its ass end and she felt a vague discomfort. She did not know what such a thing meant, but had her suspicions. She thought of her father's scorn and looked to the city walls sliding by on the right.

Her servants chattered, pointing out this and that. The goat stood quietly, looking seaward with uncomprehending eyes, ignorant of its fate. Elisha enjoyed the sun that warmed her, the breeze that cooled her, and the boat that rocked beneath her feet. Had she her headband, the day would be nigh-perfect.

"My apologies," called the young man as he pressed through the entourage. Gripping the figure across its posterior, he hitched himself up. "Oy! The boat! Make way!" A small skiff bobbed before them, making as if to cross their path. The boatman, leaning against an oar, matched glares with the seaman at her side. But the black penteconter with its emotionless bow eyes and flashing oars bested his courage and the skiffman backed oars. The youth returned the scowl with a grin as they swept past. Then his smile turned towards Elisha and she felt her breath check.

He was young and slender, competent strands of muscles standing beneath boyish skin. While not yet old enough for a beard, his black hair was long, standing out like a pendant on the wind.

"Permit me to introduce myself, my lady. I am Bitias, *shnymsht̲r* of this vessel."

"'Second-officer'?" The rush of water and wind intoxicated her, making her feel clever and adult. "Certainly this must be your ship, what with you ordering this and that."

"*Lys̲,*" he laughed, "I only borrow it from time to time. In truth, to the last oar and plank, it belongs to Commander Jabnit, the man

21

entertaining your priests. As his junior, he lets me run things from time to time, training. But I know _Sdqsh_. I've known her since I was but a boy, just big enough to pull an oar. I've been on her ever since, from Egypt to Ionia, Greece to Libya. She is my home."

"_Sdqsh_?" A giggle bubbled up. "_RearEnd_?"

"Yes, an odd name for a ship. Evidently, fifty years ago, before any of us lived, she was involved in action against Tjeker pirates. She managed to back out of danger with surprising speediness, eluding two foes who proceeded to foul one another. Her captain capitalized on their distress and took both, winning great honors. The name stuck."

He glanced over the bow, then called to another horse-headed skiff. "Way, Lord! Way!" They swept past, oars flashing in the sun. Clear of the smaller craft, he called to the tillerman to lay west around the tip of the island.

Elisha watched him closely, wondering how this boy only a few years senior afforded such command. Tillermen eased their rudders over at his word, oarsmen corrected their pace at his chiding. He commanded _Sdqsh_ and its fifty-plus crew. She, on the other hand, remained locked in her palace, frittering over lost jewelry.

Tyre lay due north, its southern harbor a confusion of shipping. He gauged its distance with a practiced eye.

"Does your ship berth in the southern anchorage?" She wished to sound adult.

"The 'Harbor of Egypt'? Nay, that is used primarily for merchant hulls. When we are at port, we dock in the northern harbor, the military one. But normally its just an empty beach someplace during a long patrol."

Elisha thought about it, how he would return to the sea and she to her echoing palace. "It sounds dispiriting."

"I wouldn't trade it for the throne of Tyre," he replied with a smile. She thought of Pumayyaton and his drive for the cold seat of their father's.

Bitias' attention had slid over to a pair of tubby merchantmen standing out from the port, their oars sliding in, their buff sails sheeting down, cracking open in the south-east breeze. Loaded with cedar planks, they passed the warship, bound for Egypt.

The waves began to pick up. One of her attendants, a girl from inland Hazor, was leaning over the side, sick; the other two comforted her. Elisha realized that she had never been this far out before. Tyre, its massive fortifications little more than a pinkish ribbon, stood well astern. A strand of hair had escaped her cap and she brushed it aside, eyes on her city. It was amazing to think of all those trading ships and caravans, spokes of a vast commercial wheel, centered on this single island. Suddenly she understood the power her brother hungered for.

A tug traveled up the lead in her hand. The goat was straining towards several small amphorae secured along the bow planking. It paused, looked over its shoulder to her with uncomprehending eyes, then leaned into the lead again. She planted her small bare feet on the ships deck, fighting the roll and the goat, using one against the other.

"Bitias," she called back, "What is in these urns? The goat seeks it."

"Cereals and water," he replied. "Provisions for long overnight runs when no shore is available. Pardon, my lady, but my attention is required elsewhere."

Unused to such blunt disengagements, Elisha could not even consider a retort when Bitias shouted, calling a minor course change. The tillerman responded. A moment later, a wave broke over a reef's crest, momentarily exposing its black coral. Bitias nodded after it as if it were an old, untrustworthy friend.

On the stern, Arherbas spoke quietly with Commander Jabnit. The captain nodded once. Elisha could sense a change come over Bitias. One moment, he'd been commanding the penteconter. Now he stood silently, ready to receive orders.

"All hold," called Jabnit. The oars dug in, bringing *RearEnd* to a halt in just over its length. Deprived of motion, it rolled in the waves. The rowers raised their oars, at rest.

The priests, with as much solemnity as they could manage on the rolling deck, started back. Elisha had been versed in her role in this ceremony. Representing Tyre's royal house, she started down the deck towards the three holy men, the goat trotting complacently at her heels. Amidships, they met. She noticed that one of the priests was slightly green.

The lead priest held out his open hand. "Melqart, god of Tyre, provides for his people. He has given them land to farm between mountains and sea. He has given them other races with which to trade for grains. The Canaanites have prospered, and Tyre has prospered. But now the Assyrians threaten our grainlands and trade routes. We call on Melqart to safeguard his people."

Elisha suddenly couldn't remember the words Arherbas had drilled into her. She glanced to where he stood in the stern. His face was easy and he gave her a reassuring nod. Her uncle's love brought comfort to her mind, stilling it. Suddenly she could hear his voice in her head. She spoke the words.

"I am Elisha, Daughter of King Mattan the Second, who was sired by Baal-Azor the Second, son of Ithobaal. I speak for he who commands Tyre. I offer this sacrifice, given from King Mattan and, hence, from Melqart, to Yam and Arsh, who dwell beneath the waves. We seek the abundance of the sea to feed the Canaanites, to provide subsistence and plenty in this time of need."

She handed the lead across to the priest. He expressed his rehearsed thanks and further requests for full nets, but she wasn't listening. Her part was finished, her words had been correct.

The priests led the animal back. Arherbas stood rock steady, the ceremonial knife in his hand. Elisha returned to the bow.

Her attendants were still hanging over the side. Elisha braced herself into the prow's concavity, watching the priests maneuvering the sacrifice onto the stern railing. Bitias stood next to her, unsupported, shifting easily against the roll.

The knife flashed down. The goat shuddered, then thrashed unexpectedly. A spray of blood blossomed into the air, coating the priests. Their grip slipped and the sacrifice, still alive, dropped overboard and disappeared beneath crimson bubbles.

"The gods certainly must understand," Bitias observed. "Mortals being mortals, after all."

THREE

As she climbed the back steps that led to the throne room, she scanned back and forth, as if the headband might somehow have been overlooked.

Some of her days were spent with tutors, some with carefully-selected playmates, but some days the lessons were more practical. Today she would watch the Royal Court conduct business. The air would be filled with heat, flies, and droning tedium. It was not something Elisha looked forward to.

She could hear the crowds as she neared the top of the stairs. A guard nodded as she entered. How different it all was from that night she and Pumayyaton had played cat and mouse.

The screen was still in place, dividing the room. On her side, the logistics of the court were well underway. Trays of sweetmeats and dates were readied for dispersal. Tea steamed from clay pitchers. Servants lined the walls, the head of staff reminding them of their duties. Papyrus scrolls were deployed like so many carpets, scribes and clerks scanning the figures, boning up the day's business. And along the screen, separated from their noble husbands, the ladies reclined on their pillows, watching the court through the latticework.

Elisha made her way down to a conspicuously open section of carpet down front, hers by birthright. She nodded to those on either side, her gold necklaces jingling. The women around her were so refined, with their long robes, their jewelry, their rings and arm-bands. Envy flickered low within her.

A short distance off sat her mother, a silently dignified woman. She had been brought at an early age from the inland town of

YaaHuun, her marriage to Mattan binding coast and highlands together. Yet the queen never had grown used to the port city's bustle nor its endless ocean, remaining withdrawn, a prisoner of choice within the palace. Elisha loved her, but found their time together discomforting.

On the other side of the screen, the men got down to business. At the head of the room, reclining upon his throne, King Mattan sat in some discomfort. His face appeared drawn and dark rings underscored his eyes. Elisha noticed his mouth was agape, his breath labored.

Arrayed behind him were the head scribes and holy men. She noticed Uncle Arherbas to one side, consulting a scroll. The high priest nodded gravely, stroking his naked chin with his large hand.

On the floor to his father's side sat Pumayyaton, his oddly-pro-portioned figure at odds with his opulent robe. His thin lips were pursed as he looked across the attendees, deep in thought.

A respectful distance from the throne sat the *mw'd*, the Council of Elders. The members who comprised it represented the various major noble houses. They provided the king with a sounding board, supporting rulings that were to their liking, vehemently arguing those that weren't. Elisha knew, from tired experience, that the Council of Elders could snarl over a minor point a whole afternoon, often while King Mattan napped.

Behind the elders were the *rzn*, the princes, filling what was left of the hall. As expected, the more powerful among them sat close behind their representatives, ready to whisper instructions. The lesser-ranked competed for what space remained, lining the rear wall.

Mapen stepped before the throne. Tall, bald, and bearded, his skull topped by a conical felt cap, the room fell silent beneath the chief courtier. His voice carried across the hall.

"King Mattan shall now hear the first order of business, which is a bid by Abimilki and his house to rent warehouses currently held by the throne."

The elder representing Abimilki gestured for permission to speak, earning Mapen's nod. The man stood, and began a humble approach that quickly turned into a recitation of numbers. Rental charges and surcharges. Fees for canal access. The value of replacing the aging cedar roof. Tax rates, escape clauses, continuous leasing discounts. Numbers numbers numbers. Elisha felt her eyes glazing over, remembering to cover her yawn just in time. It was making out to be a long day.

She shifted her position and studied the pattern on the carpet even though she'd memorized it long ago. Another member rose to speak. She stretched out a toe and played it along the latticework. After a time, she glanced over and noticed her uncle watching her, eyes intent. She guiltily snatched back from her unladylike behavior, tucking her feet once more beneath her long dress. Now two council members were standing, arguing about something. A prince went up on his knees, offering his own clarification. Elisha felt her interest rekindle at the strong words, but Mapen checked the proceedings and regained control. She sighed.

"A proposal has been forwarded for consideration," Mapen boomed, "restricting marketplace merchants from setting up stalls in the harbor area."

An elder stirred. "I would like to humbly put forward that such crude commerce interferes with the off-loading of vessels..."

Elisha's eyes went to the blue sky visible through the window so far away. If only she were up on the roof, leaning over the parapet, watching the people moving about in the marketplace and temples. She felt envy for the lowly 'bny and the freedoms she envisioned they had. And then her mind wandered to Bitias, no doubt on the prow of his beloved *RearEnd*, heading out. She imagined his black hair streaming back, playing across his lean shoulders. A feeling rose in her and she was confounded by it. She simply did not know what it was. She'd only known him for a short time, and she felt like he was a friend. But that wasn't right. She had friends, but she did not feel that way for them. Nor did she feel that way for Father and Pumayyaton. In some indescribable fashion, she felt something *different* for the young sailor. She knew that, if she could dare wish it, and Melqart somehow grant it, she would like nothing more than to sail about with Bitias, away from these plodding debates.

Mapen's voice: "A proposal has been forwarded..."

She looked to her father who slumped through the proceedings.

His tired eyes moved from one whining elder to another. But she could remember the way they flashed that night when she'd shamed herself.

She started. The women around her smiled, believing that she'd begun to doze and caught herself. She blushed at their assumption, but more to her own thoughts. Perhaps the thing that caused her such fascination for Bitias was that same thing her father had forbidden. Respectful of her father's wishes, she tried to focus on the proceedings.

Elisha squinted into the dark, attempting to see more. This shuddering confusion could not be the same act of divinity that her father and mother performed.

For a single moment, the *'bny* male became Bitias, his muscles cording across his taunt back. And the woman...

She bit her finger until she tasted blood. Her father had forbidden such thoughts. He spoke for Melqart. Further, the act had disgusted her. It was a *'bny* thing, crude and dirty and perverse. Whoever was picked to be her husband would instruct her in the proper noble ways. And she knew in her heart that whatever they were, they would be stately, logical, and pure.

The couple by the canal, the distorted figurine of Yam on the *RearEnd*, and Bitias smiling in the sun, all these things bothered her. She drew her knees beneath her chin and focused on the pattern of the latticework before her, her mind regaining its royal dignity. She knew that the *'bny* male was dead, beyond consideration. Bitias and his Yam-thing and leaky old *RearEnd* were most likely back out on patrol. All these things were lost to her, so she closed the door on them. Having mastered her thoughts, she felt a sense of pride come over her. She looked to where her father slumped and felt love for him.

Mapen shepherded the debates through the chamber, one after the other, like sheep. Servants moved about the princes, passing out treats and cups of hibiscus tea. One of her attendants appeared at her side with small items of nourishment; she ate them slowly, turning the simple act into a distraction. Outside, the sun topped the sky.

"An incident has come to the attention of the Royal House,"

Mapen announced, "that Hannon, a merchant engaged in the royal treaty-trade with Egypt, has discrepancies in his accounts. Dockmaster Jaminus has reported thus."

Elisha looked up from the last of her treats. She knew that name, but it took a moment to come to her. She and Pumayyaton attended writing lessons with other noble children. There was a young boy, Barcas; she thought him overly headstrong. But he'd spoken of his cousin Hannon who would head the family trading business someday. His training included acting as commander on one of the family's *gôlah*s.

Hannon stepped from the back of the room, waving down his council member, preferring to speak for himself. He was a tall man, slender but for the foundations of a pot belly that showed beneath his long tunic. Where younger Barcas was handsome, Hannon was homely, with a nose too big for his narrow face.

"This is unfounded," he snarled, eyes flashing. "Where is my accuser? Where is Jaminus?"

Dockmaster Jaminus had been waiting in the servant's area all day. Elisha had noticed him but thought nothing of it. A methodical-looking man with a tightly-curled beard shot with gray, he stepped through the gap in the screens near the throne.

"I am here, Hannon."

"What are these tales you tell, Jaminus? When we tied up in the Harbor of Egypt two days ago, you came aboard and examined our cargo. You looked at our listed inventory and said all was in order. We surrendered silver equal to the docking fees and royal taxes. And now you testify that I am a thief?"

"At that time, everything appeared to be in order. But later, when I looked over old records in the palace archives, discrepancies came to light." The dockmaster pulled a scroll from a nearby assistant. "This was your third treaty-trade voyage. You made one last year, and one earlier this year." He unrolled the scroll. "On your first return, you delivered 350 tons of grain. On your second, 340 tons. Does this appear correct?"

"It is as it occurs in the records," Hannon agreed.

"And this trip, you registered 290 tons."

"As you confirmed when you looked beneath my decks."

"When I looked under your hatches, I saw amphorae. They completely filled the hold."

Hannon nodded, squinting at the dockmaster as if to see where this led.

Jaminus rolled the scroll with a dismissive motion. "It wasn't until I returned to the palace to add your shipping figures to the archives that the question arose. If your ship can carry, fully loaded, 350 tons of grain, then why do your records only indicate 290 tons even when your hold was clearly at capacity?"

"So that's it. You think I am shorting the Royal Granaries sixty tons of grain." Hannon shook his head in disgust. "What happened, dockmaster, was that the Egyptian granaries ran short, and there was no knowing when the next Nile shipment would come. Rather than wait, we loaded with what we could, which was the exact figures on the scroll as documented by Egyptian officials."

"Documents can be forged," replied Jaminus. "He could have given you 350 tons and merely documented 290. Such things are not unknown. How else to explain your full hold?"

"Those were old amphorae, our own. We took our own urns to save on charges. They didn't fill all of them, and we weren't about to just leave them on the beach. Besides, they helped to keep the cargo from shifting. If you don't believe me, come and see them. My ship has not yet been fully unloaded."

Jaminus frowned, "Perhaps they have already been secretly unloaded. Perhaps the grain they contained has been removed."

Hannon threw up his hands. "Forged documents! Secret unloadings! How can I argue against your make-believe stories?" The merchant turned to the king. "My Lord, we are at an impasse. I beg for your judgment on this matter."

Mattan looked up. The heat and the long hours of bickering had drawn on him. He was breathing in short, shallow breaths.

Pumayyaton came to his feet. "Father, you are unwell. Clearly your duties have sapped your strength." He hesitated. "Do not take this as it was not intended, but someday I will be king. You said yourself that you were young and unprepared when Mot came for your father. You should allow me to judge this case, to learn my duties while you can still instruct me."

Mattan looked at Pumayyaton, then nodded slowly. To speak was an effort. "I agree with your thoughts, my son. Settle this matter as seems fair and correct."

Pumayyaton drew himself up. "I shall. But father, regardless of my judgment, you must not counter it. A true act of a king stands. Otherwise, this is nothing but a game."

Again, Mattan nodded. "Whatever you decide, it stands."

Pumayyaton turned to the dockmaster. "Let me see that scroll again. The one containing Hannon's manifest." He looked over the figures, the room silent around him. Then he looked up. "As part of our treaty-trade, it states that you departed Tyre with fourteen beams of cedar, four small urns of dye, and a sizable consignment of marketplace jewelry. Upon your return, you listed 290 tons of grain and two ivory tusks."

"The tusks I carried topside," Hannon confirmed. "I purchased them for my own use, and paid import on them, as noted."

"That is not the point. The true issue is that you used a royal ship for personal use."

Hannon stood silently for a moment. "That ship belongs to my family. It is one of four *gôlah*s that we own."

Pumayyaton pointed the scroll like a baton. "Tyre signed a treaty with Egypt. It is a matter of diplomacy and good will between our two peoples. Our wood for their grain. You enlisted your craft in our duty, agreeing to a fixed rate per trip. You were provided with incentives, provisions, and reduced port fees for your involvement."

"We appreciated the royal investment," Hannon sputtered, his face flushed. "I am not a thief, nor a smuggler. I followed our royal charter to the letter..."

"The charter states that you would carry timber, dyes, and luxury items, in amounts of our choice, outbound. In return, you would bring grain. There was nothing in the agreement concerning ivory."

The young merchant's temper broke. "There was nothing in the agreement about shitting, but you can assume we hung our arses over the stern railing, just the same."

Pumayyaton's eyes narrowed on Hannon.

"You seem to have forgotten your high-born manners. Your tone is a direct insult to myself, the throne, and Melqart. Someone find this man a sword."

For a moment, there was stunned silence. Then chaos erupted; the council leapt to their feet as one man, the *rzn* rising at their rear. From the floor, all Elisha could see were robes. She scrambled to her feet, jumping up and down to see. Finally, she slipped her toes into the screen's lower crosspiece and raised herself up.

Mapen was furiously swinging his rod at the crowd, his voice booming. Eventually he gained control.

"Sit down!" ordered the chief courtier. He held the rod threateningly over his head. "Be still! This is the royal audience chamber, not a marketplace!" Individually, and then in groups, the princes settled to the carpets. Soon only Hannon stood, uncertainty lacing his anger. Opposite, Pumayyaton watched with level gaze, arms crossed.

Mapen lowered his rod and voice, then turned to Elisha's brother.

"Young lord, there has not been combat in these chambers for hundreds of years. Would you not reconsider your demand?"

"No," Pumayyaton replied. "Kings do not reconsider."

Mattan raised a frail hand. "My son..."

He did not turn. "You gave your word, father. No interference."

The king fell back onto his throne like dust.

Mapen turned to face Hannon. "The option becomes yours, Lord. Duel or banishment."

Hannon eyed the child standing before the throne, half his own twenty years. He silently weighed the dangers of fighting and perhaps killing the royal heir. Balancing this was the thought of exile to one of the Canaanite trading stations far to the west. Either way, the bright future that had been his this morning was gone.

He thrust his hand to his side, opened. A short sword was slipped into it.

Ib had crossed to Pumayyaton and handed him his own sword. They conferred quietly, and Elisha sensed something passing between them.

Hannon made his way forward to the open circle of carpet, the nobles rising silently behind him. Elisha raised herself on the screen just in time to see the young merchant hesitate. Across from him, the child whose duel he'd accepted was advancing, sword in his right hand, a thin dagger in the left. Such a thing went against all convention. Fighting was a matter of standing shoulder to shoulder with your comrades, hacking.

Pumayyaton drew closer, pivoting his body, tucking in behind his sword arm. The dagger in his left hand pointed to the floor, a scorpion's tail. Hannon watched this all, confusion flickering in his eyes. Such techniques were alien.

"Are you going to fight me, smuggler?" Pumayyaton's childish voice reeked of disdain. "Or are you just going to stand there and let me hack you down?"

Hannon blinked, then settled into the traditional fighting stance; knees slightly bent and shoulders squared, perpendicular to the vector of his attacks. Such would bring shield and sword into concert before him. It didn't occur to him that lacking a shield, all it did was make him a broader target.

The clash of iron startled Elisha, breaking the silence of the room. Pumayyaton had made a minor foray, tapping at Hannon's sword. Hannon moved like a sleepwalker, attempting to figure a way out of this situation that did not involve killing this important child. He paid for his distraction, a moment later, with a slicing cut along his left arm. Disturbed, he took a step or two back.

"One of us dies, smuggler," Pumayyaton hissed as he advanced. "Take care not to fall into the ranks of your gaping friends behind you. This is not sport; I'll run you through should you stumble."

Hannon looked back to see just how close he'd drawn to the onlookers. He was running out of room. Awaking to the danger, he swung his blade, clashing off Pumayyaton's short sword. Rallying, he attempted to use his mass against the child, rushing in. The young lord matched him swing for swing, and then the dagger lashed out, nearly taking Hannon in the side. He disengaged, falling back, losing even more ground. Drops of blood from his wound left a trail in the opulent carpet. Pumayyaton moved closer.

"What's this, smuggler? With all your money and social standing, your privileges and training, you cannot kill a child?" To the rear, there came a chuckle from the servants along the back wall. Elisha wanted to turn and glare down their insubordination, but was powerless to turn away.

Her brother yelled and lunged, checking his action, startling Hannon further. One of the princes hissed a warning, preventing him from backing into the watching ring of men. He swung once at Pumayyaton who danced out and back, then dove right, attempting to get maneuvering room.

It was as if some demon suddenly inhabited her brother. He drove in on Hannon, sword and dagger flashing, checking the man's attempt to elude in that direction. To Elisha, it made no sense. Why should her brother take such a risk?

Hannon then went left, and this time, Pumayyaton smiled tightly, following closely. The crowd was to Hannon's right, her brother's left.

Elisha frowned, then saw her brother's strategy. With the crowd forming a concavity to Hannon's right, he'd naturally canted himself so that he could backpedal left should he be forced. This placed his left shoulder slightly closer to Pumayyaton's right. The merchant would have to swing clumsily across his body to get at his opponent. Her brother would not.

Hannon tried to swing once or twice, and Elisha could clearly see that he was in a bad position. Pumayyaton kept pressure on the man, forcing him back, step by step, around the circle.

"Slay him, Hannon!" someone shouted.

A second slash opened up across the merchant's left arm. He was fighting a losing battle and knew it. Suddenly, he made a wild swing and tried to force past Pumayyaton towards the center. The sword blades rang against one another. And then Hannon was standing still, a grimace on his ugly face. Pumayyaton's dagger was jammed to its hilt in the merchantman's gut.

A silence fell across the room. Hannon's sword fell to the carpet with a muffled thump.

Maintaining the hold on his dagger, Pumayyaton shifted his feet slightly. The sword cocked back.

"Pumayyaton, no!" Elisha didn't realize the voice was hers.

The edge of his sword caught Hannon along the line of his jaw. A grown man might have struck the head clean from its shoulders.

Given his lack of height and strength, Pumayyaton's blade managed to chop halfway through. Hannon's head tilted crazily, his ear touching his right shoulder, while a plume of blood gushed out. A moment later, the body slid off the knife and crumpled to the carpet. Pumayyaton, drenched in gore, looked down at the dead man. He let his knife, then his sword, fall.

For a moment, there was nothing. Then her uncle's voice thundered over the crowd.

"There is something wrong with the king!"

In the second before the crowd blocked her view, Elisha saw her father. Collapsed across his throne, face white, mouth gaping like a fish pulled from its element. But above all, she noticed the eyes. Eyes locked on his son, seeing him as if for the first time.

FOUR

"Ah, Princess Elisha! How nice of you to inspect your guards!"

Ib's mocking tones echoed in the dark corridor. It was unlikely that anyone would overhear his insubordination.

Elisha's scowl had no effect on him. He leaned against the palace's back door, his smile broad.

"I want you to tell me about what happened in the throne room today," she spat. "My brother is still a boy. He fought and beat a man. He has only trained with you for a few months."

Ib examined his spearpoint, thumbing away an imagined trace of corrosion. "Perhaps I am that good."

"Perhaps you are not," Elisha countered. "You are not much more than a little boy yourself. You are no warrior. You are just a guard, someone who is entrusted with the least-important duty during the worst shift."

Ib's eyes flashed. "You should remember that the greatest dangers to royalty often come from back doors at night."

"Then we should put better men at this post."

"Your brother has no complaints with my skills nor my service. It is unlikely that he will relieve me of my duties."

"He is not king yet. But you elude my question. How did my brother do what he did?"

Ib frowned at her closeness. With care, he placed the butt of his spear on the floor between them.

"I taught him the basics. Even *you* could learn them in a matter of weeks. Combat is not finesse nor an art; it's only simple swings and parries. However, for the last month or so, I have been bringing men to the palace, men who have fought in Ionia, Assyria, all over the world. Sellswords currently in Tyre's employ. They are the ones who know the techniques. How to watch a man's eyes, to predict what he will do. How to plant one's feet. A hundred tricks that will grant the edge. Like that daggerwork—a mercenary from Turushpa showed him that, just last week."

"Learning tricks from lowly *'bny*. I question my brother's wisdom."

"You should not. After all, he predicted you would come to me, seeking answers. He told me to give you this."

In Ib's hands, the golden headband glimmered in the torchlight.

"He told me to tell you that he found it on some steps. I know not what this means, but he said that you would understand."

It was as if the blood stopped in her veins. Her fingers grew numb. Her breath hung in her chest.

Pumayyaton knows! He knows I saw him that night.

Ib looked into her face, savoring her shocked expression. When she finally went to take the headband, he let it drop on the floor at his feet. She stooped to pick it up and he snickered at the image of a princess kneeling before him.

"The king has not long to live," he observed. "Soon Mot will come for him and a new ruler will rise. And with new rulers come new regimes. New princes. Hopefully, he will remember those who aided him in his ascension, who taught him valuable lessons, who supported him in his actions against his enemies."

Elisha looked up, miserable.

"Perhaps he will cement these friendships. Kings do that, you know. Royal weddings. Who can say how it will all come to pass. Perhaps, Lady Elisha, he will elevate me to general and give you to me as my wife. Image that; Commander Ib and his lovely wife Elisha, who will suck her husband's *'yr* at his command."

Elisha looked down at the golden headband in her hands. Her misery was total. Her father, with his contempt and his sickness. Her brother, a sudden enemy. She was as alone as she had ever been in her whole life.

She fiercely wished she could be like Bitias, in command of his own ship, men doing his bidding. How easy life was for him.

"*But I know* RearEnd," Bitias' words came to her. "*I've known her since I was but a boy, just big enough to pull an oar.*"

Bitias had been a rower. Somehow he'd elevated himself to second-officer. She couldn't assume that the rank had merely been given. Something told her that unlike herself, he'd made his place in the world. He'd had to fight.

She looked up at Ib.

"The king is not dead yet."

"No, but..."

"I could go up and see him. Tell him that you said the word '*yr* to me. And, how weak is the king, Ib? So weak that he could not tell his guards to crucify someone?"

"Pumayyaton would see to it..."

"My uncle is the high priest of Melqart. I could have a vision where his brother could be spared if a sacrifice were made. A dramatic sacrifice. *Y*, the Canaanites have not sacrificed a human in hundreds of years. As his favorite niece, presenting the vision, I'm certain that I could influence upon whose shoulders the honor would fall."

"But..." Ib gripped his spear, a barrier between them.

"Or maybe," she paused. "Maybe I will kill you myself."

Ib's eyes widened.

"I'm certain your '*bny* dogs taught my brother how to use fear. Hannon could not strike. Fear held him back; fear at what would happen should he kill the sole heir to the throne. So what would you do if I decided to kill you? Would you strike first? If you attacked me, you would die in the most horrible manner that could be devised. Your '*yr* would be burned away with a blazing rod. Would that be worth my life, Ib?

"And then there is the other possibility. Where I kill you."

There was a blur; Ib felt cold metal against his throat.

"This dagger, Ib? Should I press it further, into your neck? Into your brain? If you twitch, I will kill you. No matter what you do, you will die. Fast or slow. But it will be certain."

Elisha's black eyes were hard. Ib looked into them and saw death.

"Remember that," she hissed. "Always."

She stepped back, her gaze pinning him to the door. Then she smiled, a small smile of a royal to a commoner as she raised her hand to slip her headband back into place.

Without another word, she left.

"But he was your cousin."

Young Barcas turned from the sea to look at her, his elbows resting on the parapet of the city wall. His handsome face was carefully composed.

"My father explained to me the way of the world. Pumayyaton will be king someday, and we shall be forced to work with him. His disapproval could ruin our family. We are traders. All that matters is placing cargo in our holds."

Elisha blinked into his stony face.

"But he killed your cousin."

"Hannon was a fool. He brought great risk to our house." He turned back to the sparkling sea. "I do not wish to speak further of it."

The tutor paced between the low benches, sunlight from the high windows haloing his gray mane.

"...and this can be considered our most precious gift to the world, children. Not our dyes nor wood nor silver-craft, but our letters. Discarding the bulky hieroglyphics of the Egyptians, we have adapted only those symbols representing consonants. These letters form the sounds; the sounds words; the words sentences; and the sentences, history. Everything from a marketplace tally to the lineage of kings can be preserved with simple marks."

Elisha peeked over her wax-tablet. On the bench opposite, Pumayyaton spared her a cool glare. Barcas, at his side, remained oblivious. Behind them were some of the other children of nobility, boys and girls clustered in their desperate knots of fellowship. Her father hoped she would find friends with which to associate, but thus far she had failed. She found that even girls two and three years her senior were simple creatures of gossip and fashion.

The tutor turned at the end of the hall; her eyes dropped back to her tablet.

"So let us see how individual words can be used as building

blocks. The title of the king is *'mlk'*. The title of a noble is *'bol'*. A woman whose is born or married to this rank is titled *'ba'alat'*. If you were to formally address our ruler, you would call him...?"

"*Bolmlk,*" the children chorused.

"And the queen...?"

"*Ba'alatmlk*"

"And the high priest of Melqart...?"

"*Bolqdsh,*" called the children, but for Elisha's "*Qdshbol.*"

"You brutes could learn from our little *ba'alat*. Elisha is correct. Our esteemed Arherbas is our 'Holy Lord', not our 'Lord Holy'."

"She just calls him 'Uncle' and asks for treats," whispered Barcas just loud enough for everyone to hear.

"Since we seem familiar with the titles of the high-born," droned the tutor, "let us see if we can write them. First exercise: *Bolmlk.*"

With tongue peeping between her lips, Elisha carefully wrote the correct letters from right to left. Beth. Ayin. Lamed. Mem...

A hand cupped her shoulder. She craned about, thick hair spilling back. Mapen, the chief courtier, looked down on her with quiet eyes.

"The princess is to be excused from the lesson. She will accompany me."

The tutor bowed low in acquiescence. With silent care, Elisha stowed her tablet beneath her bench. As she turned, she caught Pumayyaton's thoughtful frown.

They crossed between the palace outbuildings, moving along paths winding through miniature gardens. While the sun was still strong, there was a slight chill to the air. They continued towards the main palace in silence. Once inside, they climbed the back stairs. Two flights up and a turn or two placed them before the royal apartments. The sentries standing watch at the door lifted their javelins as the courtier approached, permitting entry.

Mapen slipped aside and gestured for Elisha to continue. He remained behind as she crossed the small anteroom towards the shrouded portal, her steps inexplicably reluctant. With a hand on the curtain, she looked back. The courtier stood silently, arms crossed, eyes focused somewhere above her. She took a final moment to gather her breath and adjust her headband before pushing through the soft waves of silk.

Her father lay on his pallet, a wizened remnant of what he'd once been. His thin chest rose and fell, his breath rasping.

At the foot of the pallet stood Uncle Arherbas in his simple linens. He was flanked by the body of elders who made up the council. They eyed her silently.

One of the advisors, thin as a mast yet no longer as erect, stepped forward. Elder Shipitbaal scratched his unruly beard as he studied her.

"Yes, I know this one. So this is Elisha, eh? We've seen her often in court. Sitting behind the screen, yawning."

"That is because you are so dull, Lord Elder," she replied with a level tone and a small bow.

Shipitbaal's eyes grew so large, Elisha thought they might pop from his head and roll down his beard. Then he barked a laugh.

"'Ha! A good answer! An honest one too, I'll admit. She might do, after all."

Arherbas coughed diplomatically. "Elisha, the council has assembled thus to express concern for the events that recently took place in the throne room."

"The butchering of Hannon," scowled Shipitbaal darkly.

"The princes fear the future," her uncle continued. "Until now, the power that ruled Tyre was stable, a tripod based on the royal house, the temples, and the high-traders. Our government has outlasted the Hittites and holds firm against the Assyrians. It has placed colonies as far west as Gadar in Iberia. Now, it seems as if your brother Pumayyaton seeks to upset the balance. It is almost as if he is determined to discredit the princes, assuming their power. He seems..." Arherbas paused, seeking a diplomatic word. "Ambitious."

Elisha recalled the moon shining on the ivory throne and nodded.

Heedless of the fine carpets, Shipitbaal spat in disgust. "Ambitious? He's ravenous, I'd say. He won't be happy until he is cracking our bones and sucking out our marrow."

"Shipitbaal..." warned one of the other councilmen, nodding to where Mattan lay, silently listening.

"*Lys*! The king knows. He saw what that boy did with that sword.

As if we were nothing but cattle or *'bny*. We are merchants! Our ancestors built Tyre! What good would all that dye and timber El blessed the Canaanites with had we not learned the honorable art of transport? Our class, the *shrrzn*, the merchant princes, were the ones who worked with the kings of Tyre. The royal house provided capital, protection, and incentives. But we were the ones that ventured beyond the safety of our island. We were the ones who built ships for the Egyptians to use in the Southern Sea, opening up trade with the East. We were the ones who settled Cyprus. We were the ones who placed trading stations along the coasts of the Upper Sea, pebbles on a game board, all the way to the Columns of Melqart and beyond."

The elder gestured out the southern window to the packed shipping in the Harbor of Egypt.

"Out there, those are our vessels. They ply the waters of the Upper Sea, bringing back grain, silver, and gold to feed the voracious people of Canaan. Further, we trade with the Assyrians, iron for peace. They dare not move against us, since they could not locate the rich mines of Gadar if you pointed them in the right direction and gave them a kick in the arse. The merchant-princes, not the city walls, keep the Assyrian demons out.

"And all we ask is that our blood should not stain the rugs we imported, in the throne room we built." He shook his head in disgust.

"Elisha," came Mattan's dry voice. "We have decided that you should be queen. That you will co-rule with Pumayyaton."

She stared at her father, unsure if she had heard his faint words correctly.

"Father, that has never been done before. The throne has never been shared or divided." Concern came to her face, and she looked to the elders, her suspicion gathering. "You seek to dilute the power of the throne."

"That is not true," replied Shipitbaal, "yet it is not false. We do not want what Lord Pumayyaton seeks, to destroy power that checks him. Forces often derive benefit in opposition."

Uncle Arherbas noted, "Elisha, the nobles are represented by a council, the *mw'd*. They might bicker and argue but they eventually tend towards moderation. Imagine the chaos if Shipitbaal alone represented the upper class.

"The temples have their own council. It is not as formal nor as argumentative, but it exists. I meet with the priests who serve Astarte and Baal, as well as the lesser gods. We discuss issues of concern to us, to present a unified voice." He then pointed to Mattan. "Until now, the rulers of Tyre have been just. They understood and respected our system, the balance of royalty, merchants, and priests. But we suspect that Pumayyaton will destroy the equilibrium and become a tyrant. He must be moderated. By you."

She looked to the faces of the elders, to that of her uncle, and lastly, her father. Then she nodded.

"Very well," Arherbas concluded. "When the king has...passed on to the next world, the co-regency will begin. The crown, the merchants, and the temples are all in agreement with this. There is nothing Pumayyaton can do to oppose this decision."

Elisha took her father's hand. Finally, she felt safe.

T he wind off the narrows was brisk; Tyre a gray shape against heavy skies.

"Oy, Adon! Wake up! Are you ready for the final fitting?"

Adon started, nearly spilling the wooden tongues into the sand. At the far end of the half-completed hull, Cadmus shook his head. Adon cursed silently, pushing his worries behind other thoughts. He slipped the last three tongues into the hull-plank's pre-cut slots, checking the peg holes for correctness and finding them dead on. He drove them home with a small mallet. The plank now stood ready to receive the next member, its joining tongues lining its upraised edge like teeth in an old man's jaw.

Cadmus waved to three slaves who hefted the carefully warped plank and carried it over. As they neared, Adon looked about with an artificially casual air. The master shipwright and the commissioning prince were slowly walking along the mainland beach, heads bowed in discussion. Adon's mouth went dry. The cloth band holding the small bundle against his upper thigh constricted like a snake. He looked down, avoiding eye contact with the two men, focusing on shaving a rough section of a tongue with his shiny new iron knife.

"Pardon, master," huffed a slave. Adon stepped back, letting the man move the plank into position.

"Good. Dead on." Cadmus' voice carried on the crackling wind. "Lower it into place."

The bowed plank was eased down, the tongues slipping into the descending slots. For a moment something rubbed and Adon forgot the packet and the nearby prince. His sole concern was that the new board would fit perfectly. He motioned for the slaves to hold it steady as he crabbed from tongue to tongue. Cadmus watched from his position at the bow.

One tongue, just a little too long. Adon gestured to the slaves to raise the plank. As it cleared, he planed away a shaving with a practiced eye and a lover's touch. He studied it, heedless of the straining slaves. Finally he nodded and gestured, palms down. The board slid home with scarcely a whisper to reveal the shipwright and the prince, standing together and watching. He glanced away, calling for more pegs.

He'd gotten three pegs set when he noticed the master-craftsman and the high-born walking towards the office shed. His hand shook briefly, the peg shifted, and the mallet sent it spinning into the sand.

"Clumsy," chided Cadmus as he augered out some peg holes.

The door to the office banged closed. Adon thought about shoving his small burden into the sands, but the slaves were nearby, carefully measuring for the next series of tongue holes on the newest plank. It was fine. The prince would not notice. The *rzn* were beyond their wealth.

The next peg did not set properly. He tried to tap it in, but some minute distortion caused it to bind. He might risk forcing it in with the mallet but that could shatter or split it. Carefully, he shaved around its base with his new knife. So intent was he on his craft that he did not even notice the shadows on the sands around him.

An un-callused hand grabbed his shoulder and spun him. The shipwright stood over him, the prince at his back. "Were you in the shed?" the man barked, his fury barely checked.

Adon froze, unable to speak. The shipwright's eyes traveled down to the shiny new tool in Adon's hand. A moment later, the wright's fist slammed into Adon's head. He crashed into the sand, stunned, two broken teeth dislodged from his bleeding mouth. His kilt was flipped up; ocean breezes played across his arse. The wrappings were torn from his leg. A pause for consideration, and then the wright's angry instructions to the slaves.

"Beat him. Then drag him to the city guards."

Adon saw Cadmus turn away. Boards began to club his back, his flanks. He screamed in pain. A crack across the head brought darkness.

He woke on the dirt floor of a small room, the air foul and close. The hint of lamplight came through the heavy planks of a small door. Groaning, he pulled himself into a tight ball in a cold corner.

"Ah, my companion is awake," spoke a gruff voice. "They threw you in here a day or so back. Since you weren't eating your food, I took the liberty."

"Who," Adon paused to spit out the clotted blood from his mouth, "Who are you?"

"Me?" A coughing laugh. "A simple drunk, of no matter. You, on the other hand, are someone. I heard the guards say so."

"What do you mean?"

"Stole something from a *rzn*, I hear. Bad news, that. You'll go across to Tyre in the morning. It's the royal court for you." Another rasping cough and the smell of cheap barley beer. "You young fool."

Adon never saw his companion. He'd slipped into a shivering slumber, awaking to find himself being dragged from detainment. He still did not have his wits about him when he was frog-marched out into the weak sunlight. The beach lay at the end of a small, twisting lane, a horse-headed skiff waiting, the ferrymen accompanied by several guarded prisoners. His escort shoved him in and followed. A moment later, they were away.

Of the passage across, Adon saw nothing but the bottom of the boat. He slumped in his seat, his breath coming fast, propelled by fear. *What was I thinking? I was a craftsman. And to throw it away, for that?* He wanted to vomit. He wanted to cry.

He wished he were dead.

There was a jolt and the guards called for them to stand. A small jetty beneath towering walls, an open portal, darkness within. Gleaming armor all around.

Melqart, came the words in his head. *God of our city, have mercy on me.*

A rod across his back drove him forward. There were stairs, three or four flights. Adon wasn't sure, his attention on the ragged figure before him. And then suddenly they were in an anteroom, the guards calling for them to hold. A man, richly dressed with fine robes and a conical felt cap, faced them.

"In a moment, you will be shown into the royal audience hall where your cases will be tried. The events will be recounted to the ruling official; your punishment will be determined. Speak and it will go harshly for you. Do you understand? Guards, you may show them in."

It was like stepping into another world. Until now, it had been cramped cells, wind-swept jetties, rough stairwells. Now there were carpets beneath his dirty feet. Rich carpets unlike any he'd ever seen. His head swam when he considered their ornate patterns. His eyes came up to take in the fineries around him, the screens, the urns, the richly-attired *rzn* lounging along the wall.

"That is not Mattan," came a low murmur behind him.

"Nay, it is a child," replied another. "We are to be judged by a child."

A guard stepped closer, frowning, and there was silence.

Adon could not see beyond the prisoner before him, but he continued to peek this way and that, staggered by the opulence. It was then he saw the girl.

She sat behind a screen with a collection of other women. Hair the color of midnight was barely checked by a headband. Adon considered her face, so serious for one so young. Adon briefly forgot his peril, taken up by the girl and her intensity.

She was staring at something at the head of the room. Something he could not see but was invariably shuffling towards. Something that concerned her greatly.

On the wall opposite the screened girl, the princes were stirring. Adon felt a growing anger radiating from them.

Suddenly the guards were pulling the prisoner before him away. One moment he was there, the next he was gone. Adon stood unshielded before his judge.

It *was* a child, one who sat on the throne, looking over the court as if they were his toys. His smile was crooked. Adon felt a his knees waver.

Someone started talking; the *rzn* from the beach, robes and beard perfect, angrily gesturing at him.

"...but when the wright and I returned to his office to transfer the newest installment for my commissioned hull, it was clear that someone had been there. My urn had been shifted. Three silver shekel-weights had been removed.

"This *'bny* had been in the office. He'd gone to fetch a tool, sniffed out my silver with a rodent's instinct, and stole a portion. The wright spotted the new tool in his hand, knew he had trespassed, and struck him. We found the silver bundled to his leg.

"If it would please Prince Pumayyaton, I would ask that this *'bny* thief be sold as a slave on the market, the price he brings split evenly between the royal house and myself. In this way, all affected parties are compensated."

The boy before him smiled, scratching his chin. When he spoke, the voice was melodious.

"My father, in whose stead I serve until he regains his health, told me how the kings of Tyre owe their empire to the noble *rzn* who ply the seas, searching out new markets and opportunities for our people. Without them, this empire would not exist."

His smile grew broad.

"However, the *rzn* need also realize that the hulls beneath their feet were crafted together by *'bny* such as this. These men labor to build your fine *gôlah*s, and when you depart for distant opportunities, they turn towards the next hull to be built. In that, we owe the *'bny* our gratitude for it is they who built our empire. Not the king, not the princes. Them."

Adon felt a growing respect for the young boy before him. The words leant strength and dignity in his darkest moment.

To his side, his accuser stood silent, face set.

"And so, with all that we owe this man, how can we take his

freedom?" Pumayyaton's posture changed slightly, as if he were bowing to Adon. "Nay, he is too valuable to be sold on the market. It is our wish that he be returned to his former occupation. Inform his master that should he be cast out, it would earn my displeasure. Further, this man should be compensated for his time and concerns. Step forward."

The guard at Adon's side prodded him. The boy reached into an urn at his side and placed something into Adon's hand, something that chilled. Then he was turned and marched out. As he passed the screen, he noticed the girl. She was scowling. Her hands were clinched in her lap.

As he was herded down the stairs, it hit him. He would not be a slave. He was still a citizen. He still had his full rights and his life's work. He'd been plucked from doom by a child.

In the brilliant sunlight of the jetty, he looked into the hand. It was a gold *shql*, far more valuable than the pieces he'd stolen.

It was then he noticed the others with him, his fellow former prisoners, all smiling foolishly like survivors on a bloody battle field. And all of them had gold.

FIVE

Arherbas stood in solemn silence.

A priest pulled a fowl from a basket, gripping its neck to preserve the serenity of the chamber. With motions expert by repetition, he pressed the bird into a large golden bowl with one hand. In his other was a knife. A quick cut and the creature's essence drained.

As soon as the diminutive heart stilled, he slashed the bird open, spilling its innards into the blood.

Arherbas frowned at the results. From his experience in sacrifices, he saw mixed omens within the entrails. He nodded and the priest departed, taking the morning sacrifice with him.

The high priest looked across the temple's central chamber, feeling the touch of Melqart in the stillness. The *hekal* was spacious and ornate, as near to perfection as possible in the world of men. Golden bas-reliefs adorned the walls, separated by pillars. Small high windows allied with bronze braziers to provide a comfortable duskiness.

He felt the chill of the stones through the soles of his feet, the breath of air across his shaven skull, the wisp of priestly linens. All was in the moment. His brother's health, his nephew's schemes, all carried the weight of dust. His godly master was near.

Tetramnestus couldn't have that, of course.

Arherbas' portly assistant stood silently near the doors. His simple existence irked the high priest, pulling him out of his reverie and into the real world. He crossed the room slowly, composing himself into dignified neutrality.

"It is your niece," Tetramnestus told him, piggy eyes expressionless. "She waits outside in the *ulam*."

Arherbas nodded. Tetramnestus bowed, then pulled open the door.

In the room beyond, a huge portal stood open to the marketplace, admitting a chilling late-year breeze. The massive doors were flanked by two pillars, one inlaid with gold, the other, emeralds. Through the opening swirled the noise and confusion of the city.

Just within the door, flanked by guards, stood Elisha. Her lustrous hair was concealed beneath a felt cap and her robe was collected by a cloth girdle, carefully knotted in front.

"Sparrow, what a pleasant surprise."

"Holy Lord," she replied properly.

"First, your feet. Are they clean? You have tracked through the market." He placed his large hands on her shoulders, bracing her, allowing her to raise her diminutive soles up. He looked over her shoulder at them, nodding. "Fine."

A small frown crossed her face. As a woman, she could not go beyond the *ulam*, so she would not track dirt into the temple. Further, he'd not checked the guards...

"What is this?" Arherbas' concern cut through her thoughts. He raised his hand to his nose and sniffed. "A fig? Rotten?" He looked to her shoulder and found the stain. "Elisha, why are your fine garments so ill-treated? Have your servants...?"

"Someone threw that fig at me." It was then he saw the fear and anger mixing in her dark eyes. "As we skirted the market. Between the palace and here. There was a shout. Then it struck me. One of the guards went between the stalls, looking for the responsible one." Rage flashed. "They knew. Those common *'bny* all saw who threw it. Not a one stepped forward. An assault on the royal house and they protected the guilty."

Arherbas shook his head. "This is Pumayyaton's work. In the month since he began acting in your father's name, he has done much for the poor."

"*Lys!* He sweet-talks them. He charms them with his magic tongue, entrancing them like children."

Her uncle was struck by her seriousness. She spoke disdainfully of the capacities of children, she who was only just ten years of age. It was times like these that he was amazed at her maturity.

Looking beyond her to the marketplace, he formed words in his head before speaking.

"Goodness and truth. Evil and the lie. These are all values men place upon things they cannot see or touch. As if they can hang meaning on an event that passes through our lives like the moon crossing the evening sky. Your brother uses the lowly *'bny* for his own agenda, the reduction of the lofty *rzn*. But for the commoner's point of view, he is giving them power, so they view him favorably. To them, he is a good and just ruler."

Elisha started to argue, but Arherbas waved her to silence.

"Pumayyaton has been pardoning those accused of petty crimes. Those men go free, indebted to him. They return to their families who feel a similar bond. The praise for your brother spreads from mouth to ear."

"It is bad," Elisha scowled. "It is wrong."

"To you and I, and perhaps to the gods. But to the commoners, it is he who is right. The nobles, with their gold and possessions, are the ones who are wrong."

"Can they not see? Clearly Pumayyaton's motives are self-centered."

"All men's motives are ultimately self-centered. Besides the pardons, there are the reductions in the export taxes, which directly effects Tyre's smaller craftsmen. There are the cobbles being replaced along the Purple Way, an avenue through a poor district long in need of repairs. There are even the occasional kegs of barley beer rolled out into the marketplace, a gift stated to be that of King Mattan, but clearly seen as being from his heir. Of course these are naked attempts by your brother to win the support of the people. And they have worked. The people now favor him. A bond has been formed. Whether it was wrong or evil or corrupt matters not."

"Matters not?" She looked at him in surprise. "You are the Holy Lord of Melqart. You service the gods who teach us right and wrong, who punish the evil and reward the good. How can you turn your back on something so false?"

"I am not turning my back. I am simply not focusing on the unimportant."

"Unimportant? But how can what he did..."

"Stop being a child, Elisha." His harsh words hit harder than any blow. "The Canaanites are a race of merchants. They value gold. Not art. Not culture. Not song nor dance. Not athletics like those sweaty Greeks. Gold. It is a value they can hold in their hands. There is a lesson there. You can seek goodness and mercy, truth and love. You can let them influence you, but you cannot let them blind you. Your brother has acted. If there is anyone to blame for his ascension, it is ourselves for not seeing his stratagem before it was too late."

Elisha spoke to his back. "So you are saying that goodness does not matter?"

"No," replied Arherbas, eyes still on the flow of the market. "You should only concern yourself with the good or evil of your own acts. The actions of others are beyond your control, and the judgment of them will be the concern of the gods."

Elisha looked down, having had her first glimpse of adulthood and finding it not to her liking. "It matters not," she finally said. "When my father gets better, he will set things back the way they were."

"He will not get better." Her uncle turned to face her.

"How can you say such an evil thing? He is gathering his strength."

"He is dying, Sparrow." More gently. "He is dying. He knows this fact, and faces it squarely. He has had a sarcophagus built; it lies in the temple's store room, awaiting his final breath. Further, men expert in preparing mortal remains have been journeyed from Egypt. All these things Mattan has ordered. He knows his time is short and readies himself." .

Elisha looked into her uncle's face, desperately searching for a lie or humor that would explain it away. But deep down, she already knew he spoke the truth. Defeated, she faced into the wall, face cradled in her arms.

"What shall I do, Uncle? I have been a threat to Pumayyaton's claim to the throne. When father passes..."

Arherbas looked at the small frightened girl. He rubbed his chin, brow lined, deep in thought. Finally he turned to the two guards who stood respectfully at the opposite end of the room.

"When the princess is composed, see her safely to the palace.

Should any man move against her, in any manner, you are to kill him. Do you understand?"

The two spearmen looked into the high priest's eyes. Carefully, they both nodded.

"Elisha, I must leave now. I must speak to my brother while there is still time."

The throne room was more subdued than it had been in months past. Where once a roomful of elders had fought passionate verbal battles, a silent handful now remained. There was little respect to be gained by arguing with Pumayyaton. He would simply chide his opponent, embarrassing the councilman before the court. The heir's position ensured no rebuttal.

In truth, the balance had corrected slightly. On the onset, the *'bny* could do no wrong. Thieves and debtors were forgiven their sins at the expense of the *rzn*. The council had watched helplessly as the guilty streamed through the court. Once his position with the commoners had firmed, Pumayyaton began to rule against the worst of the defenders. In this, he was walking a very fine line; to completely abolish the *mw'd* and *rzn* would be to invite the total financial collapse of the trading empire. Yet he had to maintain the support of the *'bny*. Elisha had watched as he shifted judgments from day to day, pitting the two classes against one another. While Pumayyaton was shaping up to be the tyrant her uncle had feared, he was also proving himself capable at playing politics. She couldn't fault his skill.

The hearings were light today, largely due to the weather. Elisha sat propped on a pillow, her robes gathered against the chill, watching rain swirl past the window. The first of the winter storms had come; people forced to remain indoors were less likely to venture forth to rob, cheat, or otherwise victimize one another. Later, as the dreary months dragged on, there would be the rash of beatings brought on by the monotony and close quarters. For now, things were quiet.

As always, Pumayyaton sprawled comfortably across the low throne. Advisors stood behind him, ready to provide any information he should require. To one side, members of the temple reclined on pillows, silently watching the proceedings, Arherbas among them.

Opposite the throne sat the reduced and dispirited council, watching the heir perform his duties with little assistance from them. Elder Shipitbaal sat at the head of the group. At one point, Elisha happened to glance at the elder just as he turned to face her. Through the screen, their eyes met. He momentarily crossed his eyes and stuck out his tongue. She placed a hand on her mouth to stifle her giggle at the ludicrous image.

"A proposal has been forwarded for royal consideration," Mapen announced, "*Rzn* Urkatel feels that he was excessively taxed for jade imported last summer." One of the elders representing Urkatel stood, scrolls under his arm, bowing.

A slight motion at the end of the room drew Elisha's attention. Guardsman Ib stood just inside the door, half-turned, as if listening to words from someone just outside the chamber. He gave a small nod of understanding, turned to face forward, raising his javelin slightly; a signal. Elisha twisted in time to see her brother catch the gesture. He then leaned back and whispered to a scribe. The man balked. Pumayyaton's face clouded and he repeated his words in tones both royal and menacing. The scribe bowed low and scuttled from the chamber.

Elisha watched the man depart, wondering what was transpiring. She caught her uncle's attention. He'd noticed the interplay but seemed surprisingly calm. He returned her glance, his expression wooden, before looking back towards the elder who was reading aloud from his scroll.

Time limped by. Pumayyaton asked some half-hearted questions, dragging out the case. And then the scribe returned. At the sight of him her brother straightened, gesturing to Mapen. The courtier approached the throne, listening to his master's instruction.

Intent on his scroll, the elder had missed the interplay at the head of the court. He was midway down an itemized list of shipping charges when Mapen's voice cut over his own.

"This case will be decided at a later date."

The elder lowered his scroll. "Eh?"

"All rise and pay respect to King Mattan, ruler of Tyre."

Four slaves entered the chamber through the rear stairwell, a litter slung between them. Elisha only had time to come to her knees and turn as her father was carried past. His skin was the color and texture of aged linen. His eyes stared sightlessly towards the ceiling and his mouth gaped, puffing for air. For a moment she felt as if Mot, god of the underworld, trailed in the wake of the litter.

The council of elders were on their feet, their bows more respectful than any they'd given Pumayyaton. Elisha noticed Elder Shipitbaal. The old man stared at human wreckage on the litter, a faint wetness glimmering in his eyes.

The slaves placed their burden before the throne. At the slight jostle, a wet wracking cough erupted from the ruler. His attendants stood helplessly by as he choked around his phlegm, the sounds of his gagging filling the silence. Finally he stilled, his breath as faint as a kitten's.

"How dare you, Pumayyaton!" Elisha stood over the screen she'd toppled, eyes flaring. "Father should not be moved! You could kill him by bringing him here!"

Her brother was on his feet. "This in the royal court! A woman cannot address it! Return to your place!"

Elisha felt her small hands ball into fists. She took a step forward, the screen cracking beneath her instep. Pumayyaton's face whitened at her insubordination; his own fists clenched.

Out of the corner of her eye, she saw Ib rushing forward, weapon clenched at the ready.

Opposite, the temple priests had risen as well. Arherbas spread his arms, checking them, his eyes on Pumayyaton.

"Children," came Mattan's weak voice. "Behave."

The court froze. Mattan's dull eyes were on Pumayyaton. He seemed too tired to even blink.

"What was it you wished to show me, my son?"

Pumayyaton lowered his arms slowly, a ready smile building across his face. "Father, there is a matter that must be heard by your ears. My position prejudices me. You must pass judgment on this."

The voice, thought Elisha. *So sincere. If snakes could speak to mice, it would sound thus.*

Pumayyaton glanced to where Ib stood, weapon ready. The heir gave a small stand-down gesture. Opposite, the priests settled back to their pillows. Several of them whispered simultaneously to Arherbas. One of them, Elisha noticed, was carrying an ornate cedar box. Curious.

Meanwhile, Pumayyaton had once again summoned Mapen to him. Another whispered conference. The courtier turned and returned to face the chamber's silence.

"The throne grants an audience to the *bolh* representatives."

Elisha frowned at the title. The '*community of citizens*'?

A group of rough men entered. Their cotton tunics were simple, practical. Their mantles and conical caps were colored with cheap every-day dyes. Elisha might have passed them on the streets of Tyre with hardly a notice. Now, they were pieces in the game Pumayyaton was playing.

They filed through the seated council, sparing not a glance. Assembling into a loose row before the throne, their spokesman stepped forward. Elisha squinted—she'd seen this burly man with his thick cropped hair before. Here in this very court.

"I am Adon, and I speak for the *bolh*, the '*community of citizens*'. We represent the '*bny* of Tyre, just as the elder's represent the *rzn*. We feel that for too long, there has been little representation for the craftsmen and workers of this city. We have come together on our own to seek representation."

On your own. Elisha shook her head at the little play. *Of course.*

"We have two demands to make of the king. These demands are the following. Firstly, we seek formal representation in court. We wish to have the *bolh* present for all royal business, a counterweight to the *mw'd*. We will be given an equal chance to speak, and our words will be given equal weight. The committee of the *bolh* will represent any '*bny* brought before this court."

"Ha!" Shipitbaal climbed to his feet, grimly smiling at Adon. "You seek membership in court, do you? You wish equal speech and equal weight, equal carpet and equal pillows. More like equal gold, I would say."

Adon frowned at the scrawny noble. "We seek fair representation. Is there anything wrong with that?"

"For the *'bny*, perhaps no representation is fair representation. I remember you from the last time you were here. What is it that you do in life? Hammer pegs and steal your master's gold?" Adon flushed, his mouth opening to speak, but Shipitbaal was quicker. "Yes, yes, you were pardoned for it. I forgot. My wits are little better than my *'yr*, these days."

The elders of the *mw'd* chuckled. Shipitbaal under full sail was something to witness.

"So we will have you in our company, I am to assume? You and your 'committee' shall sit at our side and argue the finer points of court. So you understand the laws of Canaan? The order of the proceedings. The times when supporting scrolls can be called for? The structure of the presentation. The rules for counterpoint? How to address the king when you need to relieve yourself? *Y*, I forgot! You know all about hammering pegs!"

The *mw'd* were now reclining, enjoying the performance. Along the wall, the attending princes smiled like a wolf pack. Elisha glanced to her brother, delighting in his discomfort at watching his pet *'bny* fare so poorly.

"Enough, old man!" Adon had pushed back through the rough men of the committee to stand face to face with Shipitbaal. He stood a head taller than his elder, and physical labor had broadened his shoulders to twice the other's width. "I can stand before you in court and hold my own."

"Hold your own what? You own *'yr*, perhaps. *'Bl*! For twenty years I have been a member of court. I have discussed fine points of mercantilism with ambassadors from faraway lands. I have organized convoys to bring back metals from Gadar while playing a delaying game with the Assyrians. I have won fortunes for my houses and for myself through wits and oration. And you think you can match me? You would not last a single session in this place. I could crush you, steal every last shekel-weight of silver you own, every last kernel of grain. You do not have the brains, skills, or years, boy!"

"You old fool! No man speaks to me like that!"

"I do, and if you are to remain in this court, you had best become used to it. And lower your fists. You threaten an elder with violence?" Shipitbaal's voice dropped to an ominous level. "I helmed a merchant *gôlah* before you peeked from your mother's *'bn*. I have killed Tjeker pirates by the score. And if you put those fists up at me ever again, I will shove them someplace so deep you will crack your knuckles when you sit."

A rasping laugh rose from where Mattan lay. "Shipitbaal, you have not lost your tongue. I have missed your tirades."

The elder bowed low. "As it pleasures, my lord."

Mattan licked his dry lips. "You had best let young Adon finish his demands, lest we be here all night."

As the councilman returned to his place, Mattan's unblinking eyes moved to the young ship builder. "Your request for the *bolh* committee to gain membership to the court is granted."

Adon bowed stiffly, unpracticed at such gestures. "Thank you, my Lord King. Our second demand involves the issue of the throne, should something befall you. Currently, the *bolh* is aware of the plans to have Pumayyaton and Elisha share the throne. This, we think, is a poor plan. We of the *'bny* seek leadership. As we have seen, your councils can be argumentative, disruptive. There must be a point where talk ceases and a single individual makes the final decision. Although he has just turned eleven, we feel that Lord Pumayyaton represents all men of Tyre, not just those with gold.

"That, and Elisha is a girl. We choose not to be ruled by a woman."

Elisha felt her face flush. Adon continued.

"Should the co-regency come to pass, we feel that Tyre would face a downturn in fortune. The *'bny* might riot should the throne be split. The marketplace, the vessels in the harbors, all of these could be destroyed by fire should Elisha rule. The Canaanites of the mainland might even rise up in rebellion, cutting Tyre's access to its croplands. Remember, the *bolh* committee speaks for the commoners, but they in no way control them."

"If that is how your threaten," Shipitbaal muttered, "you should stick to your fists."

Mattan studied the young ship builder for some time. Then his eyes slid over to Elisha. She tried to preserve a calm exterior but inside she wished she was anywhere else. It all felt so unfair. It was all she could do to keep tears from forming.

Standing over his father, Pumayyaton studied her as well. His expression was cold.

Mattan seemed to be having trouble breathing. Finally, he captured enough breath to speak.

"We understand the issue. At this time, when faced with...Assyrian aggression on the mainland, we can not risk...internal strife." He closed his eyes, drew in three shallow breaths, and concluded. "Elisha shall not share the throne. Pumayyaton shall be the sole heir."

The council stirred, confirming among themselves, faces grim. Pumayyaton's own smile broadened. Elisha kept her face wooden as she met her brother's triumphant smirk. In her lap, her hands twisted her robe.

Arherbas pointed to Mapen. It was a simple gesture, pre-arranged. The courtier turned and addressed the court.

"The following proposal has been put forth." The room hushed. "Holy Lord Arherbas desires Lady Elisha's hand in marriage."

Elisha sat numbly, unsure if she'd heard the courtier's words. Arherbas was already stepping towards Mattan, the ornate box before him.

Pumayyaton loomed over his father. "You cannot do this! You cannot interfere with..."

Arherbas' large hand swept him aside. "Quiet, child." He quickly knelt before the king, box open and held before him. Something flashed brilliantly from within.

"King Mattan, I present this finely crafted golden bowl as a *kusata*, the wedding gift. Do you agree to the consummation of this marriage?"

Pumayyaton attempted to press around the priest. "Father, you cannot..."

Arherbas rounded on him. "Silence!" The booming voice reverberated though the hall. His nephew stepped back, alarmed. The priest returned his attention to the prone ruler. "Do you accept?"

"I do," Mattan huffed.

"I will not have you marry my sister," Pumayyaton shrilled. "I will not let you give her sanctuary! Ib, take Elisha to her room! No one is to see her! And cast this priest from the court!"

Arherbas came up from his knees, rising before Pumayyaton, a force of nature. He took a step towards the boy, his hand clamping on his shoulder, arresting his backpedal.

"Lady Elisha is now my wife by Canaanite customs. She now has my protection, and that of the temple of Melqart."

Mapen stepped up. "According to our laws, opposition to the marriage by any member of the bride's family would be deemed non-fulfillment of contract. The fine for such an act would be three times the value of the *kusata*. That item has been pre-evaluated at over two talents gold in worth, based on its content and craftsmanship." The courtier's eyes locked on Pumayyaton's. "Do you wish to protest the marriage?"

"No," snarled the boy.

From his litter, Mattan looked up over the precious bowl. Its reflection cast the ruler in golden hues.

"Arherbas, our customs dictate...that I now assign an *iwaru*, a dowry. With my daughter, I present...two fifths of the royal treasury."

"*N*'! Father! Have you lost your wits?" Pumayyaton forced his way around the priest and courtier, dropping before the litter. "Two fifths of the treasury? We will need that wealth if Tyre is to check the Assyrians! How will we pay for our fleets and trade goods? This is ruinous!"

A whitened hand fluttered up, resting on the boy's shoulder.

"Son, this is for your...own good. Elisha is beyond your reach now...As for the diminished treasury, there is but one road...that you can follow. All others lead to disaster...You must work with the *rzn*, grant them their former powers...Learn to work with them, not against them."

"I will not!"

"Then you, and Tyre, will fall."

Pumayyaton slowly rose, trapped. He fixed a hard stare at each man before him. The last he saved for Elisha, murderous in its intensity. Without a word, he stalked from the room.

Arherbas walked over. Elisha rose, faint, staggering before the changes that had just occurred.

"Uncle..."

"Husband," he corrected. "I am your husband now, Elisha. By our laws, we are married. You are young but not too young. We are of close relations but not too close. It is correct and proper by our customs and laws. As my wife, you should be safe from Pumayyaton, but we will not tempt fate. This priest will accompany you to the temple. Leave now; your belongings will follow. Seek out Tetramnestus, my aide. He will find you an apartment in the compound."

Without waiting for her reply, Arherbas turned his back on her, walking quickly over to the litter before the throne. She watched him kneel to attend her father.

My husband...

The priest at her side gestured towards the door. "If it pleases the Holy Lady...?"

SIX

They housed me with the washer-women. A princess, quartered with 'bny!

Elisha lay on her pallet, looking up at the unadorned ceiling of her apartment. In the courtyard, women chatted and sang as they washed linen and polished brasswork. Isolated in her room, Elisha simmered as the third day of marriage died.

How she'd fretted that first night. She'd crossed to the temple, a stream of servants following with her dowry. Tetramnestus, her uncle's...*husband's* aide met them on the temple steps. The escorting priest exchanged hushed words with the portly assistant. She was amazed the bulky man could hunch down low enough to address her.

"So you are Elisha, the *qdshbol*'s new wife." His lips formed a fat smile. She disliked him at first sight. "Well, let us find a place for you. And welcome to the temple."

The other inhabitants of the women's quarters had given her wide berth but she could still hear the whispers, feel the eyes. And as that first day had descended into night's indigo, she'd awaited Arherbas' arrival, fearful yet expectant.

He had not come.

Tetramnestus visited the following midday, a basket of biscuits and a jar of cool water cradled in his thick arms. They'd shared the food; he'd monopolized the conversation.

"Your father is very unwell. He has little time and Arherbas remains with him." He set down his cup and gave her a leveled look. "There are no words of comfort I can say to you. I know you are confused and sad. I was, too, when I came here. You will grow used to it."

Elisha found herself frowning. Tetramnestus had eaten most of the biscuits, the crumbs flaking his stained robe. When he made to leave, they cascaded to the floor. Not knowing who her servant was, or who to even ask, she cleared the mess herself rather than risk ants.

The women around the courtyard watched her sweepings with silent eyes.

Her apprehension grew with each day's passage. Her wifely duties existed just beyond her comprehension. At night, she would lay silently, fearful that Arherbas might suddenly appear. When the dawn came, she would find herself looking at her familiar ceiling, still Elisha, still alone and ignorant.

The women busied themselves with their chores. And every day, Tetramnestus would come.

"Your dowry has done much good," he confided as he chewed. Elisha found herself leaning back slightly. "Your husband has decided that it should be a boon to all the gods, not just Melqart. The temples of Astarte and Baal have sent their thanks, as have the lesser shrines."

She thought of the house of Astarte, of the women she'd seen there, the expectant men and strange smells. A visit to the fertility cult might shed some needed light.

"Could we see how the gold has been used? Perhaps we could visit the temple of Astarte...?"

Tetramnestus' large fingers worried a biscuit into crumbs. "You must not know what occurs there. It would not be seemly for the wife of Arherbas, the holy lady, to enter such a place."

Again, the crumbs. Again, the sweeping. She didn't need a servant. She was becoming her own.

The light of the day grew long across her ceiling. A restlessness rose within her. The days of stilted, stumbling conversations with Tetramnestus, the silence of the women, all were filling her with a charge. She felt she had to do something, anything.

She took a moment to lean over the railing and look down on the enclosed courtyard. The women sat on the stone benches, doing their little tasks, sewing, washing, gossiping. Elisha felt a stab of jealously over their simple contentment. It was secure yet closed, a prison.

She descended the stone steps, briskly crossing the courtyard along the far wall. The women looked up and silence fell like a shroud. But by then, she was in the main hall leading out.

Outside, she took a moment to orientate herself. From the palace parapets, the adjacent temple compound had revealed little save trees and rooftops. The grounds were arrayed around a number of buildings separated by ribbon gardens and creaking palms. Here and there, priests moved through long shadows, intent on their evening services. The hubbub of the city was lost in the compact tranquility.

There was an entire world here to explore. And she was the holy lady. Who could stop her?

On the stones of the walk she saw droplets of water leading away. No doubt one of the women, carrying water back to the quarters, had spilled some. It would be a good first thing to discover, the cistern from which it came.

A short distance later, she found something of interest. A little bridge crossing a tiny stream, a flat rock to one side, suitable for the filling of urns.

She'd not known of any steams on the small island of Tyre. It was a place of bedrock and buildings and people. Yet here the stream was.

She paused to look up and down the path; no one was in sight. Stepping to the low rock, she slipped a toe into the burbling water. It was chilling yet not excessively so. She glanced again, her eyes flashing and smile tight. Then she raised her robes slightly, stepping out into the water.

She thought back to happier times and the games she and Pumayyaton had played. The palace became the coastal mountains and they the explorers, seeking the hidden valley that would cut time off the trade routes and make their fortune. And here was just such a mysterious river, flowing between the heavy ferns. In her mind, it was not a foot or two in breath but a mighty watercourse. She pressed upstream, expectant of wonders.

Eventually she eased through the last of the brush to find a massive structure before her. It was the rear of the main temple. Here, the water was carefully shepherded between rock banks. She followed the course of the stream, finding that it trickled from a pipe jutting from the flank of stairs that climbed the rear face of the great building.

Holding her skirt carefully, she stooped and peered into the pipe. Blackness.

As the sky grew golden, she looked for pretty pebbles in the stream, collecting one or two. Then she amused herself by stepping from rock to stream, crossing and re-crossing. Over and back. On her lips was a melody her Syrian governess had sung her to sleep with.

From the nearby palace roof, trumpets broke the evening air. They wailed long and hard, a cacophony of grief which rolled across Tyre. From the square that faced the temples and palace came the echoing lament of hundreds of people.

Father!

The palace was little more than a purple shape in the evening light, but she felt a compulsion to see. The temple rooftop was the tallest building in the complex, equal to the palace. She started towards the nearby steps. Then she remembered Arherbas' concerns with her tracking dirt into the temple. After wiping her feet dry upon the grass, she dashed up the stairs.

The steps ended at the second story landing. A glance inside showed an audience chamber, elegantly furnished yet otherwise empty. Next to the entrance was a wooden ladder that climbed the rest of the way. She took a moment to test its security, then started up. She focused on the rungs before her, careful not to look back into the drop.

The rooftop was like those of Tyre's sister buildings. In the tight urban confines of the island, all rooftop space had been converted to gardens. She saw small fruit and olive trees, carefully potted and tended. Bushes removed the harshness of the surrounding city, turning the small space into a sanctuary.

She crossed to the far corner, looking into the city's main square. A multitude filled it, faces upraised towards the palace where the trumpets still mourned. The crowd stood still, each member reflecting upon the changes facing the Canaanite federation. Pumayyaton had experimented with the monarchy, but Mattan had always been there, ready to correct his mistakes. With the *mlk* gone, Tyre's trade routes, colonies, and distant influence had fallen into the hands of an eleven year-old boy.

There would be no speeches to the masses. The new king would meet with the *mw'd*, the priests, and the newly-instituted *bolh*. It was hoped that the transition would be seamless, that the trade ships would still sail and the Assyrians held at bay. If the nobles and masses could agree on one fact, it was that change was a dangerous thing.

Citizens were now assembling before the columns of gold and emeralds, seeking admission into the house of Melqart. Now more than ever, they sought the benevolence of the city's god. Priests controlled them, keeping the press from becoming a mob. From the inner *hekal* came the sounds of droning prayer.

She leaned against the parapet for a long time, watching the people. She felt a disembodied sadness for her father's passing, but nothing more. She was surprised that she felt more relief than grief. She could picture him, his withering wastage, the way that simple actions became great efforts. She felt a peace for the fact that he was beyond his suffering.

A swirl of white caught her eye. Flanked by two priests, Arherbas passed through the gate at the side entrance to the compound. She moved along the parapet, looking down at her distant husband, so important yet so sad. Even from here, she could see that his brother's passage had affected him. He moved slowly, his bald head down, in thought.

Tetramnestus met them at the rear of the temple. She could catch a wisp of the conversation, the fact that the aide was bringing routine matters to the holy lord at this bad time. Arherbas' words were too distant to make out but his tone was harsh. He drove the portly man away. With greater civility, he dismissed the priests. Then he turned for the steps she'd recently ascended. And stopped.

He seemed to be peering out at the grass, the rocks, and the creek.

He took a single step, peering into the gloom of the temple's shadow. Then another. Eventually he moved to the rocks where she'd played.

He knelt down, his linen robes folding around him, looking at the flat rocks that were shedding the last of the day's heat. His fingers traced something, his motions slow, reverent. Elisha leaned out as far as she dared, squinting into the dusk that leached into the compound.

Her foot prints. He was studying the wet marks she'd left behind, his eyes absorbing every detail.

She'd been ready to call out to him but something stilled her throat. Her father had told her that priests often found beauty in even the simplest things. If this were so, interrupting him would be a great wrong.

Eventually he rose, turned, and ascended the steps. As he neared, she looked down on his shaven head, feeling a great protective love come over her. This was her husband, the high priest of Tyre's most important temple, in a time of crisis. The weight of the world pressed down on his broad shoulders and yet he could still see its wonderment.

A moment later, he'd turned into the opening at the top of the landing and disappeared. She assumed his apartments were somewhere beyond the audience chamber.

Arms crossed on the stone wall, she looked out over the city. The sun was only just kissing the sea, highlighting walls and buildings in orange fire. People came and went from the temple, the droning of the priests rose around her. Contentment came to her once again, a reminder of similar sunsets witnessed from the palace roof.

The thought made her glance in the direction of the royal structure. She froze. A hundred yards away, Pumayyaton stood atop the palace, silent, still, facing her. She did not wave nor shout. She returned his distant gaze, wondering what the other felt. Had his father's death pleased him? Was he frightened of the responsibilities now his? Was he mad at her?

Did he wish she were dead?

The distant figure never moved. It continued to stare, watching her watching him. Neither broke contact until the sun dipped beneath the waves with a final green flash, casting temple and palace into darkness.

She paused at the top of the stairs to peek into the audience chamber. Several priests stood, backs to her, her husband's voice rising over them. For a moment her hand played with the ladder, tempting her with thoughts of the rooftop garden.

How much easier to face distant horizons, she thought, *than immediate surroundings.*

They didn't see her approach, so intent were they with Arherbas' words. She slipped around them to find her husband seated at a scroll-littered table. Before him stood Tetramnestus, head hanging.

"I do not see what the problem is." Arherbas' words were icy. "We gave you control of the temple inventories. It is simple work; store items for our worshipers, return them when demanded."

"Nothing is missing, Holy Lord."

"*'Bl,* it is all there. The problem is that it is 'all there' late. Lord Attis was presented with an excellent opportunity to place luxury items on a Gadar-bound ship. Such an investment could not hope but succeed. He requested the withdrawal *three* weeks ago. Not only was he unable to gain his wealth, he was unable to find you."

"I was looking for it." The aide's voice was miserable. "I eventually located it."

"The ship sailed, Tetramnestus. Shipitbaal provided the cargo once it became apparent that Attis could not secure collateral. You cost him a fortune, a fortune he would have safeguarded with us. I have just found out, from the high priest at Baal's temple, that Attis has transferred his wealth to them."

The *Qdshbol* drummed his fingers on the table, eyes dark.

"What am I to do with you, Tetramnestus? You fail every task given you." He shook his head slowly. "What am I to do?"

The aide stood silently, head down. With a sigh, Arherbas waved him away. The big man trudged off, climbing a set of stairs in the back of the room.

Arherbas turned his attention on his priests, hesitating when he saw her.

"Sparrow! I did not see you come in."

"I did not wish to interrupt you."

"Do not worry about that. You are never an interruption."

She worried her lip, then blurted, "May I speak with you? In private?"

Arherbas' eyebrows climbed his bald head. His nod came slowly.

"Of course. Brother priests, if you will excuse us?" The men bowed as one, slipping quietly from the room.

"Are you faring well, Elisha? Did that bungler Tetramnestus locate suitable quarters for you?"

"My apartment is adequate, my husband." She did not wish him distracted by her accommodations. Uncomfortable with making him look up, she dropped to her knees. "It is just that...I was feeling so..." She shook her head at her false starts, took a breath, managing to meet his eyes. "It has been two weeks since our wedding and I have not seen you. Not once. I was worried that you do not like me."

"Sparrow, Sparrow, nothing could be more from the truth. You are my niece, my brother's child. Of course I like you."

"But you have not come to see me. I feel like I am a possession, forgotten on a shelf."

"Now you are being silly." He tossed a dismissive wave. "I have been very busy with matters of temple and state. These things take all my time. Firstly, there were your father's remains. The proper services had to be performed. Now his body must be moved to the necropolis on the mainland, again observing formalities.

"And there is the matter of Pumayyaton. In emptying the treasury, your father gave his son a blessing. No doubt he was ready to solidify his power, backed by that silly commoner committee. Now he will be forced to listen to the council of elders, to work with them like a true king and not oppose them like a spoiled child."

Elisha considered this.

"What is the temple's role in this?"

"The priests provide moderation between king and nobles. We balance the needs of the throne against the livelihood of the merchants. And never before has a ruler so needed our help. Your brother still bickers with the *mw'd* and coddles the *bolh*. He is losing time and gold he does not have. If he does not soon heed our advice, the royal treasuries will empty. It would be a disaster."

"Why?"

It was the unexpected maturity of the tone in her query that caught him.

"Elisha, if Tyre's gold ran dry, calamity would befall us. The army would not be paid, nor the fleet. The royal granaries would fail. Riots would follow. The king might be overthrown."

She sat in silent consideration.

"Sparrow, he is your brother."

"Sixty-seven years ago," she recited as if in lessons, "A man named Ithobaal seized the throne. He declared himself king and forced the priests of Astarte to bestow the title of Holy Lord, *Qdshbol* upon him." Her dark eyes looked up at him. "We have had priest-kings before."

He studied her long and hard. Her returned expression was one of simple curiosity. Finally, he reached out and tousled her hair, dislodging her headband.

"These are not your dolls, Elisha. These are not toys whose make-believe lives you twist to your whimsy. These are people. They die in riots. They starve in hard times. You can not simply decide to topple the established order without blood staining the flagstones."

"I do not play with dolls," she replied simply.

He looked at her and realized that she'd grown over the last year. When the storms had come last, she'd been a small girl. But something had changed. She was growing up fast.

"The king directs the power of the Tyrian Canaanites," she continued. "Power flows from him. If a city confounds him, he can direct an army to raze it with a casual wave of his hand. Should he desire gold from Iberia, ivory from Libya, grain from Egypt, he need only speak his intent and a trading fleet will clear the breakwater with the sunrise. He can point to a man on the street and make him rich beyond his dreams. Or he can spill his lifeblood across the cobbles. That is power."

She gauged him.

"You could have that power. The powerful *rzn* support you. You could enter the palace and take it from Pumayyaton as you would fruit from a tree. He would no longer be king, simply an angry little boy once again."

She lowered her head demurely. Nothing more could be said. She waited for an angry retort to her scheme, perhaps a slap or a beating. Her hopes were for a long speculative pause.

Arherbas laughed, long and hard. She looked up, too confused to feel hurt or anger.

"*Y, y, y*! Elisha, my little Sparrow, you have me fit to burst." He took a moment to compose himself. "You think that your brother wields absolute power in Tyre? You believe that he is a living god, the nexus point of heaven and earth? *Lys*! You are simply too young to know how real power works."

Her eyes narrowed. "Of what do you speak?"

"My little wife, when it comes to wealth and power, I can assure you that we are well represented in both regards. In my possession, I have..." He paused, catching his tongue. "I speak hastily. Someday, I will explain further. But not now. You are still a child."

She placed hands on knees, drawing herself erect. "*N*! Everyone considers me a child. I am now ten. I am ready to take my place in the world." She locked her eyes on those of Arherbas, forcing her words through her fears. "I am ready to perform my duties as a wife. I am yours to command."

The eyes of the high priest widened for a moment. Then he settled back into his chair, his head shaking back and forth.

"Little Sparrow, I am touched and honored that you would say such words. But I do not think you know a thing about what you offer."

"I know what I must know, my husband." She swallowed at her boldness, remembering Ib's foul word. "I know of '*yrs*.'"

He studied her, rubbing his chin. "I do not think you do. You bluff like a blind man describing the sky." He saw confirmation in her eyes. "'*Bl*, I thought as much. You have become a wife and think that it means you are no longer a child. But you are a child, Elisha. You have probably not had your first red stain yet. Do not ask what that is; you will know it when it comes." He looked up at the ceiling for a moment, composing his thoughts.

"Sparrow, I had no inkling a month ago that I would be your

husband. I proposed it as a way to keep you safe from your brother. Your father agreed. But frankly, I am as surprised as you to find myself in this situation. Speaking candidly, it will take time for me to grow comfortable with having a wife as young as you.

"Someday you shall perform your duty. But not now. It is simply too soon for such things." He smiled. "Enjoy your youth while you can, Sparrow. Life will leach you soon enough."

"But the duty," she asked imploringly. "I know little about it."

"Remain the child," he replied. "Remain innocent. Do not speak of it to any other. If others speak of it, depart their company. I desire my wife to remain pure until the moment I call upon her."

"I understand."

He gave her a warm smile. "And now, little Elisha, you must excuse me. I have neglected my work for too long."

She climbed to her feet and bowed respectfully. On the landing outside, she paused to watch a light rain swirl through the trees.

He was touched when I offered. More than touched. Something else. He was...gratified. She started down the steps, eyes distant. *It was as if his own self-perception changed when I offered myself to him.*

She stopped on the steps, checked by a thought. Had she offered her duty and *then* proposed the seizing of Tyre's throne, would the result have been different? *Perhaps*, said a voice from deep within.

The winter rains tore across the island, closing the seas to the ships of Canaan.

The crews returned to their families or lounged away the days in the island's northside wineshops. The gold of Gadar settled into the possession of whores and tavernkeeps.

For the merchant-princes, the storms were a time of politics and planning. The temples filled with *rzn* buying, selling, dealing. The plans for the coming year were formed in the light of temple braziers.

It was also a time of parties and galas, a chance to place one's new-found wealth on parade. Almost every day, at least one noble house hosted a ball. There would be food, music, games; anything to ward off the dreary outdoor monotony.

Elisha's life filled with activity. At first, Arherbas escorted her to the parties, introducing her to the high ladies, hoping she would find friendship. While no bonds formed, she did gain acceptance amongst the aristocracy. Soon she had enough invitations that she no longer required her husband's company. For long rainy weeks, she was occupied.

Monkeys and jugglers. She leaned against the temple's back wall, shielded from the west wind and its driven rain. *Could not Lady Ayzebel think of anything new for her party?*

The sun was arching towards its zenith somewhere above the shield of cloud. She should be in her apartment, picking through all the new clothing Arherbas had provided. An enclosed sedan chair, hefted by temple servants, would keep her dry and transport her to the party. But monkeys and jugglers would not keep her amused.

She looked up the stairs to the raised landing. It was likely that her husband was meeting with princes in the temple's *ulam.* However, he might be up in the audience chamber, at war with his pile of scrolls. Perhaps he would take a moment to converse with her. She found comfort in his presence.

Reaching the landing, she peeked around the edge of the opening. The audience chamber was empty, the lamps cold.

Her nose wrinkled as an errant drop fell on it. She would be cold and wet returning to her apartment. And Ayzebel's affair held no attachment with her. She fancied exploration. What better way to spend a rainy afternoon?

She drifted across the floor, the marble chilling her feet. Her husband's bench was buried in the familiar mountain of scrolls. She opened one or two, looking across the columns of figures, finding them too somber to hold her interest. Circling the table, she looked out over the chamber from Arherbas' chair, feeling its power. Then she thought of moonlight and Pumayyaton and nervously hopped to her feet. That part of the game was no longer fun.

Along the back wall were several openings. Through one, she could see an opulent bedchamber, probably Arherbas'. Another opening revealed a flight of stairs ascending into darkness. Anticipating wonders, she crept upwards.

The room was long and low, taking up the entire top floor of the temple. Rain drizzled past slit windows along the roof. Lining the walls, marching away into the gloom, were rows of amphorae. The ruddy, undecorated containers were stacked haphazardly to the ceiling in places.

In the center of the chamber was a long, low table. Scrolls were scattered across its surface and piled high on the adjacent floor. A small oil lamp pitched a feeble flame against the cold shadows.

She slipped silently along the stacks of urns, her small hand playing across the letters cast into their cool surfaces. On others, small clay labels hung around their necks.

In the darkness, something stirred.

Elisha froze, poised midway between the stairs and the table.

On the table's far side, lost in the transition of lamplight and shadow, a humped shape stirred.

Her mind jumped to the monsters of the gods, the Aklm, the Rephaim, even the freakish Arsh. She nearly fled, checked only by the thought that she was the holy lady, the *qdshba'alat*, and this temple was part of her household. She took a step forward, small fists up and clinched.

The shape stirred and reassembled. In the flicker of the lamp, she could make out doughy flesh. Human flesh.

"Tetramnestus?"

Small dark eyes opened, reflecting the minute light.

"Lady Elisha," he replied, voice flat. "You should not be here. I have much work to do."

She stepped carefully to the table and studied the man. He seemed shrunken, deflated. The sorrow in his eyes pierced her heart.

"What is this place? What are all these containers?"

"This?" He waved with a weak gesture, a humorless smile spreading. "These are the treasures of Tyre, the wealth of Canaan, the reason behind all the sailing and trading and fighting. Lumps of gold, silver, bronze. Fine grains, roles of silk. Powdered dyes. Its all here." Suddenly his hand lashed out, scattered scrolls. "*'Yrzro!* Here somewhere!"

She came around the table. He flinched at her concerned touch.

"What do you mean, Tetramnestus? What is wrong?"

77

"Wrong?" He met her eyes, then turned away. "Nothing is wrong that my own stillbirth would not have corrected."

"Tetramnestus, you should not say such things. Astarte blesses us all with life."

"Blesses us all? Every citizen of the city? The cripples? The beggars?" His eyes flashed at her. "The failed priests?"

"You are not a failure. You are my husband's aide. You do important work."

"Your husband's aide? Do you think that young Tetramnestus left his home in Arnuun so many years ago, driven by a burning desire to be an aide? Do you think *this* is what I wanted my life to be? *N'!*"

She stood quietly, unsure of what to say in the face of his frustrated anger.

"I wanted to be a priest. I wanted to be the *qdshbol*. But it was not to be. A dropped tripod during a service. A passage forgotten from an important rite. My girth. My clumsiness. Myself. All of these brought the disdain of my brother priests. And so they put me here, minding the inventories while the others honor Melqart.

"And I cannot even do that right!" He pressed his fists into his eyes. "Lord Melqart, what will become of me? How soon before your husband tires of my inadequacies and sends me back to Arnuun. And what will my life be, then? Minding a small shrine, sweeping out the dust and inventorying the copper lumps of poor farmers?"

"But I can see that you work hard. That you *want* to succeed. That should be enough for my husband."

Again the bitter smile. "Ah, Elisha, you are still the child. Such a foolish view of the world."

"And yours," she replied coldly, "is adult?"

He nodded slowly. "'*Bl.* You are right, my lady. Hardly the way of men."

"Why do you fail?" she asked, looking around the room at the stacked amphorae. "What is wrong with what you do?"

"Only that I am a feebleminded..." Her look caught him. "My apologies. My task is to store and retrieve all items entrusted to the temple. The urns are brought to the base of the stairs. I store them here. When the owner desires the return of his good, he tells the priests the day he will pick it up. The priests record that information and bring it to me."

"That sounds straight-forward enough."

"Oh course, my lady. So you do one. Here is a request for three urns of grain, entrusted to us by the house of Mintho. No doubt they seek to replace their stores. They wish it in five days time. Find it for me."

She turned to confront the wall of amphorae. After four labels, she stopped, turning to look back at him.

"How many orders do you have to fetch?"

He smiled sadly, gesturing to the stacked rolls before him. "Egersis is a busy time. When the storms let up, the wealth flies from the temple, seeking to go into the world and multiply." He dropped into his seat. "There is no way I shall ever accomplish this. You saw how your husband was with my failure to Lord Attis. This shall be much, much worse."

She carefully sat on one of the larger amphorae, thinking hard. Tetramnestus watched, nonplused.

"More men," she offered. "Could we bring others up here? That should permit us to search quicker."

"We tried that the last time I got behind. It works, after a fashion. They tend to get in each other's way more than they find the correct urn. Further, with the activities in the temple, there are few priests to spare."

"Then just us. Suppose you were to go through the urns, and I through the scrolls. At each, you call out the name, and I will look to see if it needs to be pulled. That way, we can bring everything back up to date."

"It would take too long. There must be hundreds of demands at this point. That means I will be standing around for each pot while you run through all the scrolls. It would take us forever."

She looked down at the large urn on which she sat, fingering the letters of the family name that had been drawn into its surface before it was fired in the kiln. There were so many things the Canaanites had done. The letters her small fingers traced, taken from the Egyptians, oriented towards sound rather than image. An elegant solution.

They lay before her, the letters she'd learned as a child. The learning rhyme sang in her head.

Alpha, beth, gimel, daleth...

She stilled, eyes locked on the ground before her. Then she rose to her feet, looking up and down the dank chamber. *Yes, it could work...*

"Get bread," she instructed. "And hot tea." She started for the door.

He scowled after her. "Bread and tea? How will that help us to find the urns?"

"It's not for us. Its for the grounds-keepers."

"Grounds-keepers? What are you talking about?" He rose to his feet, scowling.

She stopped at the door. "For what we are going to do, we will need men. With the rain, there is little enough for the gardeners to do. We will give them a hot meal and start on my plan. This might go late into the evening."

"Plan? What plan?"

"We must move all the amphorae downstairs into the audience chamber." She turned to go.

"And then?"

"We must move them all back here again." She shouted over her shoulder. A moment later, she was gone.

"Move them back? What do you mean?" Tetramnestus realized he was calling out into an empty room. *Bread and hot tea?* She might be mad, but she was a princess *and* the wife of the high priest; and at least it was something. Shaking his head at the folly of following a little girl's whims, he made for the temple kitchen.

SEVEN

"Ah, Elisha, how good it is to see you again. You are a ray of sunshine in an old man's gloomy day."

A genuine smile came to her face. "Councilman Shipitbaal. It is a pleasure to see you as well."

The elder crossed the audience chamber, a slave struggling behind him to carry a pair of ruddy amphorae.

"So, girl, what brings you into these dusty halls on so pleasant a day?"

She nodded to the far end of the hall where several priests and *rzn* stood around Arherbas' bench. "I had several questions concerning the workings of the temple. I had hoped to find my husband alone, weeks after Egersis, but he is surrounded as usual."

"Like fleas on a marketplace dog," the old man agreed.

"Lord, these containers..." prompted the slave.

"Set them down, lummox. Be still."

She eyed the urns as they were placed on the floor. "Withdrawing your riches from our house, Lord?"

"These?" The old man laughed. "*N*'! Nothing but poor barley and cheap wine, something for a small gathering of friends."

"If those urns contain the Khiosian spirits and grains procured by Mazikurash the merchant-magi, it is little wonder you would store them here. Those are rumored to be worth their weight in gold."

"As I said, a small get together. Several of the *rzn*. A council elder or two." He paused. "The king." A shrug. "Gold makes more gold, I always say. I am hoping to mend a few fences and win a few contracts with this outlay."

"Pumayyaton. I have not seen him since my wedding. All those long months." She paused, her feelings uneasy. "How fares the court?"

"Well enough, I suppose. The current financial crisis has your brother behaving far more reasonably with the *mw'd*. Good news, since I have had my fill of swordplay and bloodshed."

"Is he still courting the low born?"

"Not directly. Oh, they still hang around the court. I figure most of them do it to shirk their real work. Still, the tedium has grown heavy on them; the *bohl* is rather reduced at this point. Three or four of them in attendance, yawning their way through the day's agenda. If we could teach them to catch flies like frogs, at least they would serve a purpose."

Elisha checked a smile, attempting to maintain a lady's grace.

"Still," Shipitbaal noted, "Pumayyaton keeps his *'bny* contacts warm. All manner of public works, things Tyre can ill afford, directed to the meanest of streets. The king has even taken to inviting members of his little committee to various parties. That cocksure Adon is his favorite bird to display." He paused. "In Melqart's name, I wonder if he will bring that insufferable buffoon to my party tonight?" He glanced at the amphorae at the feet of his slave. "Perhaps some cheap waterfront beer is in order. *'Bl*, those *'bny* pigs..."

The elder's eyes went over her shoulder. "Speaking of pigs..."

"Shipitbaal!" A voice boomed over Elisha, making her start. "I have not seen you in ages. Still hiding on this rock, counting your gold, you old woman?"

A figure stepped past her as if she'd not been there. He was a bear of a man, his broad frame sheathed in a bronze-stripped jerkin. His hair and beard were knotted and greasy, topped by a conical helmet of iron. Trunk-like legs emerged from his ornate kilt, encased in kidskin boots. His huge forearms held the scars of numerous campaigns.

The smell of horseflesh drifted in the dignified air of the audience chamber.

"Lord Qurdi-Aššur-lamur," Shipitbaal enjoined with a slight lack of enthusiasm. "It is always nice when ranking Assyrians take time from burning mainland villages to visit us."

"Those who do not stand with Ashur stand against it. Such men are rebels. Rebels die."

"Nineveh's influence has long been based on crafty statesmanship and diplomacy," Shipitbaal agreed. "How goes the spring campaign?"

"The Aram vassalages have taken advantage of our troubles in Babylonia. They see their tribute as optional. I am correcting that oversight."

"And Babylon?"

"Most likely afire, as we speak."

"Silk prices will be going up," Shipitbaal mused to himself. "So, Qurdi-Aššur-lamur, what brings you to our fine city?"

"Many things. I must see your king Pumayyaton and your priest Arherbas. They must agree to this year's tribute. Further, there is the matter of *ilku* duty; the coast road is growing too rough for our chariots. Your citizens will fix it."

"I am too old for *ilku*," Shipitbaal observed. "I know a young shipwright who is handy with a mallet, though."

"Ah, Shipitbaal. I sense that you humor at my expense. I would drink with you, but I only drink with warriors."

The elder glanced to Elisha. "Assyrian humor." Turning back to the huge man, he noted. "Well, you mentioned tribute and manpower, but you neglected minerals. I assume that you have also come seeking iron?"

"Of course," A shrug. "Until we can take the iron mines of Cilicia, we must court you sailor-women. The metals of Gadar are critical to our empire. We must have them." The Assyrian's eyes fell on the two urns. "Removing your treasure from the temple, old friend?"

"This? Nay, simply some wine and grain, supplies for my humble household. Like you Assyrians, we store some of our possessions in temples. Until recently, reclaiming them was like prying them from Melqart's own hands. Very, very inefficient. But then it all changed. Now you need only provide the priest with your clay marker and you gain your goods immediately." His eyes flickered to Elisha. "It is rumored that this woman here, the *qdshbol*'s wife, had something to do with it."

Qurdi-Aššur-lamur's dark eyes fell on her for the first time. "Indeed."

Elisha bestowed a bow without respect and a smile without warmth to the Assyrian. She assumed such a man would never credit a woman for cleverness, yet credit should never be wasted.

"It was Tetramnestus' doing. The idea was his, as was the implementation. I assisted him in minor ways."

The warrior measured her for a long moment. "Organizational talent. Modesty. Support of underlings. Valuable attributes for a commander. If you had been born a man, I might have offered you a position on my staff. Aie, the wastage of the gods." He returned his attention to Shipitbaal, dropping Elisha into the void. "I must speak with priest Arherbas now." With that, he moved away, pushing past holy men as if they were grass.

"Charming fellow," mused Shipitbaal at his armored back. "Perhaps he would consider a seat on the *bolh*."

Elisha watched, too. But her mind was working in different circles.

"Lord, you said that he was seeking Gadar iron."

"Aye, and luck to him. The winter storms have only just lifted. The ore-bearing transports are still months out. He can stand before the *rzn* and whistle, for all the good it will do him. The storehouses of Tyre have no iron."

"Not entirely true," she carefully corrected. "Traders speak of such metals as they dicker in the temple's *ulam*."

"Just leftover stock from the prior year. None of the trading houses have it in amounts to interest the Assyrians. I, alas, have none, so the matter interests me not."

"It should," she replied. "These individual merchants have small amounts, scattered here and there. Yet they have no contact with the Assyrian emissary."

"And this is your idea? That I should be a *srsr*, a broker to these doings? Recall that I have no iron. What is my gain for arranging such a trade? You still think the world is a place of goodness and charity, little one."

"I think the world is a place of influence and favor." Her level tone caught the older man's attention. "You will have performed a service to the merchants of Canaan and the armies of Assyria. You will gain favors from mighty Qurdi-Aššur-lamur, as well as from numerous trading houses."

Shipitbaal blinked slowly, looking at her in a new light. "By Melqart's knees, what a flatheaded idiot I have become. Thinking that gain only comes in gold. And to be told my business by a girl." He checked himself, looked to her, and bowed. "A thousand pardons. To be told my business by the holy lady. Excuse me, but I must seek that animal's disagreeable presence one more time." He started towards the distant collection of men.

"Master?" The slave stood over the two urns. "Should I follow you, or take the amphorae home?"

The elder looked back. "Take them home, simpleton." He paused for a moment. "Wait. If I arrange trade with the Assyrian, I will probably need to invite him to tonight's celebration. If I did not and he heard of it, he might take offense. No doubt he drinks wine like an empty cistern. We shall need more." He pulled a clay token denoting his ownership of another wine amphorae from a pouch on his belt. No priests were in sight.

Elisha extended her hand. "Lord, give me your marker. I can take it to Tetramnestus. Your slave could carry the two amphorae home and return for the final one."

"Good plan. You heard our holy lady. Hurry home and return; no delay, mind." The slave bowed as he took up his burdens. "Elisha, thank you again for waking me from my slumber." He shook his head in mock self-disgust as he handed her the clay token, then turned and hurried towards the distant assemblage.

Elisha smiled after him. It was true that favors were just another good to be gathered and traded; the influential old man now owed her one.

Content with her dealings, she followed the audience chamber's wall, remaining unobtrusive to the collection of men. Soon she reached the flight that led upwards.

The inventories had lost their control over Tetramnestus. The big man moved about, checking items against scrolls, nodding contentedly at the order of it all. When he saw Elisha, his face lit up.

"My lady! How good it is to see you."

"Thank you, Tetramnestus." She held up the elder's marker. "Shipitbaal wishes another amphorae of wine. His slave will return soon to pick it up. If I locate it, could you move it to the stairs for me?"

"Of course I would. Anything my lady wishes."

She nodded her thanks, moving down the long chamber with its stacks of goods. Fingering the clay token, she carefully read out the letters painted on the floor as she walked by.

"...*qopf*...*resh*...*sin*". She faced the section with its mountain of goods owned by those whose names started with "Sh". According to the rules they'd laid down, *aleph* would be on the far right of the section, *taw* to the left. As the next letter in Shipitbaal's name was *pe*, it would be roughly dead-center. So indexed, it was easy to locate the merchant-prince's holdings. She found the wine amphorae with little difficulty.

Tetramnestus came immediately when she called.

T wo men sat across the scroll-laden table from Elisha. One was the *r'shnor*, in charge of the temple kitchens. The other was the *khn*, the priest who conducted the morning and evening sacrifices.

"I am not attacking you, Lord *R'shnor*," Elisha replied as non-threateningly as she could. "But it has never occurred to you to discuss the animal to be sacrificed with the *khn* before going to the market?"

"I am in charge of the kitchen. The events of the temple are not our concern."

"The kitchen is beneath the notice of those who serve Melqart," sniffed the priest.

"Other than the fact that we feed you," retorted the *r'shnor*, eyeing the *khn*'s moderate belly.

Elisha looked from one to the other. "How much meat are we losing to spoilage when we sacrifice a cow the same day we purchase one?"

The *r'shnor* glanced to Tetramnestus, sitting nearby.

"Do not answer to me," the holy lady's aide replied. "Tell her."

The party-goers ignored the roar of winter rain overhead.

"...you should have seen him." Shipitbaal laughed into his beard as he told his favorite tale. "His face turned as purple as dye. He bellowed and raged but in the end, what choice did he have? After all, he had to have that iron."

"Shrewd bargaining, Lord," young Barcas agreed. "For all his demands on us, Qurdi-Aššur-lamur needed to go down a peg or two. And our house profited handily from your dealings."

"'Bl, if only I could take credit for it. But here is the real master of that day. Holy Lady, would you join us?"

"The wife of Arherbas?" Barcas was incredulous. "You listened to a woman? A girl?"

Shipitbaal's eye's flashed. "She provided sound council while you were learning to diddle your 'yr, boy. She has a talent for organization. It would be wise to respect your superiors."

The other rzn laughed at the joke, then greeted Elisha with courteous bows.

The torch flickered in the sweltering night air. A moth flew through it, blazing like a comet.

"Hold the light closer," Elisha ordered. Naked, she knelt on the flat rock overlooking the compound's stream. She examined the red stain on her linen sleeping robe before dunking it into the water once again.

The female slave holding the torch watched her scrub. "Such a moment this is for you. You are no longer a girl. You are a woman."

"Be silent," Elisha replied, scrubbing harder. "My husband will determine when I am a woman."

A female hand shook her awake.

"Holy Lady. Someone has come for you."

Elisha sat up on her pallet, rubbing her eyes. Then the words registered, jarring her awake.

"Who?"

"That large man. The holy lord's aide." There was a rustle of departure.

Elisha stood, her breath coming quickly. She started towards the door before realizing that she was wearing only her sleeping linens. She crossed to the pegs containing her clothing, turned to her jewelry box, then back again.

"Stop it, Elisha." She hissed, collecting herself. "Find your calm."

Far steadier, she slipped a light wrap over her linen. From the box, she collected her favorite headband. She also retrieved the finely crafted silver necklace, a present from Arherbas on her recent twelfth-year celebration.

She took a moment to study herself by moonlight in a small mirror. The wire of the headband gleamed amid her flowing black hair. Strong eyes, narrow nose, firm jawline, womanly chin.

"Astarte, bless me," came her whispered prayer. The robes swirled and the reflection was gone.

Tetramnestus waited outside the women's quarters, a silent presence. As she stepped from the entrance, he turned without a word. She followed his dim figure.

They crossed the compound, keeping to the well-known paths. A trickle of water came to her ears at the same time the blunt shape of the temple reared against the star field. Tetramnestus left the path, crossing the small glade. Before them was the single flight of stairs, the portal at the upper landing casting faint illumination. In her chest, Elisha's heart pounded.

Tetramnestus waved a halt, then pointed to the stream. "You must wash your feet."

Without a word, she obeyed. The chill water was a welcome distraction to her apprehension. Finished, she stepped back to the grass, wiping her feet dry. The aide nodded, then gestured to the stairs.

Alone, she climbed the flight, fingers knotting her robe. The night air was pure and still. It was as if the entire world held its collective breath.

The audience chamber was silent, a single lamp burning atop her husband's bench. Its tiny light refracted off the polished marble of the chamber and for a moment, Elisha was struck with the simple beauty. Then she saw the doorway to her husband's apartment and nervousness reclaimed her.

The splendor within was equal to any she'd seen in the palace.

FIRE AND BRONZE

Silk tapestries spilled down the walls. Thick rugs covered the floor. Golden figurines shimmered in the light of a second lamp, twin to the one in the chamber outside. So struck was she by the opulence around her that she failed to see him.

"Elisha." Her husband's voice was deep, calming. "Come here."

Layers of rugs had been thrown in the corner, surrounded by heaps of white pillows, a den of comfort. Arherbas reclined beneath a sheet, his dark eyes upon her, his bald head bronzed by the lighting. He gestured to a mound of pillows placed just before him.

Silently, willing herself not to trip, giggle, or weep, she stepped to the pillows and settled against them. Coverlets were strewn about and without thought, she slipped beneath one. Her knees slid up, a barrier against him. He viewed it all with an easy smile.

"Sparrow." His voice was warm and smooth. "Welcome to my chambers."

Speech eluded her. Her head bowed.

"Perhaps you should refresh yourself." He picked up a small tea urn from a tray at his side. The amber liquid steamed into a pair of bronze cups. She took it from his hands, careful not to touch his fingers, sipping. A soothing warmth descended through her. With downcast eyes, she took another calming sip.

"I can see your toes," he chuckled.

Blushing, she began to draw her foot back within the coverlet.

"Nay, tiny wife, nay. Leave it so. Do not remove such beauty from my sight." Instinctively obeying, she checked her movement, holding perfectly still. Then, self-consciously, she wiggled her toe. Across from her, Arherbas' smile spread.

"Sparrow, you do not see the encompassing beauty that you are. Frightened, you seek to hide it. You should not."

He moved with slow grace, and suddenly, she felt his gentle figures touch her foot.

"Nay," he calmed, "Do not start. Just be still."

Cupping her small heel in one hand, his strong fingers seemed to transform her very blood. A steady warmth spread upwards.

"The tiny foot of a princess." He examined it as if it were his greatest treasure. Lulled by his words, she found her own attention drawn to it.

89

"Its fine construction, its wonderful arches. From the coarse world it treads, it acquires a toughness." His fingernail slid across her small calluses. Her breath lodged in her throat—she could feel every ridge of her skin beneath his touch.

"Yet you are a true princess. There is still much that is playful and soft. *Y*, my little Sparrow." The fingers tightened and suddenly, the caress became a gentle tickle. Laugher bubbled from her, deep laughter, carrying away the tensions she'd borne. He teased her gently, holding her to the edge of comfort. She bowed in mirth, her forehead resting lightly on her single upraised knee.

Then his fingers closed around her foot, protective and gentle. She felt cleansed by her laughter, her body no longer her own. His fingers caressed her heel, her ankle, her arch.

"Perfection," Arherbas murmured, his eyes an eternity in the dimness. "El set aside the entire world, from the moment of creation onwards, concentrating all of its beauty into this single thing. *'Bl*, my heart seizes in my chest to behold it." He raised her foot as if in worship. She looked at it, suddenly seeing what it was that he saw, the sum of all beauty focused on a single physical object. How could she not have seen it before?

His breath played across her skin, raising goosebumps across her forearms. She could feel every thread of her linen clothing, every fiber of the carpet beneath her. She could smell the burned oil of the lamp from across the room. Perhaps the tea had been spiced. Perhaps Melqart had touched her. Perhaps it really didn't matter.

He kissed the top of her foot, his lips caressing her brown skin. The intense contact forced a cry from her lips. A low trembling seized her, coalescing into her belly. Nay, not her belly, lower. Within her private place, her *'bn*. Sensations flooded up her leg from her husband's touch. The mad confusion of rhythm became a fixed waveset. She trembled to a pulse as steady as oars in a sparkling blue sea.

She saw Bitias' smile, felt his touch. Something within her convulsed in pleasure.

She found herself leaning forward, forehead pressed against her knee, a low moan trickling up from deep in her throat. A bead of sweat dropped into her lap, instantly absorbed.

Arherbas' touch was gone. Her dark eyes opened. He lay on his side, shuddering as she had moments before.

"My husband, are..."

"Go," he croaked. "Go."

She bowed, even through he could not see it, and staggered to her feet. Her robe hung like draperies, entangling her clumsy limbs, and she stumbled once or twice. Leaving his chambers, her feet touched the cold marble and heaven became hell. Dazed and over-sensitized, she staggered across the endless hall, reeling towards the far door, driven by her husband's command. She fell through the opening into the cold night air. Her momentum might have propelled her over the brink of the landing had not strong arms captured her.

Tetramnestus' fleshy face appeared before her, brows knitted, eyes unreadable. Then, without knowing how, she found herself in his arms, carried like the child she was. As the aide transported her back to her quarters, she looked up into El's starry sky and beheld his wisdom. A tear rolled down her cheek, staining the man's sleeve.

He returned her to her pallet. Her sleep was deep, dreamless.

Elisha scowled as she crossed the glade to the rear of the temple. Tetramnestus shepherded her in the direction of the stairs.

"Explain again," she demanded, "why you interrupted me. The master of the kitchen and I were working out the allocation request to the royal granary."

"It is that insufferable priest," the aide whined. "He is endlessly badgered me to see the holy lord."

"For the tenth time, who? Who is responsible for this disruption?"

"*Rmkhn* Sirom."

Elisha took the steps to the audience chamber two at a time. The aide waddled after her as best he could.

"I do not recognize that name."

"He is not of our order," panted Tetramnestus at the landing. "Astarte. He is from the temple of Astarte."

She turned to face him. "What business does Astarte require of Melqart? And by what right does her priests make demands of us?" She scowled. "Why has not my husband dealt with them?"

"The rituals of this year's Egersis have yet to be completed. The holy lord and his priests are attempting to conclude it." He saw her concern. "Yes, it should have been completed two days ago. But Arherbas saw an evil portent in a critical sacrifice. They seek to confirm it."

She opened her mouth to ask another question but thought better of it. Turning on her heel, she swept into the audience chamber.

With the order's holy men occupied in the temple downstairs, the room was oddly still. Three men stood near the distant bench, lost in the great space. Elisha walked quickly to them.

"High Priest Sirom?"

A man dressed in fine robes turned to face her. Unlike most of the men of the Canaan, he was beardless. His eyes were doe-like, his chin weak.

"I am he," the man replied, eyeing her up and down. "First aides, now women."

"I am the holy lady. You will speak to me as you would the holy lord. What questions I cannot answer, I will convey to him."

The man threw up his hands. Elisha found the gesture weak.

"I seek the holy lord, not his underlings and playthings. For the last time..."

"Either way, I shall see the holy lord before you do." Her tone was cold. "Either way, I will pass along my first impressions. *My* first impressions. In that regard I largely determine the outcome."

The priest stared at her. Unsure, he looked to Tetramnestus. The aide gave a confirming nod.

"Well, yes." He blinked, then refocused on Elisha. "All right. I shall speak with you, and consider you as the holy lord's spokesman. The matter concerns colonial tribute."

"Yes?"

The priest gathered himself. "As you know, all colonies forward ten percent of their gains to Tyre, a duty paid to the mother city. Half this wealth is forwarded to the palace, the other half, the temple of Melqart. Your order keeps a portion and divides the remainder across the various shrines."

"So far, correct. It is how it has always been done."

"We do not feel that we are receiving an appropriate share. Last year, some two hundred talents of precious metals were received by Tyre. The temple of Melqart forwarded a mere five talents to us." His voice quavered in indignation. "By what right do you withhold gold that is Astarte's? We are one of the major faiths of this city, equal in numbers of followers to Melqart's temple. Our Lady is a powerful goddess. She instructed Baal to scatter Yam. The great god, the Rider of Clouds, obeyed her council. Her wrath is mighty to behold, and you seek it at your peril."

Elisha listened, nonplused.

"May I ask the Lord where he received the information concerning the tariff levels?" Her blunt question earned a blink from the priest.

"That is not the issue here. The issue is that you are cheating our Lady..."

"Where did your figures come from?"

Tetramnestus coughed politely. "I would wager the information came from the palace." Elisha arched an eyebrow towards him. "It stands to reason; the Temple of Astarte has had much contact with the palace during the recent celebration of Egersis. The king is old enough to fully engage in his duties. Lacking a queen, the Lady's temple is generally called upon to provide assistance for his task."

"Three priestesses were sent," Sirom considered his words, "to *assist* the king, to perform the rites of fertility and rebirth. The women were experienced in such matters, and were able to coax the king to perform his duties."

Elisha found a part of herself wondering what this might have entailed. Certainly it was not the act that she and Arherbas performed. Her husband's touch contained great skill and tenderness. She could not imagine Pumayyaton taking enough interest in anyone to please them in such a way. Could such have been done *to* him? Perhaps.

Could it have been that...activity she remembered the *'bny* engaged in so many years ago?

Unthinkable.

"So you met with the king to discuss Egersis, and ended up speaking of Gadar gold?" Now it was Tetramnestus' turn to arch an eyebrow to Elisha.

"He was grateful for our order's assistance," Sirom replied. "Lord

Pumayyaton simply wished to return a favor, and advised us as to the inequities between the various temples."

Elisha met the aide's eye, sharing a silent thought. *Pumayyaton had stirred the house of Astarte against us.*

"Lord Sirom, let me explain the situation as it stands. Our gods each govern an aspect of our world. El is the father of the gods. Baal, lightning and thunder. Astarte, fertility and love. Anat, war and the hunt. And Melqart? *Mlqrt* means, literally, 'King of the City'. He is the true power of Tyre. He controls the destiny of the Canaanites."

"This I know," growled Sirom but Elisha cut him off.

"When Tyre establishes a new colony, what is the first permanent structure they build? A granary? A harbor? No, they build a temple to Melqart. The reason they do this is *not* to honor our god. They do it because his house *is* the house of the Canaanites. In his house, the commercial dealings that drive our expansion are conducted. In his house, the wealth is stored. Across the breadth of the Upper Sea, the mightiest *rzn* and the lowest tribesman share the same view; the temple of Melqart is a sanctuary, and inside it, the men of Canaan will trade fairly. It becomes the cornerstone, the *grn'bn* of the new city.

"From each temple, the wealth flows back to Tyre. It flows back in the manner of which you spoke, divided between palace and temple, *mlk* and *Mlqrt*. And our temple, the hub of our entire merchant empire, distributes our wealth in the best way we see fit."

She waved her hand in emphasis. "Yes, Astarte sees less than a tenth of this. As does the temple of Baal. The lesser shines also receive their due portions. The remainder is Melqart's."

"Exactly," Sirom puffed. "And why is that?"

"Because we pay a share to the Assyrians. This is something we do that Astarte does not. And we fund new trading and colonization efforts. Melqart is Tyre, and it is in Melqart's interest to expand. The Canaanites, traders all, know that it takes gold to make gold. And that is where the gold goes."

Sirom looked to his feet for a moment, flustered at being set straight by a young girl.

"We still should get more gold," he groused petulantly.

"You want more gold?" Elisha sighed. "Is that what this is about? If so, I can have Tetramnestus take you to the temple's coffer and give you any amount you deem fair." The priest's eyes flicked for a moment. Her words grew hard. "But determine what it is that you lack. Determine what is due Astarte of Melqart, and we shall set it to rights. But if you seek to simply move gold from our vaults to yours, not for use but to hold, then you are not meeting a need. In that case, you would be prostituting your goddess for gold, and stealing from ours."

Sirom shifted uneasily. Standing in the house of Melqart, he was certain that the god could see his mortal thoughts.

"Astarte is not a goddess of thieves," he replied with quick defensiveness. "She only seeks what is due her."

"Melqart understands this. Astarte is an integral part of the Canaanites. She should be thanked for such. Perhaps if the house of Melqart were to sacrifice a golden bowl to the house of the goddess, such a gesture would not be misunderstood."

Sirom nodded. Begging for gold had been undignified. A sacrifice to the goddess was a gesture of respect. He felt far more comfortable with this.

"Tetramnestus will have the item transferred following our evening service. I believe that this concludes the matter."

"My thanks to you, Holy Lady, for settling this matter equitably." Sirom bowed with respect. "May the goddess smile on you." With that, he departed, assistants in tow.

As they descended the stairs, Tetramnestus noted, "You handled that well, my lady. You illuminated his greed, letting him discover it for himself. And you gave him a little gold to soothe any hurt feelings. When first I heard his demands, I thought that the only options were a new enemy or an expensive ally. I could not see any other alternative." They turned to follow the temple wall to the front of the building. "You have a way with people. I know not how you do it."

She shrugged. "I just see a path I would like a person to follow and show it to them."

Tetramnestus thought about this. Indeed, he was one of her greatest supporters. She had shown him how to do his work, arranging the temple and its inventories to run themselves. If she was directing him down a path of her own choosing, so be it. It was far better than the one he'd followed previously.

They reached the front of the temple with its twin columns. At their back, the sun fell horizontally across the market, pulling at shadows. Priests emerged from the temple, stretching and laughing after the long services. Tetramnestus stopped to speak with a few. Elisha asked for her husband. One of the men pointed inside; Arherbas was concluding his business with the city's god.

The door of the *ulam* thudded behind her. The anteroom to the temple was dark, lit by high windows and a single lamp. Across from her were the doors leading the to main hall, the *hekal*, a room forbidden to her sex. She leaned against a wall, patently waiting.

Eventually the door opened. With the temple lights extinguished and the sun lost in the high windows, she could see little of the inner room. Arherbas, garbed in his traditional linens, smiled at the sight of her.

"Sparrow."

She pushed off of the wall. "Husband, Pumayyaton tried to set the temple of Astarte against us."

"What?" His eyes widened in surprise. He crossed to her in a swirl of robes.

"He incited High Priest Sirom with thoughts of gold and pointed him in our direction."

"This is inexcusable. I must meet with him this evening. The temples must stand firm..."

Elisha shifted against the doors, her buttocks wedged against the horizontal bar. She raised her leg, planting her small bare foot squarely against his firm belly. He halted, looking down in surprise.

"I said he *tried*." Her smile was coquettish. "I placated Sirom with words and a gold bowl. All Pumayyaton achieved was to reveal his plans. Nothing more."

Arherbas stood still, at odds with the pleasure of her contact. "I still should speak with the other priests. We must fortify our position against future attempts."

"Now?" Her toes wiggled against his flesh.

A smile spread. "Later." He pulled her to the floor with a growl.

Her squeals echoed in the *ulam*. Eventually the tickling gave way to his wondrous caresses. On her back, she looked up at the dark ceiling through shuttered eyes, concentrating on the lips that kissed her ankles, toes, and soles. His devotions quickened her breath, fanning the fire within her *'bn*. Shè looked down lovingly at him. Then came the small eruption from deep within. A contented smile blossomed across her face.

EIGHT

Rogue hulls slid forth from a Cilician cove. The shout of a lookout. Merchantmen scattered, but the wolves were amid the sheep. An escort bore in.

A pirate bowman raised his weapon, not really aiming. His eyes were bad, he was slightly drunk, the boat rolled. Still, gods other than those of the Canaanites were in attendance. The arrow drove through flesh, artery, larynx. The battle turned on this minor event.

She lay across the pillowed floor from Arherbas, lovingly watching him sleep.

Seven months had passed since she'd headed off Pumayyaton's attempt at driving a fissure between the temples. She'd continued to administer Melqart's house, learning how men worked, how they thought. Most of the time, the priests and servants welcomed her changes. Occasionally, a man would not; he'd grumble, balk, or sulk. She would repair the damage, returning the angry lamb to her fold, learning more about men as she did.

She might see her husband two to three times a month. He had his work, she her own. But occasionally he would summon her. Sometimes he would just worship his favorite part of her. That was fine—she found enjoyment in his enthusiasm. But sometimes he would just drink tea and talk. Those were her favorite times.

She would sit across from him and listen to his thoughts on the temple, on Pumayyaton's politics, or his opinions of her changes. She would watch his strong face as he spoke, his large hands as they cradled a teacup. Sometimes, lying on the floor, she would playfully allow her feet to come in view and take hidden delight in seeing his eyes light up.

She loved her husband with iron-clad devotion.

But there was something else. She didn't know what it was, but there was something. It hid deep in her emotions like a reef beneath waves. She felt as if her emotions were a deep amphora, and something lay at the bottom, just beyond her reach.

There was *something* more to love than what Arherbas had shown her. She knew it. While he caressed her feet, she'd discovered that her body would become so very sensitive. The simple shift of her cotton robes would take her breath away. And sometimes, when her *'bn* would fail in its song, she would brush a hand across her breasts, sparking her kindling to flames.

And there was the thing that she would occasionally glimpse, the rising of his own robes near his belly. He took pains to hide it, often keeping a cover over his hips or a knee strategically placed. But seen it she had.

She thought of the *'bny* by the canal, the grimy embrace, the animal grunting. That could not be love.

No?

Her doubt was a challenge to her devotion to her husband. She crushed it, wishing it to be gone, knowing that it was not.

It was then she noticed Arherbas was awake, quietly watching her.

"Sparrow, you seemed...agitated."

"*Y*, husband," she smiled, fighting her blush. "I was simply thinking of that stupid kitchen master and his silly ways. He attempts to maintain the household as it has always been done. Every day is a battle with him. *N'*!"

Her husband watched her silently some time. Then, as if coming to a decision, he nodded. She watched as he stood. "Come."

Without a word, she followed in his footsteps. They left the apartment, passing through the silent audience chamber. The landing outside was cold; it was the darkest moment of the night. Low clouds obscured the stars, and Yarikl's orb sailed other skies. She ran a hand along the temple's wall, straining her senses to remain behind Arherbas. Carefully, they circled to the temple's front face.

The marketplace was empty, the flagstones deserted. From the nearby temples of Baal and Astarte, and the palace as well, torches burned. On the steps between the massive columns of gold and emeralds, a priest sat hunched in his robes, sleeping. Arherbas smiled sadly to her, shaking his head at the man's failure to keep watch. Yet he did not wake him. He led her past the slumbering man to the large doors which he eased open. She looked at him in puzzlement; her replied with a quick gesture. *Inside!*

The door clunked shut behind them and darkness flooded the room like subterranean waters. Elisha felt panic creeping up her throat and willed herself to be calm. She would not show girlish weakness before her husband.

A tiny spark flared. An instant later, Arherbas stood before her, a small clay lamp in his large hand. Around them, the gold leaf patterning the walls of the *ulam* shimmered faintly. A sense of peace, of nearness-to-god, fell over Elisha. She smiled to her husband to show she was no longer afraid.

He stepped to the opposite door. She stood, watching, wondering why he was choosing to enter the central room of the temple at this hour. Then he raised his hand, beckoning.

For a moment she was struck dumb. His fingers wiggled. *Come-come.* Hand to her throat, she hesitantly stepped to him, and as she did, he pushed open the door. Taking her hand, he backed in.

"Husband," she balked, "I cannot enter."

"Sparrow, it is all right."

"No, I cannot enter the *Hekal.* Women are not permitted."

"I am your husband, high priest of Tyre, Holy Lord of the Canaanites. Melqart speaks through me. I am, in part, our god. I give you permission."

She looked into his cool eyes. If she held back, she sensed that something would be lost forever. Never again would he bring her here. But if she were caught, his position would not save her. Stoning. Crucifixion.

She steadied herself, looking into his eyes once again. Then she let his strong fingers draw her into the darkness.

Much of the room was lost in the blackness, but before the tiny flicker of the lamp, gold shimmered. Two rows of bronze tripods, five to a side, lined the high narrow chamber. Delicate patterns flowed down the walls. The marble at her feet was deep as space.

He led her slowly down the length of the room. Her hesitation was not of fear but amazement. She had never considered that men, coarse and brutal as they were, could be capable of such soaring devotion. Had Melqart suddenly appeared before her, he would not have seemed out of place.

Arherbas smiled back. "Remember that day three years ago, shortly after we were wed? You spoke of usurpation, of casting down Pumayyaton and seizing the throne?"

"Then, I was but a little girl," She replied, chin raised. "I have grown."

"*'Bl!*" he chuckled. "And now you are all of twelve."

"I shall be thirteen within a span of days."

He smiled. "You spoke of the power within my grasp. How I could rule Tyre. As if sitting on that cold throne meant anything." His hand tightened. "Do not you see it, Elisha? The power? Look into the wise faces of the cherubim surrounding us. Look at the high walls with inlaid gold. Think of all who seek my favor. Your brother has taken the same blind road to power as his father. But this is where the true power lies, at the feet of the great god Melqart."

"But you could have all this," she noted, "*and* more."

"More? What more is that? The more of sitting in a drafty room day after day, listening to the *mw'd* whine, passing out rules and laws to the outside world? Nay, Pumayyaton is a prisoner to his cursed chair."

"He has gold." The light of his lamp was steady in her dark eyes. "Much gold."

"Gold? That is what is important to you? Mere gold?"

"Gold is power. It makes men do your bidding. It builds cities and causes them to be destroyed. It is the only true magic. A lump of gold can become a ship, a herd of cattle, a bevy of beautiful slaves, anything."

"How mercenary of you, little Sparrow." His smile was knowing. "Come."

He began to ascend a flight of steps leading to two massive cedar doors at the far end of the room. This time, she set her feet without thinking.

"The inner room," she gasped. "Husband, no!"

"No?"

"The holy-of-holies. Whatever man should behold it shall perish." Her voice tremored. "Only you, as high priest, may enter that room. One day a year, the Day of Atonement."

"From greedy usurper to fearful supplicant. Quite a change, little one." His hand closed on the massive golden handle. The other tightened on her own. "I said I would show you power. Come with me."

The huge door opened soundlessly. The darkness within was total. Elisha allowed herself to be led inside, a lamb to slaughter.

A huge shape leered over her, wings spread. All-knowing eyes considered her above bared teeth.

She took a step back, a tiny scream welling up from her throat.

"Behold," Arherbas stated, waving his small lamp. "The guardian of the treasure. The keeper of the stone."

She realized that the massive sphinx that towered over her was man-crafted, a thing of finest cedar and purest gold.

"The guardian is old," her husband noted in reserved tones. "Not as old as time itself, not even as old as this island, but old. He dates back to Hiram's time, a century and a half. The one it replaced, only slightly smaller, was rumored to have been there for five hundred years. And that was, itself, a replacement. *'Bl*, we Canaanites are a long-lived race."

She gazed up at the mighty statue, marveling at its grandeur.

"Look long, child. Only a dozen or so holy lords have seen this sight."

Eventually she began to take in the opulence of the room, the clever interworkings of gold and wood. The beauty of all that surrounded her was such that her heart felt as if it would burst.

Suddenly she could see true power, the power beyond kings. This was the power of her race, the force that propelled them across oceans, trading with men of all colors. It encompassed the world.

Eventually her eyes fell to the area immediately between the great creature's paws. With a shocked cry, she slid to the cool floor. The sacred stone stood before her. A rough column of marble had been thrust through a swirl of granite. From its center, water trickled through a minute fissure, bubbling into a pool whose pebbles were orbs of gold and silver.

Her eyes stared into the timeless water, her lungs compressed. When she did breath, it was more a gasp of shock.

"The water. It flows...it flows into the pool. But it must go somewhere." Her eyes rolled towards her husband. "The pipe under the stairs. The water of the holy-of-holies flows out through the compound." She collapsed on the floor, pressing her face into the marble in shame. "The women wash their laundry in its waters! I...I have played in it!"

His chuckle was deep. "Sparrow, Sparrow. Arise. Our ancestors had to do something with the sacred waters, lest they flood the room. The God provides. Man uses. So it is in the world." He lifted her gently. "But this is nothing but an aside. Come. There is something you must see."

She was now numb, unable to resist. He led her around the creature's vast paw, moving along its flank to its massive haunch. The surface was smooth, crafted from the finest cedar.

Gently, he took her hand, placing it against the statue.

"Here, between its haunch and flank. That is it. Feel that small imperfection? Press it and step back."

Fissures crossed the surface before them, seams cunningly camouflaged in the grain of the wood. It was a hatch, three feet across. It swung open and down. Within was a small space. Arherbas moved the small lamp closer.

Nine ordinary clay amphorae lay within. They could have come straight from the hold of a transport. They appeared unremarkable in any way.

The Holy Lord took one of the stoppers and eased it out. Diamonds glittered in the dark maw. Another stopper revealed perfect gems, each the size of a goose egg. Others contained golden dust, jewelry, and precious stones.

"You see my position, Sparrow? You see my power? Both lords and low-born pay for their sacrifices to Melqart. A minute portion of that payment goes to me, tiny lumps of silver and gold. You combine these and purchase trade goods, and the lumps become bigger. Invest here and there, and the lumps become more numerous. Combine them this way and that, the lumps become diamonds, emeralds, precious things."

"So now you see the truth. These nine small urns contain the true treasure of Tyre. Talents of gold, stored in this room no man may enter. There is more wealth here than the palace vaults ever held, and it's mine. All mine."

His large hand cupped her shoulder, drawing her close. "You are the wife of the richest man in the world."

She turned thirteen. The rains came shortly after, closing the port. The poor drank and fought, made babies and died. The ship-owners groused about the weather, endlessly checking their vessels lest disaster strike the moment they turned away. Merchant princes met in the temples to formulate their plans. In their opulent homes, *rzn* parties spanned the dreary days.

Elisha moved through the fetes with stately grace. Something had changed her. Even though her stature made her look up at others, the reverse seemed true. She became known as *Qtn'khn*, Little Priestess, for her regal bearing. But regardless of her fine robes and the stunning jewelry, she was rarely without her favorite headband, so very much a part of her.

Barcas, little older than she, was the first to notice the change. Her breasts had begun to form. He would have mentioned it to the other *rzn* in quiet jest but was unsure of their reaction. The princes seemed very supportive of the holy lady, and Barcas felt that he might risk a beating should he speak ill of her.

Twice at parties, the paths of Elisha and Pumayyaton crossed. Each remained within a circle of supporters, openly ignoring the other. During the second encounter, Elisha happened to glance towards her brother, to find him studying her in return. His expression was unreadable.

As quickly as they'd come, the last of the squalls scraped over the eastern mountains. Egersis was held, wine flowed, and the effigy burned. Immediately after, the booms of the harbors opened and the merchants sailed. Trade of all manner passed through Tyre, silks and dyes, ivory and horses, iron and slaves, trinkets and treasures. The Assyrians took their tribute of iron and gold, turning their attention to their growing civil wars.

Elisha passed through her life. Arherbas continued his acts of *pomhbb* on her. She met with the staff on matters of household. Amid the nobility, she became increasingly active, quietly listening and occasionally offering sound advice. All in all, she was content with the way things were.

But change drove towards her. Out of the north, borne on fifty oars, it came.

"**Y**ou looked wondrous, *Qdshba'alat*," Tetramnestus beamed. He slipped the small parasol between her and the mid-year sun.

"Tell me again about this party."

"*Celebration*," the aide corrected. "One of our captains turned the tide against a nest of pirates north of Cyprus. Killed a hundred of them, I hear tell. Took twice more as slaves. King Pumayyaton and Holy Lord Arherbas have determined that this is a victory for Melqart, not just Tyre. They are promoting the man to the rank of admiral in a celebration at the temple."

"Men," she scoffed. Tetramnestus followed her down the path with the parasol. "Wars and battles, victory and promotions. Such an involved little game."

They arrived at the rear of the temple, ascending the stairs to the high landing. Guests climbed the ladder to the roof without a thought. She waited her turn, a nearby slave cooling her with a peacock feather fan. Tetramnestus held the parasol and sweated.

Eventually they reached the gardens atop the temple's roof. All four corners were densely foliaged, surrounding a central court containing a small gazebo. Elisha chose to stand near a bank of ferns, forgoing the festivities for the simple pleasure of a breeze laden with the scent of honeysuckle and the hiss of palm fronds. She gained thin amusement watching the guests.

"*Y!* Look, Tetramnestus. It is that horrible Qurdi-Aššur-lamur. How *does* he stand his bronze armor in the afternoon sun?"

"He is Assyrian, my lady. They enjoy such things."

She watched him move through the crowds like a ponderous merchantman through a school of dolphins. He paused before a table of refreshments, quaffing the contents of three silver cups before moving on.

A finely robed figured moved past, disdaining conversation and eye contact with the other guests. Elisha squinted after him, realizing that it was the commoner spokesman, Adon. The ship builder had done well under Pumayyaton's rule. His former master had received a palace mandate to organize a shipyard in distant Gadar. He'd been bought out at cost and dumped on a boat for the Atlantic colony. Adon now managed the business for the throne.

She wondered how he could represent the city's lowly *'bny* when he no longer was one himself.

Disaster struck when Lady Ayzebel swooped down, cornering Elisha against the foliage. No excuses could extract her from the noblewoman's chatter. She was treated to an entire recounting of the prior season's social events, followed by a preview of those upcoming. Elisha watched the sun slowly fall as if weighted by the prattle. At her side, Tetramnestus moved the parasol from hand to hand.

"...and you could tell from the gummy taste that their date wine had gone bad. Such might be consigned to the servants, but to serve it to guests...."

Looking over the noblewoman's shoulder, Elisha could see the distant brown hills of the mainland. A narrow shelf of rock was just visible in the afternoon haze. She wondered what it would be like to be there rather than here, looking out over distant Tyre. Would she still hear Ayzebel from such a distance?

"...claimed it was silk. *Heavy* Rhodian silk. How could I tell the poor thing that she'd traded good gold for common cloth..."

Other *rzn* ladies began to drift over. Like the anchor-man of a hoplite formation, Ayzebel formed the centerpoint of the tiny island's gossip mill. Anyone not present was flayed for social imperfections.

They sound like chickens. Chickens in a pen. Elisha fought to maintain an attentive stance. *Cluck cluck cluck.*

She realized that she might be able to slip away, but not with the ponderous Tetramnestus and his colorful parasol. She caught his eye and made a *stay here* gesture. A look of horror crossed the aide's face, but her answering scowl invited no arguments. Moving cautiously, she eased around him, placing his bulk between herself and the others. As nonchalantly as she could, she strolled away, threading through the crowds. At the other side of the pavilion, she settled onto a bench, happy to be free of Lady Ayzebel and her harpies.

"Do not you hate it when you cannot escape a bore?" Someone plunked down on the seat next to her.

The young man at her side was finely adorned in robes, gold rings hanging from his ears. His beard was short and tightly curled, his hair uncommonly long. For a moment, she could not place the lean face.

"Bitias!" She was startled by how he'd matured. The wiry ship's boy had become a man on the cusp of his prime.

"How good of you to remember, little priestess," he smiled back, then studied her face. "Perhaps you should seek the shade. You appear to be reddening."

She turned slightly to hide her blush. Her mind had flashed the fantasies that sometimes came when Arherbas performed his worships upon her.

"So," she said with regained composure, "What are you doing here? Should not you be with your ship, the...?"

"*Sdqsh*," he laughed. "The *RearEnd*. Certainly you have not forgotten our amusing little figurine?"

She ignored his comment as she had ignored the suggestive figure-sprite four years ago.

"So what are you doing in a gathering of Tyre's elite? Hardly the place for a lowly second-officer." Something clicked. "You are part of the new admiral's escort, are you not? That is what you are doing here."

"Quite so," he agreed. "No waterfront dives for me. I always latch on to a superior's robes. Where they go, the wine is better and the girls prettier." His expression was frank.

"I am married now," she replied bluntly. "I am the wife of the holy lord."

"Reefs ho," he sighed. "I understand the warning. I shall behave. You are charming, but hardly worth a place on a cross."

"I was not threatening you. I was merely explaining changes that have taken place in your absence."

"Just in case I should discretely slip a hand over to take yours, *Qtn'khn*?" She looked up quickly at the use of her pet name. "*Y*, 'Little Priestess'. I know the nobles call you that. You can pick up so many things when you lack rank and age at an affair such as this. 'Mouth shut, ears open', as old Commander Jabnit used to say."

"Your mouth is not shut now."

"Cleaver *and* cute. I love that in a woman."

A shadow fell over her. A fist appeared near her head, holding the shaft of a parasol. Tetramnestus glared down at the second-officer.

"Is this man bothering you?" he asked Elisha flatly.

Bitias smiled up at the new arrival. "Ah, this must be the lady's eunuch."

"I am the holy lord's assistant and the holy lady's escort! I worship the great god of Melqart! You confuse me with the priests of Astarte who maim themselves in their passion to serve their goddess."

"Sorry. It was the rolly-pollyness that threw me."

Elisha heard the cane parasol shaft creak beneath Tetramnestus' fingers. For some reason, Bitias' presence disturbed her and she rallied against it.

"Second-officer, you forget yourself. Tetramnestus is a priest of Melqart, ranking high in the temple order. He is held in highest esteem and deserves nothing but respect. Especially from '*bny*."

"Such as myself?" Bitias' smile was easy.

"Such as yourself." Elisha's anger flashed. She felt boorish, as if she represented the worst of the *rzn* class. Bitias seemed to goad her to it with his handsome grace and lackadaisical smirks.

"This is my house," she continued, "and you are a guest here.

Until you can achieve distinction and rank, it would behoove you to remain silent. Be thankful that I and my escort do not report your advances to your superior."

Bitias climbed to his feet. "The new admiral. How good of you to remind me." His smile remained easy. "Allow me to offer my apologies for my actions. Lord Tetramnestus, forgive me for assuming that you were emasculated. And Holy Lady Elisha, forgive my unwanted advances." While his bow was comically deep, his eyes were serious. "Too long at sea, I suppose."

Tetramnestus watched Bitias disappear into the crowds.

"What is happening to our society? The common herd strut like peacocks, putting on airs. First Adon, and now this upstart. What became of those fine prior years, where those with age and rank were treated with respect? Our society falls into the abyss."

Elisha looked to her assistant, tinted orange by the lowering sun. "I am sorry, Tetramnestus. I do not know what that was about. When we met as children years ago, we were civil. Now we meet and everything falls apart. But he was wrong to insult you with his japes."

He returned a warm smile. "Do not worry, *Qtn'khn*. Remember, before you came to me, I was a failure. That strutting sailor boy said nothing I had not heard before. The whisperings of the other priests, the seemingly innocent remarks. If I could weather their disdain, I can easily overcome the comments of a *'bny* oar-puller."

"Very good, Tetramnestus..." Elisha saw the aide's face turn wooden. Without a word, he dropped the parasol and bowed deeply. Confused, she turned.

NINE

Pumayyaton stood facing her.

His rich robes were embroidered with golden threads. A mantle of expensive purple billowed in the light sea-breeze. His conical felt hat gave the illusion of height.

Ib flanked him, sun shimmering off his bronze breastplate. From the plumes of the helmet under his arm, she could see that he was now a Commander-of-One-Hundred, presumably the head of the palace guards.

She looked closer at her brother. Beneath the finery, he was still the same. His shoulders were a little broader but his neck was still too scrawny for his round head. Yet he was her ruler. She bowed in formal respect.

He spoke with a voice that was deeper than the one of childhood memories.

"Holy Lady, we thank you for granting us entry to your husband's estate." This was little more than a formal greeting.

She held her bow until he gestured she straighten. "Thank you, my Lord King."

He looked into the sky, as if noticing the heavens for the first time. "A fine day for such a ceremony."

"Yes, Lord." She kept her eyes downcast. "Not hot. Not cool."

He paused, then said, "I wish to speak to the holy lady alone."

Ib looked questionably to his master. Pumayyaton's eyes remained upon Elisha. Finally, with a nod, he moved back a respectful distance. Tetramnestus, too, eased away. His attention remained locked on his mistress.

"Why, Elisha?"

She met his eyes, momentarily confused. "Why? Of what do you speak?"

"Was it his gold? His power?"

She gestured to indicate she was still confused.

"Your husband. Our uncle. Arherbas. Why did you marry him?" He shook his head, bringing a hiss from his silken fineries. "I have faced hell these past years. Father growing sicker and sicker. The priests and healers applying their cures to no avail. It was like watching the last of a fire burn out. One moment he was there. And then he was gone.

"And the *mw'd*. Those of the noble council sit on their pillows, eyeing me like snakes watching a mouse. They do not respect Canaan, Tyre, or Melqart. It is gold they lust for; you can see it in their eyes."

"Pumayyaton, the *rzn* have shown nothing but support for the royal house."

"*Lys*! I have watched them in court for years. The knowing glances. The discrete whispers. They are a threat to the throne. What course was there but to counter them with the *bolh*?"

Elisha stood silently. She had never considered that her brother might have reasons for his actions.

"And so there I was, Elisha. Father dying. Nobles plotting. I had nobody to stand shoulder to shoulder with, other than you." He looked directly into her eyes. "And then comes your disloyalty."

She blinked at his hurt tone.

"You fled, leaving me to face the world alone. I needed you."

"I...I do not understand, Pumayyaton. How can you say you needed me? What gain would my presence bring you? I was only a small girl."

"You were my sister. That would have been enough."

She looked to him in concern. Inside his robes he seemed small, frail.

"But you frightened me, brother. You spoke of me as a danger. You spoke of," she looked to make sure none were within earshot, "having me killed." At his incredulous look, she clarified. "In the throne room that night."

"That?" He shook his head. "A child's game. Further, you have shown yourself adept at organizing men. I cajole and threaten, yet you simply point out the obvious and men fall over themselves to obey. Rulers need such skills among their backers. Clearly, you have value. No good would have come from your death."

She sank onto the bench behind her, confused. Finally, she looked up at him. He stood against the setting sun, lost in the glare.

"What is it that you want?"

"I want you to return to me. Canaanite wives often live outside their husband's homes; you, yourself, have dwelt in the woman's quarters for the past four years." He stepped to her, placing a hand on her shoulder. "Come back to the palace, Elisha. You will still be married to the holy lord. But you can support me, too. You can help me to organize and to better read the designs of the aristocracy." A pause. "I need you, sister."

She let her head drop. Could she have been wrong about him? Could her vision have been so clouded?

"You know I am right," he said simply. "You can feel the truth."

Feel the truth. Feel. Of course I feel that it is true. But I know that it isn't. He tracked me through the throne room with a sword. He gave Ib orders to mock and threaten me. He tried to have me seized when father and Arherbas agreed to my wedding.

She looked up into his eyes. What she saw shocked her.

He believes his falsehood. I can see it in his eyes. He actually believes his tale. That is how he charms people—he convinces himself, then argues from his heart.

"You were going to kill me, that night in the throne room. You felt that I conspired against you, just as you feel the *rzn* plot against you now. I will not return to the palace. My home is here."

"I told you that was just a game," he blurted in apparent hurt. "Why cannot you see it? Is it because you do not dare to stand by my side in the glory of our empire? Are you afraid of the greatness of ruling? Is that why you fled, to marry a man who is more a father than a husband?"

"Arherbas is a good husband. He is a kind man."

"Is he castrated, Elisha? Does he let you sit in your cold little room while he wiggles on the floor before the glory of Melqart?"

Now she remembered his other power. When it did not suit to charm, Pumayyaton would poison. He would probe with taunts, gauging reactions. The surer he became, the harder he thrust. She turned away lest he saw how close to the mark he really was.

"Is that it, Elisha? No love to warm the coldest night? No reason to give thanks to Astarte? Remember my words, sister. Fleeing me, you ruined your life. I would have seen you married to a man, someone to share passion with you. Now, you will live in that little room, never to taste what life is really about."

She continued to face away, eyes clenched shut. A moment later, his hand clamped on her shoulder, startling her. He leaned forward, whispering with false tenderness in her ear.

"Last year's Egersis was the first time I performed my duty as a man. You know, the act of rebirth. The act of seeding for the new year." She could sense his smile. "Lord Sirom of the temple of Astarte sent three priestesses to assist me. For a time, we talked. They tried three or four times to relax me, but I was like a little turtle, fearful to come out of its shell. Finally, one of them suggested wrestling in the manner of those barbaric Greeks. Naked, Elisha. They all stood before me like castings of Astarte herself. So much beauty. All mine."

She opened her eyes. Wetness shimmered the sunset into fire.

"They were masters of their craft. Before I knew it, two of them had me pinned, one to each arm. And the last, clever whore that she was, toyed with me. She played with me with her tongue and her fingers. At first, I was scared, but something came over me. I struggled. I shouted. But she tormented me until I was mad with passion. Such a glorious release, the Egersis."

He chuckled a final time in her ear.

"The *'drtnt*, Elisha. The burning passion, the thunderous release, the still aftermath. You shall never truly feel it, not with your kindly old husband. You shall be his innocent little sparrow until you turn old and gray. I could not have wished a better curse upon you."

The hand lifted as he stepped back. "I have a ceremony to perform. Farewell, sister."

She slumped onto the bench, eyes wet, ears burning. Pumayyaton's words rang through her. Was that all her life would be? Nothing but Arherbas' gentle yet distant touch? Would she forever be denied the *'drtnt?*

Another hand fell on her shoulder, softer. She shrugged away Tetramnestus' comfort. He stood next to her, unsure of what had been said and what he could possibly do to fix it. Finally he slunk off, leaving her to her own misery.

It was the fanfare that brought her out of her blackness. Trumpets tilted into the indigo sky, screaming towards the gods. She looked up to see the crowds gathering along the carpeted runway. In the gazebo, a stately Pumayyaton stood beneath the first evening stars. In his hands was a heavy golden medallion. A man walked down the runway, flowing robes rustling as he bowed before the king. It was Tyre's newest admiral, the man who'd scattered the northern pirates so courageously.

With great dignity, Pumayyaton lowered the medallion across the kneeling man's shoulders. To one side, Arherbas shouted into the heavens, calling to Melqart to reward this man and his people for their courage. The other priests took up the chant.

The admiral turned to receive the collective blessings of the crowd. A cry leapt from Elisha's throat. Bitias bowed to the onlookers, returning their respects, his medallion glimmering in the starlight.

She thought of her haughty words, the things she'd said, little realizing he had already earned the title of *Bol.* Lord.

Until you can achieve distinction and rank, it would behoove you to remain silent.

With tears of embarrassment staining her fine clothing, she pushed into the foliage, seeking a place to hide from the horrible world.

She dangled her feet over the high ledge, tears plunging into the darkness.

At her back, the party continued. Shielded by the foliage, she entertained her grief alone.

She was absolutely miserable. Pumayyaton's words burned in her thoughts, as did her own to Bitias. It was amazing that other people's evilness could strike so deeply, yet her own should rebound against her. She wished she hadn't come. She wished she hadn't spoken. Looking down into the darkness, she wished she could jump.

Time passed. The celebration went on. Elisha leaned over the edge, watching her tears fall so very far. If only there was some way to return to her tiny room...

The little room Pumayyaton had cursed her with.

...but the ladder was exposed. She could not risk her brother's scorn, Bitias' laughter, or Tetramnestus' pity.

She studied the dark strait over the city wall. The mainland was lost to the night. She wished, fervently, that she lived there. A fisherman's wife, excused from the intrigue of temple and palace. A life of tradition and routine. A *'bny* life.

Suddenly the brush crackled. A figure pushed into her leafy alcove. Her heart jumped when she made out his face in the moonlight.

"Oh, it is you," Bitias said in way of greeting. "Wonderful place you have found here. Mind if I join you? It is not healthy for me back there right now."

Blushing, she tucked her knees under her chin, firmly maintaining her attention on the dark void.

The young admiral studied her back.

"The Greek playwrights would follow that sort of stage entrance with the question, 'Why?'"

A sulking pause. A sigh. "Why?"

"Because," Bitias sighed in dramatic overacting, "Pumayyaton will order me killed if he sees me."

She twisted a glance over her shoulder. "What?"

"'Why' and now 'what'. We are making progress. Anyway, your brother is in a foul mood, one my sparkling presence might simply enhance. You see, I was basking in the glory of my medallion with our young king and his two toadies, Commander Ib and Lord Adon. Everything was going well for my career. Then this huge, clumsy armored fool..."

"Qurdi-Aššur-lamur."

"Aye, I would recognize that barbaric mish-mash of a name anywhere. Anyway, he steps up and was quite pleasant for some time. Then he fixes King Pumayyaton a knowing glance and proclaims, 'Is it not the way of kings to surround themselves with men more capable than they?'"

Against her wishes, Elisha felt a smile flicker. "Pumayyaton heard it?"

"Pumayyaton? Aye. I would say they heard it in the north harbor, so loud did that buffoon say it. The king turned purple. Had anyone else dared such an offense, his head would have been instantly struck off, but this was the Assyrian ambassador. All he could do was glare at Adon, Ib, and myself in turn as if our competency was the issue. Realizing that my neck was not above separation, I decided that the best path was to bow, back away, and dive into the bushes. I hope you do not mind the company, *Qtn'khn.*"

"No," she said, realizing that it was true. "No, I do not." She turned slightly on the wall to better face him. "That is, if you do not mind the company of a bore."

"A bore? Who, you?"

"Yes."

He looked at her in some confusion. "Are you worried about the little game I had at your expense? Of not telling you that I had been elevated to admiral?" He smiled warmly. "I was just playing with you, little one. You were taking yourself so seriously that I could not resist."

"I suppose I earned that," she sighed. She dropped a leg over in inner side of the wall, resting her chin on a raised knee. "Might I be so bold as to ask how one as young as yourself becomes an admiral? You cannot be more than..."

"Twenty? Aye, I am nineteen. It *is* an honor, I will admit, and a pleasant one at that. I just wish that it had not come at such a cost." She waited and he met her eyes. "You are sure you wish to hear it? It is nothing more than a windy sea story." She nodded.

"Fine. What happened was thus: Commander Jabnit, my former captain, had grown tired of Cilician coastal pirates raiding our outbound traders. We rowed up and down, looking for a sign of them, but lookouts posted on the various bluffs always saw us first, giving them time to pull their hulls into caves and brush.

"Exasperated, he attempted a bold plan. Finding several merchant hulls departing Ugarit for Rhodes, he slipped into their midst. He even lowered the mast to hide us better. With such a tempting target, the pirates could hardly resist. Three of them came for us. The traders had orders to hold course to maintain our concealment, but being traders, they bolted. Cursing the luck, Jabnit called the attack."

"But they were three, and you, one," Elisha noted.

"'Bl, but *RearEnd* is an elite ship, easily their match. As it stood, only one chose to engage, the others racing after the merchantmen. I can still see Jabnit, heedless of the spray of our passage and the blaring of our trumpeter. He took in the positioning and situation with no more passion that a potter facing his wheel. His plan was to pass down the port side of the enemy penteconter, calling in the oars at the last possible moment in hopes of running down the oar bank of the enemy. It requires perfect oar-handling, a light hand on the tiller, and a competent commander. All three we had, until the critical moment."

Bitias' face darkened.

"I saw the dog that fired the arrow. I was up in the bow, watching the enemy hull rushing down upon us. I was throwing signals back, lining up our passage. Of course, the enemy would sheer off. I expected it and was watching for their tillerman to lean out on his steering oar. Then the single archer and his single arrow. It took Jabnit cleanly, that much I am thankful for. It is good that he did not see what happened to his beloved ship.

"Killed instantly, he fell back into our own tillerman, staggering him. The enemy, by chance or design, realized that we had lost control and swerved inward rather than out. With no call to inboard the oars, they rode down our port aft banks."

Bitias shivered at the memory. "You cannot imagine the chaos. Seven oars, three from the bottom, four from the top, slammed back into their oarsmen. Men were thrown into their comrades, shafts splintered. Worst, there came a horrible scream as the two vessels skidded off one another. The impact threw me to the deck. I came up in a run, dashing for the stern. The tillerman had almost been thrown overboard. As it was, his port steering oar was gone, carried away by that black dog. The rear bench pits were filled with the wreckage of men. Shivered oars dangled over the side, dragging us to port.

"The pirate was also badly damaged. I could see him raising over a wavetop, one rudder bent, several oars gone. Not the clean pass we had envisioned.

"When we topped our own wave, I could see the other two pirates alongside two traders. Relying on their sails and limited oars, they lacked the crew for anything resembling a defense. The pirates stormed them easily. I saw one captain casually pitched over the side. He sank like a stone, poor devil."

He paused for a moment, eyes on the waters rolling beyond the walls. Elisha waited for him to continue.

"I wanted to attack. I wanted to burn them to the waterline. But Jabnit had trained me well, I suppose. With limited speed and half helm, any further runs would have certainly involved a ship-to-ship tangle and reduced odds. We might take the pirate, but how many more men would we lose? And what when the others engaged? As it was, those pirate bastards lubbered beam-on to the waves while arguing with one another. I called for three of my more capable men and we erected the mast. As we regained way, I plunked down on a bloody bench with a spare oar, pulling with the rest of them. The tillerman followed my orders and we ran downwind along the coast, slipping from view fairly quickly.

"A few hours later, we came across two of our own penteconters, drudging along on patrol. I explained what happened and demanded that they fall in with us. They balked, of course, as entrenched commanders will. In the end, I pointed out that their proximity to the combat technically made them part of it and refusal could be cast as cowardice. They agreed with the understanding that I command the group."

He shook his head ruefully.

"They were so worried about doing something wrong, they failed to see how right it would be. We knew where these pirates were based; we had seen them spring from their lair just that morning. With night falling, I figured that they would beach their captured ships and divide up the booty. And I had glanced at the cargo manifests before our sailing; one of them was loaded with wine." He smiled. "The result was obvious.

"We came out of the dark, the eyes of our ships glowing like sea monsters in the light of the bonfires. One moment, the beach contained nothing but drunken pirate scum. The next, our hulls where rasping in, our men were over the side, swords glimmering in the flames. We could have captured them all, but there was a certain amount of interest to be meted out for Jabnit's loss. When we were done, we had recovered the ships, the cargoes, and the surviving crew, along with a hundred or so slaves. The dead we stacked around a pyre we constructed for our departed Commander. We sent him to the gods with honors."

He shrugged. "The rest is hardly worth telling. Enthusiastic questioning of the prisoners. More dens revealed. We swept down the next night on them, repeating the trick twice more before word finally got out and the remaining pirates retreated inland. We did our job, killed a lot of men who deserved it, and they gave me this." He raised his heavy medallion offhandedly. "So now I have five ships under me, as well as command of *RearEnd*." He let the award dangle. "The circle goes up. The circle goes down. That is all."

She looked at the young man before her, so courtly in his fine robes and compact beard, trying to imagine him pulling at a bloody oar of a defeated ship. He seemed so urbane. Yet at his command, men had charged into combat. Blood had flowed. Lives had ended.

"Bitias, that was a wondrous victory you gave Canaan. An admiral's rank is not enough for such a deed. In that light, Qurdi-Aššur-lamur spoke the truth."

The young admiral seemed embarrassed at her earnestness. "Please, my lady. I was but a simple officer who did Melqart's bidding." The light of the moon played along his earrings.

The 'drtnt, Elisha. Pumayyaton's voice whispered in her ear. *The burning passion, the thunderous release, the still aftermath.*

"I should go, my lady. You might suffer should we be discovered together."

You shall never truly feel it, not with your kindly old husband.

Bitias drew himself up to bow before departing.

Now, you will live in that little room, never to taste what life is really about.

"Wait." The word came on the tail of a breath.

She bit her lip so strongly she tasted blood. Her heart pounded in her chest. In her thoughts, she prayed to Melqart lest she hear her own frightened dissensions.

Slowly, she slipped her small foot out, to run it along Bitias' calf. The muscles beneath her instep felt strong, firm, young. Reaching his knee, she slipped back down the rear of his leg, barring his retreat.

Beneath his heavy brow, his eyes were unreadable in the darkness. She lowered her head slightly, her smile small, her dark eyes calculating.

He smiled then, but this smile lacked the mockery. It was pure warmth. Then came his touch upon her leg, extended so boldly. His hand played along her smooth thigh.

She shivered, wondering what would follow.

His fingers closed beneath her thigh. The other hand shot down, capturing her other leg, pulling it out from under her. For a moment, she teetered on the edge of the wall. With a gasp, she threw her arms around his neck to keep from going backward into the void.

Holding her thighs against his hips, he chuckled. "Tactics, my dear girl. Admirals are full of them." And then his lips were on hers. For a moment, she was surprised. She'd only begun to wonder if this thing was low class or high, but then the pleasure took her and everything was moot.

He kissed her lips, her throat, her ears. It was like Arherbas at her feet, but better, far better. This was pleasure, this was wondrous. She tried to return the kisses, but found her own attempts clumsy and unpracticed. Then their lips met again and it was perfect.

She was marveling in the delightful array of his aromas, of perfume, sea, and sweat. His strong arms supported her. Her breath grunted out as the tip of his tongue traced her jawline.

She realized that her robes had ridden up in his initial rush, that her nakedness was rubbing against him.

She smiled like a cat before the pleasure. Then it *entered* her. She gasped at the delicious strangeness of his '*yr*. There came a brief moment of hesitation, a small stabbing pain.

Bitias stopped, staring.

"I do not believe it." His eyes were wondrous. "The *qdshba'alat*, the holy lady, beautiful wife of the holy lord for several years, unbreached."

She looked at him with lidded eyes.

"Never question a miracle," he smiled languidly.

His strong arms began to rock her up and down upon the thing within her. Her breath was hot, fire from a kiln. The pleasure built, spreading from her *'bn*, throbbing through her whole being. She wanted to scream in release but smothered it into his shoulder.

Astarte, thank you.

And then she understood the *'drtnt*. The passion lasted forever. It was over too soon. She lay against his chest, cradled in his arms, listening to the rapid tattoo of his heart.

The stone wall was cold on her exposed buttocks as he carefully set her down. Her breath steadied. Her eyes found their focus. Bitias seemed to glow in the moonlight.

"Thank you for the use of your harbor, dear lady." He began to rearrange his robes. "For that, I would slay a thousand pirates..."

"Hush," she told him, slowly spreading her legs. "Again."

TEN

The roof was still. The celebration had ended some time ago. Bitias was gone.

She lay in the loam of the brush, slowly cleaning herself with leaves. Her mind drifted back to his touch, his smile, and that thing that had pleasured her so. Should she die this moment and appear before the gods, she would not have regretted her life.

Eventually she finished and dropped the handful of leaves over the wall. One of them stuck against the face of the temple and she giggled. Blasphemous, yes, yet funny all the same.

Bitias would be sailing in the morning, returning north to face new pirates that would fill the recent void in their ranks. Perhaps that was a good thing, the removal of temptation. While it had been wonderfully pleasant, her appetite had been filled. She no longer felt the burning need, and probably would not in the future. Her life would return to more stable patterns.

She checked herself a final time for evidence of passion then pushed through the ferns. The gardens were still, the gazebo shimmering before the lowering moon. She crossed to the ladder and descended easily. Half way down, she halted briefly. Voices drifted from the audience chamber below. From the landing, she peeked in the door. The vast hall was empty save for two figures standing near the scroll-covered workbench. Qurdi-Aššur-lamur stood near the table, meaty arms crossed. Her husband stood to one side, back to the Assyrian, studying a scroll. Even at this distance, Elisha could read his consternation.

She slipped through the door and approached demurely. Qurdi-

Aššur-lamur spared her the briefest of glances. Her husband finally noticed her over the top of the scroll.

"Elisha, you are still up? I had thought you had returned to your quarters."

"No, my husband, I was simply sitting on the wall upstairs, looking at the moonlight fall over Tyre."

"Still dreaming from the rooftops, Sparrow?" He cast a smile back to the ambassador. "It is a little thing she does. She has always enjoyed watching life go by from a high vantage point."

Qurdi-Aššur-lamur spared her the smallest of grunts.

"Should you not return to your own pallet, my husband?" Elisha asked. "The night grows old. There will be time enough for business once the sun rises."

"Alas, this is business that must be conducted on the morrow. Lord Qurdi-Aššur-lamur has presented the Assyrian demand of tribute. Time has grown increasingly short for him; his men are demanded elsewhere. We must agree to this tomorrow."

"As must the palace," the huge man noted bluntly. "You pay your portion, they pay theirs."

"It's just...," Arherbas paused, frowning back at the scroll, "Well, it is excessive. For years, the tribute was set at fifty talents of gold. Last year, you raised it to sixty. Now you demand eighty, with an answer by tomorrow morning. There is simply no time for consideration."

"Our duty calls us. We must answer. It is now the time for fighting, not for quibbling with a merchant-race. Tomorrow you shall give us our gold, as shall the palace."

"But it is so much."

"This is not a request," Qurdi-Aššur-lamur noted.

Arherbas rolled the scroll, then tapped it thoughtfully in his open palm. "The tribute has always been seen as equitable. But now the amount rises. I hear reports of increased banditry in the hills. Caravans are routinely sacked. The cost to us grows. We pay more for less."

"You demand further benefit? Some additional gain for your cold metals? Very well, merchant-priest. I shall give you something more." Qurdi-Aššur-lamur's smile was grim. "*Qdshbol*, your wife is an adulteress."

Elisha's breath turned to ice. The scroll dropped from Arherbas' hands.

"It is true, merchant-priest." Qurdi-Aššur-lamur's eyes locked on Arherbas alone. "I saw this with my own eyes. I had drunk too much and did not wish to concern myself with your dainty screens and pisspots. Such is what bushes are for. Entering, I espied your wife in the arms of another man."

"There must be some misunderstanding..." Arherbas stammered. The Assyrian cut him off.

"Do not insult me, priest. I saw his *'yr* within her *'bn*. I heard the moans of her rutting. She betrayed you." Qurdi-Aššur-lamur's smile was merciless. "So now you have your value. Was what you received worth the asking?"

Arherbas' eyes were now on Elisha. The muscles twitched across his drained face. "Please leave us, Lord Qurdi-Aššur-lamur."

The Assyrian gave the slightest of bows. "I shall be back at mid-morning to collect our tribute. I care not of the affairs of your house. What matters to me is the gold." He turned and strode towards the distant entrance, the sound of his boots fading. Arherbas remained motionless, his eyes locked on Elisha. Her own limbs trembled in fear.

The Assyrian passed through the portal. They were alone. Arherbas' glare still held her. Then he stepped forward, the large fingers of his hand snapping around her throat.

"Whore! Demon offspring! How dare you do this to me! How dare you lie with another man!" Spittle sprinkled across her face. Beneath his grip, her windpipe closed. "I save you from your brother! I bring you into my home! And while I attend to the duties of my office, you roll in the dirt with another?"

Light flashed in her eyes and her peripheral vision darkened. Yet she could not raise her hands to defend herself. She hung in his grip, a lifeless doll.

"*Y*, little bitch, you broke your oath of marriage to me! Do you understand what paths that opens for you? I could have you stoned! I could have you burned! I could have you crucified! And, Melqart's curse, none of those are enough!" He let out a bellow of animalistic rage. Elisha's vision was nearly gone; she felt as if she were floating away in some warm sea.

The workbench caught her in the small of the back. Dimly, she realized that he'd thrown her into it. Beneath her weight it toppled, dumping her to the floor amid a shower of scrolls. Arherbas was stepping up, hand outstretched to take her throat once more. This time he would not cast her away. This time he would hold her neck, screaming curses, until she was dead.

His fingers touched her throat.

"You are..." she rasped, "...the Assyrian's fool."

He wrenched her up by her neck, shaking her again, his bellows muffled by the pounding that filled her ears. She began to slip away once more. The shaking stopped. She felt the first moment of doubt. His vise-like grip loosened. Through the dark haze, she could see his confusion. He released her and she fell to the floor.

His voice as still as water in a deep cistern.

"What do you mean."

She paused to rub her throat, a luxury. When she spoke, her voice rasped.

"Why do you think he told you?" A pant. "About me?"

"He is a man. I am a man. It is our duty to one another."

Her laugh came out as a croak. "Our traders are unified beneath the council, yet they take every opportunity to cheat one another. Men fight one another for land. Men sell the wives and children of another into slavery. There is no bond." She raised her eyes to her husband. "So, why?"

He looked down on her with unreadable eyes. "You have the answer, Elisha. Speak."

"Qurdi-Aššur-lamur commands fifty chariots and five thousand troops. He did obtain such a rank by being a *nbl*, a fool. He told you what he had witnessed to upset you."

Arherbas shook his head. "What does he gain, angering the house of Melqart?"

Elisha slowly pulled herself to her feet. The room moved like a ship's deck. Carefully, she braced herself against the tipped table.

"He seeks increased tribute. He does not want arguments or

negotiations. He wants gold for his wars. So he has forced the issue upon you with no time for consideration. And to further distract you, he told you about what he had seen."

"You put too much opinion in yourself."

"Do I? The Assyrians use their chariots to break up enemy form-ations. Their foot solders fall upon the broken remnants. He has done the same to you. Your thoughts are broken. When morning comes, he will sweep into this hall and claim his eighty talents. And you will give it to him."

"Stories, Elisha. All you tell me are stories."

"You think so? Did you not know that Lord Qurdi-Aššur-lamur also grievously insulted King Pumayyaton tonight before the court? That he questioned the king's competence as ruler? Pumayyaton is now distrustful of the very men who might advise caution against the increase in tribute." She paused. "As are you."

Arherbas rubbed his chin thoughtfully. Finally, he looked upon his wife again.

"Your words might be true. But why should I trust you, Elisha? How can I have faith in you, on this or any matter?"

"You cannot," she replied simply. "Qurdi-Aššur-lamur's words were true. I have shared myself with another man. I stand before you and your judgment upon me. However, you must decide the value my death brings you against the gold I can secure."

"How much gold?"

"Thirty talents. Perhaps forty."

"Forty talents? You are but a small girl of thirteen years."

She looked hard into his eyes. "Let me negotiate with the Assyrian tomorrow."

"Unheard of."

"Exactly. If he wishes to fight us unconventionally, we must respond in kind. The Assyrians are an aggressive race. With their armored siege towers, they can break any fortified position. One wonders if they can fight defensively." Now it was her turn to think for a moment. Arherbas watched her in silence. Finally, she spoke.

"Tomorrow, simply allow me to be present in the hall. Make no move to argue the tribute. Simply provide delay."

"You are asking me to trust an adulteress?"

"Is it my *'bn* you seek, husband? I never refused you, not in anything that you have done. If you seek that part of me, it is yours."

Disgust clouded Arherbas' face. "That interests me not."

She nodded slowly. "I know. And that is all that this man took, the part of my body you care not for." Bracing herself against the table, she raised her foot, trailing it along his leg, his loins, across his chest. Carefully, she hooked her other leg around him to steady herself, tentacles around the prey.

"This is what you seek, is it not?" She ran her small foot along his jawline. He shuddered, taking in her earthy scent. "It is yours, my husband. This part of me shall always be yours."

He shuddered, hurt mixing with lust, disgust with desire.

"Take it," she breathed.

Fingers that had strangled now closed on her ankles. She fell into the nest of scrolls, Arherbas atop her. Fingers and lips played with her feet in desperate hunger.

The sensation was pleasant. She looked at the gilded ceiling, indulging in the sensations. In her mind, she thought of Bitias. Like a cry across the sea, the passion of *'drtnt* echoed in her loins.

Qurdi-Aššur-lamur entered the temple's audience chamber. Flanked by his shield bearer, he crossed the expanse, boots loud against the tile-work. The men of the temple stood behind the bench. Peripherally, the diplomat noted others standing along the walls. Onlookers, servants and slaves, beneath notice.

He stopped before the bench, casting a hint of a bow to the holy men. He jutted a hand to his shield bearer. A moment later, a cool weight was placed there. He did not glance down.

"*Qdshbol* Arherbas, I present to you this gift, a fine silver bowl, etched with scenes of Assyrian triumphs."

The priest accepted the formal gift. After a respectful moment examining its craftsmanship, he passed it to his lumbering aide, who handing him something in return.

"*Bol* Qurdi-Aššur-lamur of Ashur, I present to you this fine dagger. The hilt is ivory, from our colony Utica in distant Libya."

The Assyrian accepted the return gift, examining it casually.

"The workmanship of the hilt is interesting, but ivory affords poor grip for a warrior. Perhaps I shall give it to one of my women."

He turned to hand the item to his bearer, missing Arherbas' brief frown at the slight. His assistant secured the gift in his pouch, then produced a scroll. Qurdi-Aššur-lamur thrust it at the high priest like a weapon.

"Our demand of tribute."

Arherbas paused silently, a comment on the mainlander's tactlessness. The crackle of its unrolling reflected off the marble walls. The priest's eyes scanned it.

"Eighty talents of gold," Qurdi-Aššur-lamur summarized. "As we had discussed last night."

"So much," Arherbas scowled. "Please, give me a moment to discuss this with my aides."

"Do not tarry long, priest, lest my demand grow to ninety. I still must see King Pumayyaton concerning his own portion of the tribute."

The priests huddled, the big aide providing hesitant answers to Arherbas' questions. Qurdi-Aššur-lamur glanced to his shield bearer who responded with an expression of haughty amusement. Clearly, if the Canaanites would not fight, they would pay. Blood or gold, it made no difference to the men of Ashur.

The chariot commander looked around the room, seeking idle amusement to pass the time while the priests came to grips with their unpleasant obligation. Around the hall, scattered princes watched the proceedings. He recognized the aging Shipitbaal. The fact that the old man now relied on a cane brought a snort to the warrior.

Then he noticed the holy lady. He felt surprise that she would be in attendance. An Assyrian woman guilty of crimes such as hers would be dead. That she still lived gave rise to further disdain for the nation of traders. He could not tell if she was bruised or battered; her scarlet robe had a high collar and her hair was tucked into a tight cap. Still, she seemed in fair spirits, observing events from her cushions, fanned by a servant.

At first he assumed that she had averted her eyes because meeting his gaze would remind her of her stain. Then he frowned. She was not avoiding him at all. In her lap, a tiny monkey cavorted. Garbed in miniature finery, it presented a ludicrous sight as it leaped for a grape she teasingly held above its grasp.

Qurdi-Aššur-lamur had a firm opinion of women. Their *ilku*, their service, was to provide sport, comfort, and children. They should not be present when men discussed business. Certainly not with pestilent little creatures.

The monkey leaped again for the grape, spinning in air. It landed again on her lap, this time facing him. Evidently the Assyrian's presence surprised it; it squeaked in alarm and burrowed into Elisha's robes.

She giggled at the little creature's antics, pulling it out. "There, there, little Samsi, do not be afraid. The big man will not hurt you." She comforted the creature, passing it the grape. It gnawed, big eyes studying the man.

"Such foolishness," Qurdi-Aššur-lamur groused, "giving a name to a dirty little creature like that."

"Do not let the big man frighten you," Elisha cooed, scratching the little monkey's head. "He does not mean to scare you; it is simply his way. Be at peace, Samsi."

"You women with your silly ways. As if that puny beast could think."

She ignored him, her words soft and comforting. "He does not believe you can think. He does not see that others can play in the game of life. Is not that right, little Samsi-Adad?"

Qurdi-Aššur-lamur paled. "What!" At his bellow, the heads of the priests snapped around.

The Assyrian took a step forward. "You mock me, woman? You mock the Ashur king, Samsi-Adad the Fifth? Our ruler whose hand reaches from the Southern Ocean to the Upper Sea? You stain his name by comparison with this beast?"

Elisha met his anger coolly. "From what we understand, the Urartu and Manneaian peoples make gains against your northern borders. To the east, Babylon stirs before the whispers of the Elam. Your own princes consider rebellion." She patted her pet. "Perhaps it is the reverse; your ineffective ruler stains the good name of my little monkey."

"How dare you," he breathed, fingers working. "Your insubordination could cost you and your people dearly. I could easily double your tribute."

Her reply was low and even. "Such would mean little if we refused to pay."

His bellow echoed off the high ceiling. "Foolish wench! I could pull down Tyre's walls! I could burn its temples, enslave its people!"

"Your armored rams do not float," she spoke quietly, that only he might hear. "Nor do your chariots. Nor your warriors. And Ashur has no fleet." His mouth latched open for another bellow but she checked it with a raised finger. "You *could* burn our inland crops. But remember, Lord; Egypt would like nothing more than to see your desires checked. She would send us grain if only to confound you. Perhaps, with great effort, your successor would retake Tyre. But as the man who lost this city, you would not live to see that day, I should think."

Qurdi-Aššur-lamur's eyes flashed. "Shield bearer!" His man stepped forward. "Give me your sword!"

There came the cold rasp of iron. The ambassador reached back for the offered blade. Over his shoulder, she could see Arherbas, Tetramnestus, and the others, horror-struck by the events.

"Strike down the holy lady?" Her smile was cold. "Within the temple of Melqart? The people would riot. Again, Tyre would be lost to you."

His fingers closed around the sword. It hissed around, steadied over her. Her eyes, shadowed by the blade, never left his.

"Our fates are shared by your next action, Lord."

He looked down on her, murder in his eyes. His sword quivered. "Well?"

The tip faltered, moved away.

"Clear the room," she ordered. For a moment there was silence.

"Be gone," Tetramnestus bellowed. Servant or noble, it mattered not to the big man. Like sheep, he drove them from the chamber. Meanwhile Elisha stood, dropping the monkey. It skittered away, clambering a tapestry to safety.

When the room was cleared, she nodded to Tetramnestus. "You too, friend. And take Qurdi-Aššur-lamur's companion with you."

The bearer glanced to his commander, who gestured towards the portal. With their departure, only Elisha, Arherbas, and Qurdi-Aššur-lamur remained.

Elisha did not allow the stillness to regain the room.

"The temple of Melqart will pay no more tribute."

The Assyrian cocked back his head and roared at the ceiling. Before this, Elisha merely frowned.

"Bellow like an ox," she chided. "Hiss like a snake. Swim like a fish; it is all the same to me. The tribute is ended. We will pay it no more."

"You cannot decline to pay!"

"You cannot afford to demand," she replied. "What I said is true and you know it. Ashur's influence is draining away. Her inner districts squabble. External forces mount. Civil war brews. This campaign season, you do not march south for conquest. You march north to reestablish control."

"Idle guessing."

"You have demanded that our own ships supply you along your line of march. You are driving on Aleppo, well within the Assyrian Empire. Its Turtan has openly broken from Sansu-Adad's rule. Other Turtans watch; some will follow."

"We shall defeat these traitors." Qurdi-Aššur-lamur growled. "We shall return."

"And when you do, perhaps we will close our gates. Or perhaps we shall pay. That is for future men to determine. But today, the temple's gold is lost to you." She raised her chin. "There is one matter you should consider."

"Yes?" he grated.

"You still have the palace. They do not know of our plan not to pay."

"They will know soon enough. They shall see that no gold has been borne to our skiff."

"They will see urns. Urns filled with rocks to make the bearers bow convincingly, but urns devoid of gold." She did not look to Arherbas for his reaction to her plot against the throne. "As long as the truth is concealed, they will pay in full. And you shall have something to fuel your efforts to the north."

The Assyrian shook his head. "We planned on 160 talents, eighty from the temple, eighty from the palace. Our efforts depended on it."

"You handled last season's campaign masterfully on 120 talents. You should be able to repeat the performance. Further, you should be able to extract one hundred talents from Pumayyaton, to lesson your shortfall."

"One hundred? He balked at eighty."

"His advisors instructed him to balk. But you have set him against them, no?" He glared at the accusation but did not counter it. "My advice is this; when you enter the throne room, it is likely that his precious *bolh* will be there. Greet them and proudly announce that King Pumayyaton has agreed to pay one hundred talents of tribute. Speak loud and long of this. Tell them how it has averted a horrible siege."

He frowned. "Why should he care what his *'bny* think?"

"I used my monkey on you. Now, it is time that you used his own monkeys on him. He will not dare to look bad before them."

Qurdi-Aššur-lamur studied her with dark eyes. "*Ba'alat* Elisha, you are a traitorous adulteress," he said

"A traitor?" she spat with such venom that the Assyrian flinched. "My brother, in his foolishness, seeks to tear Tyre apart from the within, just as you seek to harm her from beyond. To save Tyre, I must weaken him, divert you, and strengthen my own position. And thus I have done so."

Qurdi-Aššur-lamur thought hard on her words. He knew of the rivalry between palace and temple; his own spies had reported such. Her open words of playing invader against crown for the good of her city rang true yet he still felt distrust. The Canaanites were a devious race of traders, and she was beyond any he'd faced.

Perhaps, she'd had allowed her indiscretion to be "discovered", to suck him into her own ambush, just as he'd lain his for throne and temple. He could no longer divide truth from lie, so thoroughly had her twisting words bewitched him.

She'd given him his moment for consideration. Now she gave him her terms.

"You will bind yourself with your word that you will never speak of what you saw in the garden. You shall never pass the information by spoken nor written word. Should you refuse, I would send word to my brother concerning my thoughts on your inabilities to take Tyre. Think wisely, Lord. Is petty gossip worth one hundred talent-weight of gold?"

Qurdi-Aššur-lamur stood quietly for a moment, jaw working. His nod was slow.

"You have my bond. My tongue will remain still as concerns this matter." He drew himself up. "I will expect the...*gold* to be delivered immediately to my skiff. I must now go to the palace. King Pumayyaton expects me."

Only to Arherbas did he bow. It was as if Elisha was no longer in the room. Before he left, he studied the high priest a final time, his expression unreadable. Then he turned and marched from the room.

Arherbas watched him go. When they were alone, he turned to face his wife. He could find no words.

Cold rains beat against the buildings lining the narrow lane. Four cloaked figures leaned into the storm, eyes down. Their passage along the narrow way was unobserved by the residents who huddled behind their shutters and doors.

The lead and trailing figures were broad of shoulder. Their exposed hands were muscular, marred by scars. Their cowled heads moved back and forth, watching the alleys with expectant caution.

The second figure was small. Once or twice, heavier gusts threatened to blow him completely over. Only the action of the figure to its rear, whose own bulk negated the effects of the elements, safeguarded the slighter companion.

The foursome followed the twisting byways through the various districts of Tyre, keeping to the lesser streets, avoiding the avenues. The silversmith's area. The street of furniture-makers. The potter's district. There was a slight grade in the direction they were traveling; runoff water flowed over their feet like a shallow river. At the end of the lane, it coursed into a moderate avenue, flowing to the right. The four stopped in the shadows of the building, the lead figure checking the street. Empty.

With his nod, they quickly crossed the open, the larger figure helping to steady the smaller against the slick cobbles. A half-block down, the street entered the Avenue of Kings. At the northwest corner stood a two-story wineshop, its rough bulk leaning over the street. The knock on the door was discrete. It creaked open, admitting them.

Inside, benches ranked down to a small fireplace which cast a glow against the wet gloom. Elisha, Tetramnestus, and two world-weary men cast their sodden cloaks to the floor before the hearth. The holy lady held hands to the blaze while the aide stood aside with the wineshop's owner, a pudgy man with a ragged beard.

"All is in order? The shop is ours?" In Tetramnestus' hand, a small sack hung with a suggestion of value.

"Aye, my humble home is yours. My slave has been sent away. We are the only ones here."

Tetramnestus passed the sack over. "Your discretion is expected."

The keeper eyed the two rough men who'd plunked heavily onto the benches, cudgels within easy reach. "Of course. The bread is nearly ready. Let me bring you beer."

The aide nodded. He looked to Elisha, but it was as if she were alone in the room. Without a word to any of them, she crossed to a narrow stairwell. A moment later, she'd climbed out of sight.

Three mugs of barley beer were deposited before the men. Tetramnestus sat across from the others. He took a tentative sip.

"Why so glum, Tetramnestus?" This from the rough companion opposite. "We have a roof between us and the rain, and beer between our stomachs and sorrow. What more could one wish?"

"I do not like this."

The man misinterpreted. His hands closed on his club, his eyes glancing to the door.

"Nay, not that. Just the situation." He took a moment to wince into his drink. "My lady plays with fire."

"As long as she pays with gold, that is all that matters." At the man's side, his companion grunted acknowledgment into his own cup.

The shopkeeper slid into view, a steaming wheel of bread on a wooden tray. He set it on the table with the humblest of bows and retreated into the small kitchen. The mercenary tore a chunk of bread for his friend, then one for himself. As his jaw worked, his grubby face took on a thoughtful appearance.

"Let me ask you, Tetramnestus, what is this all about? Why leave our warm little rooms to cross half the island on the coldest, rainiest day of the year?"

The aide's expression turned hard. "The *Qdshba'alat*'s business is none of..."

"Ours? Of course its our business. She hired us mercenaries, did she not? But keeping us in the dark is frustrating. Not that I am complaining about the work. It is an easy billet. Compared to some of the auxiliaries' camps, it is very fine indeed. Good food. City life, and not under siege, mind. No, dry quarters and good gold. Seems almost too good to be true."

"And the problem is...?"

"No problem. It is just that the holy lady hired us as mercenaries but uses us as doormen. We watch the temple entrance. We watch the back gates. We keep our eyes open at night. She even has us out in the marketplace with instructions to keep our ears open. Funny work for men like us."

"The Assyrians have withdrawn to the north," Tetramnestus pointed out. "The times are uncertain."

"Uncertain. That is just the word for it, just the word to describe the holy lady. She is uncertain. She has deployed us as pickets and scouts. I can see it in your eyes that I'm right. No need to admit it. I have seen it before, usually in commanders moving through unknown territory. Screen and scout."

"We need guards. Nothing more."

"Fine." The small scar on his cheek turned his smile into a knowing leer. "You do not have to tell us. But it is difficult to defend against an enemy you do not know. As it stands, we will have only the time between the drawing of the blade and its swing to protect you. Maybe we can, maybe we cannot. It is for you to decide."

"My lady has powerful enemies. They are quiet now, but the situation could change in an instant. All I can advise it to keep your eyes open and be ready for anything. Bands of armed *'bny*. Mercenaries such as yourself. Even palace guards. The situation is fluid."

The man's companion grunted. "Like Miltus."

"Two years back, aye." He drained his cup, then locked eyes on Tetramnestus. "A city feud, eh? Tight work. Factions change. Assassinations. Treachery. Makes me long for the times I fought in Assyrian formations. Just a straightforward fight, nothing more. Still, gold is gold."

A fist hammered against the door. The shopkeeper crossed to it and lifted the latch. The door opened to admit a swirl of rain and a sodden figure. Tetramnestus kept his face carefully neutral as he looked upon Bitias. Ignoring the three, the admiral gave the keeper a slap to the back.

"Aziru, you old dog. It has been ages. Is that wine you carry? Good, good. Two cups, now. Thanks." He noticed the men at the bench and gave them the courtesy of a small bow which wasn't returned. Unfazed, he mounted the steps, disappearing upstairs. The timbers overhead creaked softly once, then again, before lapsing into silence.

"None of our affair," the mercenary grunted as his rapped his cup for a refill. "Aye, we understand, Lord Tetramnestus."

ELEVEN

The spring evening was as purple as murex dye. Long streamers from cooking fires hung vertically in the warm air. The sounds of the city were muted by the closely-packed buildings, but from the marketplace, voices drifted upwards to Tetramnestus' vantage point.

From the temple rooftop, he could gain peaceful respite from the day's activities. There was always wealth to document and to store, services to be attended, problems to be solved. Witty poets and philosophers might equate Tyre to a *gôlah*, a craft plying the Upper Sea, loaded with men and merchandise. The aide was more prone to believe that the temple itself was such a craft, one that required constant careening, caulking, and maintenance to remain afloat.

Still, at least some of his worries were lifted. The negation of the winter storms and the passage of Egersis had freed the ships from the harbor, the warships among them. Admiral Bitias was with his command, hopefully in some far-away place.

Heedless of the stillness surrounding him, a sour expression crossed his face. The thought of the holy lady's infidelity caused him great anguish. The risks she ran were breathtaking in their magnitude. Should she be caught, swift death would be the most favorable outcome. He might be dragged down as well. He should hate her for the danger she brought them both but could not. She'd salvaged him at his lowest point, returning to him the respect and position he'd long sought. In that, he would always support her, regardless of the path she followed.

Still, he hoped for more sense from his lady. After all, she was fourteen years old, an adult!

He'd heard that it was difficult for husbands and wives to keep secrets from one another for any length of time. Sooner or later, subconsciously or not, the spouse would pick up the signs of indiscretion. It seemed strange that the holy lord had no inkling of his wife's activities. But there it was. The high priest and his wife seemed distantly close.

Could Arherbas truly not suspect? Or did he? Either alternative seemed impossible.

The most serious concern was that she might bear Bitias' child, which could bring disaster to this careful balance. At Elisha's bidding, he'd made careful inquiries among the physicians of Tyre. A plant imported from the Libyan colonies would prevent such a mishap. Now, with the rise of every new moon, she ingested a careful dose, no greater than a chickpea in size. Yet should this magic not work...

Tetramnestus shook his head to clear his doubts. The troublesome Bitias was gone, sailing off foreign shores. The danger was lessened.

The direct danger to Elisha, that is. Tyre and her inhabitants faced other dangers. The Assyrians had disappeared. They'd collected the palace's share of the tribute and vanished north. He'd long wondered what had taken place in the room between Qurdi-Aššur-lamur, Elisha, and Arherbas. The Assyrians had gone and the gold had stayed. Elisha had sworn him to secrecy and altered the temple records to conceal the windfall. Some of the metal had gone to Elisha's mercenaries. Some had gone to the other temples. Some had simply vanished.

But with the contraction of the Assyrian empire, Tyre had found itself without a protector. Her armies, never large to begin with, were spread along the seaboard, protecting fields and granaries. A large contingent of the city garrison had been ferried across the straits. Outlaws were becoming more numerous and daring. It would not take many more raids to push the city into famine.

Thoughts of the palace brought his attention around to the proud structure. Relations between the two bodies had become strained. Nothing visible, of course. There was simply a curtailment of courtesies between the royal and theological ruling bodies. No longer did the holy lord attend court unless specifically requested, and rarely did the king ask the temple for Melqart's blessing for its endeavors. He was glad that Elisha had thought of the mercenaries but fervently hoped they would not be called upon.

Even the *rzn* sensed the strained relationship. The number of bodyguards employed by the nobility was growing.

Tetramnestus looked into the fading light, shaking his head sadly. He missed his innocent youth in the dusty streets of Arnuun. The world rushed headlong into madness, all parties pulling madly at the oars.

From below came the reverberation of a gong. The evening services were about to begin. He felt a sudden urge to pray to Melqart against the dark days that loomed on the horizon. With uncustomary haste, he departed for the temple below.

Q urdi-Aššur-lamur sweated beneath his corslet, his mind on Elisha.

The damn girl had captured his thoughts. She'd bested him, neatly outmaneuvering him out of eighty talents of gold. He could still see the set of her firm jawline, the cast of her dark eyes. She'd faced him down, earning respect and more from the Assyrian.

On the ride north along the coast route, he'd found himself thinking of her. In his dreams, he would see her hanging in the embrace of that young naval officer. Her back arched, her head tipped back, and in her sweet face, the ecstasy. Such an expression from a woman was something new to him. He'd never seen it before. Indeed, he'd never looked.

But now he did. With every whore and slattern he'd had over the year of campaigning across Ashur's western provinces, he looked for the expression he'd seen on that rooftop. Oh, the women had moaned and mewed in all the right places. He could afford such professionalism. But it was nothing like Elisha. She'd glowed like a bonfire in her lover's embrace.

He knew he shouldn't let his mind wander to those dark eyes, the river of jet-black hair. Distracted, his shoulders bumped against those of his shield bearer and driver as his chariot thundered along the rough road. He should be thinking of the action ahead, the pacification of the Queian village. For tribute, they'd sent the head of the official assigned to collect it. The usual reprisals were in order.

The village was a short distance off, beyond the river, across a line of hills. Qurdi-Aššur-lamur's twenty chariots covered the ground quickly. There were other villages awaiting their own reprisals.

She'd seen it, he thought. *She'd seen the signs of our empire collapsing. The Turtans move against one another while Samsi-Adad dithers in Nineveh.*

The first of the chariots were splashing across the narrow ford, their wheels spinning spray. His shield bearer reached over to steady him as their chariot bounced across the uneven surface.

He saw her gentle hands as they played with the monkey. He saw the hint of breasts beneath her robes.

Perhaps, when the campaign is done, I can return to Tyre and take it. The Canaanites have cast us out. In this, they are no different from any other village. I could kill Arherbas and take Elisha. In his mind, she fell into his arms.

The lead chariot upended, its shafts splintering with a sharp crash, its occupants thrown into the tangle of horses. The second and third chariots fouled into the wreckage. Qurdi-Aššur-lamur's driver managed to stop short, the column bunching behind them.

The current lifted the wreckage up and over. The armored shield bearer, arm broken and useless, bobbed briefly before swirling out of sight. Qurdi-Aššur-lamur had only a moment to think how the spring floods had carried away part of the ford when the line of natives burst from the foliage to their rear.

The driver attempted to turn. A single chariot could have cut the charging line like a knife through goat cheese. The drivers cursed, hauling at the reins, but the column was snarled. Qurdi-Aššur-lamur nodded to himself at the effort of the ambush. To carve a channel across the ford had required tenacious effort. Now the natives would reap the benefit.

Qurdi-Aššur-lamur's sword was out. Arrows hissed past. The natives were amid the useless vehicles. An Assyrian was pulled over the side of his platform. Qurdi-Aššur-lamur's shield bearer squinted upwards, then moved his shield before his master. There came two sharp rings off its bronze. Then the man collapsed, an arrow quivering from his ruined eye socket.

The Assyrian commander leapt from his chariot, knowing he was a dead man.

I deserve this. His sword shimmered in the sunlight, river water beading across its surface. *I dream of Elisha while the barbarians cut their channel. Now I die.*

A naked, lanky youth, screaming and brandishing a club, bore down on him. Qurdi-Aššur-lamur kicked a geyser of water at him. The boy threw up his hand instinctively. The sword plucked at his exposed belly, once, twice, like a snake. He fell with a little cry, swirled briefly in the waters, and was gone.

Two more men advanced on him. Leather armor, made over the long winter months. Stolen weapons of bronze. *No screaming youths, these. Village militiamen.* He swung his sword back and forth, maneuvering in. *Perhaps even mercenaries.*

He ignored the ringing of weapons and the ragged Assyrian curses from his disintegrating command. His attention was on his two opponents. A feint to the left; the man instinctively backs. Spin to the right. Catch the sword as it comes overhead. The bronze blade shatters against his iron one. The man dives away. He takes a step, swings, misses. A fire from his side.

The left man is back. His blade juts into Qurdi-Aššur-lamur's flank.

He bellows as he twists off the blade. Swings overhand, missing, his blade splashing into the water. His side opens up. Pain shimmers over him.

His opponent backs, eyes to the blood pouring from him. He could continue backing, leaving Qurdi-Aššur-lamur to drain away into this cursed river. But the man is as much a warrior as himself. He moves in. Qurdi-Aššur-lamur grips his left side, holding himself together, his own blade rising. They rush together in an explosion of spray.

It began with a single fish.

Truthfully, had it not been that, something else would have sufficed. A glare. A jostle. A word.

Animosity between *rzn* and *'bny* had been building. King Pumayyaton's direct support of the committee had been countered by the *rzn*'s council aligning with the temples. Relations became strained. A social system that had run for a millennium began to unravel between competing authorities.

The mid-year heat wave that fell over Tyre was the worst in memory. By day, the city shimmered like a tile in a kiln. The rich took to private boats or the nearby shore. The poor, tied down by their occupations and obligations, watched the daily exodus with trapped contempt. At day's end, the safety of the city walls brought the privileged class back. High born or low, royal or religious, all took to their roofs, fighting for sleep in the stagnant air.

A fishing skiff dug its heavy way through the coastal rollers, making for Tyre's southern harbor. Its nets had been blessed, taking several schools of fish early in the day. With a full hold, its captain had ordered her home. If they could sell early, they could fetch far more than those who would pass through the breakwater at sunset.

With practiced motions, his crew nestled the craft against the quay. As they secured the ship, the captain leapt across to the cobbles, whistling at the idlers to carry his cargo to market in exchange for the silverweight of a rough meal, a shabby room and a drink or two. He distributed wicker baskets to the chosen candidates. Like ants, they ported fish from boat to market stall where his seller waited.

One of the men, his drink-fuddled mind distracted by concerns that last week's prostitute had been far from clean, missed a step. Already overbalanced by the basket of fish perched atop his head, he stumbled on a loose cobble and fell. The fish scattered across the quay to the derision of onlookers and the outrage of the overseer. Distracted, the line began to slow. The overseer's bellow got the men moving again. The big man spared a moment to curse at his charge as the two stooped to re-gather the flopping, dying fish. Eventually they were returned to the basket. All but one.

It lay nestled against the city wall, shielded from casual view by an overhanging stone. The shallow puddle into which it had fallen had been heated to broth by the sun. Its tail pulsed, its fins trembled, and then life departed its body.

Other ships docked. Other cargoes were borne inside. People passed. The night fell. Its body began to stiffen.

A wharf-side cat found the long-dead fish at midnight. Pinning its meal with its paws, the feline's yellowed teeth tore at the fish's flank. However, it had not gotten more than a bite or two before the sharp scent of a female in heat drifted across the stones. Whiskers trembling and meal forgotten, the cat slunk off.

With the sun, the fishing fleet sailed. Heat blazed across the town. The puddle in which the fish lay shrank.

This time, it was a different ship, but the same men were hired to shift its load. Midway through their labor, a merchant's cart fouled the gate. While the city guard and cart owner screamed and cursed at one another, the bearers set their burdens down. One of the baskets toppled over, the man not quite fast enough to catch it. The fresh fish slithered across the cobbles. Cursing, he worked quickly to recover them, so as not to be docked for the delay. When he hefted his basket, the small puddle near the wall was empty. The basket was one fish heavier.

"Here," Agbal gestured to the men who trudged up to his stall. "Set the baskets here, just to my side. Those, place atop the planks. Hurry, you louts. You are blocking my customers."

Agbal represented several fishermen. They sailed their small craft and wrestled fish from the deep; that was their job. His was to represent them, acting as a clearing point for their catches.

"You wish two? Three! Excellent. Today's catch is the best in a week." The customer tossed a small sliver of silver into his scale. He frowned, then counterbalanced it with lead. "You will have to do better than that. Twice, I'd say. Scream all you wish. Who? Mathkart? His fishermen are inept, their catches poor and scrawny. You shall trade with him to your regret." A smaller sliver rang in the scale's pan. "Y! You cheat me. Very well, take them! I have other, more honest customers!"

Agbal's son crouched behind him, tallying the fish with pebbles in a small tray. At day's end, the profits would be shared proportionally with the fishermen he represented, as well as his sponsoring lord. Agbal always retained far more than his agreed-upon share.

The fishermen expected this. It was how things had been done for generations.

"A dozen fish! A party, you say? Melqart bless you and your guests. *'Bl*, the same rate as we agreed to last week will be fine." Silver and lead shekel-weights counterbalanced the scales. "My thanks, Lord."

The fishmonger took a moment to wipe the sweat from his eyes. *Melqart curse the heat!* He glanced to the twin structures of the palace and temple that loomed over the east side of the market and felt unease. Rumors, rumors. And then another customer. Agbal sized up the man. A potter's assistant, to judge by the clay stains. Not a usual customer who could claim from a running account. It was the most inefficient of transactions, dickering with a *'bny* over a trivial sum. With a sigh, he entered the game.

"Come, come, let us see what you will pay." Tink. Agbal frowned, then forwarded a single fish. "Robbery? I should mind not to sneeze, lest I blow away your offering. I have seen dust with more weight. And your curses, colorful as they are, lend no weight to your offering." The dickering went on, the man adding more silver to the tray. Agbal realized that it was mixed with lesser metals. Customers far more affluent stood behind the man, waiting their turn. He would lose on this transaction, but he didn't dare give Mathkart any more of his business. Without looking, he grabbed a fish from a basket, tossing another to the man. "Here. That makes two for the price of one. You have cheated me. Now go."

The man scowled at the rebuff and gathered his fish. Agbal dropped him from his mind, concentrating on his next customer, a head servant for a large wealthy family. Seven fish for the main table, perhaps another half-dozen for the staff. The heat would rush her, make her quick to close. He smiled.

Then the *'bny* pushed between then.

"*N'*! Who cheats who," the man spat angrily, tossing his two fish before him. One was a silver/blue beauty. The other was a gray, bloated monstrosity. From a hole torn in its side wafted an odor of corruption.

The servant and the others in line stared in grim fascination. A number of scenarios flashed through Agbal's mind, one of them actually true. However, to admit any of the likely ones would be to admit an inferior product. Several stalls down, Mathkart looked up.

"So what is this," Agbal replied, eyeing the horror. "You bring me scraps from the street and expect me to trade? I gave you two fine blue fish but a moment ago. You accepted them. Be gone, swindler!"

"Swindler! I labored all day, only to have you steal me blind! What am I to feed my family? Such evil meat would kill them! I paid for fresh fish, and I mean to have it!" He reached for a tuna in a nearby basket. Agbal's hand closed on his wrist. Behind him, his son stood up.

"Let go of my hand," the man grated, "or, so help me, I will strike you down. I grow weary of thieving *rzn* and their lackeys."

Agbal shoved the man back, livid for the attention he did not want nor need. "Leave my sight, *'bny* whoreson, before I..."

"Hold!" A man stepped from the crowd, two others flanking him. His robes were a contrast; fine cloth hung inexpertly. "What occurs here?"

The fishmonger eyed the speaker and his attending thugs. Without thinking, he took a small step back.

"The man disrupts my business. He brings diseased fish from the gutter and claims I sold it to him."

"Lies," the potter's assistant yelled. "He took my payment, threw this fish into my hands and shoved me away! The barter was not complete!"

"Is this true?"

Agbal squinted at the man. "Who are you?"

One of the man's companions stepped forward menacingly but the leader checked him. When his eyes fell on Agbal once more, the fishmonger felt fear stir deep within him.

"I will ask again: did you cheat this man?"

"No," replied Agbal. "No I did not."

"Yes he did," countered the potter.

"Clearly someone lies," observed the man, scratching his beard. He paused, as if considering. "As I see it, if the poor man is lying, his gain is but a single fish, an insignificant amount. Should the merchant be lying, his gain is far more. Not only does he gain the value of a fish, but he gains the knowledge that he can cheat his fellow citizens at will. He will grow rich by theft and misdirection. This we cannot risk. It is my decision that the merchant shall provide his victim a bushel of fish. Should my decision be wrong, we have only helped to feed a hungry family. Should I be right, we have fully punished a wrong-doer."

Agbal's mouth gaped, imitating his stock. He blinked out of his shock when one of the man's attendants stepped forward, lifting a bushel with both hands.

"You cannot do this!" he squealed. "Robbery! Someone call the guards!" He struggled with the man with the bushel. A moment later, the other man pulled him away and backhanded him, staggering him against his stall.

"Adon, you overstep your boundaries!"

Agbal looked up from the pungent surface of his bench. A heavy-set temple priest stood in the avenue between the stalls, flanked by his own two burly men. *So many thugs these days,* the fishmonger found himself groggily thinking. *What has Tyre become?*

"I am within my bounds, Tetramnestus," the man replied. "Issues concerning the *'bny* are to be handled by the committee. It is not a matter for the cronies of the council."

"In matters of trial, yes," the priest agreed. "But not in everyday street matters. This should be resolved in court."

"It has been resolved," Adon shot back. "We would find for the commoner anyway, so what does it matter?"

"You simply cannot..."

"Enough of this," one of the large men backing the priest growled as he shoved past. He stepped towards the man whose hands were occupied with the basket. He tried to set his burden on the table, to duck, anything, but his opponent was already on him. A meaty fist cracked into jawbone. Agbal felt the limp body collapse over him. The basket tumbled to the ground, spilling fish.

Adon's remaining bodyguard tried to fight the priest's two escorts. He doubled over when a fist pistoned into his gut. A knee to his face sent him into darkness.

Adon stood, a statue of confusion. A moment later, thick fingers closed on his fine robes. He looked up to see a fist swinging towards him. He had time enough to manage an expression of indignant surprise before the blow landed, cracking his head back. The mercenary holding him looked at his limp victim, shaking his head. "*Nss'sh*," he cursed in disgust.

Like Adon, Tetramnestus stood frozen, shocked at how quickly and disastrously the matter had been resolved. While the bodyguard let the lulling representative collapse to the dirty cobbles, the other shook the aide.

"Lord, we should be away before the guard arrives. It would not be good for a holy man to be arrested."

Tetramnestus blinked, then gave a shaky nod. Before leaving, he stepped to Agbal, pressing a lump of silver into his hand. Its weight was worth several bushels of fish.

"Take this," the big aide said in a tone reserved for apologies. A moment later, his escort propelled him away.

Agbal stood over the scattering of men and fish, fingering the lump of precious metal. He'd never really considered himself *'bny* or *rzn*. Yet looking down at the men who would have stolen from him, silver cold in his hand, he felt allegiance form.

T he prince stepped from his litter, his mind on his ships and the goods in his canal-side warehouse. His slaves stood dopey in the heat. No one's attention was on the present.

A clod of dung thudded into his back. Another whistled past his head, close enough to smell. He whirled in surprise to take the final ball in the chest.

Ragged children dashed down an alleyway, free and clear. Behind them, the prince and his attendants stood, shocked to the core.

T he tinworker looked up in alarm. People were no longer walking past his stall, they were running. Crashes and shouts pulsed down the narrow souk.

His wife looked from the doorway behind him. "Husband, what...?"

"Inside," he shouted, grabbing up the most precious of his trinkets and dumping them into her trembling hands. "Get inside! Bar the door!"

He turned as the door slammed at his back. Tin spoons, combs, and cups glimmered on his small table. Some of the sellers remained at their stalls, others had retreated into their workshop homes.

Three burley men rounded the corner. They casually made their way along the twisting alley, idly kicking over the small, rickety tables. Tin and silver adornments scattered amongst the cobbles.

"Trash," one of the men shouted, "Nothing but trash. Real craftsmen are found in the marketplace, not in some pest-ridden back alley."

"We sell here because we cannot afford otherwise," protested one of the tin-sellers. "Only *rzn*-backed craftsmen can afford stalls there." He dodged an offhanded slap one of the men threw at him, backing into his house.

The men drew abreast of the tinworker and for a moment he thought they might leave his meager stall unmolested. Then one of them smiled, looked him dead in the eyes while slowly turning the table on end. His goods tinkled across the dirty stones. With deliberate motions, the vandal drove the table into his fallen wares, bending them into ruin. Eventually, nothing remained but a shattered pile of wood. The man straightened, dusting his hands against each other in the universal sign of a job well done. He rejoined his comrades as they worked their way down towards the avenue.

The tinworker watched them go, trembling in fear and shame.

"Lords," he grated through his teeth. "Lords of shit!"

The guard detachment rushed through the narrow streets, staffs at port arms, sweat staining their leather armor. Normally the high summer months were quiet ones for the constabulary; it was simply too hot for mischief. But they'd been out since first light, breaking up brawls, fights and disputes.

"Keep up, curse you," the commander bellowed. Like his men, he wanted nothing more than the shade of the guard house and an afternoon nap. He didn't like what was happening, and he certainly didn't like where he was going at the moment.

They raced down the street, citizens backing clear into doorways and alcoves. At the mouth of an alley, a woman beckoned frantically.

"Here we go, lads," he gasped as he dashed the ever-present sweat from his eyes. "Watch for knives."

They barreled down the narrow way, emerging into a common courtyard. Women rolled and tussled about the central fountain, water urns shattered and broken. Hair was pulled. Flesh was scratched.

Ordinarily such bedlam would be met with derision. But the commander and his men were too hot and tired for that. He felt the urge to order his men to wade in with their staffs, to pulp flesh, crack bones, to punish these citizens for their foolishness. He had only to say it and his men would obey; their eyes confirmed it.

"Break them up," he spat.

The women were pulled apart. Servant girls of noble households exchanged hot glares with low-class wives and daughters. Beneath the mud and tangled hair, they were indistinguishable from one another.

"I shall save words with you lot," the commander told them. "Do not have us summoned again. Do you understand?" The one or two women who attempted to meet his hot gaze looked down. The implication was clear.

A distant voice rang over the jutting rooftops.

"Guards! Summon the Guards!"

"Astarte's bodice," the commander cursed over his men's groans. "Come on."

TWELVE

"Y, Lord Shipitbaal! I would wager you did not expect us back before storm season."

The wizened merchant-prince looked up from a discussion with a stall-keeper, his eyes falling on the two traders who were supervising the securing of their sea-stained vessel. He crossed the quay to their berth, his cane ticking across the cobbles. In his wake trailed a large bodyguard.

"'Bl, you are correct. I would have thought you had weathered in Utica." His rheumy eyes flashed briefly. "You two know that I am not partial to commanders who risk my hulls needlessly."

"No risk, lord. Just fair winds the length of Libya and some night sailing along the coast of Canaan. Good luck and sound sailing."

"Good luck, anyway," the old man agreed. "What do you bring me?"

"Iron, of course. We have also ivory and furs, some bulk grains and oils, and twelve slaves. In addition, the Libyans were more than happy to trade away their gold for those beads and trinkets. We did very well, I can assure you."

"Your records will assure me. Have them brought to me tomorrow morning."

"Indeed, Lord," agreed one of the commanders. The man's eye traveled to the thug standing behind the elder. "Is this a new, ah, pet?"

"He is my companion. I suggest you anger him not."

The commander tilted his head back to meet the guard's quiet stare. "No, I think not."

"We shall forward the slaves to your broker immediately," the other merchant noted. "As for the balance of the cargo, we will keep it on board overnight. Tomorrow we will set up in your reserved stall in the marketplace. The grain and oil are of good quality and should fetch a fair exchange. The iron, I assume, is consigned to the Assyrians."

"You assume incorrectly. It is ours. Place half of it in my warehouse. The remainder, sell."

The two men exchanged glances. "But the Assyrians..."

"You are a Canaanite. I assume I do not need to tell you what 'sell' means."

"No, *Bol*, you do not. Your goods will be bartered at the most favorable rates."

"I expect nothing less, Commander." Shipitbaal turned to go, then hesitated, looking back over his narrow shoulder. "One thing, gentlemen. Tomorrow, you will keep two, no, three strong men in the stall with you at all times. You will watch every person who touches our goods. Especially those rascally *'bny*. Expect the unexpected. If it helps, imagine that our property has tiny little feet and will dash off if unwatched."

One of the merchants blinked. "Watch our goods? But certainly nobody would attempt to steal from us. Not in the marketplace, before the palace and the temple. It would be unthinkable. The guards would punish them severely."

"Do not count on the guards. Trust no one, do you understand? Assume every man intends evil upon you."

"Yes, Lord. We understand."

The old man tapped away, his large guard following closely.

A merchant looked to his companion.

"What has happened to Tyre in our absence?"

"**C**ease your hammerings," the boatman cursed around his door. "Why do you disturb my evening's rest?"

A stranger stood in a travel-stained cloak, drizzle swirling around his broad shoulders.

"I require crossing." The accent was strange.

"In this?" the boatman nodded at the waves rolling from the

descending gloom. On the beach, his horse-headed skiff lay canted. Beyond, just visible against the iron sky, stood Tyre.

"This will be enough?" In his palm, a sizable lump of gold.

The boatman thought of his sons reclining in the other room. He weighed the danger and effort of such a crossing against a simple assault.

The man returned his gaze, his hand casually dropping to his utilitarian short sword. Leather armor was visible through the lips of his cloak.

"Lads," the boatman called, "we have a late traveler. Fetch the oars."

Another scroll crackled open.

"These all show the same," Arherbas noted, scowling at the words. "Offerings at all temples are down. Citizens have been reclaiming their wealth, storing it in their own houses. The people sense the discord between Pumayyaton and ourselves. They are afraid."

Elisha reclined on pillows strewn across the audience hall's floor.

"It matters not."

"Matters not? I wish I could share your blithe outlook, Sparrow, but this loss is beginning to effect us. With limited assets, we can no longer invest in trade. The temple's finances grow stagnant."

"You worry too much, husband," she smiled. "If we are hurting, imagine Pumayyaton's plight. His tribute was ninety-five talents of gold. His coffers are straining at the cost of maintaining garrisons on the seaboard as well as in Tyre. Eventually he will ask for aid. And then we will have him."

"Have him? What is there to have?"

"The dismissal of the *bolh*. Once the commoners have returned to their occupations, the old order will return. The king, the princes, and the temple." She leaned back, letting her robes draw across an ankle. Arherbas' eyes flickered downward.

She smiled as she watched his reaction. Sometimes men were so easy to control. As long as her husband got what he wanted, he was content.

She looked past him towards the dark window where the first of the seasonal rains fell. Soon the ships would roost in their ports. Bitias would return. She felt an aching need for him.

"Evil conspirator!"

The shout from the temple's doorway caused them both to whirl. From the darkness rushed a skull-like visage; for an instant Elisha thought Mot had come to drag her into the underworld. Then the lamps fluttered brighter and she recognized Pumayyaton. Rage cast his bony head in a self-caricature. His hair was plastered across his forehead, his cheeks flushed with anger.

Ib flanked his master. The head of the palace guards wore none of his ceremonial gear, not even a cloak. He'd been pulled from court and dragged into the rainy night. Another guard, similarly disheveled, trailed the two.

"How dare you burst in here!" Arherbas's hands were fists. His bald head flushed in rage. "This is an affront to Melqart and to myself! Not even the royal title of *Mlk* permits this outrage!"

The ruler ignored him, hefting a battered scroll in his hands. "Do you know of this?"

"Of this? Of what! Have you taken leave of your senses?"

Without a word, Pumayyaton tossed the scroll to the priest. He caught it, dropping his own. It fell to the ground, rolling away like a frightened creature.

Arherbas' squint turned to shocked surprise. "Is this...? It is! Blood! Mercifical gods, it coats the scroll! It stains my hands—"

"Read it," the ruler commanded.

Arherbas looked up. He seemed to noticed the guards flanking Pumayyaton for the first time. Ib's javelin was level. Elisha could feel her husband lose momentum. His eyes returned to the scroll. He read aloud.

> These are the words of Shaknu Qurdi-Aššur-lamur. If you are reading them, I am dead.
>
> The scroll has been entrusted to this man, to be delivered un-opened to the Mlk Pumayyaton of Tyre. Once they are read, the bearer will likely be killed.

With my death, I desire it to be known that the Temple of Melqart paid not its tribute as due to Ashur. They sensed our distractions and claimed advantage.

Further, the Qdshbol and Qdshba'alat instructed me as to the manner of setting the supporters of the Mlk against him. Additional tribute was thus gained.

I spit from the grave at the accursed race of the Canaanites. Thus speak I, Qurdi-Aššur-lamur.

Arherbas lowered the scroll, his face carefully guarded.

"What say you of this, priest? And you, wife? What words will excuse your actions?"

Elisha remained coiled on her pillows. Standing would be an admission of rank she would not make.

"What do I say?" She forced a smile. "I say that Qurdi-Aššur-lamur was a coward. He could not face me in life, so he struck at me from death."

"Strike he did." Pumayyaton's smile was grim. "Not only did you shirk your duties to Tyre and Canaan, but you did so at a dark time. Your actions alone cost me an additional fifteen talents of gold. You have acted against the royal house. You shall yield 120 talents of gold."

"You are the king." Elisha noted. "You are ruler of Tyre and its colonies. Yet you could not pull yourself away from your distractions to see your enemy's weakness. You never thought to look at them anew as their numbers dwindled and their columns slipped quietly north. You could have barred the gates against them at any time over the past five years yet you did not. Your activities alone cost you, Tyre, and the Canaanites hundreds of talents of gold. Fifteen talents is a drop against that golden sea." She fixed him a final glare. "You do not deserve the throne."

Pumayyaton's hand shot out, plucking the javelin from Ib. Its point shook.

"I will kill you for your words, viper."

"You could not kill me when I was a child. You tried that night, and failed. Father died of his afflictions; you only could assist by moving him. Hannon was too scared to strike, and that killed him, not you. As for Qurdi-Aššur-lamur's envoy, I assume you struck him down where he stood."

A wildness had overcome her. Years of caution, of holding back, were overcome in an instant. She smiled cruelly into his flushing face.

"Perhaps that *'bny* you killed, the one by the canal when we were children? The one making love? Certainly *that* was an act of valor!" She leaned back into her pillows, her dark eyes scornful.

"You are not the king. You are an unblooded boy."

Pumayyaton hefted the javelin to his shoulder. His hot eyes calculating the throw. His fingers shifted into position. Muscles bunched.

Four mercenaries burst through the portal.

"Forgive me, Holy Lord, for my tardiness," rattled Tetramnestus from behind them. "When we saw these three push through the gate..." He saw the trespassers clearly for the first time. "The king!"

The mercenaries before him brought up their bows, leveling them on the three.

"Lower your weapons," bellowed Pumayyaton over his shoulder. "This woman is a traitor! She dies now!"

"Your orders, Holy Lord," the mercenary leader asked calmly.

Elisha felt a command form on her tongue. She drew her breath to shout.

Arherbas' words were quicker.

"Pumayyaton, leave this hall lest blood be spilled."

The boy-king stood for a moment, weighing the javelin, weighing his fate. Then he tossed the weapon down against the marble floor.

"Someday, sister, it will just be the two of us again. In the throne room, in the moonlight. This time, I shall not give up my search so easily." With that, he stormed out, the mercenaries parting to permit the three to exit.

"You have done a foolish thing, Sparrow," Arherbas sighed. "You have made a very powerful enemy."

"Pumayyaton was always my enemy," she noted flatly. "He just displays it openly now."

Too much had happened. They could not simply return to their separate pallets after such a confrontation. Arherbas dismissed the guard, ordering them to watch the compound's walls. Then he pulled down a tapestry, tossing it over Elisha's pillows, a makeshift bed. He extinguished the light and settled against her in the darkness, holding her close.

"Sparrow," he commented, "you are shaking. Do not be afraid. Our guards will keep us safe. There is nothing to fear."

She clung to his shoulder, watching the rain fall past the open window. In truth, she shook, but it was not fear that drove it.

I should have been quicker. I should have given the order to release their shafts. Her fingers kneaded her husband's shoulder. *I should have slain the king.*

T he merchants sipped their tea, warming their insides against the chill that permeated the *ulam*. Tetramnestus circulated among them, his tray bulging with treats and delicacies.

In one corner, Shipitbaal held court with the upper echelons of society. With their words, goods shifted ownership, alliances were formed, and the destinations of fleets were decided. Lesser merchants hung close, hopeful for any scraps.

Elisha paused in the high portal, making a show of shaking rain from her cloak to let the men adjust to her presence. No one stared openly but the conversations became stilted, the laughter measured.

She moved through the crowd, nodding to the members of her class. Men bowed in return, their expressions guarded.

"*Qtn'khn,*" Shipitbaal wheezed, patting her shoulder. "What brings you here? If anything could be more dreary than rain, it is rain in the company of traders."

The other *rzn* began to move away.

"Stay. I must speak with all of you." She took a moment to gain the measure of each man. "I realize that most of you have seen your profits dwindle year after year. That the interference of the *bolh* and the conflict between the temple and palace have hurt you greatly. Am I right?"

No one spoke. Shipitbaal watched, his yellow teeth grinning at the interplay. Finally Kotilus, an importer of northern horseflesh, returned her gaze, defiance edging his wooden expression.

"The holy lady is correct. My household has begun to lose gold. My servants steal from me and mock me when they think I am beyond earshot. In the streets, the poor grow bolder." His words seemed to intoxicate him. "These troubles began when you opposed the king, marrying a man he did not choose. He strikes at you through us."

She looked to each one. "You all believe this?"

There was a rustle of opulent robes. One by one, the bearded faces nodded.

"And you, Shipitbaal?"

"Me? I am just a foolish old man."

"Let us all remember what really happened. I was never my brother's to give away. My father, Mattan, bestowed me to Arherbas. He was still alive then." Her eyes grew hard. "You will remember when the marriage agreement was made. It followed the death of Hannon."

The men around her grew still.

"*'Bl*, you remember now. Pumayyaton butchered one of your own while you watched. After that came the *bolh* and the court's corruption. Then years of increasing abuse and hostility."

"What do you seek, Elisha?" The voice was quiet, the source lost. "The death of the king? Yourself on the throne?"

Possibly.

"It is not what I want. It is what you want, and what Tyre needs. With the withdrawal of Ashur, the king will grow stronger. If we are to return power to the factions that once held it, we will need to act now. For us to succeed, I must ask that you alter the price of grain."

"You call upon us to raise its price?" a prince asked. "You wish us to starve our fellow citizens into submission?"

"Such an action would be petty and pointless. No, I wish to drop the price of grain by half. Fish, too."

The danger to their profits caused more concern to the merchants than the threat of famine. For long minutes, the men jabbered angrily to one another. Elisha waited for them to subside.

"The temple will credit half your losses against your tithe. But think, lord-princes; what better way to reduce the king's power?

As the people grow content, they will forget his petty gifts and treats. They will see us as their benefactors. In court, the committee will lose credibility and purpose. The council's powers will be fully restored."

The merchants conferred quietly to one another, unsure. Shipitbaal watched the dickering for a while before rapping his cane against the marble.

"Listen to you. Men willing to put their wealth behind the most risky of voyages, yet unable to commit to this venture. Do you young fools not see? Elisha is right. Should things continue, Pumayyaton will grow stronger and stronger until he holds ultimate power. Every ounce of gold you save this year will be taken from you in the next. There is only one course of action, that of slashing the cost of grain we import to Tyre. Such a move will cut young Pumayyaton off at the knees."

The men grew silent. Kotilus finally spoke.

"It will be a sacrifice, one that must be made. We will import grains and fish as the holy lady prescribes."

"I appreciate your support," she replied. "This strategy should work. However, there is one final thing I must ask of you before we commit."

"Another request? You bring the *rzn* to the edge of ruin and yet desire more?"

"Give us half of your mercenaries." Her voice was somewhere between a plea and a command. "Consign half your hirelings to the service of the temple."

"So should trouble start, you will remain safely behind your walls while our own households burn?"

"Lord Kotilus, you are a master trader. You know of economies of scale. A fleet of merchantmen beneath one master will show more profit than those same ships working independently. Their efforts can be directed in unison to greater effect. Likewise with mercenaries. I am fully confident that our efforts regarding the grain will succeed. But should they not, it might be better for all parties if the force opposing the throne was unified."

"Under you," someone noted.

"Under the temple of Melqart," she corrected.

To one side, Shipitbaal smiled. *Same thing.*

The men discussed the matter quietly among themselves. Elisha gave them space, standing in the portal, watching the patterns the rain made across the marketplace's empty expanse.

She sensed someone behind her. Kotilus' voice was resigned.

"As unpleasant as these times are, they will not simply go away. You are correct. We shall yield both our prices and our guards to your bidding. We stand fully behind you, Holy Lady. Do not fail us."

She nodded, looking out over the wet paving stones to the palace. Fiscal ruination was the worst that faced the nobles. She suppressed a shudder at what her brother might do to her.

Elisha stood at the parapet, looking down on the masses surging across the marketplace. There was no commerce taking place this day.

"I spoke with Sirom, priest of Astarte." Tetramnestus stood behind her. "King Pumayyaton has performed the Egersis."

"The priests of Melqart were adamant concerning this. It was not time yet. It rained this very morning." Her eyes remained locked on the wooden shape resting in the midst of the mob.

"The king told the court that the priests of Melqart were stalling, interfering with his god-assigned tasks. He claimed that the storms had ended, that what fell was summer rains, not winter storms."

Below, a rope slapped taunt. Twenty men cheered as they pulled.

She frowned as the beam rose out of the crowd. "*Khn* Sirom would not dare provide priestesses. The temple of Astarte would not risk our displeasure."

"Sirom was not consulted. The king engaged the services of *drkhy*, claiming such would suffice."

"Concubines? He excludes the temple and the people from the ceremony of rebirth and claims it to be Egersis?" Below, countless arms steadied the crossbeam as the construct lifted.

"He told the court that Melqart wished the service to be a private affair as a punishment to the Canaanites. That Melqart was unhappy for what happened to the granaries. 'Grains are Melqart's gift to His people. Such an act is an affront to Him.' These were

Pumayyaton's very words. Elder Shipitbaal was there and reported them to me."

The thud of beam into pocket carried to the top of the temple. The cross stood quivering in the center of the square.

Elisha looked down on the stained cedar beams a moment longer. "What of the *rzn*? What do they say concerning Elibaal?"

"That young fool? They are too busy hounding us for the return of their sellswords. The lower orders are growing more dangerous since the razing of the granaries. They roam in packs. Several members of distinguished houses have been threatened. No beatings, but it is only a matter of time now."

The crowd cheered as the palace doors swung open. A line of guardsmen emerged from the darkness, a young man in their midst. His elbows were bound behind his back. Even from this distance, Elisha could see the fear that bleached his face.

From the crowd opposite the guards, a group of men stepped forward. All wore their mantles over their left shoulders. This was the symbol of the *norbolh*, the militia of the people's committee.

The guards stepped back, yielding the prisoner to the masses. The young man, Elibaal, saw the cross looming over the crowd. Even bound, he attempted to escape. A grinning guardsman slapped him down. A moment later, the militia took possession of him. Their tight formation shepherded the young man forward through the press. At the cross, ladders clattered into place. Men with mallets climbed into position.

"Do they not see reason?" Elisha scowled at the thousands below. "Why would the merchant-princes cut food prices during the winter months when grains are their most scarce, only to burn down the granaries when the storms lift? Should they wish to deprive Tyre of grain, they would simply not ship it. But then, in one night, four of the largest granaries go up in flames and a nobleman's son, a wastrel who has not been seen in this city in months, is found drunk in the ashes. Do the people not see it for what it is?"

"What might they see; that the king is behind the destruction?" Tetramnestus paused. "That the ruler of a city might risk horrible famine rather than have his power base shift to his enemies? My lady, if one's belly is empty while others feast, which is easier to believe? The *'bny* simmer in resentment. Pumayyaton has poisoned them against their betters. And now he throws young Elibaal to them, an offering to their rage."

The *norbolh* clustered at the base of the crucifix. Ropes soared up and over the crossbeam.

"Summon Anaphes."

The ropes flickered like a fisherman's line. There came a shout and the Elibaal was hauled, struggling, into the light. The lines about his wrists were raised until they rested against the crosspiece. More ropes were lashed around his elbows, securing him to the beam. The men on the ladders consulted with those below, taking their time, prolonging the event.

Elisha watched, dark eyes dispassionate.

Iron spikes were passed hand over hand up the ladders. Elibaal tilted his head back and wailed for Melqart's mercy.

A figure climbed midway up a ladder. Elisha made out Adon by his foppish trappings. A fine mantle of expensive purple lay across his left shoulder. She knew he was making a speech to the crowd but could not make out his words. Not that it mattered.

"My lady requested me?"

She turned to face Anaphes, the commander of the temple's mercenaries. He was dressed in northern fashion, a sleeved tunic jutting from his bronze scaled vest. A dagger lay strapped down along his right thigh. His shoulders were covered by a short cloak. The eyes beneath the felt cap were like those of a snake.

"You know what is occurring?"

"I know the situation worsens." His sentence was punctuated by the distant rap of a hammer. Elisha ignored the trilling scream.

"Have the *rzn* tempted you with gold to return to their service?"

"They have," Anaphes noted dispassionately. "We have a contract with the temple. We will honor it."

"Good. What do you know of these *norbolh*?"

Anaphes' laugh was devoid of humor. "The 'militia'? Citizens playing at soldiers. Bullies seeking victims. They march around town at night in groups of six, 'securing' the peace by banging on *rzn* doors and yelling threats."

"Tonight, you will form your men in groups of eight. Send them out. Find as many *norbolh* patrols as you can."

"My lady, three of my men could best any six of theirs."

"I want them to feel overpowered *and* outnumbered. I want them to taste fear."

The mercenary rubbed his chin. "Kill them?"

A hammer pounded again. The screams were fainter, nearly lost in the excitement of the crowd.

"No deaths. I want bruises. I want broken bones. Dead men require only burial. Wounded ones require attention and effort."

"I see not what difference it makes," the man said with a shrug.

From behind her, the tormented wailing had faded.

"I wish to give them a lesson they will understand. Tomorrow morning, meet me in the temple's audience chamber."

Anaphes nodded, turning to leave.

"Commander, one last thing."

"Aye, my lady?"

"Your mantle. Wear it over your right shoulder. Inform your men of this, as well."

The mercenary nodded, moving his garment as instructed before leaving.

Elisha did not return to the wall. There was nothing more for her to see.

THIRTEEN

He had made women's caps in the time before the madness.

He'd completed his apprenticeship, deciding to make his living devising caps and cowls for the ladies of the *rzn*. Ostrich feathers, baubles, interesting patterns. He'd learned to make use of them all. His business had been profitable, his stall generating wealth.

Nobody bought his caps now.

The noble ladies huddled behind their stout doors or went about their business escorted by men-at-arms. There were no more parties, no more social gaieties. And no more reason for his caps.

Inactivity had forced him to remain at home with his nagging wife and squalling brats. Food was running short, tempers high. And then the *norbolh* had demanded his participation.

He looked to his group of six. They came from all walks of life. A shipbuilder, a potter, a laborer, a sailor, and a wineshop slave. The shipbuilder was their leader, no doubt on the influence of Lord Adon. It was he who carried the torch, and he who decided the streets they would patrol.

He had no imagination, of course. Night after night, the same streets.

The capmaker thought back over the weeks. There had been the thrill of watching the militia move across the city, so frightening to the princes, so worthy of praise. Then the beatings. Entire patrols, every man injured. Lord Adon had responded quickly, raising the patrols to ten men. The mercenaries moved in packs of twelve. The militia to units of twenty.

And then the attacks stopped.

The *rzn* gained a respite. Larger patrols meant fewer patrols. The upper classes could slip to each other's villas, gaining camaraderie and companionship. There were even reports of brave little parties.

Adon had been furious. The patrols were cut back to six men each. The inward siege had returned.

The royal house was no help. King Pumayyaton praised the efforts of the *norbolh*, but praise was a poor substitute for gold and grain. His own city guards may well have eliminated the mercenaries, but he kept them back, guarding the palace, watching the temple of Melqart.

Some thought the mercenaries were cornered in Arherbas' compound. Some thought they had fled. Two weeks had passed since a patrol had been buffeted.

The shipbuilder froze, torch high. At the edge of illumination, a man stood. Fine robes. An amphora beneath his arms. A grain amphora.

"Hold, *rzn* dog!"

The man did, for but an instant. Then came the blur of robes and the slap of feet.

They tore after the fugitive. The torch flickered in the wind. The capmaker was jostled by the others as they tore along the narrow lanes. The fine robes were tauntingly close. The man ducked down an alley.

"Now we have him," panted the laborer at his side. "The end of that alley was walled off long ago! It goes nowhere!"

The rzn checked himself just short of the mortared barrier, turning to face them. The *norbolh* stopped, filling the alley.

"A merry hunt, Lord," the shipbuilder allowed, his torch wavering as he caught his breath. "It is over now. You have lost."

The capmaker felt a thrill pulse through him. The club in his hand trembled.

The cornered noble reached into the amphora, a curiously easy motion, given his plight. From it he drew his own club. The empty amphora, he tossed into the corner where it shattered.

The capmaker frowned at the club. It was not a crude length of cedar like their own. It was finally crafted, ornate iron knobs studding its surface.

Hulking shapes rose from the darkness, disarming and disabling them like so many children. The capmaker saw the sailor's arm break. He saw a fist slam into the laborer's face, teeth spinning against the darkness. The torch fell, blocking out the horrible vision, giving birth to sounds of the underworld.

Then the dreadful noises ceased. The torch rekindled.

Mercenaries moved easily about the narrow battleground. Someone sobbed quietly. The capmaker gradually became aware that a mercenary was standing over him. That he himself was huddled in a corner. That the sobbing came from his own throat.

"Here is one we missed. This little fellow went to ground."

The capmaker grinned weakly at the jest.

"Smart lad. We will leave you to fetch one of your boy patrols to clean up this mess. When you leave the alley, bear right and follow the lane. There is a cistern three streets down the militia water at."

He nodded understanding. A wondrous thought arose. They were going to spare him!

He moved through the loose ranks. The last two men stepped aside. The alley beckoned! Glorious freedom!

A meaty hand thudded down on his shoulder. He was turned. The mercenary commander smiled down at him. He felt his hand gently taken.

"One thing, lad. We make it our business that every militiaman we come across suffer some discomfort. It has become our custom. Just this one thing, and you shall be on your way."

The capmaker felt thick fingers close around his index finger. Another hand pinned his wrist, bracing it.

The commander smiled warmly, then yanked.

Beneath the coarse linen covers, the air was superheated. A hand moved across her breast, playing with a nipple. She twisted, struggling for freedom, desirous of entrapment. His weight bore down, locking her to the sleeping pallet. She clinched her jaw against the scream threatening to burst from her.

He penetrated her roughly. She moaned in delirious abandon, wishing the moment would last forever. She felt the *'drtnt* rise within her, a glorious wave. Her orgasm shook her like a doll. His own came and went while hers rolled on. Eventually it trailed off. She found herself nestled in his arms.

For a long time, her eyes studied the rough wall. Finally she whispered, "That was wondrous."

"I have no option for otherwise," Bitias chuckled into her ear. "Not with your mercenary thugs downstairs."

"You have no cause to fear them. Not with that club you carry." She giggled.

"Perhaps. Still, they make me uneasy. What if one of them should jabber? What if the *qdshbol* should hear?"

How could she tell him her husband already knew. That he would extract his own *'drtnt*, which she would enthusiastically provide. Their unspoken contract.

"Do not worry about it, brave admiral."

"*Lys*, Elisha! Do not worry? We continue our affair while the city crumbles around us. Melqart help us all should the militia or sells-words resort to edged weapons. Now, its just a children's game, beatings in dark alleys. But we are one step short of blood on the cobblestones. What will happen when blades are drawn?"

She snuggled deeper into his arms, rubbing her buttocks against him. "Think about something else," she suggested.

"I should not be here," he sighed, eyes far away. "I should be out on patrol, following endless coastlines, sleeping under the stars. Yet here I am, ordered about by a nervous boy. Day after day, my men grow flabby and my ships dry out. This is not work to which I am suited."

She felt his breath whisper across her neck.

"Be wary, Elisha."

"What do you mean?"

"What do I mean? *Y*, when Pumayyaton talks about the *rzn* elements, he occasionally slips, referring to them as 'hers'. He knows you are the strength behind the nobles. He will not admit it, nor will the *bolh*, but everyone knows. But how long can this game go on between the two of you? How long can you continue to hide behind Melqart's graces?"

"My situation is secure. There is nothing to fear."

"You think your mercenaries can continue to best Adon's thugs in the streets? How long before Pumayyaton releases the city guard upon your men? Or brings in mercenaries of his own?"

"He cannot do either. His forces are spread across the mainland, trying to keep food shipments safe amid the lawlessness. As for mercenaries, he has not the gold to lure them here. His granaries and treasuries are empty. Soon he will have to deal with me. But not as king to holy lady or even brother to sister, but as equals."

"And what will you have him do? Make you co-ruler?"

"It was my father's wish."

"Yours too, I would wager."

She twisted to face him. "'Bl, as if you are one to criticize. Only a few years ago, you were pulling an oar. Now you command five ships. As if you are not grasping for power yourself."

"Bah!" he exclaimed, climbing from the pallet. "You cast the world in your own image. You do not see that when you love your occupation, success and power follows."

"Perhaps you fool only yourself, Bitias. All men crave power. You can wrap it in your proclaimed love for the sea, but how euphoric would you be if you were still on a rower's bench?"

"Whatever you say, Little Priestess." He ducked into his robe. "Living as close as you do to Melqart, it's not unlikely that some of His omnipotence has rubbed off on you."

She watched him dress, hating and loving him at the same time. As his robes took his lean body from her sight, she felt an urge to apologize. Anything to lure him back.

His robes were in place. He pulled his short sea-cloak over his shoulders.

She bit her lip. Backing down, even a little, would be humiliating. But then she remembered how his body felt against hers.

With a flick, he pushed his cloak from his right shoulder, leaving it to only cover his left.

She leapt up, feet braced apart amid the crumpled sheets, her small body a statue of perfection.

"What is that you do? Do you not know what that means?"

"This?" He gestured to his cloaked left shoulder. "Of course I know what it means."

171

"You ally with that, that beast? Still wet from our lovemaking, and you flaunt such before me?"

"You honestly think I would be neutral in such a struggle? Elisha, I am not a mercenary. I do not pick my side. I am a man of Canaan. I am a subject of the king. My efforts are his to command. Do not tell me you did not realize this."

"I thought that you cared not for the politics of Tyre, just the security of its sea-routes."

"What I care about does not matter. I am an admiral; my orders come from the king." He took a step towards her. She felt herself tense. "Listen, little one. I warned you to take care. The game is about to change. Tomorrow, Pumayyaton will order my men into the streets, to track down and capture your outlaws."

"*N*'! Sailors. My men know every street, lane, and alley in this city. Yours know nothing beyond the quay wineshops."

"It matters not. I have two hundred and fifty men in my command. They will sweep the city. Any mercenaries captured go into the slave pens." He shook his head in frustrated desperation. "Make your peace with your brother before he is in a position to dictate terms. It is your only chance."

She crossed her arms across her breasts. "Sending sailors into an urban battleground is a desperate act. Pumayyaton knows his time runs short. When you see him next, take the advice you gave me and give it to him."

He desperately thought for something to say that might change her mind. But she'd turned away, gathering her own clothing. It was as if he were no longer there.

A moment later, this was true.

The roof hatch slid aside. A trio climbed into the night, their leather armor blending with the gloom, their clubs stained black.

Commander Anaphes cast a practiced eye over the forward parapet of the House of Astarte. The marketplace before the temple was studded with individual torchlights, men of the city guard standing in rough lines around the temples of Melqart, Astarte, and Baal. Their goal was to keep the mercenaries penned in.

Melqart's temple was no good; the compound was too open and

watched. Its sellswords were only there to protect Arherbas and his household. The balance of the mercenaries were carefully secreted in the houses of Baal and Astarte. The primary reason for this was the proximity of neighboring buildings.

Another figure emerged onto the roof. She was slender with a delightfully hooked nose and almond eyes.

"Everything proceeds," Zdenka said with her husky voice. "The girls have gone to the cistern, drawing off the guards from the rear alley."

"Good," Anaphes replied, his mouth dry, a familiar feeling before a dangerous endeavor. "We will be back before the sun rises. Have the usual distractions ready to distract the watchers."

She placed a hand on his leathered chest. "Be careful, Commander."

"Warm our pallet for my return," he smiled, then turned away to his two men. "Ready?"

They nodded, hefting a plank of light, strong wood. Like their clubs, it had been stained. Darkened linens sheathed its ends.

The three were old hands at this. They swung the plank to a nearby building, its padding muffling the noise to a faint scrape. A moment later, all were across. Anaphes took but a moment to look back to Zdenka, watching silently from the temple roof. The board slid across the next alley. In short order, they were a dozen streets from the temple, in the heart of the city.

Given Tyre's discord, the rooftops were devoid of sleepers. The citizenry had pulled into their houses like turtles, barring doors and windows against the nocturnal conflicts. The trio continued unobserved.

They paused on a rooftop, the men giving their arms a rest. Anaphes cast about, squinting in the moonlight. There. Small rocks, carefully stacked by the *rzn* dwellers of this house. The mercenary commander could not read words, but this held meaning. It spoke of a picket of sailors, three streets up, arrayed east to west, a larger collection behind them. Militia patrols in the area as well, but they were useless, a danger only if you tripped over them in the dark. Anaphes considered, then whispered orders.

They descended through the unbarred hatch. Whether the family was truly asleep or silently watching from their pallets was of no concern. The three men slipped into the street.

They located the sailors easily enough, their linens brilliant in the gloom. The weak point of the line was a sailor too sleepy to mind his overly broad avenue. They eased past him, looping behind. One of his men held a strip of cloth garrote-fashion. It would be easier to kill the lad, but Elisha's orders were firm. The cloth snapped across the man's mouth, gagging him. The clubs descended. Methodically they worked him over, leaving him bruised and bloody.

The picket line was now compromised. Twice more, they circled north around the pickets, taking them silently. But their luck could only hold so long. Two blocks over, a naval trumpet shrilled.

Without a word, they dashed headlong down familiar alleys. There were only their quiet gasps as they ran. No words were wasted concerning the six *norbolh* in pursuit a half-block back.

They reached the spot. Anaphes dove into a roll, tumbling along the street. His two men followed suit. An instant later, they were all on their feet, running full out again. They turned right, then left. They were just slipping through the door of the house they'd used earlier when they heard the sharp twang of the rope they'd set up neck-high across their retreat route. The door's closure cut off the distant choked cursing.

A lamp illuminated a small plate of dates and a jar of cool water. Anaphes and his men paused to wolf down the offering before ascending to the roof once more. In a moment, they were across the alley. After another, they were gone from view.

Every day, he was getting harder to find. A year ago, Elisha could count on her husband being at the temple, either in the audience chamber or the *Ulam*. As of late, she was having to look for him further afield.

She'd once found him in the storage chamber, his melancholy nature unnerving Tetramnestus. Or haunting the kitchens or the quarters of the servants. And there had been the time she'd had the entire compound searched, only to find him standing on the adjacent city wall, looking out over the straits. Ordering out the staff to find the holy lord was becoming a matter of routine.

This day, she'd not gotten to the point of engaging the priests. On a hunch, she'd ascended the ladder to the temple's roof gardens. Peering over the ledge, she saw the familiar white-linened figure sitting in the stone gazebo, staring towards the distant mountains of the mainland.

At her touch upon his shoulder, he smiled.

"Sparrow."

"Husband, are you well?"

His smile remained, shadowed by sadness.

"Is that what worries you? My need to commune with my god?"

"I fear it is not Melqart with whom you speak."

He laughed. "Aye, you are perceptive. It is my own heart to which I converse. Things change. Tyre changes. The Canaanites change. I am a man of thirty-nine years, too old for such things."

"You are not..."

"You are young. You do not understand. I always assumed that my life would be centered upon my service to Melqart. That I would conduct the services. The Egersis. The Day of Atonement before the sacred wellstone. I never thought there would be politics and infighting. I could not have conceived that the palace and my order could become estranged."

She ran a comforting hand along his broad shoulder. "Husband, it will soon be over. Pumayyaton's treasury is depleted. The people grumble over the lack of grain. The city guards are unpaid. He must concede. The committee will be abolished and the council renewed."

"And if he should not?"

"He will."

He shrugged beneath her palm. His attention was still distant, focused on the brown mountains. She glanced along his line of sight; he seemed fixated on a distant shelf of rock that jutted from the nearest hill. It was the same one she'd studied when trapped by Lady Ayzebel at that rooftop party so many years ago.

"The city tears at itself, Elisha. Every night, rival gangs battle in the streets. The militiamen end up in the care of healers, the mercenaries on the slave blocks."

Elisha sniffed proudly. "The militia loses far more than..."

"This is not some game, played with a ball in the street, for you to cheer over. This is our city. It is devouring itself."

"I stand by my belief that it will soon be over."

"Over? It's too late for being over." He looked up sharply. "Have you not considered what this means to me? I am the *Qdshbol*, the Holy Lord of Melqart. He is the god of Tyre. His essence is this city, the buildings and lives that encompass it. So think, child. What does it mean to the high priest of a city god when his city collapses in riot and dissension? Where is my god? Has He turned his back on his people?" Arherbas realized that his hands had balled into fists and carefully released them. "Have I failed Him?"

"Melqart is still with us. The city still exists, does it not?"

"Does it? As one people, the Tyrians of Canaan? Or as a collection of rich and poor, eyeing each other with distrust by day, fighting like animals by night. A city without a collective spirit is nothing more than a loose association of people. It was not our dye or cedars that made us great, it was our uniformity beneath Melqart. And suddenly, it is as if He is gone."

"If He is gone, He will return."

"He is not some day-traveler, here one moment and gone the next. I feel as if He is truly gone." He reached up and patted her hand. "As should I."

Elisha started at his words. "What do you mean?"

"My city falls apart. My god has moved on. Perhaps it is time for me to go as well." His hand tightened around hers. "We could leave. There is a large population of Canaanites living in Egypt, a trading community. They have a small temple there, one where I could perform services. With our gold, our lives would be comfortable."

"You would never get your gold out of Tyre. Pumayyaton watches far too closely. He would swoop in the instant you moved it."

"Who says it has not already been moved?"

She stood quietly for a moment. "I thought that your wealth was secure in the holy statue within the temple's inner chamber."

"Perhaps." His attention went back to the rocky scar across the mountain's face. "Perhaps."

She dropped to her knees before him, his hands clinched in hers. "Husband, do not leave, not yet. Pumayyaton will yield. The city

176

will mend. Melqart will return. A moon's passage, perhaps two, will see this concluded."

Arherbas looked down at her distantly.

"All right, Sparrow. We shall stay a little longer. But I plan to depart before the winter rains."

She nodded her thanks, giving his hands a final squeeze, then departed. As she descended the ladder, she realized that time was now as much an enemy to her as it was to her brother.

Ship's trumpets wailed in the night.

"Up, lads," Bitias bellowed. Around him, men scrambled to their feet. They fell in behind him as he raced up the narrow lane towards the screaming horns.

They were getting good at this, the young admiral reflected. Not as good as the mercenaries, but not too bad. They'd learned the streets, and were learning the ins and outs of close urban fighting. The cost was broken heads and shattered bones, but they were learning.

They poured into the small square where several men from one of his ships staggered about. His own second officer and another seaman struggled to hold down a bucking mercenary. Chains were rushed in, clamped home.

"Now, you bastard, you will pay for your games against us." The second's bronze knife gleamed in the moonlight.

"Put that away, Werketel," barked Bitias to his *shnymshtr*. "The slavers pay naught for dead men."

"But it is time those bastards paid for what they have done to our crew. Those damnable traps, the ambushes..."

"Do you want to be paid in blood or in gold?" Bitias grabbed the man's knife, ramming it unerringly home into his scabbard. "By the scattered pieces of Yam, *RearEnd* and her sister ships are rotting in the harbor. No prizes have been taken and the ship's funds are low. Taking mercenaries is our only income. So get this man to the pens and be quick. Should something happen to him en route, you shall take his place."

"I understand," Werketel grumbled.

"Now, which way did they flee?" His *shnymshtr* gestured to a maw of a lane. Bitias detailed ten of his men to accompany his second officer. They would not lose *another* slave to an ambush. The rest he led through the narrow opening.

Their eyes pierced the darkness, watchful for triplines, chokelines, or any of the other unpleasantries the mercenaries tended to employ. They could not move as quickly as the sellswords, but they were learning to move damned quick, regardless.

"A street fight ahead," one of his men shouted.

They poured into the small square, its stones blueish beneath the moon. A militia patrol lay about, the *norbolh*s battered but not abused. Sounds of running drifted from the lane opposite. Bitias whipped a hand forward. The hunt was on.

The mercenaries laid a twisted trail in their attempt to shake them. Now the sailors could see their quarry in the moonlight, four men running, one of them favoring an injured leg.

"Keep 'em in view," Bitias shouted. "Watch them close! If they duck or jump, watch for a wire!"

The distance between the two parties dropped. Two of the mercenaries had taken up their wounded companion but they were just not fast enough. The slaver's gold was as good as theirs.

"Wall ahead, Admiral," one of his men shouted. "We will have them before they can shimmy over it. They are ours!"

True to the man's words, a wall blocked the far end of the lane. The first man leapt up, straddling it, reaching a hand down to help his injured comrade over.

"Take 'em, men," Bitias roared. "To the slave pens with them!"

The men assisting the injured man heaved him up, then backed away for their own run at the wall.

The screaming sailors charged, clubs waving through the night air.

"Now!" the man on the wall shouted as he hauled his comrade up. "Now!"

Bitias glimpsed motion above. Several men rose up along the roofline. Bows shimmered in the moonlight.

"Cover!" shouted Bitias. There came a humming of arrows and a scream from a sailor before him. The admiral hit the rough flagstones, rolling.

His men had all fetched up against the buildings lining the lane, glancing nervously up. The boy kept screaming, holding his shoulder. The wall was empty, the mercenaries gone.

Bitias thought of the moment before, of the hissing of arrows. Something was wrong. He fetched up one of the shafts, feeling its tip. Then he slapped the young sailor to shut him up.

"You young fool. You are unharmed. See, no tips on these arrows." He looked at the empty roofline. "Damn them."

FOURTEEN

Tetramnestus hunched over a scroll. The lamp at his side cast a tentative glow across the storeroom and its urns.

Elisha frowned from the stairs, looking around the room. Finally, she coughed politely to announce her presence.

"Tetramnestus, have you seen Arherbas?"

He looked around quickly. "No, Holy Lady, I have not."

"I must speak with him. Word just came in that nine of our mercenaries were taken. The city guard forced its way into two noble households and captured our men as they descended from the roofs. They will be on the slave block by morning. If Arherbas will give me gold, I can have the men purchased by temple agents and returned to our service."

Without looking up, the aide replied. "I am sorry, Highness, but I have simply not seen your husband."

There was something in his tone that caught her attention. The forced disinterest.

The voice of one of the lesser priests echoed up the stairs.

"Holy Lady, we have searched the entire compound. The holy lord has not been found. In fact, nobody can recall seeing him this day, nor the last."

"Very well," she called over her shoulder. "Send the men to their pallets." She looked at the aide's back for a long time.

"What is it that you know, Tetramnestus?" Her tone was flat. "What is it that you are not telling me?"

"I was ordered to silence. By the holy lord himself."

"Hirgab's eyes! My husband is missing and you hold information from me?"

Tetramnestus winced before her tone. He licked his lips nervously before speaking.

"At dusk, three days ago, I was in the *ulam* with Lord Arherbas. I had temple watch that evening. We were just discussing some routine matters when they came."

"They? Who?"

"King Pumayyaton. With a group of guards, led by Commander Ib. The soldiers waited respectfully outside while the king entered alone. He spoke with Arherbas. Something about ending the strife that was pulling the city apart. Your husband seemed open to the idea."

"They spoke of our feud? And I was not summoned?"

"He ordered me to silence, my lady. Then he sent me away."

"You left him there?" She took a step into the room. "Alone with my brother?"

"It was his choice. Later, one of the mercenaries on the roof saw the king and his escort return to the palace. I had just assumed the holy lord had gone about his business." He found the courage to turn and face her, only to see her disappearing down the stairs.

Elisha ignored Tetramnestus' cries as she crossed the empty audience chamber. Scenarios swirled about her head. Had Arherbas gone through with his plan of departing for Egypt?

He would have taken me. I meant too much to him.

She could hear the aide's flat-footed pursuit. She continued to ignore him as she swung out the portal into the chill night air. The year was dying. Soon the storms would come and it would be truly dead.

She took the steps three at a time, plans forming in her head. Search the compound once again. Check with all the guards on all the gates: had the high priest departed? Had a skiff been summoned to the royal dock?

But there was one place she had to check first. And only she could do it.

Huge cedar doors stood between shimmering pillars. She shoved one open with her shoulder. Inside the *ulam*, a sleepy acolyte came to his feet.

"Holy Lady?" he blurted, "Is anything wrong?"

At that moment, Tetramnestus entered behind her.

"Nothing at all. You are relieved of your night's duty. Tetramnestus shall watch over the temple."

"Very good, Highness."

Tetramnestus watched him depart. "My lady, why have you...Melqart's grace! You cannot do that!"

Elisha stood at the door leading to the *hekal*. She'd just started to pull it open when the aide blocked it..

"Holy Lady! It is forbidden for any woman to enter the inner room! Should you be caught, you would be killed!"

"Stand aside, Tetramnestus."

The aide remained before her, not meeting her eyes.

"I said stand aside!"

He withered before her demand. Finally he stepped clear, his face averted lest he witness the violation of the temple. There were no further words. A moment later, he was alone in the outer room.

The *hekal* was as cold as death. The chill of the marble sucked the warmth from her feet. Around her, the braziers sat in their rows, cold and silent. At the head of the room, a single lamp fluttered.

She moved through the chamber, eyes probing its opulent gloom. It was as wondrous as the other time she'd been here. But then, she'd had Arherbas to guide her. Now she was alone.

As she neared the final stairs leading to the huge cedar doors, she felt her fear returning.

Forgive me for this, God Melqart. Forgive me for violating your sanctum. But I must find my husband. I must know if he has fled.

Once, her father had ordered snow bought from the inland mountains. Relays of riders concluding with a fast skiff had seen the delivery of a sloshing bucket of water and ice. She'd stuck her hand inside to collect some of the slush, gasping at its cold fire.

In her hands, the gold handle to the inner room was every bit as cold. Even though the door was well maintained, it was opened but once a year. It took all her strength to gain entry.

She stood in the inner room. Silent. Watchful.

The door eased shut, cutting off the weak lamplight.

The darkness was absolute.

She stood for a long, long time, her eyes closed. Faintly came the trickle of water that bubbled from the sacred stone.

She let her memory feed her eyes. Once again, she could see the huge sphinx that towered over her in the darkness. She could imagine its cold gemstone eyes observing her trespass. The stone, the guardian. It was all before her in her mind.

Her nose twitched. She frowned.

The air in the chamber was stale. Dead. Aside from the high priest performing his services during the Day of Atonement, the room remained sealed against the outside world.

Yet she smelled an odor of the world of men. A faint, bittersweet corruption.

A tremble shook her small frame and she cupped her hand across her mouth, not daring to cry out. Carefully moving her feet, she maneuvered around to the guardian's broad flank. As she did, the evil smell grew.

A tear trickled down her cheek.

Her hand reached out tentatively, running along the beast's artificial flank. Its gold plating was cold. Her probing fingers found the catch Arherbas had once guided them to. She pushed.

She heard the panel ease open. A stench washed over her, the smell of urine, feces, clotted blood, ripped organs.

Her eyes were blinded by the darkness. Her mind provided an image of how a body would have to be disassembled to fit into such a tight compartment.

A wail rose in her throat and she clamped both hands over her mouth. The portion that escaped echoed against the marble walls, rebounding her grief at her. Strength departed her body, her knees folded, and she fell to the floor. The coppery smell of her husband's dried blood washed over her, a wave of guilt and decay.

P umayyaton's triumph was clinched in his wolfish smile.

"My dear sister! How good of you to come. You have been absent from court far too long."

Across the throne room, across the heads council and committee,

Elisha stood in the entryway. The ruler of the Tyre was pleased to see her, this much was true. But it was her appearance, not her presence, that brought forth his skull-like grin. She was haggard, appearing as if she'd paced the night away. He found her dull loathing wondrous.

From their pillows, the men twisted to look at her, nobles and commoners alike.

She ignored them all. "I know what you did."

He reclined easily. "You should be careful, my sister, with accusations and details. Should you admit to certain trespasses, you could be struck down. A simple admission from your lips, a single command from mine, and you would be dead."

At his post behind her, Elisha sensed Ib stirring.

"You were with my husband. You charmed him with your cursed serpent's tongue."

"The holy lord had grown disillusioned with Tyre's strife. He spoke to me of leaving the city, of traveling to the Iberian colonies or perhaps Egypt. It appears that since we spoke, he has left. Is not that correct, Adon?"

The one-time shipwright stood and bowed respectfully. "It is, my Lord. A skiff-man reported that a man matching Arherbas' description was ported across the straits yesterday. He was traveling light and disappeared into the mountains."

"Arherbas is lost to us." The king's small smile was for Elisha alone. "It would be impossible to find him in such rough terrain. Further, his defection from Melqart was his choice. Retrieving him would solve nothing."

"He did not leave," Elisha growled. "Not his city. Not his god."

"You have proof of this? Evidence you would like to share?"

There was a long moment where the siblings matched stares. A single word would bring death, riots and insurrection. The Canaanite empire lay on the tongue of a girl not quite sixteen.

Finally, she shook her head. No.

"I thought not. So all agree that the our priest is gone. This leads to our next order of business: his wealth. It is clear that a single man could not carry any significant amount of gold from the city. His fortune must still be here. As the temple's activities have drained

ROBERT RAYMOND

our treasury, it is only right that his estate should be entrusted to me. The holy lady shall yield Arherbas' gold."

Elisha frowned, the realization coming that Pumayyaton had not gained her husband's fortune. Only her brother knew what really took place that night in the temple, but she could see the likely events. The gentle words to lull her husband deeper into the building's darkness. Then the demands for his wealth. Arherbas' attempts to mollify his nephew, the revealing of the empty compartment. The murder, followed by the butchery on the temple's marble floor. The concealment of the remains. The cleansing of the blood with water from the sacred spring.

The fortune had not been there. Arherbas had hinted that it had been moved. He'd carried his secret to the nether world with him.

"You will give me his gold, Elisha," her brother repeated. "Here and now."

Truth gave her courage. "I do not know where it is. I only know where it was kept, before it was replaced with other things."

"Ib!" Anger flashed across the king's face like lighting across the coming storms. "Summon the palace guards. All of them."

She heard her brother's lackey calling down the stairs and the clatter of gear as the soldiers responded to the summons.

"I can not tell you what I do not know, Lord," she said with level simplicity. "I am my husband's wife. He did not share details of his finances with me." Behind her, she felt the presence of the soldiers. Ib stood at her back.

"No idea where he hid his wealth?" Pumayyaton studied her dispassionately. "None at all? Well that is unfortunate. Your imprisonment and torture would not likely force such a recollection." He scratched his round soft chin. "But you have a strong sense of commitment, my sister. So perhaps other means would heighten your recall. Ib! Arrest the council of elders. And their supporters."

The merchant princes leapt to their feet at the command. Some pulled daggers from their robes, a pointless resistance. The guardsmen were armored and far better equipped. They moved past Elisha, surrounding the pockets of protesting men, taking away their puny weapons and fragile freedoms.

Pumayyaton was on his feet, witnessing the mass arrest with

186

grim satisfaction. Elisha noticed Adon to one side, watching with hungry eyes. It was clear he was anticipating the formation of a new nobility, a benefit for men such as himself.

Only when the detainees grew silent did Pumayyaton speak.

"It is clear that the lords of the nobility conspired against the royal house in its disputes with the temple. They shall be held in our dungeon. As our treasuries are empty, we can ill afford to feed them." Shouts rose at this. Ib's men restored control with the butts of their weapons.

"The holy lady can purchase their freedom. She can save them from starvation. She need only produce her husband's wealth and these men shall be saved." The king's smile was firm. "Otherwise, their deaths are certain. Take them away."

Under escort, the noblemen were herded down the stairs to their cells. As they passed her, each looked upon her with a differing expression. Some silently pleaded. Some scowled their hostility. Only Shipitbaal, the old council member, was unique. He smiled at her, as if curious to see how it would all play out.

The prisoner's shuffling faded. Elisha stood alone at the rear of the room. Mapen, the high courtier, began calling items of business. The committee of the *bolh* moved up onto the recently deserted pillows. Pumayyaton listened to the opening arguments but his eyes were still on his sister.

With slumped shoulders, she turned and left the court, never to return.

She lay on the floor of Arherbas' apartment, the marble sucking the heat from her body.

She'd lost. Arherbas was dead. Pumayyaton still held the throne. Her mercenaries had scattered. Her power was gone.

Elisha wondered how the *rzn* captives were faring. Like them, she had not eaten this day; her appetite was gone.

She thought of her husband and wept softly to herself. In her mind's eye, Arherbas stood before her. His gentle smile, his kindly ways. While he was strong, he lacked the faults that made her brother stronger. Before Pumayyaton's audacity and unconvention-ality, he'd not had a chance.

She thought of her husband's body, still entombed within the guardian. What would become of it? Doubtless, decay would continue. In a half-year's time, at the next Day of Atonement, the odor would be gone. The new high priest, a lackey of Pumayyaton, would not dare raise an objection should he even suspect.

News of what had occurred in the palace was sweeping the town. Tetramnestus had organized searchers to comb the compound, looking for the treasure that would save the captives. Elisha gave a bitter laugh at that: even with the gold, Pumayyaton would still kill them all. They'd opposed him, herself and the nobles. They'd stood up and checked his attempt to shape the world to his whims. As soon as the treasure was secured, he would order their deaths. From his *bolh* supporters, a new upper-class would be formed.

Like a ship passing through thin squalls, she drifted in and out of sleep. In her dreams, Arherbas came to her. She could see his sincere smile. She could hear him call her Sparrow. She could feel his firm fingers upon her. And then she would wake and he would be gone, dismembered in his golden tomb once more.

There was guilt. She felt darkness in her heart at how he'd been pulled into this storm. He'd only wanted to serve Melqart, to follow the rituals of the temple. In aligning with her, he'd doomed himself.

She was not sure if she was asleep or awake. A ghostly Arherbas stood before her, a sad variant of himself, troubled by the city's conflicts. They sat in the gazebo once again.

She stood quietly for a moment. "I thought that your wealth was secure in the holy statue within the temple's inner chamber."

"Perhaps." His attention went back to the rocky scar across the mountain's face. "Perhaps."

The ceiling of her late-husband's chamber was before her eyes once more. She stared without seeing until she heard a stir in the audience chamber.

"Tetramnestus?"

A pause.

"Yes, *qdshba'alat?*"

"Do not call me that. I am no longer the holy lady." She closed her eyes for a moment. "Inform the king that I know where the treasure is."

They shivered in the murky dawn. A day before, they had been men of the world. Now they stood on the stone quay in the swirling rain, eating fish paste from crude bowls with dirty hands.

At the end of the quay, *RearEnd* rolled in the low waves. Water dripped from the Yam's raised posterior, bearding his grin. On her benches, the rowers lulled, watching the fallen nobles and guards with indifference. Bitias and his second, Werketel, stood on the rear deck.

"Poor stupid bastards," Werketel judged, then spat over the side.

There was a heavy door set into the city wall. It grated open to admit a finely-dressed royal party. Pumayyaton laughed into the cold rain, his merriment echoing across the dreariness. His courtiers huddled in his wake, bedraggled peacocks. Watched closely by Ib's guards, Elisha and Tetramnestus followed.

She wore her finest robe, its fabrics glowing the purest purple. Her favorite headband contained her hair. She lent an air of nobility to the grim proceedings and the *rzn* who watched her stood taller in her presence.

Bitias strode down the gang plank, his second officer following.

"We have brought our ship to the royal dock as ordered," he reported in mid-bow.

"Very good," his king replied, smiling into the day's starkness. "I have a short mission for you. Convey Lady Elisha to the mainland. She will lead you to a hidden cache of treasure. Retrieve it. You should have no trouble returning before dark."

Against his better judgment, the admiral frowned.

"Lord, for the last few months, you have used us as irregular troops. Now you wish us to dig in the mud, to fetch and carry? I fear that the morale of my command is in jeopardy."

"I would not ask such from the heroes of Canaan. These twenty-seven prisoners will accompany you. They shall grub for the treasure and carry it back to the boats. You need only to accompany them."

"So many? *RearEnd* is a small vessel. So many men might cause her to turn turtle, especially if my fears on the coming weather are true."

"No, no, my Admiral. You misunderstand. You are to leave half your men here. Let these traitors face a day of work, in the mud *and* behind an oar. Tyre has supported them long enough."

Bitias looked at the bedraggled nobles. "Are you sure that is..." he paused, then opted, "*advisable?* That would leave us equal in numbers."

"But not in strength. They are pudgy princes, cowed by a cold night in my cells. You and your men are fit and armed. Nothing would please me more than to force a day's labor out of these *'yrzroy.* No more arguments. Be off."

Bitias bowed once more, then turned to Werketel. "Clear the lower oar benches. Give those men silver enough to see them through the day. The others, make sure they have their daggers about them." He glanced at the sodden nobles. "Ensure there will be no hesitation should the need arise."

Oddly, the excused men left their benches grumbling. For too long, they had been away from the sea. The short run from the northern harbor to the royal quay had given them a taste. Now they looked to the misty waters of the straits with reluctance. Those remaining on the upper benches settled in, content to be about their business.

The *rzn* filed in, Werketel directing them to their seats with disrespect. At the gangway, Shipitbaal paused, rainwater jewelling his grizzled beard. He gave the royalists a long, cold stare as he settled his mantle over his right shoulder.

"Why, that old bastard," Werketel snarled. "I will not have him flaunt..."

"Leave him be," Bitias ordered. "He is just an old man. Place him into the bow with the Lady and her aide."

"May Rephaim's flatulence fill your sails," the old man shot back, dropping to a bench of his own. "I started my life before an oar. It is fitting it end there."

The second stood poised to object but Bitias headed it off, calling for the clearing of lines. Moving like a disoriented beast, *RearEnd* edged out into the open waters of the straits. The long time ashore had robbed the men of their crisp experience. The clattering of oars carried over the slow waves, bringing a grimace to the admiral. He looked at the walled city retiring in their wake, cursing the cost of politics.

"Across to Ushu," he instructed his tillerman. "Try not to hit anything." The man nodded grimly.

A heavier shower swirled over the penteconter, briefly hiding both shores from view. Bitias squinted to the bow where Elisha and her stocky assistant huddled amid the urns of provisions. He wanted to go to her, to speak words of pity and compassion but knew it would be a waste of breath. Elisha looked forward into the gray scud, eyes narrowed, a grim figurehead to their sad journey.

As customary, they grounded stern-first into the sands of Ushu. They were met by an escort of guards and a large collection of scowling citizenry. Most of their food had gone over the straits to feed Tyre. The official account for this necessity had placed the *rzn* fully to blame. The condemned debarked the *RearEnd* amid a fury of muddy clods, the guardsmen keeping well out of the way. Tetramnestus did his best to shield his mistress from the worst of it.

"The rain shall wash us clean," she noted flatly as they moved through the streets, ringed by sailors and guards.

At the edge of town, Bitias appeared before her. "Which way, my lady?"

She nodded to a narrow trail that ascended the gentle slope, traced by generations of woodsmen and herders. "A cliff juts from the hillside, a mile or two inland. I believe this is the way."

They continued, the mud, the chill and the grade all in league against them. The commander of the guard was insistent: no stops. He'd been instructed to safeguard the party and have them back before nightfall. Given the wild nature of the hills, he was only too happy to oblige.

Eventually the stony outcrop pressed through the mists. Thick brush surrounded it. Bitias looked back to her, questioningly.

"I do not know where it is located, or even if it is here," she told him. "I told Pumayyaton that this was little more than a guess."

"For your sake, I hope it is here," Bitias replied grimly. "Werketel, hold the men here. I shall scout the position." With two oarsmen escorting, he moved into the brush.

Elisha stood in the mud, forcing herself not to shiver, to keep her chin raised. Even now, she would remain the holy lady she once had been. Nearby, the men of the guard studied her lithe form and exchanged low jests. She ignored them, focusing her attention on the cold rock overhead.

"I believe it is here," Bitias panted as he pushed clear of the brush. "There are words of protection carved into the rock and the ground is covered in disturbed shale. I would stake my arse on it." He paused to look over the column. "Here is what we shall do. The guards will establish a perimeter in the brush to keep us safe. My men will oversee the prisoners while they dig. Commander if you would detail a few men to watch over Lady Elisha and Elder Shipitbaal..."

"Do me no favors, pup," the old man replied, shoving a guards-man out of his way as he joined the other prisoners.

Elisha, too, made to join them. Bitias attempted to intercept. "This is not woman's work," he protested.

"What you do is not sailor's work, no? More the work of shep-herds, I think."

The ragged nobles and the city guard shared a laugh at the sailors' expense. Werketel growled, a dog on a tether. Only Bitias appeared unaffected.

"Fine. Labor if you wish. Let us finish this work and be done with it."

They pushed through the tight shrubs, the oarsmen carefully flanking them, making sure none wandered. Elisha paused as they entered the small clearing at the base of the rock wall. Shale sloped away, unmarked by weed or brush. Upon the vertical face before them glimmered letters, carved with recent chisel strokes: *MLQRTYBRKH.*

"*Melqart's blessing,*" read Tetramnestus. "It is the holy lord's invocation for the protection of his treasure."

"I doubt our god will protect my husband's gold any more than he safeguarded his life," she replied darkly.

"Enough gabbing," Werketel stated. "Start moving the stones down the slope. And should any of you entertain ideas of clubbing us with rocks, please try. Here in the wilds, we deal with rebellion far more directly than King Pumayyaton chose to."

The former members of the elite began their long ordeal. Stooping.

Scrabbling for rocks. Carefully transporting their loads to the growing pile downslope. Then back in line for another pass. The slimy ground grew treacherous; painful falls more common. Amid the laughter of the sailors, blood mixed in the quagmire.

Bitias watched the efforts, his face grim. Downslope, the mound grew while more of the outcrop's base was exposed. Every so often, he would look upwards into the gray void, attempting to judge the fall of the sun.

Elisha struggled down the slope, her mind dulled by the cold and the labor. Occasionally she would slip, spilling her rocks. She would leave them where they fell, climbing back for another load. Blood oozed from her cut hands and slashed knees. Her hair hung wetly across her face.

How quickly we have changed. She looked into the dull faces of the others. *How quickly we have become slaves.*

A cry halted them. A prisoner knelt before the exposed face.

"Lord Bitias! There is an opening here!"

At the bottom of the hole against the cliff face, a minute opening lay exposed. Werketel roughly pushed the laborers clear, ordering a trio of sailors to finish the excavation. The rocks flew quickly. The cave mouth grew.

Off to the side, Shipitbaal slumped on a log, his gray head hanging from limp shoulders. Elisha sank down next to him.

"He loves you," the old man said, not looking up. "You can see it in his eyes every time he dares look in your direction."

"He hangs his cloak over his left shoulder. My mantle hangs on my right."

The elder studied the ground between his gnarly feet. "Does that mean anything anymore?"

"Nothing matters." Her voice was flat. "We die tonight."

Shipitbaal raised his eyes, taking in the toiling sailors. "True."

"Enough," Bitias called. "Stand clear." With no thought to dignity, he lowered himself prone into the muddy pit and carefully wormed into the maw of the cave. Sailors and nobles stood shoulder to shoulder, watching the opening with a breathless quiet.

His head poked out, his long hair grimy. "There are ten amphorae within. Take them as I pass them to you."

ROBERT RAYMOND

Elisha watched her husband's treasure emerge into the feeble sunlight.

FIFTEEN

RearEnd plowed into the dark waves, sea-water trailing from its bow-eyes.

"I do not like this at all," Bitias commented into the crimson dusk.

Before their bow, Tyre lay backlit by the sun. The gathering winds had molded the black clouds with the skill of a potter. Their forms withered and convulsed in the scarlet light.

The cloaks of the two officers crackled in the gusts. Behind them, the tillerman leaned into his oars. The rowers pulled clumsily in the pentecounter's pitch.

"We shall be snug in the harbor soon enough," noted Werketel. "Just as soon as we turn over these rebellious dogs to the king." He spoke confidently, the wind whipping his words over the stern. "Commander Ib tells me that they will be murdered in their cells. As for Pumayyaton's whore of a sister, a cross stands in the marketplace."

Bitias remained silent, his eyes on the distant quay bristling with guards. To the world, he appeared to be judging the kicking waters, working out the tricky approach. But his view included Elisha and her servant, huddled in the bow.

"Row, you women, row," bellowed Werketel into the wind. "Once we get within the shadow of the walls, it will be calm enough."

Elisha came to her feet in the bow and Bitias was struck by the sight of her. Her purple robes streamed back in the wind to reveal her trim form. Against the glare and spray, she was a ghostly goddess, Astarte come to earth.

A moment later, she dropped back into the prow's limited shelter.

Looking beyond the raised ass of their figurehead, Bitias noticed the quay was shifting to port. He called back to the tillerman.

"It is the chop," the man replied. "The blades are dry as much as wet. The water in the narrows is confused."

The admiral stepped back to assist the steersman. True to the man's word, the steering arm's feedback was chaotic. One moment, the blades bit the water, sure of their course. The next, they rattled impotently in the pin sockets.

Shoulder to shoulder with the man, Bitias glanced forward, searching for the calm beneath the city walls. Against the bow, Tetramnestus rose against the gathering sea and failing sun. A moment later, he dropped to the cover of the decking.

A man was down, one of the sailors, his face smeared with blood from the butt of his milling oar. Werketel pulled the groaning man from his bench, caught the errant shaft and the cadence of the stroke. *RearEnd* drove on. The calm water grew closer.

Bitias steadied himself as the tiller bit deep. The stern was settling. They were almost clear. He looked to the sailor laying prone on the central runway, concerned about his sheathed knife and the *rzn* rowers. Should one of them gain that blade...

Once again, Elisha was up, steadying herself with one hand on the figurine of Yam. The other was close to her chest. She leaned forward. As she settled once again into the gloom of the prow, Tetramnestus rose to take her place.

The *RearEnd*'s bow dropped heavily, nearly pitching the bulky man to the decking. He remained upright, but Bitias saw something leave his hands, falling into the dark waters of the narrows.

"Tetramnestus!" Bitias did not know whether the heavy man had not heard him or simply ignored him. The aide reached down and helped Elisha stand again. The admiral felt a stab of panic. He pushed off the tiller, taking a step onto the runway.

"Elisha!"

She stood, braced by her assistant, clutching something to her breast, glancing back at him. Her eyes were dispassionate, calculating.

He took a step, then another, suddenly finding himself running, shouting her name into the wind.

She looked once more to Bitias. An urn lay in her arms, similar to those he'd pulled from the cave this very afternoon. She smiled, turned, and tipped the last one over the side. The cylindrical shape disappeared immediately from view.

"Elisha! What have you done?"

She turned back, her smile flashing in triumph.

"It is complete! My husband's wealth lies in the mud of the deep narrows!"

Men were twisting at their benches. *RearEnd* lost headway, lulling in the confusion. A noble cheered. A sailor's knife hissed clear of its sheath.

"Elisha, are you mad? You brother will kill you for such treachery!"

Her tinkling laughter was borne on the wind. "We were all dead anyway. Our lives would be forfeit the moment Pumayyaton had the gold. And we will still die, but *you will die with us.*"

Bitias stood frozen on the decking, heedless of its pitch. The truth of her mockery struck home. The king was unforgiving. How would he reward an admiral who lost upwards of a hundred talents of gold? A man who allowed his hated sister a final triumph?

Bitias would die. He knew it as sure as the breath in this chest and the beat of his heart. A pyre. A cross. A sword thrust. The sun was fading, and he would not live to see it again.

"So row, you slaves." Her eyes flashed beneath the headband. "Row, you sheep, to your death. Your king awaits you."

Bitias had gained his rank by quick action. He'd taken command amid the hiss of arrows and screams of confusion. But he was struck mute by the peril this girl had plunged him into.

"Bitias," shouted Werketel from somewhere behind him, "What will we do?"

When Elisha spoke again, her voice was level.

"There is one path you can follow. One way in which you can avoid the fate awaiting you in Tyre. We must become outcasts. We must flee beyond Pumayyaton's grasp."

"Where?" shouted Bitias. "Where is this dark haven you force us to? Where are we to go?"

She crossed her arms, chin up. "I am no oracle, providing advice to those seeking audience. I will not chart your course and then be discarded. In seeking my council, you accept my leadership. Swear by this, or cross to the quay and accept Pumayyaton's mercy instead."

"You are our commander, Bitias," Werketel shouted. "You cannot let a woman lead us. It is not..."

"Silence!" Bitias faced Elisha across the rolling deck, face flushed, emotions churning. On the quay at her back, the soldiers milled, visibly concerned by *RearEnd*'s wallowing. Atop the palace rooftop, heads came and went. The anthill had been upset.

"Where," he finally grated, "do you propose we go?"

"Do you accept my leadership?"

Distantly, a trumpet sounded recall. Figures now lined the palace rooftop. Bitias imagined he could make out Pumayyaton's rounded head.

"I accept your leadership." Voices raised around him. Some shouted in joy, others in consternation. Bitias rounded on them.

"I have pledged my word, and such a pledge extends to my crew. If any man among you desires otherwise, stand and fight me now. But should I stand or fall, only two paths remain: death or exile."

The men remained silent. Some had dropped to their benches, reclaiming their wild oars. From the stern, Werketel glared in checked silence.

Eyes on his crew, Bitias called out, "What course, my *mlk*?"

"The colony of Citium on the isle of Cyprus." Elisha's voice was thoughtful. "With the oncoming storm season, Pumayyaton will be unable to pursue us there."

"Granting we do not flounder in the attempt." He called to his second. "Werketel! Into the wind shadow of the wall, then swing north! We must get clear before pursuit is raised!

Hands desperate, grateful, worried, and angry pulled at the oars. The dark penteconter leapt forward, swinging into the calm beneath the fortifications. The tillerman leaned into his blades, bringing their bow starboard. There were still 600 yards before they cleared the island for the open seas.

"Faster, you oafs!" Werketel's voice called over the angry blare of trumpets from the nearby walls. "Damn you rich *rzn* bastards, keep your pace! Do not foul those around you! We must get clear!"

"Steady there," Bitias called, as much for the benefit of his *shnymshtr* as the others. There had been a panicky tone to his second's voice.

More trumpets shrilled, raising the alarm. Bitias could imagine the scene at the northern tip of the island, within the military harbor. How soon before other pentecontexts could be launched?

They tore along the wall, foam spuming from their flashing oars. Bitias looked up.

"Mind! Arrows!"

Several shafts hissed down, plinking at the water around the fleeing *RearEnd*. Two thunked into the deck. With theatrical disinterest, Bitias pried them up and flicked them over the side. Forced chuckles rose from the oarsmen.

Elisha watched his leadership, nodding to herself.

"The northern end of Tyre is coming up," Werketel called. "Open water ahead."

Bitias looked forward. Sure enough, heavy gray rollers lay beyond the island's tip. Lightning flashed against the darkness.

"At least it will be a sailor's death," Bitias noted as he viewed the heavy weather. "I was tired of the city and her ways."

"Your words are true, Commander," someone shouted. "Let us see what Yam's minions can throw at us!"

The oars bit into the water with growing determination.

"The entrance to the harbor is coming up," shouted the second officer. "The boom is opening!"

A heavy beam hung across the narrow entrance to the military docks. As *RearEnd* ripped past, its crew could see it ponderously swinging aside. Inside the enclosure, a pentecontex cleared its berth, swinging for the opening, its painted eyes fixed on them. Men swarmed over two sister vessels.

The first heavy roller struck *RearEnd*, flinging a geyser of vertical spray. Elisha fell heavily against the planking. The oarsmen cried out as the deck heaved upwards. Werketel bellowed like a madman, keeping them focused, keeping the vessel moving.

RearEnd adjusted quickly to the flood, rolling rhythmically as the crew propelled her north. Waves crashed distantly as they paralleled the beach.

Bitias rode the mad deck. He took in the oarsmen, the weather, and the situation with sharp eyes. In the stern, Werketel and the tillerman strained at the steering arms. Beyond them, the first penteconter cleared the channel, striking after them with grim purpose.

The second bellowed something but Bitias ignored him, scurrying forward with a monkey's grace. He leaned out over the bow, gripping the ship's figurine. His sharp eyes scanned the swirling confusion.

"Werketel! To port! Out to sea!"

The man could not possibly have heard his words but the admiral's gestures were clear. Still, the second hesitated before pushing the oars over. Elisha saw fear whiten his face.

Tetramnestus was useless, hugging the deck, coated in his own vomit. Elisha came up as a wave broke over the bow, soaking her. She grabbed one of little Yam's legs with both hands. At her side, Bitias darted a glance to her.

"Get back down! It is too dangerous!"

"We sink, I die! All the same!"

"Melqart's grace, fine! Just hold on tightly!" He peered forward into the gloom. Endless waves raced past, giving the sense of great speed. Bitias strained forward, then frantically gestured to starboard. A moment later, his arm shot to port. Through the deck, Elisha could feel *RearEnd* twisting to follow his commands.

She glanced at the stern. The two men on the tillers were focused on the admiral's gestures. Behind them, a black penteconter slammed through a wave, three ship-lengths off. Unlike Bitias mixed crew, their oars were manned entirely by professionals. Their rate of closure was visible. In their prow, archers huddled, bows readied. Two other ships followed in their pursuer's wake.

She looked forward, a cry breaking from her lips.

A line of black rocks bit through the belly of a wave, casting brine into the wind. The reefs!

Bitias steadied an arm high over his head. She could hear Werketel's shout, "Await my word...wait..." The rowers gathered themselves, watching the officer with grim intensity.

The rocks appeared and then vanished. Not seeing them, knowing they were there, was horrifying. Bitias' keen eyes watched their reemergence. His arm flicked to starboard. The rudders answered. He steadied. A roller rose from the darkness.

Releasing his hold, Bitias jammed both arms forward.

"Full stroke!" At Werketel's call, the men hauled on their oars, muscles twisting across their backs. *RearEnd* galloped down the back of a wave, gaining speed. And suddenly she was climbing, the roller shoving her keel up.

"*Ns'! Ns'!*" came the bellowed cadence from fifty throats. The oar-shafts creaked under the loading.

The roller was past and they tipped downward. A harsh squeal sounded from below the planking, screaming like Tnn, Yam's aquatic dragon. And then they were clear, the men still lugging the oars, the *RearEnd* still afloat, flying into the eye of the wind.

Elisha took the following crash to be thunder. Then she saw the pursuing penteconter staggering back, its bow punched in. It fell away in the tide, decks in confusion. Before it was lost to the gloom, they caught a glimpse of its sister craft coming to its aid. Neither looked as if they would challenge the reef as the fugitives had.

Bitias let out a heavy breath and gestured towards the north-west. The bow swung smartly onto the new track. He watched his crew labor for a dozen strokes before looking over to her.

"Well, we are on our way."

D awn found them carving across a gray wasteland.

It had been a hard night. Given the rough seas, the lower oar positions had been secured. The crew had been mixed into two sections, one to row, one to nap. The storm hindered both attempts.

Bitias pulled himself from a truncated sleep. All night, he and Werketel had rotated at the tiller. Beneath the clouds, it had been black as pitch. Their navigation had been based on the feel of the steering arm, their knowledge of the waters, and an occasional muttered prayer.

The admiral groaned, stretching the kinks out. He took in his vessel's surroundings, the marching squalls and grain of the waves. He studied the arc of his piss as he urinated off the stern.

"Werketel, what do you say to some sail?"

The officer had been applying ointment to a *rzn*'s blistered hands. He didn't look up.

"It's a fickle wind, nearly abeam as not. Chancey."

"If we lose the mast, at least we will not have to answer to the royal chandler. Let us try a quarter sheet."

The mast was raised and a short amount of sail lowered from the yard. True to the second officer's words, the wind ran between north to east. The tillerman did his best to maintain headway but even Elisha could feel their gradual fall to starboard.

"We will keep it up for a while. It will give both sections a chance to rest before we pull ourselves back on course." Bitias yawned. "Well, let us break out the provisions."

"No," stated Elisha.

He blinked in surprise. "Pardon, my lady?"

"We shall not feast. Not until we reach Cyprus."

Several of the crew looked up, their faces drawn from a night in the elements. Bitias scowled in confusion.

"We have food, oh Queen." A trace of mockery in his voice. "Enough for two nights at sea. And I figure we will make landfall sometime tomorrow. There is not need for rationing."

"I am not speaking of rationing." She held his gaze. "I am calling for fasting."

"Fasting? Are you mad? There is no religious observance for this day."

"You will speak to me as an adult, Admiral. You will speak to me as your leader. To this you gave your bond."

"My lady, the winds force us eastward. And they are contrary; it is likely we shall lose the sail before nightfall. The men will be at their benches then, and much happier with full bellies."

"Are you finished with your whining?" Elisha's dark eyes were as cold as the surrounding sea. With a quick motion, she delivered a stinging slap across his cheek. Bitias staggered back, more in surprise than pain.

"I am your queen. And even though my husband is dead, I am

still the holy lady, a direct servant of Melqart. I am the throne. I am the temple. My word is your law."

She took in the men around her. The simple oarsmen. The outcast *rzn*. She looked at each one in turn. Not a few of them blinked or fidgeted before her scrutiny.

"I am the holy lady," she repeated. "Melqart's tool. Melqart's voice. He steered me as He steered you, bringing us together on this small ship in this great sea. He saw the corruption of Tyre. He saw the overpopulation, the stagnation, the Assyrian rule. He saw these things and it displeased Him.

"So by His manipulations, we find ourselves setting forth, in search of a new land. We will establish a new city, a *qrthdsht*, a Carthage. This is His wish."

She grabbed at an oarsmen, holding the man's wrist before he could back away.

"I am not speaking of establishing a dreary trading station on some foreign shore. I speak of a golden city rising on a virgin coast. I speak of the establishment of farms and fishing fleets, of trading vessels and war ships. This city shall grow to eclipse Tyre. Unchecked, it will grow beyond the bounds of the nations that squabble along the Upper Sea's eastern coast. There is no end to the power that will be ours."

She released the wrist but the man did not back away.

"This is a holy task. This is our Egersis, our rebirth. We must purify ourselves through our fast. In this, we prove ourselves worthy of His favor."

There was a long silence. Then a sailor stepped over to the stack of oars, carrying one to his bench. Another did, and another. Driven by wind and muscle, *RearEnd* gained speed.

Lord Kotilus, the former princely horsetrader, watched the common sailors labor.

"A holy task? Does she really believe this is Melqart's doing?" He disdainfully spat over the side. "This is all because she lost her feud with her brother. And for this, my wealth and my family gone."

Shipitbaal looked up from the bench he rested on. "Is that it, Kotilus? You mourn the loss of your opulent life and blame her for it? Do you not remember Pumayyaton's plots against us? Do you not remember the committee? Do you forget shivering on your pallet while the militia pounded on your door? Do you forget Hannon's blood? Elibaal's cross?"

"No, Elder," the noble guardedly replied. "I did not forget these things."

" '*Bl*! Then perhaps you forgot how you felt yesterday when you sat on your bench and saw Elisha throw the last of the treasure overboard. Perhaps you forgot how you felt when you realized that you were not going to die. Is that what it is you forgot?"

Kotilus' eyes dropped. His head shook.

"Then I dare not think you forgot that you agreed to follow her. When you swore, as Bitias swore, that she would rule us. That she was our commander, our holy lady, and our queen." Shipitbaal stooped to pick up his own oar. "You did not forget your honor, did you, Kotilus?"

The rzn raised his eyes to meet those of the elder. "No, old man, I did not. Give me that oar."

Shipitbaal slipped the shaft's leather strap over the thole pin. "Find your own, *'yrzro*."

With the rough seas, they continued to row in shifts. When the winds would blow from the south, the sail would be deployed. When rain fell, the men would cant their heads back and catch the moisture. They ignored the complaints from their bellies.

Bitias and Werketel remained on the stern, working with the tillerman to establish their course from the occasional glimpses of the sun. In the moments he was unoccupied, the second officer felt his stomach growling. He saw the miles of exile pass. He began to feel regret at the life and rank he'd thrown away. But Bitias' stern expression stilled his tongue. He kept his growing misgivings to himself.

The storm took them without warning.

One moment, they were cutting through a light shower. A sudden chilling swirl and then the maelstrom struck. In an instant, the sail was gone, the mast a splintered stub. Icy rain stabbed at the exposed men. On the stern, the tillermen and the officers threw their shoulders against the steering arms to keep *RearEnd* pointing downwind.

"Keep rowing," Bitias shouted. "We must keep way or go under!"

The men rowed, the teams switching out after short intervals. Darkness fell and the winds continued, combing the spray horizontally from the waves. The constant rowing began to take its toll. Even with rests, the weaker men began to drag their oars, more a danger than a benefit.

With the night, the winds dropped somewhat, allowing the tillerman to hold their course unaided. But the seas were high from the stern and they had to maintain forward motion. The cold and hunger leached strength from the exiles. Bitias found himself at an oar, as did Werketel, endlessly pulling the shafts through their cycles. Even Elisha and Tetramnestus did duty on the benches. The aide failed within the hour, a seasoned veteran taking his place. But Elisha matched Bitias stroke for stroke, a grim determination driving her wiry body.

Bitias jolted awake from a short nap. The darkness was absolute, a chill rain falling. He opened his gummy mouth and slacked his thirst. Around him, the ragged grind from the oars continued. He pulled himself from a low bench, looking to see who needed relief. On a nearby bench, handsome young Barcas was floundering. He slapped the young man on the shoulder, relieving him. The lad collapsed on the lower bench, instantly asleep. As Bitias found the rhythm, he noticed Shipitbaal manning the steering arm. The elder's gnarled hands held the shaft with practiced authority, his sharp old eyes challenging the darkness.

Time was measured by the overtaking waves. Bitias knew that he should be worried about making Cyprus. Should they miss it, it would mean another night at sea. Beneath his leaden exhaustion, he was too tired to care.

"The star!" Shipitbaal's croaking laugh sounded from the stern. "The beacon star! Melqart's 'yr, can I helm a ship or can't I?"

Bitias glanced over his aching shoulder to see it glimmering through a break in the clouds. It was just off the starboard bow, right where it should be. Their course was dead on.

The overcast began to fragment, flying like ribbons before the night breeze. Wave followed wave. The stars shimmered like ice.

The eastern horizon was glowing faintly when Bitias felt *RearEnd* stray. He looked up from his labors to see the old councilman sprawled limply in the stern, his arm draped over the wandering steering arm. The admiral shipped his oar and made his way back. The elder looked peaceful, but no breath stirred in his thin chest. Bitias felt a presence behind him, turning to find Elisha looking down at the old man's body with sorrow.

"He always trusted me," she said softly. "He was a companion on the path of my life."

Bitias said nothing. Carefully, he lifted the lean body and slipped it over the stern. By the time he'd brought *RearEnd* into proper alignment with the beacon star, Elisha had returned to the bow.

Dawn brought some warmth to the laboring men. They were still cold and hungry and the seas were still running high, but they'd made it through the night. Someone had heated rainwater in a kettle and was passing it about.

The air was cold and clear. The sun broke the horizon, casting distant peaks in orange tones. The crew cheered; Cyprus was in sight. They were dead on course with Citium just beyond the horizon. The oars stretched and dug with renewed strength.

Bitias came to the bow where Elisha stood, looking at the distant land.

"Well, Highness, we made it. Soon we will be ashore. But what then?"

"What then? We weather the storm season in Cyprus, then set out to found our Carthage."

"Fifty men and a single leaky boat? *Qtn'khn*, such things take many resources. Such we do not have. You must start being practical about this."

Elisha turned her head, favoring him with the faintest of smiles. Then she knelt, picking up one of the provision urns. Carefully, she pried open the stopper. The rising sun shimmered like fire on Arherbas' treasure.

"One urn looks like another. A person will believe what he is lead to believe. My goal remains: I will have my Carthage."

THE SECOND BOOK
ENTITLED ASTARTE

ONE

Ribbons of cloud rode the sharp wind. Waves heaved before an uncertain dawn.

From the portal of the rundown stone warehouse, young Barcas took it in, unimpressed. Wrapped in a woolen blanket, he looked out over the silted harbor. A beard shadowed his young face. His life as a boy was over. Manhood had begun.

And here he stood in a tumble-down ruin on the edge of a colony town, his family's fortunes gone, his future empty.

His anger simmered at the unfairness of it all. Whatever it was, ill fortune or a god's meddling, the result was his life had been taken from him. He couldn't blame Elisha directly; he suspected that if it hadn't been for her, his body would now be resting in the family necropolis, if not some muddy pit. The same winds that had driven her had swept him along. Fault could be placed on no one's shoulders.

Still, he thought. *Still...*

He was not sure how his fate had become tangled in those of the hers. His life-path, as he saw it, should have been direct and to the point. Blessed by birth, he would be trained as a trader, to take his place in his family's business. Longer and longer voyages, an increase in responsibilities. Eventually he would be commander of his own vessel and turn its gold into more ships, adding to his family's wealth.

But not now. It had drained away like wine from a punctured skin. First, his cousin Hannon, struck down by Pumayyaton in the throne room six years ago. Relationships between the merchant princes and the throne had worsened. His family had grown concerned, keeping him safe in their compound. Years in which he should have learned his trade had been spent watching his father fret. Then the time of turmoil. The rise of *'bny* hatred. The midnight battles between militia and sellswords just beyond his window. And then, as if it could not get any worse, being taken hostage with the other nobles.

He'd remembered rowing the pentaconter across the straits that wet morning. His brave little thoughts telling him that the unpleasantness would soon be over and his freedom would be returned. After all, he'd been Pumayyaton's companion, at play and lessons. The young king would not consign him to an undeserved death. They had been friends.

But he could remember the trembling of his hands, the dryness of his mouth. Evil had been all around him that day. And deep down, he knew what waited for him upon return from their mission.

When Elisha had faced down Bitias and saved them all, he'd dashed away the tears that had come so unexpectedly lest the men on the nearby benches see. His life, with all its years and potential, had been returned.

The consequences that extended beyond that moment had eluded him.

There had been the excitement of landfall in the Cypriot city of Citium. The men cheering and slapping each others' backs. The hesitant looks from the locals as if the Sea People had returned. While the men cavorted on the beach, Elisha stood in the prow of *RearEnd*, watching.

The hospitality of the town towards the newcomers was reserved. The fugitives were a difficult issue, too politically-charged to openly welcome, too numerous to drive off. Quarters had been provided, an old warehouse to the north of the city, facing an abandoned harbor. Ruins surrounded the old building, the bones of a section of the city lost to fire two centuries before. Only lepers and madmen prowled the jumbled stones.

Under Elisha's direction, the men of the *RearEnd* chased out the animals, human and otherwise, from the old warehouse. The rest of the day had been spent cleaning their new winter quarters. It had come to a complete shock to Barcas when he found himself on the end of a broom, sweeping out scraps and feces left by the former inhabitants. The young *rzn* had never contemplated that he might, some day, perform the labor of a domestic servant.

The next day, the sailors stripped the penteconter of all its gear. Benches, mast, oars, and fittings were all stored away. By midday, Barcas was on a line, helping to pull the lightened vessel through the muck of the old anchorage. Much effort was required to shift *RearEnd* above the stormline, settling her in for her long winter's hibernation. Barcas couldn't remember collapsing to the cold stone floor. Someone had tossed the old cloak over him.

That morning, he'd awoken from more than slumber. He'd slowly opened his eyes to see the age-stained ceiling. His back was stiff, his muscles cramped. Dried mud encrusted his legs. Fleas tickled his ribs. The realization came that his life was ruined. The villas, the servile servants and slaves, the wealth and golden future; all were gone.

It was a good time for self-pity.

So he stood in the doorway, muscles protesting, stomach growling, morning chill nipping around the edges of his dirty cloak. He looked out across the sea and absorbed its nothingness.

"If you frown any more," came a voice from the darkness behind him, "your chin will fall off."

Barcas focused on the horizon.

"At least get some of that stew. It will warm your bones and keep the demons away."

"I am not hungry."

"Then there still must be lions in Cyprus, what with all that growling I hear."

"I am not hungry, Aleyn. Not for any food Elisha might provide."

Ever practical, the men of the *RearEnd* had placed its benches along the wall, just as they had been aboard ship. From the nearest one, an old oarsman sat, his pot belly at odds with his ropy muscles. His tangled hair ringed a bald spot.

"Won't eat her food, eh?" Aleyn's small smile mocked. "But you sleep under her roof. And shiver in her cloak. And your heart still beats. All are gifts of hers, yet you reject one favor and consider yourself pious." The smile went away. "Do not be an idiot, boy. Eat."

The tone was that of a parent to a child. Barcas flushed, but realized that balking would only make him look worse. Grunting, he moved over to the small fire where the contents of a clay pot bubbled. He only meant to ladle one small dash of soup but found his hands filling his bowl. As nonchalantly as he could, he returned to his post by the door.

"So where is *Qtn'khn*, anyway?"

"'Little Priestess?' Heh, as good a nickname as any." Aleyn scratched his belly with a hoary hand. "She, Bitias, and a contingent of the men are taking the treasure to a local temple for safekeeping."

Around a mouthful of stew, Barcas asked, "Is that wise? Why not keep it here?"

"Lord Bitias argued that fact but the queen decided against it. Too much chance that some of the exiles might take an urn and disappear into the hills. With regards to my commander, I agree with her."

"Bitias openly disagreed? I thought he was her supporter."

The oarsman gave a horsy laugh. "He will protest everything she might say, but end up doing her bidding. It is going to be rough seas between those two."

"What do you mean?"

"Just how young are you?" A laugh. "You must be the only one in our party that didn't know. She and Bitias have lain together. I've heard tell that they were carrying on even while their respective minions battled in the streets." He chortled again. "Damned funny if you ask me."

"But if they are in love, why should they be at odds?"

"Bolt of Baal, but you are even younger than I thought. Look, lad, they may have shared a pallet or two, but they were on opposite sides of that tussle in Tyre. With Bitias' help, Pumayyaton won, so that must lodge in her gullet. But your so-called 'Little Priestess' tricked him by tossing the provisions over the side, pretending they were the treasure. That cost Bitias his rank and homeland, so he probably smarts a little over that. They shall probably kiss and snarl, kiss and snarl, over and over again. And mark me, boy, only a fool would come between them."

Barcas digested the news along with his meal. The news of Elisha's affair with the Admiral came as a shock. A second shock came when he realized that she had been married across that time period. The thought of Tyre's holy lady laying with a man not the high priest was deeply disturbing.

But what bothered Barcas the most was that, in his young life, he'd only coupled with a household servant a few times. Elisha had far outstripped him.

He shook his head, trying to make sense out of his jumbled emotions.

"This news confuses me greatly, Aleyn. She is supposed to be our queen. She is to lead us to some unsettled place beyond the realms of civilized men. But now I hear these tales of her behavior and...and...I do not know. It seems against all reason to be led by one who is so...so..."

The old oarsman waited, his smile back.

"Well," Barcas continued, "She seems so 'unladylike'."

"So that is it, eh?" Aleyn briefly studied the centuries-old flag-stones at his feet. "Look, boy. Shortly we will leave these shores, striking west across the Upper Sea. Who knows how far we shall go. Perhaps the Tin Islands, or the western coast of Libya. Wherever landfall may be, one thing is for certain: we will be on our own. We will need food and shelter in short order. We must be able to face any animals or men who threaten us. If we are to survive, we will have to grow quickly to become a nation that can stand against any other. The one who leads us must be strong and ruthless for the good of all." The smile turned grim. "Would you rather the one who determines our success, even whether we live or die, be 'lady-like'?"

Barcas tried to think of something to say. Failing, he shook his head.

"I thought not," replied the older man.

The party halted in the main square. Ten amphorae hung on

213

carrying poles between pairs of men. Ten more men, armed with daggers and clubs, kept an easy watch on the curious locals.

Tetramnestus had already started towards the Temple of Melqart bordering the southern boundary of the enclosure when Elisha's hand checked him.

"No," she told him. "That one there."

"The Temple of Astarte?" The aide was visibly shocked. "My lady, you were the Holy Lady of Melqart's Temple in Tyre. Do you dare risk His displeasure, at the start of this great gambit, by securing our wealth in the temple of that..."

"Careful, Tetramnestus," Bitias cautioned. "It looks like the locals take worship of The Lady seriously here."

A casual glance would confirm this. While Melqart's house was moderate and utilitarian, Astarte's temple sprawled. Its wide portal, gracing the right side of the building's entrance, was flanked by ornate columns.

The aide spared the building a judgmental glance before turning back to his mistress. "Highness, I only think it wise that we place our goods in Melqart's keeping, if only to earn greater blessings."

"No. I've done a great many things which may have displeased our god. Perhaps it is best to hold our wealth in the house of another, if only for a short time. We will endeavor to re-earn His favor in our new homeland."

"Lie low," Bitias observed. "Good plan." Tetramnestus glared at the admiral but Elisha ignored him, making towards the entrance. The party snaked after her.

Short of the portal, the bulky aide blocked her again. "My lady, perhaps it is wise that you do not enter this house. You should remain outside while Bitias and myself negotiate the storage. It may be..." he glanced to the nearby locals. "...unsavory."

"Thank you, Tetramnestus, but I think I can cope with it."

Bitias had sailed these waters and knew of the variations of Astarte's worship. He watched carefully for her reaction when she entered, detecting only the smallest of hesitations. That she did not freeze earned his approval.

The interior was spacious. Four lines of stone columns marched towards the distant alter. Fine marble graced the floors. Statues of the Goddess smiled from alcoves.

And the room was filled with women.

They lounged on benches beneath the windows. Many of them reclined, breasts bared. Others wore fine slitted skirts that displayed sensuous thighs. Several women were completely naked.

The room quieted as Elisha entered. Painted faces sized her up, assessed her beauty to theirs.

"Yes? Yes?" A fussy little man crossed the floor, his robes fluttering around him like wings of a landing bird. "Do you come to perform your service?"

"Service?" Elisha frowned at the thin priest. He was oddly unbearded, his carriage soft, almost feminine.

"Yes, your Duty. To the Goddess." He stared at her. Behind her, the men crowded in, gawking at the display of femininity. The women took an immediate interest in the crew, placing themselves in poses ranging from fetching to indecent.

Elisha glanced at the women posed so becomingly. She sensed Tetramnestus' agitation and Bitias' smirk.

"I am Queen Elisha, leader of the Tyrian exiles." Her voice rang with the command she'd learned from observing Bitias. "Who are you? What service is this of which you speak?"

The man blinked at her sudden hard tone. His voice, when it came, was subservient.

"I am *Rmkhn* Scylax, High Priest of this temple. The service is one which all women of our community perform at least once in their lives. It is the ultimate act of devotion to the Goddess. The woman leaves her family and comes to this temple. Once she has performed the rites of entry, including the cutting of her hair, she remains in service to the Goddess until the sacred duty is complete."

"And that duty is...?"

"She must entice a foreigner to toss a silver or gold piece into her lap and say 'The Goddess Astarte profit thee'. The woman, under service to the temple, cannot refuse the man. They pass, hand in hand, to the temple's sacred ground, a beautiful garden, and perform the holy act of worship."

Elisha nodded, knowing full well what worship Astarte, goddess of fertility, would demand. The *'drtnt*. The great radiance.

"And if no man comes? If she is ugly or infirm?"

"Then she stays," the high priest replied simply. "Some women depart for home within a matter of days. Others remain longer. There have been women who have waited in the temple for years. That is a problem we are currently facing; with the disruption of Tyre, trade has dropped off. There are less foreigners landing in Citium these days. With the time of storms upon us, it is unlikely that any of these women will be returning home soon. Of course, should you be interested in rewarding some of your followers..."

"I have ten amphorae of great value," she replied curtly. "We need them safeguarded until our departure. I assume you have a secure place for them?"

"None would violate the Temple of Astarte."

"Show us to your vaults."

"But of course," Scylax replied with a rejected merchant's disappointment. "If you would follow me?" He gestured to a portal along the left wall.

As they moved along a compound path, Tetramnestus pushed up closer to Scylax. "I am a little surprised at what I find here, brother priest. I am somewhat familiar with the Astarte's temple in Tyre through my liaison work with them. I did not anticipate such a level of, well, community involvement."

The priest frowned. "I believe High Priest Sirom still presides over Her house there? With his priestess-prostitutes? Do you think true love and devotions flows from professionals? They have lost the light that is Astarte's love. It is only my opinion, mind, but to me their order has become little more than a quay-side tavern..."

Scylax's words and forward momentum were checked by a small figure that stepped out of a doorway directly into his path. The entire column stopped short; two urns swung together but fortunately did not shatter.

"Os'sh! What are you doing outside the temple?"

The small woman who'd nearly collided with the high priest flinched at his words, the scrolls beneath her arms tumbling to the ground. "I'm sorry, High Priest. I'd run out of things to read and had gone to the archives for more."

Bitias had automatically stooped to recover the parchment tubes. He straightened to hand the documents to the girl and froze in a way that Elisha, in the temple's entrance, had not.

She was small and compact, and unlike the bright clothing of the temple females, she was garbed in simple white linen. Most striking was her complexion, skin the shade of burnished wood, hair an offsetting tan. She nodded apologies to Scylax, thanks to Bitias, and scurried in the direction of the temple.

Bitias watched her trim form recede. "What did you say her name was?"

"*Os'sh.* 'Wood woman'; an apt name for one with such coloration. Skin a touch darker than ours, hair far lighter. Very, very strange. Came from a barbaric tribe of nomad horsemen, someplace far to the north, I believe. Nothing but trouble."

"Really," Bitias asked, genuinely curious. "Why?"

"Well, for one, there is the issue of that disturbing hue. Most men think she looks more like a carved wooden statue than a real woman and choose not to lie with her. But worse is her station: she's a slave in the governor's house. There are..." the high priest coughed diplomatically, "rumors that she was his favorite, that he used her in all manner of unseemly ways. As such, none dare the governor's wrath by touching her. None of the other women like her; she is below the station of the high born and too despoiled for the low. So she remains here, eating our food and disrupting order."

"How long has she been here?"

"Two and a half years." Scylax sighed. "We may never get rid of her." He pulled himself out of his temple's troubles and returned his attention to his patron. "And now, my Queen, if you would follow me? The temple repository is right over here..."

The pitch was in tatters, the wood clawed and torn. Bitias' fingers probed the damage to *RearEnd*'s flank.

"That trick over the reef nearly sent us to the bottom." Werketel noted disapprovingly. "A little less water is all it would have taken."

"As opposed to certain victory with a half-trained crew against three penteconters?" Bitias pulled at the splinters, exposing more damage.

"Tomorrow I will have the crew strip the pitch from the damaged panels. We will replace the center plank and all its pins."

"Pull the pitch from the entire ship. Inspect every plank." Without turning to face Werketel's frown, he explained, "We are the little priestess' flagship now. She has gold and we have time. *RearEnd* has been leaking more and more over the last year. Before her hull kisses foreign waters, I want her as tight as a boy's sphincter."

"We shall start in the morning."

Bitias left his second, crossing the muddy beach in the cold twilight. The hills over the city were black against the orange sky.

His entry into the warehouse elicited good natured cat-calls from his crew. Men sprawled on their makeshift benches, playing simple games and instruments. The smell of hot food hung in the air.

"Be comfortable, louts. Tomorrow, I want every man turned out after breakfast. Work detail on the *RearEnd*. Werketel will direct." Theatrical groans rose.

Barcas, sitting in a corner, had an air of exclusion about him.

"*Rzn* too," the Admiral clarified.

"But..."

"Only crew members work. But only crew members sail in the spring. Would you like to greet Pumayyaton should he come sniffing up the coast for his gold?"

The boy nodded acquiescence.

Bitias cut a chunk of meat from the spitted lamb. He chatted with several of his men, indirectly quieting their growing fears of exile. A draw from the water butt slaked his thirst. Stretching, he made for the back of the warehouse. Blankets draped across storage alcoves provided a minimum of privacy for the more elevated of the exiles.

His own alcove was as he left it: a bundle of meager possessions propped against the wall, a crude blanket covering his straw pallet.

A poppy petal lay in its center.

Bitias examined the scarlet fragment, a smile on his face.

He made his way back through the crew, patting his gut as if he had to relieve himself outside. Stepping into the crisp night air, he looked at the petal once more before tossing it aside. Carefully he circled the old building.

An ancient oar, discarded in the time of his father's fathers, lay propped against the wall. He studied it for a moment, spat into his hands, then shinnied up it. At the top, he wiggled onto the warehouse's roof. After a moment of straightening his tunic, he pulled the rod after him, laying it carefully aside.

He crossed the uneven surface, his head cradled by the brilliant stars. The wind was easing to the south, its chill rising goose bumps on his arms. A poor night to be adrift.

"Bitias." Her voice came as a husky whisper.

His eyes, adjusted to the darkness, made out the dark blanket. Clothing lay neatly arrayed on a parapet. Her face peeped over the cover, eyes cool in the night.

He tossed his tunic into a heap, defiance to her tidiness, before slipping beneath the blanket and into her embrace. It was warm there, the points of her nipples hard against his chest.

He attempted to coax her legs apart with a conciliatory stroke or two. She giggled at his haste, then reached down and grasped his 'yr with her tiny yet strong hand. A semi-playful squeeze elicited a grunt of pained pleasure from him.

"Slowly, my Admiral. Slowly. Do not spend your oarsmen yet. Pace your stroke."

He thought of wrestling free. Elisha studied him, her grip firm. Bitias returned her gaze and then, carefully, shrugged. With great care he brought his hands up. Callused fingertips traced the line of her ribs, the curve of her breasts. She shuddered at his attention, her own hand moving ever so slightly on his captive member, guiding him like a rider would a horse.

She shuddered under his touch, nuzzling through his tangled beard to nibble a bronze ear. In return, she felt his breath play across her exposed neck, dragonfire in the chill. In her grip, his manhood swelled until she could barely contain it.

They played with each other beneath the cold stars, taking their pleasure in their mutual attentions. Eventually Elisha released him, spreading her legs. When he eased into her, she moaned from the back of her throat. Her arms and legs coiled around him, her grip growing desperate.

As always, the moment of *'drtnt* was wondrous.

They lay together under the rough blanket, looking up into the night. There was a quick flash as something fell across the heavens. Elisha watched it drowsily, wondering what sort of an omen it might be.

"*Qtn'khn*," Bitias murmured at her side. "Little Priestess. There is something I must ask you."

She smiled. "So soon? Of course I could." Her hands began to play with him.

"No, no. Not that." He captured her errant fingers. "It concerns our plans for settlement."

"I had thought about that, too. Our band possesses much knowledge of the Upper Sea. We should not let that go to waste. Tomorrow night, I wish to sit down with them collectively and discuss where we should go."

"Elisha, that is why I want to talk to you—before plans are cast."

She twisted slightly to better see him. "What do you mean?"

"Elisha, our exiles are made of two classes, the common oarsmen and the nobles. Neither of them are true colonists. None seek your dream; they were simply thrown into it."

He waited for a reaction. Finally, she said, simply, "Continue."

"Pumayyaton seeks them for their associations with your actions. They have been torn from their families and lives simply because of the feud in the royal house. My rowers are men of the sea—they want nothing more than their bench and oar. Your *rzn* do not seek the hardships of settlement—they desire a return to their games of gold. You are the only one in this collection that seeks a utopia in the west."

"What would you have me do? Return to my brother?" Her voice was devoid of emotion. "Beg for forgiveness on my knees?"

"The king will never forgive you. I know him well enough to see that. But he might forgive these men should they prove themselves to him." He paused, then his words came in a rush. "A single urn from our trove would permit a person to live in luxury for the remainder of their days. You could go anywhere you choose; Egypt,

Greece, even the western colonies in Iberia, forever beyond Pumayyaton's reach. Your escape would be assured.

"The men, on the other hand, could return with the balance. Given Tyre's desperate state following the troubles, the king would treat them as returning heroes. From their outing, the *rzn* would be far easier to control. Everyone could return to their lives."

"As you could return to yours, *Admiral*?"

There was hurt in his voice, but hurt could be faked. "It is not that at all."

"Is it not? You are an Admiral, but only of five ships. Rather a puppy-admiral, I would say. No doubt you hunger to return to royal service, to regain the king's favor, to grow your command. You might say that five ships are enough, but one hundred would truly be grand, would it not?"

She felt him roll away. His form appeared against the star field, his breath steam in the air.

"Am I the only one who desires rank, *Qtn'khn*? What of you? An escape into luxury is not enough for you. You tasted power as a princess, and were served a helping of it as holy lady. You sought the title of Queen of Tyre but failed. Now you must settle for Queen of this new city, this Carthage of yours. And it matters not how many people you drag into this madness."

She looked up at him, her expression neutral.

"You gave me your bond, Bitias."

He looked down at her, silent and still. She continued.

"In the shadow of the walls of Tyre, you agreed to follow me. To hold me as your ruler. You gathered your crew's loyalty and handed it to me, seeking deliverance. And now you seek to return to Pumayyaton's service, transferring your trust from me to him?" She studied him for a long time. "I can not hold you to your word. No one can, except yourself. You must be a man, Bitias. You must choose."

He returned her hard stare. Then, without a word, he donned his tunic before slipping away into the darkness.

She lay alone on the roof of a ramshackle warehouse, gazing up into the foreign sky. His scent clung to the blankets about her. She tried not to think of the action she'd been forced to take. Doing so reminded her of the possible cost.

She found her own clothing, dressing quickly in the descending chill. She crossed to the pole Bitias had replaced in his descent, carefully letting herself down. Wrapping the blanket like a cloak, she circled around to the building's entrance.

At sight of her, the conversation drained away as princes respectfully bowed and sailors averted their eyes. She could not tell if Bitias' mood was shared by many. The only show of weakness she detected was in the second officer, Werketel. The man seemed hesitant to meet her eye, even after the others had paid proper courtesy and returned to their conversations.

Bitias was nowhere in evidence.

She crossed the room to the curtained alcoves. Pulling aside the hanging blanket of her own, a glint of gold instantly caught her eye.

In the center of her pallet lay a medallion, bestowed by the king of Tyre to an admiral of highest esteem. It was now hers.

TWO

The men were in good spirits following their day of honest labor. *RearEnd* had been stripped of pitch, revealing several rotting planks. Over the next few days, new boards would restore her sea-worthiness.

Yet even with shared trials and labors, the party was still divided.

Elisha sipped water from a cup in the back of the room, watching them. It was so obvious. To one side, the sailors lay in easy repose, laughing and joking. Bitias and Werketel stood in the back ranks, arms folded. Opposite, the nobles awaited Elisha with quiet respect. The surviving elders of the council sat in the front row, as customary in Tyre's throne room.

The only one to break ranks was young Barcas and that was only because it was his turn to clean the dinner bowls and cups. He scrubbed at the grime with a handful of sand, face set.

Shipitbaal would have known what to do, she thought. *He would have made some disarmingly offensive statement and brought them together.* But the old man was not here. She was on her own.

Handing her cup to Tetramnestus, she stepped to the center of the group. She took a moment to look into as many faces as she could. Her eyes briefly fell on Bitias; his expression was stony. With care, she placed herself apart from both groups, back to neither. She could not afford the most minor of slights.

"I understand that you all had a long day working on our ship. For that, I thank you. But the time of labor is past. Now is the time for careful contemplation.

"In a manner of months, we will leave this island for our new home. It is important that it be perfect in all regards—a wrong choice would doom us from the start. In that, I seek your knowledge. We must choose wisely. We must choose well. With a good location and our blood coursing through the veins of generations to come, there is nothing that our people could not do. So speak. Tell me your thoughts."

The worst outcome was realized. A distrustful silence came over the group.

I am within a knife-edge of losing Carthage. No one will speak, the group will remain fractured. Eventually it will break, if not now then on some lonely shore.

She looked to Bitias but he remained aloof. He had committed to follow, and follow he would.

She studied each member of the assemblage in turn, taking them in, searching. And in the face of Lord Kotilus, the importer of northern horseflesh, she saw it. A man on the verge of speaking.

"What is it," she prompted.

The man looked at her, then to the men opposite. He stood with the slightest of bows.

"Highness, we of the *rzn* assumed you would seek our opinions alone. We did not know that this was to be one of those Greek democratic events..."

Angry voices rose from the sailors. Without looking at them, Elisha thrust a hand back, snapping her fingers as if to check a troublesome kitten. The sharp crack echoed in the room. Surprised, the oarsmen stilled.

She held Kotilus pinned in her dark gaze.

"Lord, what know you of the coast of Egypt?"

"My dealings in procuring stallions deviates my attention to the northlands..."

"What do you know of it?"

His face remained impassive. "Nothing."

She turned her head, lowering her hand to point to a random sailor sitting cross-legged on the floor. To him she asked, "You are two days west of the Egyptian delta. Night is falling. Where do you land?"

"That is easy, my lady," the man replied with the yellow smile.

"There is a distinctive outcropping which thrusts into the sea at that point. At its summit is an old Egyptian watchtower which overlooks the approaches from land or sea. Just inland, within a grove of wild olive trees, is a spring. As landings go, it is favorable."

Elisha spoke again to Kotilus, but it was for the benefit of all.

"You see, Lord? Our race is a race of seamen. Between these twenty-five sailors, we likely have knowledge to every aspect of the Upper Sea."

He smiled at her minor victory. "Then why do you require the nobles?"

"Carthage's foundation is not just a matter of springs and protected headlands. The trade lanes of the Canaanites cross the known world. We must graft to them to gain goods and gold that will fuel our growth. The merchant-princes understand this network; they must determine which site is most feasible."

Kotilus studied her a little longer. Then he gave the smallest of nods.

"Should I put forward an observation: Canaan needs horses. For their own cavalry units and the chariots of the Egyptians. Perhaps we should look north, beyond Ashur. Mayhap in the lands once beneath the Hittites, or even further afield."

"What of the mountains," Werketel called out. "What of the Black Sea, north of the Phrygian Kingdom? Would these not be barriers to us?"

"Is there not a water route to that sea? A narrow ribbon we could transverse?"

"The current and wind are against any north-bound vessel. Greek pirates haunt its passage. I doubt we would win through."

Elisha captured the conversation before the two men could tear it between them. "So North is unlikely. South, the Egyptians and Nubians squat along the Nile. As we assumed, we must look West."

"If it is West you seek, Highness, there is plenty to be had." This from an old weather-beaten oarsman. "I've been to Gadar. All along the Great Ocean are small mining settlements. We would have no problems settling there."

"All of those settlements are established," Mintho, recently Lord of an influential trading house, replied. "They already have the best locations. They already have treaties in place with the natives."

"We would not fail," the oarsman pointed out.

"Nor would we succeed. Gold is not found on a beaten path. We will not profit by doing what others have done. Our Lady touched on it—we *must* find new trade opportunities. We must find our own place in this world."

"But there are Canaanite stations all around the Upper Sea," someone called out. "Our ancestors have considered every opportunity."

"We have an advantage over our fathers," Elisha lightly mocked. "They did not have Pumayyaton pursuing them. They could afford failure. We cannot." Bitter laugher rose at this.

"If the Iberian coast is not to your liking, why not the Western coast of the Libyan continent, along the Great Ocean? Occasional lone ships venture along it, returning laden with exotic goods."

Lord Kotilus shook his head. "I've spoken to a commander from one such voyage. Such goods were gained by numerous landfalls. The coast is poor and will not support sustained and concentrated trading. No empire will ever form in such an inhospitable place."

"What of the islands rumored to lie beyond, in the Great Ocean? Canaanite sailors have reported it to be the richest anywhere. Fruit hangs thick on the trees. Gold lies exposed on the ground."

"If such a place existed," Bitias observed, speaking for the first time, "then those sailors would never have left. Those islands are probably no more than windswept rocks."

"But beyond?" Nobody was sure who spoke, but the thought was quickly shared. "Is there not a land beyond?"

"Nothing exists beyond the Great Ocean," Bitias replied with flat confidence. "Nothing but sea monsters. Think not of it."

"Then there is nothing," Werketel spat. "The world is closed to us, every spot claimed by some other man. There is no place for us to hide from Pumayyaton's fleets."

Without looking up from his tub of greasy water, Barcas asked, "Why was it said we could not settle along the sea north of the lands of the Hittites?"

Werketel flashed in anger. "I told you, little fool; the accursed Greeks have a stranglehold on the straits."

Barcas ignored the insult. "Why could we not gain our own stranglehold? Could this not be the basis of our power?"

The second officer looked at him as if he was mad. "What? Take on the Greeks in what is virtually their home waters? The only question would be whether *RearEnd* would burn or sink."

"Not the northern passage." The young man set down the cup he was scrubbing. "A passage of our own."

Elisha looked hard at him. "Where then?"

"Sicily." Thoughtful silence met his proposal. He looked at the sea of faces. "There are two narrow passages, north and south of the island. All ore-hauling Canaanite ships must take one or the other. As do the growing number of Greek vessels, to the growing displeasure of the Canaanite kings."

Kotilus looked hard at the youth. "Are you implying that we might strangle our motherland? Deny passage to Tyre's vessels?"

"That is not what he is implying," Bitias leapt in. "Not at all. We could deny passage to Greek ships, throttling their incursions into our western preserves. But we would also be resting our hand lightly on the Pumayyaton's throat. Do you not see—this is perfect! We would provide a valuable service to Canaan by safeguarding her interests. The distance from Tyre prevents any assaults from being launched, and the blackmail of safe passage further insures Pumayyaton's good behavior. The island of Sicily would be perfect!"

"It would not," Elisha responded.

The ex-admiral rounded on her. "*Lys*! How could it not be? From my understanding, Sicily is a fertile island, its soil rich, its timberlands lush. It has quarry-able stone in abundance. Its rugged terrain would be a boon towards defiance. And none hold it now save a rabble of disorganized tribes who could be brushed aside with hardly a thought."

"A Carthage placed there might initially do well, but how far could our borders expand?"

"It is roughly the size of mainland Canaan," a sailor observed. Elisha nodded and continued.

"Should we settle on the island, in a century or two, our descendants will find their growth hemmed in by the sea, just like Tyre. We should seek the openness of the mainland just off the straits. North or South, it matters not."

"The peoples along the north coast of the Inner Sea understand iron working," Tetramnestus added quietly from the periphery. "The tribes along the southern coast do not."

Bitias frowned at him. "So very learned you are, my pudgy friend. But there already *is* a Canaanite station on that section of Libyan coast. Utica, I believe its called."

Leaning against the back wall, the oarsman Aleyn gestured for attention. "Commander, if I may be so bold? Years back, I worked a merchant tub through those waters. We landed at Utica; she is of no real concern. A dilapidated temple and a cluster of shabby houses on a promontory. The inhabitants are a slovenly lot, hardly empire-builders. They exist to service any vessel that calls; Canaanite or Greek. Their only other contact with the outside world is with the natives, mainly for fermented drink and an occasional woman."

Elisha rubbed her small chin in thought. "We could land at Utica." Her speculative gaze took in the men ringing her. "We could make the settlement ours easily enough. There wouldn't be any bloodshed. It would simply be a new hand on the reins."

"My lady," Aleyn inserted, uneasy with the visibility. "There would be nothing to gain from that. Utica lies hard against an inland mountain range. There is some land there but not much. Similar to Canaan in that respect. We take their burden, we end up just like them, I would wager."

"But if there is no place for us there, then where..."

"But there is," the old oarsman insisted. "A half-day's sail east of that settlement is a large natural bay. Hilly enough to be defensible, but still farmable. Large salt marsh to the south, limiting access from the interior. Good defenses and smack on the straits."

"'*Bl*, Aleyn speaks the truth," another oarsman added. "I know of this place. I've landed there too. It's got a spring, hardwoods in abundance..."

"There is a small beach where a decent harbor could be dug with little effort."

"Not our efforts, with those natives about."

Elisha cut over the excited chatter. "Those who have knowledge of this coast, and specifically this place, assemble along the back wall. Tetramnestus, fetch a table and benches. And the papyrus and writing tools."

The group huddled across the long hours, laying the foundation of Carthage with their words. Around them, the others sat silently, respectful of the formation of their future. The night slid over the Levant and the world slept, unaware of the power that was forming in the light of a single flickering lamp.

It was a miserable ascent.

Clouds rode low, their black bellies pierced by scattered sun shafts. Showers fell with little warning.

The two priests lead the procession, bickering all through the long climb. Scylax had proved petty and argumentative on the topic of gods, Astarte and otherwise. To his credit, Tetramnestus had borne his reedy harangue for the first quarter hour before speaking in defense of Melqart. From that moment on, the two had waged their little battle. Words were carried away on the wind. Angry feelings remained.

Elisha trudged behind the two, tugging wet hair from her eyes, her attention more on the slick track than the wrangling holy men. Bitias strode at her side, saying little.

Six men, their escort, trailed behind, a mixed collection of oarsmen and one-time princes.

Elisha spared a glance to the man at her side. Bitias' easy-going spirit was gone. Two days ago he'd suddenly decided on a new plan for his *RearEnd*. Over Werketel's objections, he'd ordered the belly planking removed and the keel reinforced. His reasons remained his own, but Werketel had freely distributed his misgivings. With their penteconter disemboweled on the beach, they were effectively trapped in Citium. The option of escape into the storm-tossed seas was gone.

"This makes no sense," the second officer had pointed out as the planks had been wrenched away. "The belly wood is sound. Why buttress the keel? It will not make *RearEnd* faster, stronger, nor the least bit more seaworthy."

"Trust me, my friend. I have an idea I might incorporate once we find our princesses' mythical Carthage." The easy smile he'd beamed had been his last. As the penteconter was torn apart, his tension mounted. When he wasn't berating his work crews for speed, his eyes nervously scanned the tossing horizon.

The party cleared a low tree line, Citium opening up below them. The town, shabby in comparison to the cosmopolitan Tyre, huddled around its harbor and central square. North lay the bones of greatness, ruins denoting a more prosperous past. The lines of ancient walls were little more than fossils in the peat.

Like all Canaanite settlements, Citium lay on a defensible peninsula, open sea to the east, brackish marsh to the west.

Elisha had paused for breath, taking in the view. "This must be how Melqart sees the world."

"*N'*, it is just another backwater town. Come, come, let us meet this savior of yours."

"Bitias, one day away from your precious ship will not differ the outcome. We cannot sail during the time of storms, and you have assured me you will be ready long before Egersis."

"A day wasted is a day lost. With Werketel's carping, we'll be lucky to get *RearEnd* rebuilt with her bow right-side up. Why did I let you talk me into this silly errand?"

"Werketel will be fine. *RearEnd* will be fine." They renewed their wet trudge. "And this is not a silly errand. We are speaking of the safeguarding of Carthage."

"*Lys*! At very least, we number fifty. With our iron weapons and Canaanite hearts, what danger could Libyan savages hold?"

"I would rather my last thought in this life not answer your question. Besides, you have been complaining that we will need more people if the settlement is to succeed. This Hêgêsistratus shall be our first."

"Some start. Scylax claims the man has seen over forty summers. What good shall he be to us, if not just the first to be interned into Carthage's necropolis?" He spat disdainfully at the side grass. "What is more, he is Greek!"

"He was a general. According to Scylax, he commanded troops

in Lycia and Arzawa. He defended Miletus against incursions for years. I need someone to direct our defense, to lead our men."

"Do you not forget? Before my enforced exile, I led men."

"You are an admiral. Once you get your boat reassembled, you will have your fleet. But I need a general, someone versed in the tactics of defense on land."

"Pah, he is nothing but *mshtr*–military brass. Likely tarnished with age."

Before them, Scylax gestured a halt. "We have arrived. Hêgês-istratus' dwelling is just ahead." With that, he stepped aside, allowing Elisha, as queen, the honor of leading.

She took a moment to wring rainwater from her hair, an effort towards presentablity.

"What sort of man is this Greek, Scylax?"

"I have only met him a handful of occasions, my lady. He retired here after a lifetime of campaigning. He secured his wealth in our temple, taking only enough for a small abode. He also purchased the services of a herder and his daughter to see to his needs. They provide him with meals and maintenance to his cottage. Evidently he is happy to bask out his golden years in the peace our island affords."

"Meaning you might not win him over, Elisha," Bitias noted. "He might be content with his roasted lamb and wine, and perhaps an occasional romp with his chambermaid."

"We shall see." She straightened her damp robes as best she could. When she was ready, she nodded to proceed.

The path rounded a low line of scrubs, breaking through a tumble-down field wall. At this threshold, Elisha stopped.

"Scylax, this cannot be right."

A ramshackle cottage lay before them. The roof was weather-stained, a corner of it missing all together. Mildew coated the walls in plague-like green. A scattering of trash encircled the building, broken pottery and rags visible in the high grass. The front door was hanging limply open, all but obscured by thorny brush.

"There must be some mistake," Scylax claimed, looking over the desolation. "I *know* this to be his abode. I visited him here when he first moved in. A more charming place for one's golden years I could not imagine."

Bitias cupped his hands around his mouth. "Ho! The House!" His hail echoed beneath the low rolling clouds.

Elisha's dark eyes continued to study the house. The homestead felt cursed, as if dark omens radiated from it. She felt a little-girl's need to turn and run from this haunted place, if only to keep the evil from spreading to her quest.

Bitias scratched his chin. "Could he have died? He was certainly of the age for it."

"It is possible. I do not think it is true." The priest of Astarte's voice wavered as if undecided. Finally it found its iron. "No, he could not be dead. Certainly Monca, the girl tending him, would have let it be known."

"She is no herald," Bitias shrugged. "Why would she bother?"

"Hêgêsistratus, Monca, and her father had an agreement. They would see to his needs while he drew breath on this earth. With his passing, whatever he left behind would be theirs." A pause. "His gold is still in our temple vaults."

"Someone has kept the path up." Aleyn looked up to see all eyes upon him. "Well, it is true. The house might be in shambles but someone has been coming this way daily." The aged oarsman stooped. "Not today, though. There are footprints in the mud but the rain has softened them."

Elisha shook herself from her forebodings. "We shall not discover what has transpired by standing here like fishwives around the cistern." She stepped from the break in the wall, marching towards the black opening. The priests exchanged flat glances and followed. Bitias hung back long enough to instruct Aleyn to set up a perimeter.

Her drive took her as far as the door. An evil smell checked them.

"Highness, come away," Tetramnestus quailed. "I fear what is within."

She shook her head. "This is not the smell of death. Nay, it is the smell of beggars and offal." She balled her tiny hands into fists and pushed into the darkness. The priests balked; Bitias shoved past.

The room inside was close, the air rank with corruption. Brush had grown past the windows, casting the interior into uncertain shadows. Then a cloud break passed overhead; golden sunlight shimmered through a gap in the roof.

"Over here," she called to Bitias.

In the room's far corner was a pallet, a crumpled shape upon it. Before the wavering sunlight was swept away, he gained a flash-image of pale skin and tangled beard. Gloom fell over them.

"Tetramnestus," he called out. "Bring light."

"All is damp outside," the aide wheedled from the doorway. "Nothing will burn!"

"Numerous curses upon your limp *'yr*! Scrabble near the door—this woman who tends to him must have a lamp. Find it!"

A deep voice murmured in the darkness, its Greek slurred and alien.

From behind came the sound of the aide groping about. A clink of clay. A moment later, dim light hissed into being.

Elisha beckoned for the lamp, then studied the prone man. His frame was compact, his skin a collection of old scars. The face visible above the matted beard was angular, a beak-like nose, cheekbones high. Yet the projected strength was like an empty fortress; dull eyes tracked the lamp's flame. The mouth dribbled mindless mutterings.

"It is as if he is a witless fool." Elisha scowled at the man, seeking some sign of cognizance.

"More like a baby," Bitias shook his head, "in that he has fouled himself. Some demon or sickness has taken him. Nothing remains but the ruin of a man."

Scylax stepped closer, scowling. "No demon this, not ailment nor plague of age." He knelt beside Elisha, taking Hêgêsistratus' chin, peering into his eyes. "*Hul gil.*"

Elisha looked to him. "The words...old Sumerian?"

"Indeed. 'Joy plant'. In our highlands, the tribes grow a certain poppy. You have no doubt seen its blossoms around Citium. Its extract is used for various religious ceremonies. It is exported as well; a handy trade, I am told."

The Admiral nodded. "Aye, I know of this. You see it along the Phrygian coast. Its ingestion brings something that feels like

Melqart's blessed touch. But to some, the touch closes to crush them. Their lives are discarded; they become drooling wastrels."

A commotion sounded from outside. A moment later, Aleyn and a fellow oarsmen entered, a woman struggling between them. A noble companion followed, an empty bowl in his hand.

"Monca?" Scylax raised the lamp to the girl. She was equal to Elisha in height but her body was built along thicker lines. Her face was blunt, eyes hard. Her hair was black as evil, utilitarian bangs in front, free-falling in back.

"Lowland priest! Why do you bring foreigners here? This is not your business."

"And what business is that?" Bitias asked contrarily.

She torqued free of the oarsmen's grasp but did not flee. "I have an agreement with the old Greek. I feed him and see to him. Upon his passing, his effects will become mine. It is our word-bond. I would not break such. In that, I was bringing him his afternoon meal when your men took me."

Scylax sniffed the bow, nodding in confirmation.

"You polluted Hêgêsistratus' essence with *hul gil* extract."

"He complained of aches from age and war. I offered him solace which he freely accepted. I broke not my bond."

"Such is not the result of a single evening's succor," the priest replied, gesturing to the figure on the pallet. "This comes from prolonged ingestion."

"My bond is intact."

"Your bond," Elisha grated. "So important that you remain within its verbage. He asked you for relief; I assume he did not specifically order its cessation?" The girl said nothing. "So you kept passing him this foul extract, mixed in his food. Why? Why ruin such a man?" She looked down at the invalid, understanding growing in her eyes. "It made him easier to control, did it not? Perhaps he spoke of leaving the arrangement, of moving on, or simply replacing you. Whatever the reason, you felt the need to tie him down with this drug, making him easy to control while keeping your precious word."

Elisha slapped the bowl from Scylax's hand. It shattered across the floor.

"Does such an extract shorten his life? Was that your game? Continue to raise his need until life fled his body? A legal shortcut to the old man's gold?"

Monca's eyes remained hard on Elisha's.

"Scylax," she said, turning her back on the native girl, "is there a cure for this debilitation?"

The priest shrugged. "Some highland tribes, seeking greater assurance by gaining favor of gods not their own, send their womenfolk to perform Astarte's duty. Some of these women have the taste of *hul gil* in their minds. Our little Os'sh knows northern herbology; she is usually able to wean them from the drug's grasp. It takes time and patience, but it can be done."

Elisha nodded grimly. "Bitias, see to it that six shekel-weight of silver are withdrawn from our holdings and delivered to this girl. Her bond is absolved; the *RearEnd* exiles will see to Hêgêsistratus' welfare."

"You cannot step in and take him from me," Monca hissed, muscles bunching like a cat's.

"Six shekel-weight of silver or a dagger's weight of bronze. It is for you to decide. But speak not of duties and bonds; such piety wears thin."

"The silver then, *mzhshrsh!*" She stormed out.

They stood in the dark silence. The Greek moved slightly, releasing a shuddering fart.

"It might not be wise to bring this man into Citium," Scylax opted. "As his cure takes effect, he might become desperate, even combative. Then there is the matter of Monca's agreement and whether we were legally right to supersede it. Add to that the citizens who dislike you exiles and would do anything they could to cross you, including taking Hêgêsistratus from your care. The risks are not small."

"Understood," Elisha replied. "We will keep Hêgêsistratus here until he is cured. At that time he will be free to choose to join us or not. Until then, four men will be posted here, day and night. We must keep Monca and her *hul gil* out, the General in. Bitias, set up watches as you see fit."

She left, priests in tow. At the floor at Bitias' feet, the general moaned and shifted, releasing another drawn-out flatulence. Bitias grimaced, both at the smell and the task he'd been assigned. First had been the street fighting in Pumayyaton's name, now this. As he stepped outside to gather his men and pick the first detail, he found himself wondering what god he'd annoyed.

THREE

She looked into Bitias' alcove; it was empty.

He wasn't with the men gathered on their benches. She crossed to the portal and looked into the rain-streaked night; nothing. With Citium's growing animosity towards the exiles, it was unlikely he would wander their streets.

RearEnd sprawled on the beach. The dagger-wound gaps of missing planks were visible against the stripped hull. Sailcloth had been rigged into a makeshift tent in the bow; the daily task of pin-fitting planks went on, regardless of weather.

Before stepping outside, Elisha picked one of the common cloaks hanging from the nearby pegs. It reeked of man-smell, sweat and toil. Rather than disgusting her, she found it comforting, even intoxicating.

As she neared the vessel, the scent of her cloak was overridden by the sharp tang of cedar. Shavings dusted the muddy sands. Wood lay in neat stacks. The sea beyond the ancient breakwater swirled and surged but the silted harbor shared little of this enthusiasm. All was still.

A crude ladder leaned against the vessel's flank. Elisha started up this with a care towards the loose foundation and wet rungs. At one point, it shifted slightly, the scrape harsh in the silence.

At the top, she looked across the *RearEnd*'s dark deck. Her eyes peered into the cave of sailcloth in the bow, unsure if she'd seen motion.

"Elisha," came a voice from its darkness.

She smiled confidently and eased onto the decking. The newer planking was slick beneath her soles. With care, she crossed to the bow, her pupils expanding in the darkness.

Bitias lay within, propped against a peg-bucket, a clay urn of wine cupped in his hands. Rain drummed against the tent. She could not see his face in the gloom but a wry smile rode his words.

"So you have found me."

She settled against the concavity of the hull, the wood cold and hard against her back. "Why are you out here? Do you not spend enough time with your ship as it is?"

A gurgle of wine in the dark. "She's one of my mistresses, aye. Great pity should be afforded the man claimed by two mistresses. A single one might be content to claim his life. To satisfy two, he must yield his soul."

"I do not ask for your soul, Bitias. Simply one part of you." She eased a foot forward, resting it in his lap. Beneath her instep, his *'yr* awoke.

He lowered his clay urn, patting her ankle. Somehow, he'd shifted so that she was no longer in direct contact with his member.

"What are we doing here, Little Priestess? What is the point of all this?" He gave a wine-sloshing gesture.

"You know what the point is. The formation of Carthage. The founding of the Empire."

"*'Bl*, so it has been said." His fingers traced the urn's lines. "It is a strange malady that holds me now. I feel dislocated. Here we are on this muddy beach. Our new general weeps through his nights. The men tasked as nursemates hate their duty, and begin to hate me for assigning it. The townsmen glare at us, wishing we'd not included them into Pumayyaton's possible wrath. Werketel mutters openly of home. Even *RearEnd* hates me for what I've done to her keel."

"You've been far from home with less-happy crews," she replied. "The battle that elevated you to admiral. You rallied ships to your cause and destroyed foes several times your number."

"True. But there is a difference. There we had a home to return to." A pause to raise his wine and drink. "Always before, no matter how cold and windswept the beach, no matter how dreary or dangerous the duty, there was always Tyre. But this time...." He gestured with his wine; she saw it raised against the dim light. "Nothing. Once we wait out the season here, we move on, pushing west into the unknown. We will land in Libya with nothing but what we carry in with us. No warm shelter, no fine foods, no friends. Every day will be toil, erecting the colony's infrastructure. *N'*, it's likely we will spend out our lives huddled in makeshift shacks, nothing differentiating us from the natives beyond."

She listened to his words carefully. Similar doubts crept through the darkness beyond her thoughts, lions in the night. She knew she was the sole conviction for the new city; should she falter, the endeavor would fail. Her only recourse when the doubts rose was to force them away. To distract herself.

Which is why she sought Bitias.

She shifted her weight slightly, letting herself slide down the hull to nestle against the young admiral. Through the cloth of her robe she could feel his body's heat. Lying beside him, she fit perfectly, like *RearEnd*'s crafted planks.

"Give me the wine," she said in a low tone.

She hardly ever consumed inebriates. Her rank, position, and sex generally forbade it outside of celebrations and festivals. In those times, it was more duty than pleasure. Never before had she taken a drought without reason.

The clay was cold to her lips. The wine was of poor quality, and Bitias had not used much water diluting it. It was bitter over her tongue, hot down her gullet, and burned in her stomach like pitch.

Eyes watering, she attempted a second pull. Bitias took back the urn, mindful of her inexperience. It mattered not—the warmth was in her. The light rain pattered across the cloth overhead. All was right in the world.

She reached over and ran a hand along Bitias' flank, trailing up along his ribs until she felt a nipple. She fingered it through the robe, wondering if it gave him the same pleasure such attentions gave her. The wine burned low in her gut, the *'drtnt* in her loins. The dangers of foreign shores were lost to her now; all she wanted in the world was the man at her side.

"Not now, Elisha," he said, pushing away her hand. "I take wine when I am morose. I mix it to heighten my despondency. It is how

I cope—I deal with my melancholy nature in a single setting." He shifted ever so slightly away. "But as for intercourse, I am disinterested."

"I can make you interested," she whispered. "I can do things I've heard slaves speak of. I can take you into my mouth. We can rut like commoners."

"By your measure, I am a commoner."

"Of course you are," she murmured, attempting to recapture his nipple. "No matter how high you rise, you will always be low-born. Just as I will always be nobility, no matter how deeply I sink."

"And that is all that matters to you, is it not? Being a noble. Never faltering, never falling. You are displaced by your brother; resulting in an ill-considered scheme of colonization." He cupped a hand to his head. "*Rb qbhn!* The wine speaks for me."

She lay still. "No, Bitias. You speak for you. The wine makes it easier."

"You make it easier," he mumbled. "You with your disdain for the lower classes. It leaks from you like venom."

"Perhaps I am poisonous by need. It was the incorporation of that lowly committee that tore Tyre apart. They challenged the order that had lasted a thousand years. They elevated themselves to pinnacles ill-suited to them. Remember Adon aping at being a lord?"

"The commoners would have been happy with their lot at the bottom of the heap, had it not been for schemes of politics. Your brother was prince, yet he saw a way to shift power to himself. He played his committee against the council. And what was the result? A couple of lords fell from their perches. A handful of peasants rose to replace them. The poor still labor while the rich idle. And a collection of idiots sit in rundown warehouse, ready to launch themselves into oblivion in a single boat."

"By Egersis, there will be more than one boat."

"One boat or fifty, it matters not. Placing a city on a heathen shore is madness."

"Gadar did it. Utica, likewise. There are a half-dozen colonies along the southern Iberian coast."

"Trading posts, Elisha. Small collections of hard men, bartering with natives and victualling passing merchantmen. Flyspeck communities. And yet you see your Carthage growing into an empire, surpassing all? You are as lost to your dreams as that Greek of yours, Hêgêsistratus. The effort is doomed."

Lying in the belly of the unfinished *RearEnd*, Elisha moved her eyes from Bitias to the canvas overhead.

"You think I am wrong to differentiate between low class and high? That there is no difference between the classes?"

Bitias turned to look down at her. "I think that anyone can be as simple as a commoner. And anyone can be as greedy as a prince. People are people."

She spoke to the raincover, not to him. "People are people. And classes are classes. But do people determine classes, or classes determine people?"

"What?"

"The class makes its members. Look at the commoners—they do not question their place in the world. They perform their services and live out their lives with no thought to advancement. Yet to a noble trader, such stagnation is death. They are constantly looking for new opportunities, new ways to gain wealth. Fortunes are used to secure rank, privilege, and contracts. They might stand together as a class, but each is constantly vigilant against the other houses. Nothing shields them from the fall save cunning and panache."

"I am common yet gained the title *Bol*—Lord. Nothing stopped me."

"Then you were a noble born of low station."

"There is nothing magical about being of noble station."

"The nobles create the power of their class. It is they who take the chances and put their lives and fortunes at stake. It is they who open new trade routes. It is they who dream, architect, and finance the great structures of Tyre."

"Lowly craftsmen built the temple of Solomon."

"Solomon approached our King Hiram. Our nobles made it a reality. They designed it, transported the men and materials into place, and made the structure appear. Common men might have swung the mallets at their chisels, but it was the nobles who put them on the scaffolding, placed the blocks before them and the tools in their hands."

"History and stories. Clever words weaving justifications. I task you; show me one example in our world that justifies the differentiation between our classes. One example."

Her eyes dropped to lock on him. Her answer, when it came, was coldly measured.

"You quaver at the thought of colonization and pine for our lost home. You chafe at your tasks and need to be driven like an ox. Meanwhile, I drive for our future. I will raise Carthage from the mud. It will be built by the wisdom and commitment of the nobles, and the labor of the commoners. And that is my living example, Bitias. The gulf between you and myself."

The admiral stiffened as if slapped. He was nothing but a shape against the dark rainfall. When they came, his words smoldered.

"I will transport you to your shore, Highness. I will raise stone blocks to build your palace. I will till the fields that supply the bread to grace your golden plate. You will direct Carthage, and I shall build it. I stand by my bond to you."

He came to his feet and stepped into the rain. It hammered across his back. He turned a final time.

"But there is one fallacy in your argument. You say prince and peasant are of different classes. Yet lovers are equals. By your words, we can never become that." He swung over the side. She could hear the sand crunch as he strode away.

She lay in the belly of *RearEnd*, looking up at the snapping sail-cloth. Her hand found the wine Bitias had abandoned. It tasted sharp and unpleasant. She drank deep. The pain within her dulled.

She began to stroke herself. With *rzn* commitment, her cold fingers toyed with herself. The passion that grew was one of chilled loneliness. When the *'drtnt* overtook her, she met it with tears.

The opulence of the governor's hall did not surprise her.

Cyprus was the first stop for most outbound shipping. Two days from the chief ports of Canaan, it provided traders a chance to shakedown crews and re-shift cargos prior to the long westward run.

Citium was affluent enough to warrant the luxury goods trader-captains were happy to supply. The locals felt more cosmopolitan with their trinkets, the merchants more comfortable with gold useful for keeping crews satisfied in the year-long runs.

"We should have come sooner," Tetramnestus hissed as they waited in the anteroom. "The summons arrived two days ago."

"I could not appear before this man in the ragged robes I began our journey in," she replied low, eyes forward. "Cloth was required, and time. Besides, it pays not to respond too quickly to a summons."

"But Zinnridi is the royal *skn*, the governor, assigned this post by King Mattan."

"And I am a queen. I simply pay the governor a courtesy with my visit."

The aide shook his head, uncomfortable with delaying a direct summons. Still, he had to admit that Elisha had done wonders in a single day. She'd been assisted by the oarsman Aleyn who possessed skills at mending sails. Together they'd created a fine garment, a petticoat affair that tucked into a sash beneath her trim breasts. The basic fabric was ordinary enough, but expensive ribbons of purple cloth, imported from Tyre, added stunning simplicity. A cap contained her raven hair, the finest jewels from her late husband's treasure graced her chest.

A courtier stepped through the portal, gesturing admission. Elisha detected disdain in his brisk motions.

She paused in the portal to take in the hall. Wooden pillars shimmered, holding aloft a brilliantly painted ceiling. Cloth hung in shifting columns. A fountain burbled cheerfully.

She sensed Tetramnestus' small surprise; women loitered along a wall, unscreened, clearly a part of the proceedings. Several were heavily painted. One had a gown cut to display a single breast.

Governor Zinnridi's rotund form reclined on pillows, a clay pipe smoldering at his side, the greasy smell of *hul gil* hanging in the air. After witnessing the plight of Hêgêsistratus, Elisha wondered why any sane person would chance the drug.

He smiled warmly to her but did not rise, a minor affront. Her own bow was perfection.

"I see thee and greet thee, giving thanks for your radiance," she spoke in formal greeting. "I come as summoned, to answer any inquiries my Lord may put to me. If it may please you, I should present to you this gift, suitable for the respect and honor I pay to you."

Tetramnestus handed forward a crafted set of grapes, the orbs cast in silver, the leaves in gold. Removed from her husband's horde, they represented considerable wealth.

Zinnridi gave them the same attention he would their organic counterpart, handing it to an assistant, taking up a gift for her in return.

"Highness Elisha, your presence beings me happiness. Please take this crafted article as a token of our esteem for you."

Elisha felt a slight start at the object handed her. It was the same ivory knife her husband had bestowed to Qurdi-Aššur-lamur two and a half years before, when she'd stood against the Assyrians and denied them tribute. Its presence hinted that regardless of their internal troubles, the men of Ashur were exchanging gifts with the governor of Cyprus. And gifts were the first formal steps of diplomacy.

She considered the slim weapon in her hands, her mind conflicted by several turmoils. The strongest were the memories of Arherbas. Suddenly, more than ever, she missed his kind manner and gentle strength. Guilt flushed through her at the thought of her betrayal for the simple joys of Bitias, joys that had come to naught.

She also thought of Pumayyaton and was shocked at the fondness unearthed. She recalled him, not as the deadly adversary she'd faced over the years, but the headstrong yet frightened boy with whom she'd careened about the palace. This knife held a subtle danger for Canaan. Clearly, the Assyrians were courting Zinnridi, sniffing him as if he were a bitch in heat. They wanted westward ports; perhaps Citium could supplant Tyre. Even given their divide, he was still her brother, the Canaanites were still her people. If possible, she would send word of this threat.

"I thank you for this wondrous gift," she responded, "and all that it means to me."

"I am so happy you fled to us in your moment of need. We have watched with horror as your city struggled. Our flow of ships was severely reduced, mainly hulls out of Byblos and Sidon. No empire based on commerce fairs well when trade is interrupted. Certainly you agree?"

"Your words are wise, Lord."

"I can only image the disruptions and turmoil of my beloved mother city. With gold, iron, and grain shipments reduced, no doubt the city's vibrancy plummeted. Trades and crafts faltered, the ranks of idlers swelled, riots became commonplace. I've heard travelers speak of such."

Elisha nodded.

"And, of course, when economies falter, certainly the monarch's power becomes tenuous. Treasury moneys are diverted. Branches of his rule are not funded, and like a tree without sap, they fall away. I'm certain you must have witnessed such." Zinnridi shook his head in consternation. "I would wager that King Pumayyaton was desperate to reduce his costs. For example, a navy is an expensive tool of statecraft. Each ship employs fifty men. The cost of keeping hulls and crews can be prohibitive. When sailors are not paid, they often leave their benches, hamstringing their vessels. I could well imagine the hulls of warships rotting in Tyre's military port."

"Well, some of Admiral Bitias' crews were reassigned urban duties."

"Exactly," Zinnridi agreed enthusiastically, slapping a hand against a fleshy thigh. "And this leads to my own concerns. We must know if Tyre can maintain patrols in these waters. Vessels of other nations appear off our coasts. As a Canaanite outpost, it is critical to know where we stand. Should foreign powers threaten our fair island, what level of response, if any, could we expect?"

Tetramnestus' eyes came up, flashing suspicion. Her confirming nod was slight; the Assyrians were not the only ones who sniffed.

"Lord Zinnridi, I cannot speak to Tyre's military readiness. I was absent from the royal court for years, and know not of her strengths and standings. All I know was that penteconters were at a moment's readiness to intercept our flight. Their seamanship was superb, their ships in top shape. Had it not been for a sudden storm, we would have been overhauled and taken."

"Continue," Zinnridi dryly encouraged.

"As far as the overall status of the fleet, I know not much. Tyre's military harbor is walled, its activities shielded from onlookers. I could not speak as to the fleet's readiness. However, there is one thing to consider: Pumayyaton has a restless, hungry population. He also has large stands of hardwoods at his disposal. His domestic foes, those constituting my fellowship, have been cast out, and the Assyrians have melted into the north. The entire eastern coast is open to him. A strong navy, its ships new, its people hungry for victory, could achieve much. I would assume that its construction would be his paramount objective."

It would have been hers, had her revolt succeeded. The shipyards would have echoed to the pounding of mallets across a hundred hulls, the storehouses filling with supplies for a hundred more. Such had been her dreams.

"No doubt," she continued, "his navy will be hungry for victory. With ships so new they still carry a scent of cedar, crews vibrant with the thought of prizes and spoils, they will be eager for combat. In that, I should not wish to be counted among Pumayyaton's enemies. None could stand before such might and prevail."

And you may smoke that in your pipe, she mentally added.

"Of course, I am but a woman, and not wise to the matters of men."

The governor gave his aide a measured glance. The man dutifully wrote upon his scroll.

"We thank you for your clarifications. The strength and well-being of the motherland are always of concern to her dedicated offspring. Our wishes, of course, center upon support for the Canaanite city states and loyalty to our king. We exist to serve."

"Of course."

He took a moment to draw from his pipe. Elisha awaited the next question.

"My lady," he continued, "I would now like to speak on matters closer to home. I understand that you exiles have thoughts of creating a new city to the west. Such a goal is admirable." He licked his fleshy lips. "Of course, colonies require settlers. You might be tempted to canvass the citizens of Citium to fill your ranks."

"That is not entirely true...," Elisha began, treading a lie.

"You attempt to restore Hêgêsistratus. No doubt you have your eyes on others."

Elisha held her tongue. She had forgotten that in a small settlement, even the daughters of herdsman might gain the governor's ear.

"As I said, you might be tempted to approach our craftsmen, tempting them away from their honest labors with talk of your golden city." His beady eyes fixed upon her. "This would displease us greatly. In this, we instruct you not to approach our townsmen, nor tempt them in any way. Instead, we will gather those wretches that are unable to function in a city such as ours. The drunkards, the drifting semi-tribesmen who live in the ruins. You will take them with you. The simple labors of building a new world from the ground up will redeem them. Both Citium and your Carthage will benefit."

"This will forge a bond between our cities," she agreed. "Our blood will mix and be the stronger for it."

Inwardly, she vowed that Carthage would not be poisoned with Citium's dregs.

"The old general you may keep. It will take the love of Astarte to set him to rights."

"My thanks for your benevolence."

"It is all I can do to help you in your bold endeavor." The last words came out on a yawn. "And now, if it pleases the lady, it is time for my midday nap. Astarte's blessings."

She and Tetramnestus stood. "Astarte's blessings to you," she replied. With a bow, she turned to go.

"Oh, and my lady, one last thing?"

She turned, her face a composition of simple acceptance. "As it pleases my Lord?"

"As you know, we of this island pay great homage to the goddess Astarte. If your men decide to pay tribute to the goddess, that is fine. But they are not to turn the temple into a brothel."

"Many of my followers are nobles, of the finest Tyrian families—"

"*Should* they enter," Zinnridi overrode, "they are to control themselves. But above all else, they are to stand clear of the girl known as Os'sh."

"Lord, I understand your concern. But as High Priest Scylax told us, selection of a woman is the choice of any gold-bearing foreigner."

"Os'sh is different," the Governor replied bluntly. "She is being held in reserve. There are guests coming to our lands next year, mainland guests with mainland tastes."

Assyrian tastes, Elisha clearly heard.

"She is trained in her art. She is an asset in place, and is to be left undisturbed. Is this understood?"

"Yes, Lord." An acquiescent bow.

"I am glad we had this talk, my lady. I am certain you can control your people."

FOUR

Nobody likes wiping shit off the old Greek's arse.

His feet splashed through the puddles of the muddy track leading back to town.

Nobody likes the new centerbeam in RearEnd*'s keel.*

The forage in his shouldered sack rasped across his neck.

Nobody likes my lineage. A swirl of rain. *Just my 'yr.*

The day was cold and wet but Bitias had still volunteered for fetch-n-carry duty for the little Scythian in the temple. Scylax had mentioned that she had eased several of the temple-girls from the grip of the poppies. It was a duty for the lowliest of oarhaulers, a ship's boy's detail, yet Bitias had opted for it himself. The alternative was to loiter about the warehouse camp, caught between Elisha's silence and Werketel's scowls. He'd even taken a turn at watching Hêgêsistratus but found his men sullen, viewing his presence more as transgression than support.

No matter where he went, people were unhappy.

He trudged down the muddy lane, threading between the first rude houses. Locals lounged away the rainy winter days under the roof-edges. They quieted as he passed, muttering when he was beyond. At this point, he would have welcomed a thrown rock; a good clean fist-swinger would improve his outlook.

Citium's central plaza depressed him as well. A handful of run-down stalls clustered against the temple to Astarte, using it to block the worst of the wind and rain. The merchants hunched together, speaking in low tones. In Tyre, they would have leapt to their stalls, bidding for his business, be he Canaanite, Assyrian, Pirate, or

Kushite slave. But in this provincial settlement, he was one of the outsiders, and that spoke louder than gold.

His only warm reception came from the women lounging about the temple's central hall. They called to him, some warmly, some indecently. By lamplight in the far corner, High Priest Scylax looked up from tutoring a handful of girls on their letters. The outpouring of greetings rankled the priest. He attributed it to the disruption the officer's presence caused, but in truth, it was a matter of base jealousy.

Bitias pushed through a heavy door into the temple's kitchen. Two servants deboned fish with lackluster interest. Os'sh stood behind a table at the opposite end of the room, grinding away with a mortar and pestle.

"Here are the plants you sought," he said, swinging the sack up onto the table. "The wild alfalfa I found on a plateau in the hills. Much grows there, so it will provide a ready source. As for this..."

"Feverfew," she prompted, sorting through his findings.

"Aye. Found a stand of it growing along the salt marsh. Not much there, so if you need more, we will have to go further afield."

She examined the daisy-like flowers. "This should be plenty for now. It should break the drug's grip."

"The watch-details will be by, at sunup and sundown, to collect Hêgêsistratus' porridge before starting out. Send a boy up to our encampment when you need more plants fetched." He turned towards the door.

"Are you going to linger with the women in the temple?"

Her blurted question brought him up short. He turned but her attention was on her work, mud-colored eyes lost in a spill of coppery hair.

"Melqart's knobby knees. What was that you said, little Os'sh?"

She ground the forage weed for a breath or two more. Then her eyes came up.

"They are quite friendly with you, are they not, Lord Bitias? Do you wonder why that is? You are a desirable catch, a young man with wealth. And a broken heart."

"Broken heart?" His attention centered on her. "Of what do you speak?"

She went back to her grinding. "Do not play the fool, Lord. They know. *They know everything.* They know you fought with your Elisha and have broken with her for good."

The admiral tried to keep his jaw from dropping but failed. "*N'!* How could they know such?" His eyes hardened. "How do you know?"

"A week back, you were out with her in your vessel. Your men made sure to remain indoors, to give you the privacy you deserved. But when you entered the warehouse and crossed to your alcove without a word, they knew. Many of them take their midday meals below the temple windows so as to chat with the women within. The information passed."

"Those whore-sons! I might lay a stripe or two across their backs! Werketel is likely the hub this wheel revolves on, with his carping and backtalk. I will bust him back to an oarbench. I..."

"No harm was meant," her eyes remained downcast. "They care for you. Your unhappiness spreads to them."

"My unhappiness? Why should that upset them?"

"They pledged to follow Elisha, mainly due to your acceptance of her terms. They trust you with their lives and hence care for you with their hearts."

"And the women out there?" He flung a gesture over his shoulder. "Why should I worry that they know?"

"As I said; you are affluent and upset. You might seek solace in a female's embrace. Should this be your intent; fine. Someone will receive your blessing and return to their family tonight. But if you only seek to balm your wounds with flirtation, it is unfair to them. It dashes their hopes."

Bitias stood in silence over a lengthy pause, scratching at his beard in thought. Os'sh sprinkled feverfew into the pulped alfalfa and resumed grinding.

"And what of you, little Os'sh? What gain you from such warnings?"

"I have no gain." Her eyes remained on her labors. "Lord Zinnridi forbids me to lay with any man."

"A very elusive answer."

"My people are elusive. It is our way."

"All peoples must eventually stand their ground." Bitias moved over to lean against her table. "No matter how badly an army is outnumbered, when its mother city is threatened, then there they must stand."

"You do not know the Scythians then." She looked up, meeting Bitias' eyes. "We are a nomadic people. Our nation exists north of the Black Sea, an expanse twenty day's hard journey across. It is as flat as this table, not a hill or a tree to grace it."

"So where do you hide if threatened by force of arms or an impertinent question?"

"We hide not. We move. Our houses are our wagons or our ponies' backs. Our herds move with us. Our capital is wherever our evening firepit is placed. We elude the strong, envelop the weak." A tiny smile mocked from brown lips. "Cities and battlelines are the marks of fools."

"If you are so mobile and elusive, how were you taken a slave?"

"Canaanite merchantmen landed on a beach near our camp. They beguiled our tribe with beads and trade goods. That evening, I slipped back to see more of their magic. They captured me and promptly sailed. I was a wild thing then, but that was ten years ago." Her voice held no malice.

"And what of being a slave?" Bitias felt a wicked urge to pin her down, to seat an uncomfortable barb. "Does it bother you to be locked in this temple of fornication? What think you of grinding your herbs for mad Greeks while your people roam free across their grasslands?"

"And what of you, Lord? Does it bother you to be Queen Elisha's slave, following her dream rather than yours?"

Bitias felt anger flash, but surprised himself when honest laughter erupted from his lips.

"Wonderful," he boomed, "Who would think to find a Scythian oracle in a temple kitchen? Mot's little yellow friends, but you wield truth like a lance, do you not?"

At that moment, the door was flung open. Scylax glared at the two.

"What is the root of such hilarity? Lord Bitias, what are you doing in here, alone with a temple host?"

Bitias tried to catch himself. "Not alone, High Priest. There are servants here with us." The servants at the far end of the room tried to slouch into their stools.

"They matter not. Should you wish female companionship, there are many in the temple who are desirous of Astarte's union."

"No, no, just passing the day with Os'sh."

"She is not within consideration. I made that clear to Lady Elisha."

"She must not have considered the fact pertinent." With that, Bitias' laughter redoubled. Os'sh ducked to her work, struggling with her own smile. Scylax petulantly glanced between the two, seeking mockery. Eventually Bitias gathered his control.

"I must see to my other duties. Good day and Melqart's blessings to you both." He tossed off a sloppy bow and departed.

"Such impertinence," Scylax fumed. "It is no wonder that he was hounded from his homeland. Brainless peacock."

Distantly came the mass voices of women calling desperate greetings to the admiral. The priest's frown deepened. Os'sh centered her attention on her mortar.

Bitias called an assembly on the beach next dawn. He walked down the line, berating every pot-belly and chicken-arm. The men winced before his criticism.

He ordered the belly-less *RearEnd* moved down the beach to the black waters of the dead bay.

"Launch her," he commanded.

"But her hull is still breached," Werketel noted. "She will not float."

"Launch her!"

His orders were carried out. The men watched as their penteconter took on water and settled to the lower oar-ports. Water swirled over her decking. Her keel lay anchored in the harbor mud.

Bitias barked for benches and oars.

Confused, the crew fetched their gear, settling seats and shafts, ignoring the water that came up to their thighs. Their oar-blades were totally submerged.

Bitias mounted the stern, disregarding the water lapping against his shins. He gave them all a hard look.

"By Melqart, that was sloppy. I've seen Egyptians do better." He turned to his second officer. "Order a moderate stroke."

"Commander?"

Bitias gave him a hard sidelong glare.

"Moderate on my mark," Werketel bellowed. "*Ns'*! *Ns'*! Pull! Pull!"

The men gained the stroke instinctively, the shafts creaking in the water. Mud frothed behind the grounded ship. Water swirled around her, but she did not move in the slightest.

Bitias held the pace, striding up and down the submerged deck. He called battle-approach. Starboard banks in. Full stroke. On his command of hard port turn, the oar banks churned in mirrored perfection. Bitias glared sternward.

"Port!" he thundered.

The tillerman stood dumbly until Werketel cuffed him. Together, they threw themselves against the steering oars, shifting them in the mud.

Hearing the commotion, townspeople began drifting down to the beach, bemused by the grounded penteconter churning mud. Mocking laughter and ribald advice began to sound from their ranks. One or two oarsman exchanged *what are we doing* expressions.

"Aleyn, you lazy whoreson," Bitias bellowed, "Have you faded so quickly? Clear your bench!"

The men blinked at this. Aleyn might be old, but he was strong and steady, *RearEnd*'s best oarsman. Yet Bitias had pulled him, taking his bench.

"Again, battle speed," he called, leaning into his oar. Confused by the replacement, those around him were not quick enough. Even submerged, the oars clattered shamefully.

Bitias, face flat, said nothing.

The crew steadied, calling out the stroke with resolve.

"*Ns'*! *Ns'*! *Ns'*!"

Water swirled around the stern. Bitias nodded silently to Werketel. The second began calling his own maneuvers. *RearEnd* serpentined through imaginary battles. Blood ran down the shafts. The harbor frothed.

The men of Citium continued their mockeries. Several clods of mud were thrown, ignored by those they splattered.

"*Ns'! Ns'! Ns'!*"

Three young men, restless with the show, slipped into the water and attempted to clamber into the bow.

"Enemy marines!" bellowed Werketel. "Boarders forward!"

Aleyn was there in an instant. The men made the mistake of putting up a fight.

Other townsmen fished out their unconscious bodies before they could drown.

The ship raced in stationary majesty.

"*Ns'! Ns'! Ns'!*"

The onlookers began to see *RearEnd*'s true form. Not a half-planked cripple turtleing in the shallows. She was a warship, low and deadly. Her crew her brain, claws and sinews. She was hard as cedar, certain as death. There were no further clods nor comments.

"*Ns'! Ns'! Ns'!*"

For the crew, they'd found their stroke. The commoners recovered skill, the nobles gained inclusion. The sun moved slowly across the sky.

"*Ns'! Ns'! Ns'!*"

No ship could keep such a pace, not in water to its oarpins. Men cramped, hauling oars in until they could work the knots from their muscles and rejoin the pace. Shafts began to clatter together but the stroke continued. Voices grew hoarse from the chant.

"Quay ahead," called out Bitias. "Five lengths."

"In sight," Werketel confirmed. "Quarter stroke. Easy, lads. Tillerman, don't let us fall downwind to starboard." The man on the steering oars corrected for the imaginary.

They eased into their imaginary mooring, landing as if at the Royal dock. The townspeople watched *RearEnd*'s flawless execution. The oars drew in as one. The beast rested.

"Crew to the beach," Bitias ordered. To his second officer he called, "*Shnymshtr*, you may forgo mooring lines."

They ascended the sands, oars vertical. The crowd respectfully edged back. Dripping with sweat, Bitias looked each man in the eye, nodding.

"It will do." He flicked blood from his hand before pointing. "Aleyn. Barcas. Moloch. Come with me—we will watch Hêgêsistratus tonight." Moloch was the youngest, clumsiest oarsman in the penteconter's crew. Both he and Barcas beamed at being included in the admiral's detail. Aleyn watched the two race into town for Os'sh's porridge, nodding in satisfaction at his commander's little exercise.

The remainder of the crew returned to the warehouse, bone tired. Inside, a servant turned a flank of beef on a spit. Three amphora of sharp wine awaited their cups.

That night, the men drunkenly toasted their commander's health.

Elisha listened to the celebration from her pallet, her face expressionless.

R*earEnd* was hauled from the harbor bottom the next day. The crew threw themselves into the repairs. By week's end, she was being leak-checked in the marshy lagoon.

The storms rolled over the mountains above the city, marking the passage of days. In his cottage, the Greek general sweated and suffered. Several times he attempted to escape, to seek out the *hul gil* his body screamed for. In each case, the sailors beat him until he stopped, dumping his bruised body back inside his rude little cottage.

Elisha began to learn about shipping. Her initial entry into a waterfront wineshop brought forth a thunderous silence. But time and many rounds of drinks eroded the isolation. For over a week, she listened to the mariners talk, gaining a fair understanding of the trade. She learned how to identify rot and worm, defective masts, sprung planks; any number of ills that could befall a working merchant ship. She began making polite offers for transport to the west, finally securing a medium-sized freighter. A second vessel was waiting out the season in a bay a short distance up the coast. It, too, was enlisted. As soon as the weather permitted, it was shifted downcoast to Citium. Bitias' crews gave the two tubs the same treatment they had the penteconter, replacing any component that might fail during the voyage.

Tetramnestus had worked day and night, calculating supplies

needed for various-sized settlements. Grain, wood, clothing, tools, tradegoods; his stack of scrolls grew and he worked his figures. Elisha had felt comfortable with the storage capacity she'd arranged for until the aide reviewed his lists. Her three ships would barely cover half the colony's initial requirements. More hulls would be needed.

A second warehouse, this one just off the town's true harbor, was rented. All secured supplies were forwarded to it. With work and guard details at the three ships, two storage houses, and the upland cottage, the crews began to feel stretched.

The morning was crisp and cold. Frost dusted the beach before the warehouse. Men wandered about, scratching, yawning. Elisha washed a threadbare robe in a tub of freezing water, her mind on dozens of items requiring her attention.

Young Moloch fetched up against the portal, panting. He was battered, blood trailing from his nose.

"There is.... trouble..." he panted desperately.

Bitias sprang to his feet. "Damn these men of Citium! I knew they were not to be trusted. Point out the clod-turners who did this, lad, and we'll sort them out."

"Not from town." He collected his breath. "The general. He's broken out."

Bitias would have rushed inland with his entire crew but Elisha dictated otherwise. There was work that needed doing in camp. In the end, Bitias, Aleyn, and six strong oarsmen set out in a distance-breaking trot, Elisha at their head.

The sun played across their shoulders, glimmering across the distantly heaving sea. The sky was brilliant, the mountains crisp and sharp.

An ominous wisp of smoke trailed upwards.

"The cottage is alight," Bitias noted. "Bastard Greek."

Midway, they encountered two of the guard detail descending. One man limped. His supporter cradled a broken nose.

"What happened," the admiral demanded.

"I'm not sure. The sun was just coming up. Suddenly, someone sings out that the cottage was on fire. We rushed in to save that

old *'yrzro*. He was just inside the door, waiting with a table leg."
The man spit out a tooth, looked at it sitting on the green grass,
and cursed.

"Where is Kotilus?"

"That stuffy noble? I think he was off in the bushes laying a cable
when it all started. *Y*, all was quiet. Then the fire. Then the club.
That bastard whoreson!"

Elisha: "Did Hêgêsistratus get away?"

"Melqart only knows. Moloch was first inside and I saw him go
down. Astarte's love, I hope that boy was not still in the cottage..."

"He is safe," Bitias replied. "He ran to port and alerted us."

Elisha shook her head at the delay. "I have put too much effort
into this Greek to have him fall into his pit again. We must start at
the cottage and try to track him."

They jogged the remainder of the distance. The smoke grew
thicker. When they got to the broken farm wall, the cottage was
totally engulfed.

Elisha would have charged ahead but Bitias stopped her. A body,
its once-opulent robes worn and muddy, lay face down in the
clearing before the blazing hut.

They approached cautiously. Aleyn rolled Lord Kotilus over. The
horse-trader had suffered a clout along the side of his head. He was
alive, but no one envied the pain he would feel when he awoke.
Aleyn, experienced in rough-and-tumble fighting and the sub-
sequent medical follow-ups, began to bind the noble's head with a
strip of cloth. Bitias and his men crossed to the cottage, circling it
like a pack of dogs, looking for the track. Elisha stood back from
it all. It was only when she turned that she noticed Hêgêsistratus
perched on the stone wall, watching her with crow's eyes.

She approached carefully, studying the figure in the cold light.
He was wiry, his arms criss-crossed with uncountable scars. His
beard was shot with silver, his head bald from the chafing of
countless helmets. He would have been a depressing, broken-down
figure but for his eyes. They reminded her of the pool within the
Melqart's sanctum; dark, calm, unreadable.

At the proper distance, she bowed formally. "Commander
Hêgêsistratus."

"A Canaanite," the old man observed, shaking his battered head. "I thought it was all part of my delirium, those Canaanites forcing that mush down my gullet. But here you are." His laugh was harsh. "Your people are like sea-slugs; they rarely venture above the high-tide mark."

"Elisha," called Bitias as he raced up, club threatening. Hêgêsistratus watched his approach with interest, eyebrow cocked.

"Bitias, hold!" Elisha stepped in his path, checking him. She turned to the general. "Do not be worried."

"I am not," he replied, head cocked birdlike. "My mind has awoke from its slumber. I know not what occurred, but Monca is not here. Was it her spell that placed me in that living death?"

"No spell. A plant extract."

"I see. My spirit craves it. Perhaps seeing her steaming innards would abate my hunger."

"Not yet," Elisha countered. "Not until we speak."

"I would have expected no less. You barbarians do naught unless gold be at the crux. Speak your bargain, little sprig. I grant you my attention."

"I am Elisha, queen to a group of exiles seeking settlement in the west. We are assembling colonists, transports and supplies, readying for departure when the storms are exhausted."

"A fine story. Quite stirring. Continue."

"We are a people of transport and trade. In warfare, we are ill-versed. We need someone to organize our defense, to safeguard our colony while it grows."

"'Bl! Truth be spoken! I've fought amongst you barbarians for years. You fight like mincing women."

"A care, boy-lover Greek," Bitias growled. "Elisha is our queen. You will show respect to her. She is the one that pulled you from your dreamstate."

"Who is to say that my dreams were not superior to reality," Hêgêsistratus countered. To Elisha, he tossed, "You said your colony will be in the west. Where?"

"The Libyan coast."

"Has the site been fully scouted?"

"It has been selected."

"That is not what I asked."

Elisha shook her head, no.

"I see. Have you sent parties inland, to parlay with the local tribes? Have you determined their power alignments? Do you know who can be threatened, who bribed, pandered, and defeated?"

She remained silent.

"What level of support can we expect from your mother city? How many troops will they forward? How much gold will they commit."

Bitias gave a low mocking laugh.

"To sum your position: You have no sponsor-city, no gold, no troops, and only the haziest idea of where you are settling. Is that correct?"

Elisha agreed. "Our situation is dire, yet not impossible. We have gold. Also, it should be noted that such are the situations that lend rise to the champion. Should you succeed, men around the Upper Sea will sing your praises."

"Do not appeal to my vainglory, girl. I discarded it years ago." He rubbed a finger along his hooked nose. "Ares preserve me in my foolishness. I accept the command."

Elisha remained silent for a space of heartbeats.

"Why," she finally asked, "did you accept?"

"I can only hope that the accursed plant of Monca's has not spread to the lands of Libya. My soul calls for it and should I remain here, I will inevitably succumb to it again. My only escape would be to open my veins. That, or join your colony." His smile was bitter. "Quite the same thing, considering."

"Then we are in agreement. You will become our general. You will arm our men and train them to fight. You will secure our landing and safeguard the colony. If there is anything that you require, you need only ask."

The roof of the cottage collapsed in a swirl of sparks.

"For now, merely a place to lay my bones. My former abode no longer suits me."

FIVE

"**S**ail!" Moloch's voice piped from the warehouse's roof. "Sail round the point!"

The exiles piled outside. With *RearEnd*'s restoration, they could fight any royal warship that chanced storms to find them. A lookout had been established.

"What do you make of her?" Bitias called up.

The young oarsman squinted beneath a shading hand. "*Gôlah* sail. Greek rigging. A trader ship. She's hugging the shore."

"I do not believe it," Bitias frowned.

"What I believe," Hêgêsistratus told him as he meandered up, "is that you have lost."

"*N'*. We shall weigh out the silver of our wager tonight. Elisha!" She appeared in the portal at his call. "It appears Telamon the merchant braved storms to trade with you."

"The rider departed for Paphos eight days ago. He must have launched directly upon receiving the message."

"He smells profit," the general smiled. "Canaanites are not the only wolves. Even Greeks can be greedy."

"Speak not of it," Bitias groaned, thinking of the silver he'd lost in his bet against the man. "Come, he will dock at the true harbor. Let us see his cargo."

They walked south along the beach, heading towards town. Other than the small contingent whose duties kept them at the warehouse, most of the exiles had come. The merchantman's arrival signified entertainment.

"Explain again how you knew this man would be in Paphos,"

Elisha asked, tucking a windblown strand beneath her gold head-band.

"Telamon has it all worked out," the Greek replied. "Most ships from Greece bring arms and armor during the shipping season. However, their arrival in Asia Minor coincides with the end of campaign season when such goods litter the ground, encasing the dead. Why part with much gold when your late comrade will 'donate' his equipment? Telamon's trick is to sail at near the end of the season, laying over in Paphos in Cyprus. When the weather permits passage, he will be first to Miletus and the like, selling his weapons to anyone, Greek or barbarian. Everyone thinks he is mad, doing things backward like that, but he has hordes in a dozen temples now."

Bitias watched the tubby vessel weather the breakwater with professional interest. He nodded as the sails tucked up against the yard and the oars came out in crisp fashion.

"I do not see why we should deal with him. Why not buy our equipment later?"

"We will need it now if we are to sail in the spring," Elisha told him. "We cannot wait years for arms we may need the moment we step from the boats."

"Why *his* goods? He's a Greek. There is a perfectly good Canaanite weaponmaster in Citium."

"*Lys!*" Hêgêsistratus spat. "Wicker shields and naval prickers. This man has the best equipment Greek armories can fashion."

By the time they stepped onto the stone quay, the trader's lines were being made fast.

"Hêgêsistratus! I could not believe my eyes when I received your message!" This from a rotund man whose beard had been shorn to disturbing shortness. "It was my understanding you had retired."

"That was business," the general called back, nodding to those around him. "This is a hobby."

"Pah! As if those ragged Sagalassonians were not bad enough. Now Canaanites. What next; marshaling washerwomen?"

The gangway slid down. Hêgêsistratus went aboard, bear-hugging the broad merchant. "It is good to see you, old friend. This is Elisha, queen of these people. I speak for her in matters military."

The sea merchant cast a judgmental eye to the ragged exiles. "My friend, I came because I thought that a man of your reputation would be Polemarch to a crack mercenary unit. My cargo is beyond the means of this ragged litter."

"Certainly you overestimate the value of your pig-stickers."

"Nothing so ordinary this time. I carry hoplons."

"Hoplons?" Hêgêsistratus arched a gray eyebrow. "I once captained a Greek free unit armed such. We mowed through barbarians like scythes through hay."

"But Hêgêsistratus, such armor is costly, beyond the means of such scarecrows."

"If it suits," Hêgêsistratus cut in, "we shall take all of it."

"All?" The merchant's dark eyes widened. "Can you afford...?"

"She can," the general confirmed. "Bring it forth."

Telamon bellowed to his second to fetch the goods from the hold. Soon bronze equipment sparkled on the deck beneath the pale winter sun.

The merchant chose Aleyn as his model. He clam-shelled a bronze corslet over the oarsman, armoring chest and back. The elder seaman looked down at it in puzzlement, rapping his knuckles on it. Hêgêsistratus had picked up another corslet and strapped it on with practiced motions. Barcas and Moloch watched the transformations with keen interest. Several grinning crewmen noted their excitement and, to the delight of the boys, fetched equipment for them as well.

Elisha, Kotilus, and the elder nobles watched the armoring. They exchanged quiet words between themselves.

"How does that feel?" Telamon inquired of Aleyn.

"It feels...heavy," the oarsman noted. "But good. A man could punch me in the chest and I would like not feel it."

"Good. Now, the helm." The merchant raised a hammered bronze helmet. Its opening would expose a narrow slit of the wearer's face. Diving cheek-plates descended almost to the collarbone.

"He looks like a shellfish," Bitias groused, stepping up. "Shellfish might do well against other shellfish, but not against the agile." He gonged a fist against the big man's head, staggering him.

"Such will not hurt him," Temamon pointed out.

"Aye, but he sees little better than a crab. Aleyn, protect yourself."

The admiral danced about, slapping the man's exposed arms and thighs while the other blindly staggered. As an encore, Bitias flicked the oarsman's nose. "With a dagger, I could have killed him a dozen times."

"You see the world through your misunderstandings, Canaanite," Hêgêsistratus rebuked. "You place a single ass behind a twin-ox plow and claim evidence of failure. Telamon, the hoplons if you please."

Large round shields were produced, hardwood faced with bronze. Aleyn hefted his with little trouble. Moloch staggered slightly beneath its weight. Barcas groaned when he lifted his.

"We shall have to train with these," the general observed. "The oarsmen are capable but the nobles will need to build their muscles." He slipped on his own shield, settling his left shoulder into its inner face. "Ah, I missed that old feeling; cedar to the shoulder, bronze to the chest. Telamon, help position the others on me; I shall be the *grn'bn*, the cornerstone,"

The merchant maneuvered the others to him, overlapping their shields like scales of a gigantic fish. Elisha found herself visibly moved by the display; behind their armor, eyes lost in the darkness of their helmets, the men became a living fortress of bronze and muscle.

"Can you take us now, Bitias?" The general's voice boomed with reverberation. "In a line of battle, with no chance of flanking, could you take us?"

The admiral was silent, stunned by the transformation.

"Display the spears, Telamon."

The merchant produced one of the weapons; its shaft six feet of heavy cornel wood, a murderous foot-long blade at one end, an iron butt on the other. Against this deadly weapon, the javelins common along the Levant coast were as toys to tools.

Hêgêsistratus stepped forward, breaking ranks, a living statue. Elisha chilled at the figure's power.

"We will be alone on this shore of yours, Queen Elisha. We will be few, the enemies numerous. Should we appear with flimsy shields and discrete weapons, they shall annihilate us. They will throw their masses at us and bury us. One man down for each of ours, even two or three, would hardly register as a cost. Our soldiers they would slay, our women they would rape, our children they would kill, our town they would burn.

"But armored and formed as hoplites, we stand a chance. Against lightly-armed foes, hoplites are eternal. They are the rock against which the ocean roils but never defeats. I've stood in such formations against barbarians ten times more numerous and found victory.

"We will have no walls, my lady. We will have no cavalry to flank, no numbers to stand at our backs. We will be few against the weight of the Libyan host. If Carthage is to survive, it will do so in the shadow of our hoplons."

Elisha stepped up to the armored giant, a child before its parent. She traced the curve of the heavy shield, ran a hand along the plated breast. He was no longer a scrawny old man; he was brute force. He was raw power. He was victory.

She stood as close as a lover's embrace, looking up into the helmet's dark recess.

"I must have this armor, Hêgêsistratus," she whispered. "I must have my men armed as you, shoulder to shoulder. With this, no foe can break us. All of Libya will be ours for the taking."

"I can train your men. I can lead them into battle. But I am no trader. You now know the power of what these represent. You must gain them."

She placed her hand flat against his armored chest. "We *will* have these arms." She turned to where Kotilus and the other *rzn* stood; her nod was definitive. The horse-trader acknowledge it, beckoning over his Greek counterpart.

"Lord Telamon, that which you have shown us is most impressive. Perhaps not quite what we wish, but interesting. For my own knowledge, how much gold could it take to arm and armor a man thus?"

The bargaining went on through the night. Both parties concluded the negotiations, exhausted yet satisfied. Elisha had her armor. The vessel and its crew were hers as well. Telamon looked forward to his return to his homeland and his imminent retirement.

One of her transports had wormy planking. It just showed Elisha was not infallible.

Werketel considered this as he made his way towards the ship chandlery, the packet on his hip containing a list of needed items and several shekels of silver with which to bargain. He was a second officer, a *shnymshtr*; Bitias trusted him, and through him, Elisha.

His head was down, his thoughts dark. Chief among them was his coming exile, the banishment to the west. His place was with Tyre's fleet, in command of his own ship. There was nothing for him in Libya. No ship, no life, no future. He envisioned a hard-scrabbled farm on a rocky slope and felt his fists clinch.

A woman passed, going the other way. There was a swirl of robes; he automatically shifted to bypass her. He'd gone several steps beyond when something pulled him from his pensiveness. He turned and looked back.

She had stopped and was looking at him, no expression save curious eyes.

She reminded him of Elisha, though huskier, features coarser. In place of a thin headband, her hair was sheared into sharp bangs. She was not pretty in the way of the queen, but there was something deeper, an animalism the young leader lacked.

"You are one of the *gly*, the exiles?" Not so much a question as a statement.

"Aye." He felt vague confusion.

She continued to silently study him.

"I go to the chandlery," he explained, attempting to fill the void. "Gear is needed for our vessels."

"They trust you to barter?"

"Aye."

"And they have given you hard metals with which to do it?"

"Aye."

"So, should you barter for less, but report more, it would be unlikely the shortfall would be discovered. Just as if the barter took a quarter day, and you were gone for half."

"They trust me." It sounded weak even to Werketel.

"Masters trust slaves." She shifted slightly. "You are unhappy."

"Yes," It slipped from his lips, unstoppable.

"Come. I know a place."

It was a bolt-hole a block off the harbor. To one side, an establishment produced pitch. The granary opposite made rats. It was unlikely any exiles would happen this way.

The keeper knew her. Monca ordered drinks, a mixture of coarse barley beer tinged with *hul gil*. He made halting small talk, slurping down his drink. She listened, watched, sipped. When he'd finished, she led him up a set of creaky stairs to a tiny hay-lined alcove. Below, the keeper poured her drink back into the pot.

The hot air of the alcove made his head spin. In the uncertain lighting, it was as if he was screwing Elisha herself. This excited him in ways unexpected. She pumped him with steadfast passion. Afterwards, she cleaned him with hay, its friction agonizingly intense. To his shock (and secret delight) she then took him in her mouth. He gripped her raven hair, thrust for all he was worth, and resisted the urge to take her neck with beefy hands and strangle her.

In the end, he lay flat on his back, feeling a vague need to weep. At his side, Monca discretely turned to spit.

It bubbled up from him then. He'd hardly suspected its existence, but it came up all the same, pus from some festering wound. The pride at rising to second officer of *RearEnd*. Watching Bitias rise to admiral, realizing that he could soon become commander. Then came the recall and the street-fighting, a check to his advancement. Thus his life and Elisha's first touched.

Soon it became obvious that Bitias and Elisha were lovers. While the battles continued, the two continued their clandestine meetings. Talk of it swept the benches. The oarsmen were pleased by their commander's panache. To Werketel, frustration begot jealousy.

Then the trip to the mainland. Watching the whore dig in the mud with the traitors. He'd planned to stand at the foot of her cross, laughing up at her as night fell, then drink himself stupid in some wineshop. Pumayyaton's rewards would follow, and likely, *RearEnd* as his own.

He'd watched in horror as she'd turned reality on its ear. The gold overboard. The arrows from the wall. Their flight. That first night had been the worst, realizing what he'd lost, and what little lay before him. He would look to the bow, see *her* standing there, and feel hatred. Her trim figure and angelic face excited him. Her stern commanding nature frightened him. Her life-force eclipsed his own. She was the worst thing that had ever befallen him.

He'd run out of words. He lay on his side, looking at the irregular wall before him, spent.

"And you do nothing about it?"

Her voice hinted at disdain and he felt the urge to serve her a slap. Weariness intervened.

"What am I to do? Knife her? She is surrounded at all times, and even should I do such, the crew loves her and would kill me. My life is not so bad that I wish to end it beneath the blades of zealots."

"You are a seaman, correct?" Her words were smooth as wine. "You are good?"

"Good? *Y*, I am the best. Given Bitias' *distractions*, I rule our penteconter."

"I am not speaking of warships. I speak of small punts."

He rolled to face her, his confused expression meeting her cool one.

"My father was a fisherman. I could handle a boat since I could stand." It was the beatings which had driven him into naval service.

"And foul weather? Could you navigate a small craft through such?"

He shifted upwards upon a buttock, looking down at her. "What are you suggesting?"

She turned her chin slightly to bring him into view once again. "It is unlikely that Pumayyaton of Tyre will intercept his sister before she flees to the west. There are too many places she should could have wintered. His fleet, through sizable, cannot check them all. But should a man brave storms in a fishing smack to carry information to the king, his vengeance would be a controlled thrust, not a blind sweep." Her smile was deep. "And his generosity would be boundless."

"Elisha controls the harbor. Her men have duties all across it. Should I set out, the alarm would quickly be raised. Bitias would launch *RearEnd*, all risk aside. And there is no way a smack will outrun a fifty."

"The nearby salt marshes are a haven of smugglers bent of eluding *hul gil* export taxes. If Zinnridi cannot control it, neither can Elisha. A boat can be procured and placed there for you." Monca was no longer smiling. "All it would take is gold."

"How much gold?"

"A half-pound. No dickering on this amount."

"*Lys*! Sixteen shekels of gold! How am I to find such wealth? I am a simple officer, not a noble!"

She nodded to his satchel. "You told me they trusted you. Certainly you could ferret away that amount."

He bit his lip. "How soon until my boat is in place?"

"You must wait. If you leave too early, you will put the exiles into flight. You must depart just before the storms abate, so that Pumayyaton can launch without delay."

"But they will still know I have departed. They could still flee."

"My price includes a false trail, farmers who would swear they saw you making for the hills. Such a defection would be shrugged off on the eve of departure."

He climbed to his feet, donning his robe. "Make it happen. Give me the boat to carry me to Tyre. Give me the means to strike at that slut!"

"I shall provide you with all those things." She sat up, unmindful of her nakedness. "But you still owe me for our little romp. We had an understanding."

"You claim for incidentals beyond your half-pound?"

"I am a practical woman," Monca replied. "Life has made me such."

Werketel paid and departed, his despair replaced by dark anticipations.

Elisha stood just behind the general, the sea breeze crackling her robe.

"This time," he bellowed into the gusts, "let us see warriors. Not children nor old men. Not commoners too thick-headed to do anything right; not nobles too pampered to do anything at all. For your Melqart's sake, for Queen Elisha's sake, and for the sakes of your wives, children, and your own hairy asses, let us see men."

He glared across the beach. Between him and the churning sea stood two groups of trainees. Both formations were double ranked, five men across. Garbed in hoplite armor, they should have been fearsome to behold. But to even Elisha's untrained eye, they lacked the unity and power Hêgêsistratus had projected that day on Telamon's decking.

"At my call...advance!"

The two lines began to rumble forward, shields in an almost continuous frontage, trot nearly uniform. Their momentum swelled to the jingle and clatter of their bronze as the two formations closed on each other. Elisha locked fingers before her lest she cup her hands across her mouth in girlish dread.

Just before they came together, a man sprawled with a crash. The opposite formation developed a discernible gap as the second rank failed to keep up.

Still, the impact was as horrific as a merchantman going aground. One moment, there were two double lines of men. The next, the lines were cartwheeling around each other. Both right flanks had cleanly missed striking anything.

The remaining chaos threatened to further degrade; buffeted men attempted to prang their offenders with their own shields. A middle-age prince spit blood and chastised a lowly oarsman opposite, threatening the whip. To the side, Barcas recovered his helmet as discretely as possible, only finding out too late that it was full of sand.

"Enough!"

At Hêgêsistratus' bellow, all fell silent. At his gesture, they fell into formation. He looked over them for a long time, his face openly saying what he thought of the lot of them. When he did speak, it was into the cusp of a hand that massaged his hooked nose.

"Why did you shift?"

The men stood silently, not sure of their answer. The wind whistled around the armor's hard edges.

"You started directly opposite one another. Yet by the time you came together, it was your respective left flanks that collided. Can any man among you tell me why this was?"

More silence.

"Well then, my warriors of bronze, I shall tell you." The hand fell away, revealing hard eyes. "It is because you are cowards."

The line stirred at that. Muttering drifted from dark helmet slits.

"Aye, whimper all you like, you ladies. The fact stands: your lines shifted." His voice rose like a wave. "And I'll tell you why that was. Each of you, every frightened whoreson one of you, sought the refuge of the shield of the man to your right. Like little chickens, you each tried to tuck yourself beneath the wing of a mother hen. Twenty men, tucking right. And so your lines shifted at the killing moment, breaking formation. Do I need to show you what happens to a hoplite on his own?"

Silence met that. None wished for their mentor to illustrate the vulnerability of a single unsupported infantryman. Moloch was still recovering from the beating.

"To the north of Greece lies Macedonia. Like you, they are barbarians, unschooled, unwashed, and unbeautiful. But unlike you, they advance into battle with a surveyor's precision. As straight as a farmer's furrow, straight as arrowflight, directly into hell's maw. Not a one of them shirks right. Their formation is as tight as a bride's 'bn.

"I am going to give you one last chance to be men. One final chance to justify the armor hanging from your pampered hides." He gestured for Elisha to move aside, backing with her, his haranguing continuous. "Should you do as I ask, you will be able to retire to your nightly meal, look at your comrades, and declare yourselves men. Should you not, on the morrow, we will begin your training anew, back at the level Spartan children easily master."

He and Elisha were now clear of the armored line that stood with their backs to the sea. Before them lay the broad side wall of the warehouse. Idlers leaned against the sun-warmed stone, watching with curiosity.

"Dress your formation," Hêgêsistratus demanded. The unit contracted slightly, ten men by two.

Elisha looked over his shoulder, wondering at his intent.

"At my call...advance!"

There was a moment's hesitation. Hêgêsistratus flared as if struck.

"Advance, or cast away your armor and be done with it."

There was a burning shame to the line now, as clear to her as the scent of brine. Shields locked, they started forward.

The men along the wall watched the oncoming hoplites, unsure what sort of drill this was. Certainly Hêgêsistratus would wheel them away. Certainly.

Elisha could feel the sand pulse beneath her feet as the armored line gathered in its rush.

The onlookers felt it too. They could see the eyes of the men looming towards them. There would be no break nor halt. They began to scatter.

Elisha's hands flew up to her mouth unchecked.

There was a thunderous crash as ranks of infantry impacted ancient stone. The second rank slammed into the back's of the first, crushing in, holding the line.

"Enough!"

The armored figures extracted themselves, stunned physically and mentally. One man's shield hung low on a useless arm. Two failed to get up at all.

"Better," the general nodded. "Some shift, but not as much. You *'yrzro* might become soldiers yet." He held them long enough that they might register his complement. "Barcas, to me, boy."

There was a long pause. Finally an armored figure stepped away from the others, hurrying over to the commander.

Elisha could see beyond the armor. Through the helmet's slit, the white skin, the darting eyes. Beneath the corslet, his chest heaved. Not the heavy breath of a man regaining air. It was the quick breath of a frightened boy.

"You were in the second row," Hêgêsistratus observed. "You stopped short of impact. Your comrade before you did not have the benefit of your bracing. In battle, the line might have failed. While the others retire, run to the city harbor and back. With your armor."

"I beat you once, old man."

Elisha blinked, shocked at the hate that carried in the boy's voice.

"I beat you when you were a boneless invalid. Back when you cried for your precious *hul gil* and reeked of your own shit. I was on nurse-maid duties with some others when you tried to get away.

I cuffed you twice on the head and once in your potbelly. I laughed at how you wept into the dirt."

Silence fell over the men. Barcas words were brave but Elisha could see fear dilating his eyes. When Hêgêsistratus finally spoke, his tone was disturbingly conversational.

"Should a worthy adversary wrong me yet later find himself within my power, I might be expected to extract revenge. But you, Barcas, are not worthy. I withdraw my punishment. Return inside with the others."

Barcas stood, his hoplon quivering. Then he whirled, running down the beach, heedless of Hêgêsistratus' absolution and the armor's weight. Elisha was certain that she'd heard a muffled sob as he bore past.

"Well, what are you all standing around for," the general demanded of the onlooking men. "See to your napping fellows and return the queen's armor to storage."

Elisha stood at Hêgêsistratus' side, watching the men disperse.

"Are they really getting any better?" She did not look at him. "Are they really the men you seek?"

"No," he sighed. "They still shift, they still shirk, and they still blink. Their class divisions isolate them further. A trained hoplite force would break them like iron against bronze."

"But we will not stand against hoplites. Merely untrained, ill-equipped Libyans. Should they not carry through such?"

The general turned to follow the lone armored figure that struggled south along the beach.

"It is not an issue of force of arms. It is one of commitment. Your people are individualists. They lack the ability to see beyond the self, to become the phalanx. In battle, they think of tomorrow, swing when it is expected, and nestle into their comrade's armpit." He looked down and kicked at the sand. "I need men who will support the man next to him, regardless of class or social standing. I need men who will *cease to be* in battle."

He started towards the warehouse, turning one last time.

"It is far more important that you can imagine, Highness. Should they be unable to discard *self* in combat, they will be, at best, parade soldiers. But the greater burden falls upon you. As individuals, they will prove poor material for the foundation of Carthage. A single man is not really a citizen. It takes a body of men, committed to their community, to be *citizens*."

Elisha sighed, feeling her own frustrations. "Is there anything we can do for now?"

The Greek shrugged. "Merely keep drilling them and hoping for unity." He looked again towards the distant figure. "Young Barcas is by far the worst. The way he flinches through his drills, it is as if he lacks confidence to face life."

She followed his gaze. There came a flash of sunlight on bronze and Barcas turned at the distant harbor.

"For him, as well as the others, do whatever you must. We cannot afford our line to break."

SIX

Aleyn generally got the last watch of the day. It was the time of greatest danger for the exiles, the time when ships would seek port before nightfall.

Bitias was familiar with the older oarsman and his trancelike state. Unlike others who became mesmerized by the dancing waves, Aleyn gained focus. The slightest change, the tip of a sail on the horizon, and Aleyn's call would boom forth.

As such, the oarsman didn't know Elisha was there until she spoke.

"Beautiful evening," she noted, looking out over the tossing sea. "Chilly."

"Aye," he stammered, his mind slowly shifting back from its sixteen-mile vistas to the young woman two feet away. "The winter winds clear the air. One can see forever."

His words were not pure boast. East, across the straits, the orange peaks of the Canaanite seaboard were just visible.

He followed her wistful view. "Ah. Home. It pulls at the heart to see it there, just over the horizon."

"It might be within sight, but it is forever out of our grasp. Pumayyaton would kill any who returned. Our new home is to the west."

"West I cannot see," Aleyn said in a way that was both simple and deep. "A man can only focus on what is before him. I shall only know Carthage when her soil is beneath my feet."

"Soon enough, old friend. The storms are driving clear. In a month or so, we shall be on our way."

"To a place we cannot see." He shivered as the sun settled amid the hills at their backs.

She shivered herself, thinking of the growing number of people unhappy with her. Bitias frowned when he saw her, Werketel seemed to be withdrawn, and everyone under Hêgêsistratus's training seemed to hold her responsible for their own shortcomings. Suddenly, she just wanted someone to like her. She knew it was a childish thing, a little girl thing, but she felt it all the same.

"I shall watch for a while," she told the older man. "Until your relief comes. Go down and find some soup."

"Highness," the older man sputtered, surprised at such royal generosity.

"Go," she replied. He gave her a clumsy bow, a *'bny* bow. She watched him descend and turned back to the darkening sea, to look for unlikely ships of pursuit. Because she was not Aleyn, the waves lulled her, and her mind drifted over her own troubles.

Simply put, they still lacked colonists. Supplies they had, and three transports and a penteconter to haul them. But her party numbered sixty, of which she was the only woman. She figured she needed two or three times that number, and women, to attempt her settlement.

She sensed that many townspeople might be willing to move west. They were frontier stock and the growing influence from the Levant states were chafing them. A good push and she felt that many would join her. But she'd given her word to Governor Zinnridi that she would not approach them. So that was out. She would have to depend on her limited population to get the huts up and the seeds down before the year advanced and the settlement failed. With sixty souls, it would be a near thing.

Instinctively, she looked to the nearby ruins. Several bonfires roared in the night, course laughter drifted in the wind. The *sh'mmhnt*, the people of the encampment, had settled for the evening. These were the colonists she would be permitted to export, these helpless cast-offs and drug-befuddled natives. Already word had gone forth and the gathering had begun. She figured they numbered fifty, maybe more.

Bitias referred to them as the 'dregs'. She was inclined to agree.

She did not include them in her rolls for colonization. She was certain that they would be worse than useless, a drain on supplies. There was simply no way Carthage could support them. *Rzn* had a place in her city, as did *'bny*. But these people; worthless.

She would not have them, but Zinnridi watched. He was certain to force them onto the exiles, to cleanse Citium at Carthage's expense.

The sea before her purpled like the dyes of home, the far-away coastal range orange against the coming night. A sense of longing stabbed at her, a sense of homesickness Aleyn had hinted of. She missed her people. She missed the familiar life; palace, temple, market, walls. The longing to see the massive seagates, the twisting lanes, the fleets of horse-headed scows pulled at her. It was heartbreaking to realize that all that she loved existed two days hard sailing south-east. *RearEnd* could be launched, and with luck, survive the crossing. She could exchange gold for Pumayyaton's mercy, allowing him to choose her new husband, to let her remain in the city that she loved.

A chill blast blew over her, crackling her robes, standing her hair out like a pendant. Its rawness brought tears to her eyes. Beyond the beach, waves crashed.

Fear replaced regret. She would be taking sixty souls into that. They would land on an alien beach with nothing but tools, raw planks, and seeds. So many things would need to be done, and so many could go wrong. A single mistake could doom them. There was a very real chance that they would die huddled in the ruins of their boats before the year was out.

The sun was down now, the sky shimmering with newborn stars. She canted her head, taking them in, seeing them as she never had before. Their endless depth, their harsh chill. It was as if she was looking into the nature of her own folly. How could she have imagined that she would place a colony like a gardener places a plant, giving it little more effort than night soil and an occasional watering? How could she, a woman...

A woman!

...of sixteen years carry such a mad scheme?

Hêgêsistratus smiled in her mind, equating it with suicide.

Bitias chafed, allowing his word to lead him to his imagined death, a bull to slaughter.

Werketel, Barcas, all the others; fear in their eyes, grimness in the set of their jaws.

The winter's cold cut through her robes, sucking away the heat. It was as if life was fleeing her body.

"My husband," she choked. "Help me."

Arherbas was in her mind, quiet, comforting, trustful Arherbas. She could see his firm smile, his calm eyes. She could see the noble line revealed in his shaven head and beardless chin, more statue than man, a study of warm confidence. Should he be with her now, all would be fine. He would point to this or that, order a few changes, and everything would settle to the better. His city would grow, and she would watch the ascent of its towers with pride, celebrating his accomplishments, loving him in the manner he preferred.

A frigid blast bucked her; she was forced to steady herself against the parapet lest she be thrown into the night.

Arherbas was dead. Pumayyaton had bested him, killing him in his own temple. Yet she had won out over her brother, stealing life and gold out from under his very nose.

Arherbas was fallible. For all his love and devotion, he had gone under. She had not.

Nor she could afford to now.

The wind chilled her, but the loneliness of her position chilled more. Regardless of what she wished, wanted, or feared, the raising of Carthage rested upon her shoulders alone.

She crossed her arms and looked over the dark seas towards invisible Tyre. Her longing faded before cold reality. To return was death. She could never go home.

With acceptance came freedom.

She looked along the beach towards Citium, distant lamplights and torches. She thought of her boats, her people, her situation.

A single voice rose from the encampment of the dregs, a dirge in the darkness.

She felt herself shift from looking back to looking forward. A plan formed in her mind, an assemblage of situations and possibilities. She examined it from all angles with a critical eye.

It could work.

She was reviewing it for the third time when a voice rose in the darkness before her, Moloch calling up to Aleyn.

"Sorry I am late, old man," the ore boy called. "I only just got back from stripping rot from those clapped-out merchantmen. Let me dash down some soup and I'll be up to take the night watch."

"Take your time," Elisha smiled down.

"Highness!" He bowed instinctively. "You hold Aleyn's watch? Forgive me! I shall be up at once."

"Get your soup. It is cold; you will need it."

The boy stood for a moment, then nodded. "Thank you, my lady. I shall take soup and be up presently."

She raised her eyes to the black seas, her mind on her plan.

Indeed, it could work.

"**H**ere. More plants for you."

Os'sh looked up from the alfalfa and feverfew strewn across the kitchen table. Concern flickered in her mahogany eyes.

"Has Hêgêsistratus succumbed once more?"

"That old boy-lover?" Bitias' lengthy hair flickered at his head shake. "Hardly. He's still chasing his army of bronze crabs up and down the beach."

"If not him, then who...?"

"Who else. Those worthless *sh'mmhnt*, the dregs. I nosed around their camp—disgusting place. Most of the natives there were pushed off their hilltops by their own tribes. Who wants a *hul gil* slave? Like Zinnridi, they see Elisha's voyage as a way to offload their worthless members. If they are going to be any use in Carthage, they will have to be cleaned up. I don't want to go through what we did with the Greek, this time in an open boat with crazed nomads."

Os'sh shifted through the plants in frustration. "It won't work, you know. You can't go into an open camp and give them porridge. There is no way to control them. Any one of them knows a dozen stands of *hul gil* in the hills over Citium. One finds the plant, the rest shall share in it."

"What am I to do?" Bitias snapped. "The dregs are nothing more than drunkards and poppy heads. I agree there is no way to clean them up. But Governor Zinnridi continually reminds us that they are now part of our party." He looked up to catch her flinch. "I am sorry, girl. I did not mean to bark at you."

"Should not Elisha handle this? Is she not queen?"

"Elisha." The laugh was bitter. "I would like to hand this whole mess to her. But she is gone."

"Gone? Where?"

"That is something we exiles would like to know. A few days ago, she told us she had important work inland. Took some sailors, provisions, and a couple of donkeys and disappeared. This leaves me with ships to repair, soldiers to train, and natives to wring out."

"Well, certainly it must be important. She would not leave for no reason."

"She had better not," the young admiral growled. "The situation grows more dire every day. We barely have hulls to transport our goods, much less our settlers. Half of our contingent are those worthless cast-offs. As far as defense, our people cannot hold a tight enough formation for those expensive bronze suits to do much good; I fear that Hêgêsistratus will begin gonging heads together before long."

"But certainly there is time to correct all these things."

"Time? Have you looked across the square, ponygirl? At the temple of Melqart? The priests sniff the air daily, waiting for the advent of Egersis. When the storms abate, we must go—the pente-conters of Tyre will be scouring the waters of the Levant for us, and we dare not greet them here. They are quick-tempered men with a unhealthy zest for crucifixions."

She waved a small brown hand, shushing him. "Take care, Lord. Your voice carries, and you might bring High Priest Scylax down upon us."

"That ball-less wonder? I'd almost welcome it. A fist to his gob might do him some good, I would wager. Girl, what are you doing?"

She'd turned away. There came a tinkle of liquid. A moment later, she presented him with a bowl of wine.

"You are beside yourself with worry, my Lord. Calm yourself."

"Easy for you to say," he replied, pausing to drain half the bowl. "You do not sit on the oar bench I man. Elisha pulls me into her hopeless scheme. My command threatens to come unpegged. Everything mounts against me."

"Stop," she instructed, raising the bowl with her fingertips. "Drink." He did.

"Now," she continued, "I want you to change subjects. No more gloomy stories about today. No more dire tragedies of tomorrow. I want stories of your past."

"My past?" Bitias blinked.

"Yes, Lord, your past. Focus on when you were happiest."

She settled across the table from him. His expression was confused.

"What service does prior happiness serve? It is gone like the rains of last year."

"Humor a humble servant." She cupped her chin in her hands and smiled warmly. "When were you happiest?"

Bitias looked at her in some confusion. Then he leaned back, looking at the chipped plaster of the ceiling. He was one to stride towards his future; it was not in his nature to look over his shoulder.

"Well," he started uncertainly, "there was the first time I took the steering oar of *RearEnd*. What a proud lad I was. Her bow was all over the horizon." The smallest of shadows crossed his face. "Commander Jabnit was so displeased."

Os'sh remained silent. He set the bowl down quietly, crossed his arms, his eyes lost on the horizon.

"My first battle, then. I was still an oarsman. I was proud to be there, but I was also scared. I can still remember how warm the piddle was on my leg. One moment, we were rowing to blazes. The next, the oar was ripped from my hands and a black hull was alongside. Most of the men were across in an instant; I remained behind and shouted encouragement." He shook his head. "The blood was so red. I recall being surprised. Like dye, it was; bright and sharp."

"That is battle lust," Os'sh noted. "Strong emotions, ones that stay with us. But when were you happiest?"

"Happiest," he mused and thought long. A chuckle arose.

"What?" she prompted.

"No. Nothing."

"It is not nothing. If it is a happy moment then a god gave it to you as a gift. It is noble to share great gifts."

"Right. I had been rewarded by my city's king. I had been cheered by my crew. All of these things were blessings. But my happiest moment was midway between boy and man. I had earned the title of second officer and was damn proud of that. Then came the command to take a party of priests offshore for a sacrifice. I was drunk with my minute powers. The day was perfect, the men were rowing as one. We shaved into the royal dock as if Melqart's hand was guiding us, and there she was. Elisha. So small and proud. So noble. Standing there with her goat, as if the priests were assisting her rather than the other way round." His eyes focused into the past, seeing again that perfect day.

Os'sh's eyes became frank. "But you had her, Bitias. You have lain with her. The woman of your dreams. Most men see such a woman one time in their lives. Few are fortunate enough to speak to her. And one in a thousand might be so blessed as to become intimate. Certainly such a consummation would be the happiest moment of your life."

Bitias was silent for a moment. Then he laughed. "One would think. But when I reconsider it, I see it clearly. Of all the women I've known, she contains the greatest flame. When aroused, she burns you with her touch. She yields herself fully to Astarte when the *'drtnt* takes her. Truly amazing.

"But she is not that proud little girl I saw on the quay all those years ago. Something has changed within her. Something drives her now, first towards the throne, and now this Carthage. Whatever the thing within her is, it consumes her. She can never be content with any man, not in body *and* soul."

He gave the bowl a small spin, watching it wobble.

"She is not a goddess. But she is no longer human. She exists...*in-between.*"

The bowl wobbled to a stop. Bitias picked it up and stared into it in consideration.

"Os'sh? What was in this wine?" Her eyes flickered nervously.

"You have no pony here," Bitias noted, eyes on the dish. "No wagon. You cannot evade. I find myself curiously cheerful. What was in the wine?"

She nodded. No pony nor wagon. "We keep this wine on hand for women facing the culmination of their duty to Astarte. The ones who might be too nervous, shy, or anxious to perform. It calms them."

"*Hul gil?*" he asked simply. She nodded.

"I should be angry but I am not. I have heard my own words and found answers to questions I never thought to ask. Everything suddenly makes sense. The love. The fights. It is as if I have backed away from a cloth and can now see its pattern."

"You were hurt," she explained simply. "You were sad and angry, and my heart went out to you. The drug is not dangerous, not in small amounts, and not to those foreign to melancholy. I felt it would help you."

He leaned back in his chair. "Aye. Such a peace is fallen over me. It is the first true rest I have had in days. The angers and worries—poof! Gone. Everything comes clear."

"Do not worry about what you have said. I know to keep such things to myself."

"Including the fact," he said, eyes coming to rest upon her, "that you are beautiful?"

"Me?" She laughed, faintly bitter. "I am a northerner. I am no dark beauty like Elisha. My eyes are mud. My skin is mud. *Os'sh*—Wood Woman. How can I forget what I am?"

"But now I see it, Os'sh. I see your beauty for what it is. I see it with my soul, not my eyes. You help others, you complain not. You endure with grace. Your beauty shines forth."

"You hold *hul gil* poorly." She reached to take back the bowl.

He grabbed her wrist. "Hardly."

Brown eyes dropped to captive wrist, then rose to meet his determined stare. "*Hul gil* provides insights. In that it is powerful. Perhaps you love me. Perhaps you are merely foolish. But it all matters not. I am a slave of the governor. He uses me as he sees fit. I am not yours, nor will I ever be. Close your eyes to your newfound truth and forget it."

"Perhaps I shall remain here until the drug wears off. Shall we see if my love is true?"

She gave him a long, sad look. Then, with her free hand, she reached back for the urn of wine. A nudge sent it over the sideboard, to smash on the floor with a loud concussion.

Bitias dropped her hand in surprise. A moment later, Scylax charged into the room.

"What fell? What broke? We cannot afford...Lord Bitias! What are you doing here?"

"I came to inventory my treasure. It is all here."

"Inspecting your party's wealth is one thing, but it does not give you rights over the temple grounds. Especially the kitchens, and not with this woman. She is the property of the governor and should word get back to him, things could be dire for you."

"That concerns me not."

Scylax nodded slowly, then gestured to Os'sh. "And for her."

"Warning or threat, I shall heed it." He bowed to the priest. To Os'sh, he gave one last speculative glance before departing.

The men sat on their worn benches in the warehouse, savoring the warmth of the fire. Rain sheeted through the frigid night outside. As oarsmen, they had been offshore on enough nights like this to appreciate the benefits of shelter.

Still, men fill their time with talk.

"She's been back three days, and not a word about what it was all about."

"Aleyn, you accompanied her. Where did you go? To whom did you speak?"

"I cannot say. She swore us to secrecy. 'Carthage's fate rests on the stillness of your tongues', she said."

"Why do you not just tell us? Then we will be still."

"Why do I not just strike you on your yapping head with an oar? That way, you shall certainly be still."

"It is the hill tribes," Moloch opted. "She seeks to raise an army against Zinnridi, to take Citium by storm. Carthage will not be found in the west—it will be here!"

"One thing is for certain," an oarsman noted, ignoring him, "the nobles know nothing more than we do. They huddle in the opposite corner, muttering about Elisha's silence."

"What of Bitias? He is a charmer and they have been intimate. Certainly he is as curious as the rest of us."

It was Aleyn's turn; he looked to where the admiral mended a torn robe. "Something has changed for him. He keeps to himself. He thinks a lot. That is never good for a man."

"Such, no doubt, explains your wealth and position."

Distantly, the watch called a challenge from the rooftop. A voice answered. From the corner where he serviced his armor, Hêgêsistratus looked up.

"Melqart's grace," Moloch groused. "It had better not be one of those cursed dregs. Always begging for food or cast-off clothing. We should just drive them away from us."

Disgust crossed an oarsman's face. "They are our *hbr*s, our colleagues. Governor Zinnridi has made that clear. When we depart, they depart with us."

"It is odd, though," Aleyn mused, "that Elisha has not attempted to train them. No oar practice. No drills with Hêgêsistratus. It's almost as if..."

At that moment, two cloaked figures entered the building, water puddling about them. One cast his hood back: the priest Scylax. His beardless face conveyed worry. His comrade's hood fell away.

"*Mzhshrsh!*" Hêgêsistratus' bronze dagger rang from his sheath. He crossed the room in long strides. Monca watched his advance with unreadable eyes.

"Stop him," bellowed Bitias. The men in his path had trained with the general at length. They knew his moods and nature. All scrabbled clear of his burning eyes and naked blade.

Cursing, Bitias launched from his mendings, slamming into the general, bringing them both to the floor. The man hissed something in Greek and shifted his dagger to cut clear but froze as Bitias thrust a bone needle close to his eye.

"Drop the dagger, boy-lover. Or bid your view of the world farewell."

The man looked over the sliver at Bitias.

"You saw what she did to me, barbarian. You saw what I had become. Allow me to strike. The world will be the better for it."

Elisha strode past. "Thank you, Bitias. General, compose yourself or retire." She stopped before the newcomers, eyes on the woman. "This visit is unwise. Your presence creates disturbance."

"My visit is not in friendship. In truth, I hope you find death in your quest. However, we are Canaanites, both of us. We are traders. I have something you might find of value."

"More *hul gil*, perhaps?"

Monca remained expressionless. "A drug more powerful than any mere poppy. Ambition. And I come not trading for it, but warning against it."

Elisha remained silent.

"Where is your second officer this night?" Monca made a play of looking around the room. "Where is your man Werketel?"

Elisha frowned and looked to Bitias.

"I know not where he is," the admiral replied testily. "*N'*, I am his commander, not his owner. I did not even notice his absence. Most likely he is in Citium, drinking and whoring."

Now Monca looked to Scylax. Away from his temple and power, the high priest was only a weak little man.

"He came to the temple earlier this evening," the priest replied to her unspoken prompt. "He claimed to represent you, Lady Elisha, and carried away a half-pound of gold."

"The gold he gave to me," Monca confirmed. "It is hidden in town, beyond your recovery."

"Perhaps you should have hidden yourself as well," Elisha scowled. "None here would feel sorrow if Hêgêsistratus repaid you for the treacheries you conducted upon him."

"Then the gold would remain lost," she smiled, "and Pumayyaton will have you all."

An outburst rose from the watching men. Elisha waved for silence. "You have played this game long enough, friend. You spoke of trades. What is it you wish? And what is it you give?"

"Simply this—Werketel purchased a boat from me. It is a small fishing boat, sound enough to provide a fair chance of reaching Tyre. He seeks to appeal to Pumayyaton. He wishes to exchange your lives for his own."

The roar rose again. Elisha waited until it subsided, holding Monca's eyes.

"The boat," the inlander continued, "is secreted in a tiny cove. But the path I told him to follow meanders. Should you leave now, you should be able to intercept him before he launches. If not, then you will never find him at sea in the dark. Your only option would be to scatter before Pumayyaton arrived, leaving your supplies unloaded. Such would doom any dream of Carthage, would it not?"

"How much?" Elisha asked coldly.

"A pound of gold."

"I thought islanders held their word."

"I provided him with his boat. I did not agree to be his confidant. My word is unbroken." Her eyes grew hard. "A pound of gold and a promise to remain unmolested. You will not track nor kill me. Your word, Lady Elisha."

"Given." She turned to look over the crowd, eyes lingering on Hêgêsistratus. "Given for us all. High Priest Scylax, return to your temple and give this woman her gold. For now on, provide no wealth to any but Lord Bitias or myself. Understood?"

The priest nodded, trembling. Elisha confronted Monca a final time.

"You have your gold, from Werketel and from ourselves. There is much bad blood between us. I have given my word but there are many in my party. It would be best if you left Citium until our departure," Elisha's eyes flashed, "lest my word be broken."

Monca nodded, accepting the advice.

"My part of the bargain: west of town lie the salt marshes. Along it are tangled groves of stunted trees. Should you take the path that leads directly west from Citium's temple square, it will lead you to a stand. A tall tree, dead from lightning, towers over it."

She tossed on her cloak. Before stepping into the downpour, she noted, "Be quick. Your man advances on it even now."

With their departure, Elisha turned to find Hêgêsistratus returned to his corner, fetching his battle spear and cloak. Looking to her, he confirmed, "A party of angry sailors, bumbling through swamps, will warn Werketel away. He might find a boat elsewhere. I shall handle this."

"Alone?"

"Nay. I shall take him." The Greek pointed to another.

Elisha followed his gesture. She remained silent, deferring to the general's wishes.

SEVEN

Werketel suspected Monca had played him for a fool.

The path she'd indicated ran south behind the beach line, slowly curving inland. It eventually wandered west.

He'd stopped, considering. The salt marshes drained into the sea south of Citium. He'd scrabbled for Os'sh's feverfew across the peninsula between sea and swamp. There were no clumps of trees like those described this far south.

Rain suddenly swept over him. He felt lost and alone. Why would Monca have diverted him this far south? Had it been to avoid any chance encounters with the exiles?

Lightning flickered over the black hilltops.

He came to a decision, leaving the path, striking northwest across the scrub lands. It was hard going. Once or twice, he tumbled into dank ponds. In the back of his mind was the image of himself floundering into quicksand and screaming helplessly as it drew him under. A light-headed fear fell over him.

Then the tall grasses fell away. A path, running north. He scouted the opposite side, quickly realizing from the wet ground and odor that the marsh was close at hand. He backed to the path and ran north, not sure if his gambit of shortcutting across the trail's arc had gained or lost time.

Beneath the night storms, the darkness was total. He was unable to determine if any of the clumps of trees encountered contained the mast-like trunk. He ducked into each grove, groping around for the boat. Once or twice, nesting animals tore from their shelters, further jangling his nerves.

Blue lightning lit the night sky. Its brilliance traced the tall dead trunk a hundred yards ahead. He ran headlong through the rain.

The grove formed a leafy shelter. Inside, the rain drummed comfortingly overhead. He leaned against the dead trunk, panting. Then his head came up; he knew that smell.

Fishgut and pitch. Suddenly he could remember every scratch and buff of his father's boat. From this dovetailed other memories. The rank odor of barley beer. The hard fists. The night he'd fled their hovel in pain and fear, to find *RearEnd* grounded stern-first on the nearby beach. He'd begged Commander Jabnit to take him, then and there. For years after, he'd pulled his oar with a fanatic's strength, secretly fearful that he might be returned home should he prove unworthy. It was only when he witnessed Bitias' rise to second that he discovered ambition.

And now that ambition had been wasted, all because of that evil Elisha.

But the boat was here.

He found it in the dark. She was small and tubby, made for blunt runs out to the sea, to fill her broad belly with fish before returning to port. She was not suitable for open water and heaving waves. But should he reach Tyre, the risks would be worth it. Pumayyaton would respect his bravery and hear his words. Werketel might even command one of the warships that would sweep down on Citium and capture the exiles. Melqart's blessing; such vengeance would be wondrous!

A true fisherman had secured this boat. Werketel could tell such as his hands probed through the darkness. The oar on the seat, the mast ready to be stepped. It was as if he'd left the boat for himself.

It was time to be away. He stepped around to the bow and leaned into it, shoving. The boat began to slide. Something hissed out of the darkness, tugging across the back of his legs.

He collapsed face first into the mud, the boat slipping onto the dark water. Confused, he rose after it and fell again. His legs were useless, dead. Probing fingers discovered the deep gashes across the back of his thighs.

Hamstrung!

Hêgêsistratus pushed from the nearby brush, spear low, a trickle of blood drooling from its head. Someone followed. Werketel recognized it as Barcas, face white, eyes wide.

"Bastard offspring! *Y*, you have ruined me!"

The Greek looked down at the withering man. "You have ruined yourself, fool. You saw what came from trusting that whore. You saw what it earned me. And yet you entered into an agreement with her."

Pain clamped Werketel's guts. He'd assumed death would come on some burning deck, arrows hornetting past. Not laying in swamp mud, rain pattering the leaves overhead. Not this.

"Help me," he grated. "Wrap my legs. Get the boat." His breath came in desperate gasps. "We can return to Tyre together. Glory can be shared."

Hêgêsistratus hunched before him, spear horizontal across his knees.

"You are *nwh*. Dead. Your blood drains. Soon your breath will still. Darkness will fall over you and you will be no more." He stood. "But you can still be of use to me. Barcas!"

The young man looked up, face masked in horror.

"You shirk and flinch. You back away from being a man. This must be corrected." He used his speartip as a pointer, lightly touching Werketel's forearm, careful not to prick.

"Strike him here."

Barcas looked up, mouth gaping.

"His time grows short," the general demanded, his foot pinning the second officer's hand. "You must be blooded. It is the only way to salvage you from your delicate ways. Strike." The spearpoint came around. "Strike or be struck."

The weight of the ironhead forced the boy to his knees. He held his blade limply, looking into the second's eyes, teeth chattering.

Werketel used his command voice. He ordered the boy away. He flung curses and threats. He verbally raped Barcas' mother.

The sword touched his flesh, icy, gauging.

"Do it," Hêgêsistratus demanded.

"Little Bastard!" Werketel bellowed. "I curse you! Curse you!"

A clumsy stroke, hacking flesh, divoting bone.

The howl echoed against the foliage cover.

"A girlish strike," Hêgêsistratus berated, hauling the sobbing boy up, shaking him. "The sword I gave you is razor sharp! *Lys*, there is no excuse!" He shouted directly into Barcas' face. "I grow tired of your fumblings, boy! Strike his other arm and strike it through! Otherwise I will kill you, here and now!"

Barcas stumbled at Hêgêsistratus' shove, falling over Werketel. Something patted off the prone man's cheek. Tear or raindrop, it mattered not.

Werketel withered in the pain. The darkness loomed, the end of everything.

"No," he whimpered. "Please."

Cold fingers braced his arm. Another gauging touch. Barcas' face was screwed in fear and hate. The spear hovered, ready to strike.

Werketel did not feel his arm come away. He knew it was gone but felt nothing. The fear had vanished. He was as light as a feather.

The spear came down a last time, pointing at his throat.

Barcas' blade swung in, without waver or hesitation.

A moment of rolling confusion. Werketel found himself staring at weeds along the dark water's edge, marveling at the beauty of their construction and the wonders of the world.

And then the brain in his severed head stilled and he knew no more.

The next day, a new fishing boat lay amid the transports of Elisha's growing fleet. No one spoke of it.

Men labored on Citium's quay, hauling goods from the warehouse to two transports. They carried urns of grain, plows, any number of items required for the new colony. From a nearby table, Tetramnestus tracked the flow of provisions, making sure that everything was loaded as his scrolls dictated. Aleyn, frowning, watched over the high priest's shoulder.

All this stopped at the distant call of the watch horn.

Elisha felt her heart come to her throat. So close. Even now, the priests of Melqart argued about the declaration of Egersis. If Pumayyaton's warships had sailed early...

Aleyn was staring northeast along the coast, keen eyes locked on the tiny sail gracing the horizon. The portage line set down their burdens. Should it be a Canaanite warship, all their efforts would be in vain.

Finally, Elisha could stand it no more.

"*Shnymshtr*!" she called. No one answered. Again, she called for the second officer. Finally, with a grimace of exasperation, she added, "Aleyn!"

The elder seaman started. "My lady, a thousand apologies. I am uncomfortable with this new rank."

"Bitias thought that you were the best choice for second. I concurred. The men respect you and I have found I can trust you. Now, what can you tell me about that distant sail?"

"Well, it is not a warship. She is a merchantman, or Melqart take me by the *'yr*."

"Likely our last ship," Tetramnestus observed. "The trader Moryshot."

"I trust him not, Highness," Aleyn added.

"We need every hull we can gather for our effort."

"But my lady, not counting the two transports we are loading, three more rest upon the beach. And there is that coastal lugger of tinkers. And the fishermen."

"All who follow us know the value of their loyalty. Every cargo vessel that comes with us will get favorable trade concessions with our new colony. For the smiths, they will become quite wealthy supplying the colony. Same for the fishermen."

"But you gave them our spare fishing hull."

"Their clan is numerous enough to put it to use. Their catches will extend our food supplies."

"The others I can understand. I was with you on your mission when you swayed these crews to our quest. But with Moryshot, I have misgivings."

"He will serve his purpose."

"I am not an articulate man," Aleyn groused. "I cannot argue my position against this man well. If only I were Bitias."

"Bitias is currently loitering under the windows at the temple of Astarte," Tetramnestus petulantly put forth, "talking endlessly with the slave Os'sh." He glanced up to catch Elisha's dark look. Grimacing, he dove back into his scrollwork.

"Come with me, Aleyn," she commanded. "We must meet our latest arrival."

"But my lady, I should remain here to supervise the loading."

"Tetramnestus has this task well at hand. It would be unseemly for me to appear before Moryshot alone. I need you with me, *shnymshtr*."

Aleyn reluctantly bowed acceptance.

They made their way to the beach between the old and new harbors. The hulls of the various craft lay grounded. Several sailcloth tents were pitched on the sands above the vessels, shelters for the crews. Nearby, smoke rose from a forge set out before the smith's craft. They were casting all manner of items, anticipating the colony's needs.

The dregs had also moved their camp closer, their pitiful tents nestled among the sea oats. Governor Zinnridi had ordered the move as if he thought Elisha might overlook the outcasts in her final loading. Aleyn noted that Elisha did not give the mean collection of shelters so much as a glance.

To seaward, the tubby ship closed. Elisha waved towards the distant craft, catching their attention. The helm came over and it nosed through the surf.

"Too soon," Aleyn observed. "He was too eager to make landfall."

Even to Elisha's untrained eye, this readily became apparent. The vessel of Moryshot wheeled back through the surf, oars milling with poor coordination. It moved closer and made another false start at the beach. Again, it was forced to work its way back out beyond the surf.

"One gains an eye for such things," Aleyn noted. "As soon as we encountered this Moryshot, I knew he, his crew, and his ship were not worth a shekel of tin. My lady, I beg you to reconsider. Even should your recent mission bear fruit and the inlanders come, I don't see why we need this lubber."

Elisha's eyes remained on the laboring merchantman. "You gave your word to remain silent concerning my mission. Should a hint of my plan leak out, all could be undone. Speak not of it, even to me alone."

"Lady," Aleyn bowed, shamed at being reminded of his oath.

Aleyn's assessment proved correct. Moryshot's vessel came through the surfline with all the grace and control of driftwood. It ground across the sand at a crooked angle, grating along the flank of one of the beached transports. The crew dashed down to the waterline, screaming oaths at the newcomers who returned the verbiage with gusto. Elisha waited patiently through it all. Finally, the crew of the impacted freighter retired back to their tent, glowering at the arrivals.

"There will likely be a knifing or two over this incident," Aleyn noted. "Should I have Hêgêsistratus assign men to keep order?"

"No," Elisha replied curtly. "Allow them to settle it on their own. Such matters not."

Her eyes were on the man who had leapt from the newly-beached craft. He'd landed clumsily in the sand, apeishly brushing himself clean. Moryshot was as she remembered; a mongrel mixture of Levantine races. Even the scent of stale barley beer was unchanged.

"Lady Elisha," he greeted, staggering through a parody of a bow, "I have come as we agreed."

"It is good to see you can hold a bargain, Lord."

"*Y*, that is something that has plagued my mind through my perilous journey here. I still agree to service your colony. However, I need something more than a promise of a golden new city and its river of trade. I provide my fine ship, but in exchange, you yield nothing but words. I require more."

"How much?"

"Two mina of gold before we depart. Such would only be fair."

"*N'*," Aleyn protested. "We had an agreement, sealed with your word!"

Elisha waved him to silence. Meeting the eye of the ragged captain, she replied, "I understand your need to cover expenses before they are incurred. Such is the nature of business. I, too, am experiencing a shortage of wealth, what with outlay for supplies and provisions. What if we gave you a single mina now, and two upon arrival? Would that suit?"

"You would not break your word with us, would you?" Moryshot scratched thoughtfully at his tangled beard. "You would not try to trick us from our gold once we arrive at Carthage?"

"As soon as your hull touches that beach, the wealth will be yours."

He considered her words at length and finally bowed acceptance. "We are yours to command."

"Aleyn shall oversee the delivery of your gold. Until I command otherwise, you are to wait on this beach with the others. Be at the ready; we launch within days."

They ascended the grade from the beach in silence. Aleyn worried his lower lip until he could stand it no more.

"Highness, forgive the impudence of a simple sailor, but I think you have erred. Moryshot's company and capacity is not worth three mina. We can do well enough without him."

"My agreement stands. His services will be well worth the gold he collects. But there is one more thing. When you deliver his wealth this evening, you will provide him and his crew with several urns of beer with our complements."

"But such feeds fuel to the fire. His men will drink themselves senseless."

She nodded, then spoke more. He listened, his eyes growing large. Then a smile spread. He nodded.

Egersis came.

Citium yielded to the celebrations. The world was awakening from its rainy slumber.

The sea chop had diminished. Bitias paced, gnawing his knuckles, certain that Pumayyaton had already launched his pentenconters.

"We shall not replace the god Melqart with the god Expedience," Elisha told him. "One does not sail before honor has been paid. Rest assured; today we celebrate, at dawn we depart."

Equally restless was Tetramnestus. He'd taken his loadmaster duties seriously and now climbed through the hulls of the two transports along the quay, checking and rechecking the placement of the cargoes. Elisha peered down through a hatch at the frantic aide.

"The scroll, Tetramnestus. Did you assemble the names I requested?"

"Those of the craftsmen of Citium? Aye, my lady, it sits there with my inventories. But why do you need the names of all craftsmen of this settlement? You told Zinnridi you would not approach his townspeople with proposals to settle Carthage."

"Yes, but should he lift that restriction, should we not be prepared?"

"The governor is unlikely to change his mind," Tetramnestus groused, his mind on missing axeheads.

In the city, the celebrations spread. All day, farmers from outlying plots had drifted into town. Egersis was an important part of their planting and harvest. Everything rested upon Melqart's graces. They gawked through streets, bumpkins amid the cosmopolitan Citium. As with every year, the balance of them ended up beneath the windows of the temple of Astarte, speaking quietly with long-absent wives and daughters. The priest Scylax watched with displeasure—should their conversations grow too emotional, he would call Zinnridi's guards to disperse the family members. Such displays were bad for business.

With night's fall, a single trumpet sounded from the palace; Zinnridi had performed his sacred act with one of his concubines. With this signal, a Melqartian priest lodged a burning brand into the straw effigy of the god. It went up in a rush, highlighting the revelers in the square.

The glow of the pyre flickered down a side street, briefly illuminating Elisha, gleaming off the swords and breastplates of the men with her. She watched with feline patience, waiting for the festival to conclude, for Citium to fall silent.

The fire died away, filling the narrow street once more with darkness.

The pounding continued. Summoned by the night attendants, Scylax staggered to the door, blinking away the excesses of Egersis.

"Who disturbs" he croaked, "the house of Astarte?"

"Queen Elisha," came the voice though the wood. "We seek to

reclaim our wealth, as is our right. We also seek to honor Astarte, as is our duty."

He turned to look across the hall. The women were stirring, murmuring at the nocturnal disruption. Above them, the windows showed a sky purple with distant dawn.

"Can you not come at a more...conventional time?"

"You deny us our gold and our worship?"

Scylax muttered a curse. She was always so right and so tricky. Of course he could not deny either. With a gesture, he signaled to his attendants to unbar the door.

Elisha entered. She was not alone. Thirty men followed her in, breastplates shimmering in the lamplight. The insufferable Bitias and the portly aide were also in attendance.

"What is the meaning of this? Do you have plans to assault this temple, to carry away its goods?"

"Not at all," Elisha reassured him. Tetramnestus handed her a bundle of clay tokens which she forwarded without hesitation. "These are our markers for our wealth. Please retrieve it all. We sail shortly."

Scylax handed the clay slabs to attendants who scurried off. Lacking Tetramnestus' system of organization, recovering the urns took time. An uncomfortable silence came over them.

The high priest noticed some of the men eyeing the women huddled in the recesses of the great hall. Their expressions were too frank for Scylax's tastes. Worse, the women were smiling back.

"One of the urns, my lady," a temple attendant panted as he lugged it before them. Tetramnestus checked his own token and the seal. He nodded in confirmation.

"Highness," Scylax managed, "These men with you. So many. And armed with swords..."

"The streets are dangerous, especially in the dark. You do not expect me to risk my fortune, do you?"

"Your urn, my lady," prompted another gasping acolyte.

"But such bold measures? Are you sure?"

"How is the seal, Tetramnestus?"

"Intact, my Queen."

An armored man fluttered fingers at a woman from a poor woollier family. She blew her admirer a brazen kiss.

The priest frowned at the interplay. "My lady, perhaps your men should wait outside. Their behavior is unbecoming..."

"Mind it not, Priest," Bitias blunted. "My men shall control themselves." He casually stepped between Scylax and Elisha, physically blocking further protests. Sulking, the priest moved away, content with contemplating life without Elisha.

Eventually the last urn was delivered. Bitias broke its seal, revealing gold shekel-weights. He looked expectantly to his queen. She, in turn, glanced to Second Officer Aleyn stationed near the open street door. He glanced outside, then returned a nod of confirmation.

Something is happening, Scylax realized.

Bitias reached inside the container, pulling forth a handfuls of shekels, filling the impromptu pouch of his robe-front. Tetramnestus produced a scroll and walked towards the silently watching women.

"When I call your name, please signify yourself. Phoenix, wife of Straton."

"I am she."

Bitias stepped forward. "The Goddess Astarte profit thee." With his words, he tossed a shekel into her lap.

Meanwhile, at the doorway, Aleyn called out, "Straton? Come, man, move quickly." A man slipped into the door, crossed the room, and embraced his wife.

"What," Scylax shrilled, "is the meaning of this?"

"High Priest," Elisha asked, formality in her tone, "where is that sacred garden? They must consummate their duty to the goddess."

"Through the door, to the right," an attendant blurted. The couple scurried in the indicated direction. Tetramnestus called another name. Another husband entered. Another shekel-weight was tossed.

"You cannot do this!" Scylax's warbled, face flushing.

"We are within the canons of the temple. A foreign man places wealth into the lap of a temple woman. She repays him with *'drtnt*, a devotion to the goddess." Elisha smiled at the frantic priest. "There is nothing that says the act *must* be performed with that foreigner."

The priest stammered over the time needed to transact three more women. Finally he blurted, "But then, *who* are these men?"

"In some cases, lawful husbands. In others, would-be suitors. Most of them are farmers, people I need for Carthage. We came to an agreement to each: I would purchase freedom for their women so no other man would tarnish them. In return, they join my exiles."

"But they would be throwing away all they have worked for here!"

"A hovel and a handful of acres? In Carthage, I have land beyond measure. They will find their situations greatly improved."

Straton and Phoenix returned, bumping into a outbound couple. Good-natured laughter echoed through the dark hall.

"You play word games with me, my lady! This is *not* the way temple business is conducted!"

"What difference does it make if the gold and *'yr* belong to different men?"

"The entire service becomes compromised." The priest's voice rose to a desperate whine. "The foreigner must provide both payment and seed. It is how it has always been done. It is what Astarte expects. Otherwise, the service becomes little more than a meaningless tithe paid to the temple."

"In Tyre, Astarte is serviced by *khn-drkh*, priestess-prostitutes. They are professionals trained as artisans, not wives pulled from husbands."

"My Queen," Tetramnestus called, "the garden grows crowded. Couples cannot find the space nor privacy they require."

"These are temple grounds; anywhere should suffice. Direct them to any empty room at hand."

A squeal from Scylax. "You overstep your authority! This is an insult to our goddess."

She looked to the constant stream of couples moving past. "I should think such an outpouring of devotion would rank highly with her." She turned and called to Aleyn. "Time grows short. Take half your men and secure your choices. When you are done, let the other half go forth"

"Aye, my lady!" With a smile, the officer picked fifteen men. Bitias handed gold to each. Women stood to meet their suitors. The nobles approached it solemnly. The commoners were all grins. The goddesses' will was done.

Scylax pushed past Elisha, collaring a gawking priest. "Seek out Governor Zinnridi. Tell him what occurs, that the Canaanites are making off with his farmers!"

Several of the armed men looked to Elisha for orders to prevent the priest from departing. She shook her head. It was still before dawn. With luck, they would be away before Zinnridi reacted.

The hall was refilling with reunited couples. Elisha's men also returned, their women remaining at their side. Scylax observed this, shoulders falling.

"Allow me a guess; the women your men selected have agreed to journey to Carthage with them, to be colonist-wives?"

"All reached understandings during their daily chats at the windows. It was all pre-arranged."

The room was growing crowded. The smell of '*drtnt* hung in the air. The women appeared flushed, the men satisfied and cheerful. Aleyn stood nearby, cradling a plump tanner's girl as if she were a fragile doll. Lord Kotilus spoke cordially with his wife-to-be, a rich merchant's daughter. Some eighty women had accepted the bid to become Carthaginians. Fifty of them would go west with husbands and lovers. The remainder had accepted bonds with Elisha's crew. The handful that remained, women unwilling or unable to journey west, clustered beneath Astarte's statue.

Scylax stood to the side, looking at the offering bowl which overflowed with Elisha's gold.

Finally the last couple rejoined the group, eliciting catcalls. Through the windows, the sky was orange, dawn just short of the horizon. Elisha stepped before the crowd which fell into a respectful silence.

"My friends, shortly we set out to our journey to the west. Building new homes and new lives will not be easy. Hardship shall be our constant companion. But when it is done, our city shall rise from the Libyan plain. Our fields shall be bountiful with crops, our orchards heavy with fruit, and from our shipyards, merchantmen and warhulls will issue forth. We will be able to look at this and know that we built it. We, who are not Cypriot nor Canaanite, not rich nor poor. We will be the people of Carthage. We are *Qrthdshty*!"

The men bellowed whole-heatedly. With wives and farmers, the colony now had a solid chance of success.

"Let us waste no more time. Soon the sun will rise and we must depart. As discussed, Hêgêsistratus waits by the boats. Proceed to him and secure the beach. Tetramnestus will direct the embarking of the farmers and women."

The crowd streamed through the doors and into the chill morning air. Elisha watched them go, intending to be the last one out. To one side, Scylax stood before the mound of gold in defeated silence.

In the center of the temple, Bitias studied her. In his hand lay a single lump of gold.

"You owe me this, *Qtn'khn*, Little Priestess." His tone was flat. "I have given up my world for you. I go into the west, and go willingly. However, this one thing I must have."

She stared at the gold in his palm.

"Is there no chance that we can reclaim what we once had, Bitias? Could we not find the *'drtnt* we felt for one another, back when we were sane and the world was mad?"

"You own my loyalty. You own my skills, my service, and my life. But there are things a queen cannot demand. You are the first of the Carthaginians, a new race. But you are not the Elisha I knew in Tyre." A shrug. "That is how it is."

Her jaw trembled briefly.

"Do as you wish."

He looked at her for a last lingering moment. Then he turned and advanced on the women huddled beneath the statue. Stopping, he dropped his gold into Os'sh's lap.

"The Goddess Astarte profit thee."

She looked at the bright lump of metal as if it were a poisonous snake.

"Bitias, you cannot do this thing. I am Zinnridi's slave. My services have been reserved for the Assyrians."

Without turning, Bitias called out, "High Priest Scylax, when a foreigner casts his gold, the woman must lie with him. Is this not true?"

"It is true," the priest listlessly confirmed. "It is the goddesses' will."

"If you lie with me," Os'sh replied, "my master will kill you."

"I will be in the west. With you. Beyond his reach."

"I cannot run."

"You are Scythian. Have you forgotten how to run, how to evade? You told me it is the strength of your people." He took her hand.

A moment later, she rose. Bitias led her towards the sacred garden. As he passed Elisha, he noted, "You should leave now. The truth had been spoken; Governor Zinnridi will fly into a rage when he finds what you have done. We shall meet you on the beach."

Elisha did not watch them depart the room.

"You will need a priest," Scylax spoke, still facing the gold. "Someone to organize the temple of Astarte in this Carthage of yours." He turned, eyes hollowed. "If you escape Zinnridi's vengeance, he will turn it upon me. It is I who provided the avenue for the exodus of his farmers. It is I who permitted his prize slave to be stolen. You must take me with you."

"Understand me, High Priest. Carthage's city god will be Melqart. Tetramnestus shall be holy lord. Further, Astarte will be serviced by trained *khn-drkh*, not women consigned to her service. We shall follow the customs of Tyre, not Citium, in this regard."

"I feel obliged to agree; perhaps it is Astarte's wish all along." He looked at the mound of gold he was leaving behind. "Life is odd. Our moments of triumph are often our most bittersweet."

"Perhaps, High Priest, it is the other way around. Let us leave this place."

EIGHT

The beach was ordered chaos.

The breaking sun forged the sands into copper. The air was sharp and fresh, a favorable breeze mounting. No clouds marred the vault of sky.

The town had been roused. The cavorting parade of the reunited couples had brought the people of Citium forth. They stood along the high tide mark, mingling, muttering, watching. Between them and sea stood Hêgêsistratus' men. The hoplons and helmets had been waiting on the sands for the return of the temple expedition. Within moments, they had changed from a boisterous rabble to a hard bronze line.

Beyond them, four tubby freighters stood ready for launch. Deckhands waited for the command to shove clear. A mass of farmers and wives milled at water's edge, seeking direction.

RearEnd worked its way out through gentle swells, half her oars manned. In Bitias' absence, Aleyn stood in the helm. The penteconter moved slowly up and down the beach, watching over the confusion with wise painted eyes.

Further out loitered the final two transports, riding low under their cargoes of tools, provisions, and supplies. The lugger of the tinkers held easy formation. The two fishing boats coursed through the formation as if at play.

Elisha pushed though the Citiumians, Tetramnestus and Scylax trailing. There seemed to be a growing confusion around the hoplite line. As she descended the beach, she realized that it was the *sh'mmhnt*, the dregs, who milled short of the shield wall.

"Elisha," called Hêgêsistratus over the crowd. "Come sort our mess out."

Mot, the Cypriot native who served as crude spokesmen to the group, turned to face her.

"You promised us passage, '*Sh*! You promised us a place to live, food to eat, and citizenship as Carthage. Do not renege on your words!"

Elisha's face remained neutral before the man's disrespect. "I agreed that you could sail with us, and that a ship would be provided. As for Carthage, you will have to work for full privileges."

"Of course," the man replied, too quickly, too easily.

Fine, she thought. *It makes my decision easier.*

"We shall load you shortly. Of that you have my word." Hêgêsistratus' shield swung aside like a gate to admit her, cutting off Mot's further demands.

"I see warriors forming up beyond the townsmen," the Greek noted as she pushed past.

Captain Moryshot waited beyond the hoplites, nervously eyeing the milling rabble of dregs and the townsmen beyond. He, too, had spotted the distant glimmer of weapons.

"With regards, my lady, we shall push off now and form up with the vessels offshore."

"You will remain grounded until I say. Move off the sands and you forfeit your two mina."

"But such risks were not part of our arrangements. I now demand three mina upon arrival..."

"Oy!" Elisha called up to the nearest grounded freighter. The deckhands smiled to one another at the sight of a lady shouting like a sailor. "Are you ready to load?" With the captain's nod, she turned to her new colonists. "Pay heed—I have assigned two hulls for you. There is room for all. The only ones that will be left behind are those who bring disorder to our boarding." She gave it time to sink in, sobering the crowd. At her signal, rope ladders were dropped over the side. Men and women clambered up.

"Elisha!" A distant bellow sounded. She slipped through the ranks to stand before the shields. At the top of the sandy incline, from within a small formation of guards, Lord Zinnridi glared angrily.

"*Ro'lhy*! Breakers of your word! You take my people, even when you vowed not to. Such is our anger that we could drive you into the sea."

Such words seemed fearsome. A younger Elisha might have faltered, but this Elisha had faced King Pumayyaton in far more dire circumstances. She was surprised with her own calm. Her dark eyes traveled across Zinnridi's formation, noting the flimsy wicker shields, the mismatched leather armor. While he had an edge in numbers, the advantage was constituted of nervous men reluctantly facing hard bronze.

"Lord Zinnridi," she called in reply, "your anger confuses us. You said not to approach townsmen. To that I agreed. But the people who have decided to share my quest are not such. They are farmers, living beyond your walls. Some of them have come great distances to become Carthaginians."

He stood silently for a moment, stunned by her trickery. Finally: "That is not what I said..." A pause. "That is not what I meant..." A gull cried overhead, breaking the second lull. "You twisted our understanding. Return my people or suffer my vengeance."

Elisha faced his boast, sea wind ruffling her robes, pausing to consider. The Governor had backed himself into a corner. She could laugh away his demand. Should he launch an attack, his men would die in their trim little ranks. But these men were Canaanites, and she had no desire to stain her path with the blood of countrymen.

"My Lord, I am afraid our loading is too far along." This, the lamest of lies. Only a third of the farmers were aboard. "I cannot disrupt our embarkation. I am sorry for our misunderstanding, but certainly you can afford to lose some of your outlanders."

"You make assumptions on matters you know nothing about. Those traitors you have collected are critical to our harvest efforts. Fields will now stand vacant. Citium will face famine. All because of your trickery and word-craft."

He falls back on guilt, she realized. *Like Pumayyaton. He asks for his enemy to solve his problems.* She half-turned and beckoned for Tetramnestus. *This is what we hoped for.*

As her portly assistant pushed between hoplites like an ox through standing crops, she turned back to her opponent. "Lord Zinnridi, the men of Carthage wish no evil to befall the men of Citium. We would do anything to avoid placing our brothers in such circumstances. A famine is the flame for unrest and revolt. We would not wish to have you pulled from your throne and horribly murdered when a simple solution exists."

Zinnridi watched her closely, fully cognizant of the truth in her warning.

"As I said, we can provide assistance. You have lost fifty farmers. Such could be counterbalanced by the export of, say, twenty to thirty townsmen. Every man who sails with us is one less who will draw from your granaries and take up arms against you."

From within his little formation, Zinnridi visibly slumped, now realizing how Elisha intended to leverage craftsmen from him. While her words were as twisted as snakes, they were as true as eagles. His city faced famine, and only by reducing his population might such unpleasantries be avoided.

The worst of it was that he had no time to deny her the best of his craftsmen. She was forcing his decision, yes or no, all or nothing.

At least, he conceded to himself, she would carry off the *sh'mmhnt*. Such dregs Citium could do without.

"We thank Queen Elisha for her kind offer and permit..." he weighed risk versus return, "thirty citizens to join."

Elisha now spoke directly to the people of Citium.

"Should any wish to join our ranks, step forward. Those who do must realize that there is no time for scurrying back home for possessions and little treasures. The decision must be made on the moment; you must come aboard with nothing but the clothing on your back.

"But note; Carthage is a virgin opportunity. The treasures of Libya wait to be plucked by the bold. True men can win their fortune there. So should you wish to gamble your fortitude and skill against this raw coast, join us. We will put roofs over your heads, food in your bellies, and tools in your hands. You will be Carthaginians, true men of the west."

At first, not a man moved. There came a murmur as couples consulted and brothers conferred. Then several young men, apprentices in crafts monopolized by their elders, started forward.

Reluctance broke. Suddenly hunger for the west swept over them all.

Tetramnestus saw the multitude approach and nervously backed against the shields.

"You have your scroll?" she asked, "The one with the names of the craftsmen we seek?" He nodded and produced it. "Gather those you can. Use your judgment on the rest. Pick thirty and send them through the line to the ships."

"What of us, Highness?" Mot's tone was bitter mockery. "You promised that we would launch with you."

"You shall. As you continually remind me, I promised such." She pushed through the bronze ranks once again.

The farmers were mostly aboard. A loaded transport pushed off, crew scrambling up her hull. A cheer rose from those crowding the decks.

A motion caught her attention. Two figures dashed along the horn of the breakwater. At its end, one of them waved to sea. She recognized the trim athletic form; Bitias. As *RearEnd* put about, he dropped into the water. Os'sh hesitated for a moment, then slipped into his arms. With an easy stroke, the admiral made for deep water, the horsewoman clinging to him, her trust total.

Elisha watched, her emotions flat. She felt nothing. This caused her some concern.

The penteconter slowed, the bow coming within a man's length of the pair. Aleyn cast a line, assisting them aboard. A moment later, *RearEnd* moved off.

Three merchantmen remained. One was almost loaded, its crew ready to shove it clear. Farmers waited impatiently to board, joined by townsmen still shocked at their own sudden impulsiveness.

"My lady," Moryshot blustered, "We launch now."

"Launch empty and *RearEnd* shall sink you." She bore past the man. "Cease with your whimperings." On tiptoes, she looked over the armored men. "Tetramnestus! How do you fare?"

The priest stood ringed by hopefuls, consulting his scrolls, his attention focused on his task to provide Carthage with the best.

"Twenty-five," Hêgêsistratus answered for the aide. "Five to go.

There is a goldsmith with a wife and three children, or two horse trainers, two wives, and a babe."

"What is the age and sexes of the three children?"

"How should I know?" the Greek retorted, "A boy, perhaps fifteen. A girl of maybe ten, and another boy still younger."

"Take the goldsmith," she decided. "His son can apprentice through Lord Kotilus to learn the trade of horseflesh."

Tetramnestus nodded and brusquely re-rolled the scroll, gesturing with it at the goldsmith. The man hesitated, then led his family through the parted hoplites. The horse traders tried to push after them, wheedling their skills and value. Bronze shields eased them away.

"Elisha," bellowed Mot. "You must take us! It is our right!"

The farmers were aboard and another transport was away. The crew forced them below while they got the tubby freighter moving. Two hulls remained. Craftsmen swarmed aboard one, some of them looking back for a final glance at their city before going below decks.

She placed a hand on Hêgêsistratus hard shoulder. "Be ready." The helmet nodded.

The remaining townsmen had gotten a taste of her dream and were loath to relinquish it. They pressed against the hoplons, calling to her, begging, pleading, promising. Lumps of gold sailed over the ranks to land at her feet, desperate offerings.

"Zinnridi is moving his men closer," Hêgêsistratus noted. "He is considering hitting us when we break for the boats. A number of archers have joined his ranks."

"You must hold."

"Of course."

Fewer than ten craftsmen milled in the low surf beneath the cargo vessel's stern. A woman had become hysterical, sinking to her knees in the water, pulling at the sands. Her husband reasoned helplessly with her.

In the shadow of his own hull, Moryshot pranced about, not daring to speak, terrified of the gathering conflict.

An arrow thunked into a stern post. Elisha whirled. The city's formation was closer. Zinnridi watched imperiously. Another bow raised. He made no move to stop it.

The woman in the surf screamed again, a warbling cry of wretchedness.

"Get her aboard," Elisha demanded. The husband darted a glance to her, pulled his wife to her feet and slapped her. She thumped against the black hull.

An arrow rang off a hoplon.

Elisha looked back to see the woman being half-dragged, half-carried aboard. Her husband scrambled after her, followed by the others.

"Moryshot," she shouted.

"Aye, my lady."

"You are to load the dregs! The other craft will take the hoplites!"

"But my Queen, they are animals. They are less than..."

"Mot, load your people on that boat!" She gestured to Moryshot's craft. "Quickly!"

The hoplites opened enough to permit them entry. Several townsmen slipped into their numbers. One of them screamed and went down, an arrow shaft jutting from his back.

She glanced back to see Moryshot scrambling aboard his vessel, a wave of unwashed humanity on his heels. The commander of the other craft stood high on his stern, eyes on her, waiting.

"Hêgêsistratus!"

At her call, the general bellowed. "Lads, we are going to withdraw. The man who breaks faces me. As we drilled—_Sd_!"

The line backed to the water, a difficult maneuver. An arrow whizzed overhead.

Half the dregs were now aboard Moryshot's vessel. The crew drove them below with kicks and blows.

The Greek general had trained the men specifically for what was to follow. At his command, his left and right flanks turned and rushed for their boat. Shield and swords were flung recklessly aboard. The men swarmed up over the sides.

The enemy's wicker shields seemed close enough to touch.

"Get aboard, Highness!"

"I go when you go."

311

"Barbarian whore! I've no time for kingship games!" A portion of Zinnridi's line false-charged, keyed by bravado and a growing numeric advantage.

The last of the dregs were aboard. Moryshot screamed for his men to shove their hull clear.

Hêgêsistratus flung his sword at the enemy. It spun in a glittering arch. The city guard backed, shields up, skittish. A second of disruption was all he needed.

"To the boat!"

Again, hoplons, helmets, and swords rang across the deck as the men clambered up the hull. Hêgêsistratus literally threw Elisha up to the railing. She kicked her trim legs up, propelling herself aboard. The horizon began to move. Their ship free, the crew clambered up to join them.

Zinnridi's men stood at beach's end, shields aloft, bellowing after the exiles.

"Brave enough," Hêgêsistratus noted, "after we retired the field."

Their ship was only just gathering way. To port, Moryshot's vessel wallowed, its crew tripping over themselves to get oars out and sail deployed. A muffled disturbance carried over the water, growing louder as the hatches sprang open and the dregs swarmed back on deck. Mot, his legs dripping wet, looked across to Elisha and shook a fist.

The transport slowed, settling. Less and less freeboard was visible. The milling dregs interfered with Moryshot's crew, the ship losing all way. Before the gentle waves, the slowly sinking hull drifted backwards, a tremble marking the moment the stern ground into the sand. Pushed by wind and current, the bow slowly came parallel to the beach, a single oar flailing. Then the vessel settled, deck awash.

Moryshot ran in frantic circles, arms gesturing, feet kicking up a spray. His crew stood in numb realization of what little could be done.

"A timely accident." Hêgêsistratus observed wryly.

Elisha watched the crippled vessel rock in the cross-currents, saying nothing.

"Of course, I must admit I was suspicious," the general continued, "when I found that Aleyn carried a jug of wine to Os'sh, and then returned with it, only to immediately give it to Moryshot's crew with your blessings. How curious that the crew became almost comatose upon drinking it. One would expect more capacity from such a crew of mongrels."

"And what else did your keen eye observe?" Elisha inquired.

"Only that Aleyn and two trusted men rooted through the *Rear-End*'s carpentry box. I could not tell what they had taken, but I could clearly see what was missing—the saws used to cut away the pegs which hold a hull plank in place. Remove a number of pegs, low in the overhanging shadow where they would not be noticed, and the vessel will appear sound. Only when stressed, such as in launching into rough seas, will the plank fail. Then the sea rushes in and problems are solved."

Dregs were dropping from the ruined craft, wading ashore. Moryshot screamed after the departing fleet, words lost but meaning clear.

"Carthage could ill-afford the wastrels of Citium which Zinnridi attempted to foist upon us," she replied. "Mot and his people were disembarked, as promised. Moryshot will be paid his balance of gold when his hull touches Carthage's sand, as promised. Our word is kept."

"You remind me of Monca." The general's tone was flat. "Are there any other promises I should be aware of?"

The words stung, especially in their truth.

"The only promise I hold is to my people, my gods, and Carthage. It is my duty as queen."

The ship settled onto its tack. Farmers and craftsmen ventured onto the deck, crowding the railing, looking back at their receding homeland. As Elisha and Hêgêsistratus watched, the vessels of Carthage ran south in loose formation, driving for the distant headland. Sky and sea combined to turn the day glorious. The ships heeled before the wind, running hard, impatient for the west.

"A promise such as that, I can respect," Hêgêsistratus finally replied.

THE THIRD BOOK
ENTITLED TANIT

ONE

The small fleet sailed the final leg of their journey, the rising sun shimmering through tattered sails.

The hulls were salt-stained and waterlogged, the odor of unwashed bodies carried away on the breeze. They'd been five long weeks at sea, endless days of cautious beachings, bad rations and brackish water. Sickness and storms had challenged their determination and spirit. In the end, it made them into Carthaginians. Elisha's dream was shared by all.

They'd cruised past the western tip of Sicily the afternoon prior, swinging their bows southwest against the lengthening sun. Through the night, the ships had remained close, following each other's lamplights in headlong rush. Anticipation was rewarded with the dawn: twin peaks flared orange against a royal sky.

Elisha allowed herself a weary smile. They'd made it. Such were the landmarks Aleyn has described. From the supply transport rose Tetramnestus' prayers of thanksgiving. The colonists cheerfully called between the boats, reduced to children in the face of their success. Even the livestock, weary from their long confinements, raised a cacophony at the faint earth-scent.

Elisha's vessel lead her four sister ships into the vast bay. *RearEnd* held easy station, its multi-class crew grafted together by their journey. The two fisher craft followed like nervous ducklings. The tinker's lugger brought up the rear.

From the bow, Elisha's dark eyes took in the western hills, adorned with stands of hardwoods and outcroppings of stone. Opposite, a rugged peninsula capped by twin peaks formed the eastern coast. Their hard faces were softened in the haze of dawn.

South, the land flattened out. Distant reeds marked a vast marsh that all but separated the western landmass from the Libyan mainland. It was a site the Canaanites dreamed of.

RearEnd pushed past, oars at quarter speed. In the bow, Aleyn scanned the near bank for the landing he'd visited so many years ago. He nodded excitedly to Elisha and gestured forward. They were very close now.

Elisha saw Bitias in the penteconter's stern, conversing with the tillerman. His long hair and beard, so refined in courtly Tyre, fluttered in tangled disarray. With the burden of keeping the mismatched flotilla intact and moving, he'd lost weight. His long face now had a wolfish cast.

"There!" Aleyn's hoary hand lanced out. "There is the stream. This is the spot. Here shall be Carthage!"

Elisha leaned against the railing, taking it all in. Heavy trees hung over the cheerful rivulet. Beyond this, the land sloped upwards to form a hill promising visibility and defense.

Melqart, she thought, *it is everything I could have hoped for. If Arherbas could be here.* Then, strangely; *If only Pumayyaton could see my success.*

A call brought *RearEnd*'s oars up. The tiller eased her clear to port. Bitias looked back over the stern, a quiet smile on his face. He met her eyes, nodding to the beach.

Her ship's commander was a good man, knowing what to do without a word from her. The steering oars came over, the bow swung beachward. In respectful silence, the crew eased the ship in.

The grinding of Libyan sand beneath Canaanite wood echoed across the bay.

Elisha no longer needed a rope ladder. With an easy motion, she slipped over the side, dropping to the cool sands. A step, then another, and she stood clear of the *gôlah*'s prow, alone on the empty beach.

Birds chittered in the trees, the brook's whisper a backdrop. She closed her eyes and breathed deeply.

The sands felt cool beneath her feet, the sensation reminding her of Arherbas' love. She wiggled her toes playfully. A stillness cupped her soul, a personal silence that cradled her like the loving hand of her god.

To the colonists watching from just offshore, no speech could be more dramatic. The image of the raven-haired woman standing alone on the untouched shore would stay with them across the span of their lives.

The moment was timeless, but it could not last. A bow ground into the sand at her back, then another. Elisha's dark eyes opened once again, her breath easing from her lungs. The peace was over.

"My lady, we are ready to disembark." Hêgêsistratus was oddly subdued. "We await your word."

"Come ashore, general." She smiled. "Welcome to Carthage."

A grinding of sand beneath sandals. "Not much to look at, really. A bit rustic for my tastes. Still, a good enough site." Others were coming up behind him, men breastplated and armed, ready for anything. He stationed them with quick motions, three north, three south, three on the treeline, three in reserve at the boats. With the landing area secured, he turned to the colony's ruler.

"I'd like to send out three-men teams to investigate the immediate vicinity. Nothing much. Team south to look at the marsh, one to the top of that hill. Perhaps another north to follow the beachline."

Elisha nodded his suggestion into being. He quickly set forth his scouting parties. She was surprised to see Barcas entrusted to lead the team up the hill. A change had come across the boy she'd known since childhood. With surprisingly mature competence, he nodded at Hêgêsistratus' instructions. In moments, he and his two men disappeared into the thick brush.

Hêgêsistratus paused long enough to see to the affairs of his command before leading his own team towards the southern marshes. The other team moved north, cautiously following the beach.

Other ships grounded, one by one.

"Tetramnestus! Aleyn!" she called. "To me!"

The two man came as faithfully as dogs homing on their master. The priest rocked slowly; he was having problems readapting to land. She spoke first to the older seaman.

"Take ten men and remove the sails from all ships save the fishermen and one transport. Use the cloth and the ship's oars to construct tents on the upper beach."

"Aye, my lady!" Hunching forward in conspiracy, he flashed her a yellow grin. "Tents to warm and shelter us, and no sailing gear onboard the ships to tempt any from looking homeward, eh?"

"Second Officer, see to your duties."

"'Bl, my Queen! Moloch! And the rest of you! Forward to me. We have work, lads..."

To her aide: "Tetramnestus, I need the critical supplies unloaded in an orderly fashion. We cannot afford to spend time looking for lost items. The long-term stocks will remain aboard, the hulls serving as warehouses. The exception to this is the transport with canvas remaining. Have it emptied and ready to sail as quickly as possible."

"Of course, my lady." His eyes spoke of the obviousness of her statement. "I shall assign teams to do so. We should have the boats emptied by nightfall." A bow. "One thing, Highness. Construction of Melqart's temple should take precedence to all others."

"Of course. As soon as you get the supplies ashore, you may start searching for a suitable site."

"I have one in mind already." His piggy eyes played across the hill before him.

"Have Scylax assist you with the manifests."

"Of course. It is just...." Elisha flashed him an impatient glance. "He seems to balk at everything. It is as if his spirit has left him. I do not know how helpful he will be."

"If he tarries, tell me and I shall have someone detailed to deliver a kick to his posterior. We had no time for the dregs of Citium. Nor have we the time to coddle him." She turned from his final bow, spotting the penteconter's second officer passing armor down to the garrison.

Colonists lined the railings, looking over their new homeland. Others slid over the side, hungry to stand on solid ground after the weeks of travel.

"What can I do to help, my lady?"

She turned to find Os'sh standing respectfully. Elisha faltered for a moment. Something about the brown Scythian girl seemed different. True, she'd seen little of the former slave once they'd set out, the latter having spent her time aboard *RearEnd* with Bitias. Still, there was something about her that looked...

She checked her mental drift. There was simply no time for even a moment's idleness. She detailed her wishes; those sick and enfeebled by the journey would share one of the tents. The girl would center herself on seeing to their welfare, using whatever arts she had at her disposal.

"I can do little more than comfort them." Os'sh noted. "All my herbs and remedies are used up."

"Do whatever you can," Elisha responded as she turned away.

Others were directed to numerous tasks. Bakers built a fire for the first meal. Smiths assembled plows and tools. Younger boys herded their hungry livestock to a nearby patch of lush grass. Activity abounded.

Bitias leaned against penteconter's prow, arms crossed, smile lackadaisical.

"And what of me, Little Priestess? You've stripped my crew, my sails, and my oars. *RearEnd* is little more than an empty hulk. Shall I use her as kindling?"

"Of course not." She refused to be drawn by Bitias' baiting. "Someone needs to take the farmers inland along that creek. I am assuming the soil there will be the most fertile. We must clear the land."

"By 'we', I am assuming the royal 'we'."

"Yes, the farmers will clear the land. You shall supervise."

"The only supervision I know is to work alongside my subordinates." His smile challenged her. "I do not suppose you will be wielding an ax, will you, my Queen?"

"No, I shall not."

With a shrug, Bitias took a group of farmers a short distance inland. The afternoon passed on the butt-end of an axe, measured by the trickle of sweat. It was only when they returned to the beach at the end of the day that Bitias was thankful for his role and not hers.

They had just brought the boy's mauled body to the beach. It was placed at Elisha's feet.

The cold Libyan wind moaned around the boat. Within its hold, the newly-formed council of elders huddled over their evening meal. Outside, Tetramnestus led the Carthaginians through the burial prayers.

The assemblage was silent. Elisha cradled her clay bowl of soup, its warmth a balm to her chilled hands. In the light of the small lamps, she could see the weariness across the other's faces. Their first day had been met, but not without cost.

"Tell me," she said slowly, stirring her soup with a finger, "how we came to lose Abibaal?"

Across from her, Barcas slumped against the hull's slope, bowl and bread untouched. When he looked up, his face heavy with sorrow.

"We never saw the creature. Not until it was too late."

"I understand." Weariness doubled the effort of her patience. "I know you are reluctant to speak of it, but we must know what happened."

The young man nodded. "Very well. The three of us worked our way up slope. It is a good site—steep enough to aid in defense but not so much as to prohibit construction. However, halfway up, we found the remains of a small campfire."

"Describe it." Hêgêsistratus' gaze was intent.

"Old enough to have weeds growing amid the charred wood. Small enough to comfort two or three men. Probably hunters."

The Greek nodded, content with the level appraisal.

"As we climbed, the trickle of the stream dropped away. The spring is likely south of the hill. There were also some low rock outcroppings—not much. Probably enough stone for a small building or two. More will have to be found elsewhere."

Elisha thought of Tetramnestus' temple but said nothing.

"Eventually we broke through the treeline at the crown. There is a small meadow with good visibility in all directions. There were some scattered droppings, game-animals by the looks of it. Our minds were on the possibility of more recent campfires, and without thinking, we drifted apart as we searched." He paused. "Forgive me, Hêgêsistratus. I failed."

The Greek said nothing. He simply chewed his bread and motioned to continue.

"*Y!* And suddenly, the roar. I spun. There was a yellowed blur. Abibaal was down, the '*rw* hunched over him, tearing, clawing. The thing was like a demon, ferocious and devoid of pity."

"Such felines prowl the hills above Tyre," Bitias noted. "There, they fear the Canaanites and slink at the approach of men. The lions of Libya will have to be taught such lessons."

"To be truthful," Barcas confessed, "my only desire was to drive the beast away and recover Abibaal's body. Hirgab and I came at it from two directions. The creature turned towards him, roaring a warning. His neck was open to me—'*bl*, I simply stepped in and trust with my sword. There was a shower of blood and the thing was dead. As was Abibaal. And all because I did not exercise care."

There was a long silence, broken only by the wind playing across the deck overhead.

"Nonsense," Hêgêsistratus replied dismissively. "You were not dancing about the glade, picking flowers and cavorting like satyrs. You were looking for further signs of hunting parties. It was simply bad luck that one danger held your attention when another sprang."

"But I failed."

"Do not be an idiot." The Greek's words were harsh yet not unkind. In denying Barcas' self-pity, he was also denying Barcas' failure. The elder warrior gave it a moment to sink in before further observing, "Abibaal's death is unfortunate, but others will follow. Such are the dangers. On the other hand, I know of few warriors who would stand up to a lion without a spear and hunting party. To kill one alone is a mark of distinction." He took a noisy slurp from his bowl. "And, let it be said, the creature's meat is a welcome change from the brown bread we've subsided upon across the breadth of the Upper Sea."

"So Barcas has brought us meat and information." Elisha looked to her general. "What have you returned with?"

"Information only, my lady. But important information. As you know, I headed the southern team that advanced to the end of the forest, where it broke against the marshes. It was hard to see, what with the reeds and such, but my men and I agree. Far on the other side, well out on the plain, we saw crude buildings."

"A Libyan village." Elisha stared at the deck in thought. "So close."

"We believe there is evidence of farming. It appeared to be surrounded by uniform growth, most likely crops. And then we saw something that further disturbed us."

Elisha's dark eyes met his.

"A road, my lady. We saw a rutted road leading south across the low hills."

"Y, ill news indeed," Bitias opted. "Ruts imply carts. The natives understand wheels. And carts imply more surplus or trade than can be carried on one's back."

"Worse," the horsetrader Kotilus added. "A road means other villages. A network of trade, perhaps a Libyan kingdom. Once they learn of us, they could easily drive us into the sea."

"How large was this village?" Elisha asked bluntly.

The Greek shrugged. "Hard to say, given the distance and low angle. Perhaps a dozen crude stone houses. Twenty at most."

She sat for a long moment, face set. "A great deal may be gleaned from this. Even with fertile farmlands, their village is still small. They are civilized to the point of forming communities, but not to a level that will allow them to support a denser population. Our technology might give us an edge."

"An iron edge, if it comes to that." Nobody argued with Hêgêsistratus' observation.

"And you were not seen?"

"No. We remained low, the marshes are broad, and the village a long way off. However, that is not to say we can remain beneath their noses for any length of time. Aside from the occasional hunting parties Barcas identified, there is also our own encampment. Today we had cooking fires. Within a day or so, we will have to burn the fields clear to permit the planting of our crop. And should a villager come far enough east to see into the bay, he would be certain to spot our fishing boats at work." He collected the last of his soup in the crook of his finger. "I figure that soon, my little Elisha, you will have to deal with the Libyans."

"We will face this when it occurs. Until then, I want men posted at the marsh's edge. Remain out of sight. Report anything observed." The general nodded at the instructions.

Footsteps clumped across the decking overhead. A moment later, Tetramnestus eased his bulk through the hatchway. He was surprised when all stood in respect.

"Welcome, Holy Lord," Elisha said solemnly.

"Sit, sit," he told them, clearly uncomfortable with the rank he'd gained. "I am still not used to being the chief servant of Melqart.

"Give him time," Bitias observed, "and he will grow to fit the rank."

"You have given Abibaal to Mot?" Elisha asked, ignoring her ex-lover.

"Aye. Honors due to the dead have been bestowed. As for the colony, the supplies have all been off-loaded. The tools are distributed, the people organized. Tomorrow I wish to begin work on the temple. It should be placed on the hill behind us, looking out over the bay."

"How many men will you require?"

"Five men to clear and level the site while I perform the consecration rites. Following this, the initial temple can be raised with wood from a transport or from the newly-felled trees. While this is taking place, we will need a source of blocks."

"Barcas knows where there is stone and is familiar with the hillside. He and two others will be detailed to guard you."

The holy lord nodded absently; his safety was not his primary concern. "We need blocks cut as quickly as we can. Carthage's survival depends on Melqart being satisfied with the speed with which we erect his true temple."

The listening council nodded, knowing this to be true. Elisha added, "As soon as the fields are cleared and the seed in the ground, we will detail a larger body of men to assist you." The holy lord nodded in satisfaction.

This done, she returned her attention to the admiral.

"Bitias, are you ready to begin your task tomorrow?"

"'Bl. The gifts have been selected. The crew has been picked. At

dawn, we will take this transport and depart the bay to the west."
He hesitated. "I still think that I should take *RearEnd*."

"I wish to make contact and exchange greetings with the community of Utica, not threaten them into submission. Since they are Canaanites, it should be simple to gain their support. Remember, they have dwelt on this coast far longer than we. Their knowledge is critical to our success."

"*Y*, worry not. I shall control my common mannerisms and gain them as allies. A day to reach them, a night to chat, and back to Carthage on the following. No doubt you will have towers built and ramparts erected by then."

Elisha ignored his wit. "Is there anything else...?"

"One last matter, my lady." It was Bitias again. Elisha almost rounded on him before realizing that his manners were true, his expression earnest.

"Yes, Commander?"

"There is something I would request before I depart. This very night, if I might be so bold." He met the eyes of every member of the council. "I wish to be bound to Os'sh, husband and wife. We seek the service of marriage."

Elisha felt a chill run down her spine. She could accept that Os'sh now occupied her place at Bitias' side. Yet she'd always entertained the thought that there was still a chance to regain his love. Once Carthage was established and the dangers overcome, she would be free to follow her heart.

But not now. The door to Bitias had slammed directly in her face.

With the same control that had kept her motionless beneath the rug while Pumayyaton hunted her, she maintained her composure. Her face was stone, her breath steady, her eyes unblinking.

"Can this not wait? You could wed her upon your return."

Perhaps you might reconsider. Perhaps you will once more discover your love for me.

"Highness, my Os'sh is with child. Astarte blessed us that night in her temple. Our infant will be the first true Carthaginian."

Elisha sat quietly for a moment.

It is truly over.

"Very well," she replied. "Who shall conduct the service?"

"We had hoped that High Priest Scylax would do us the honor. After all, Os'sh was in Astarte's service. The child was conceived within the temple's walls. It would only be fitting for Lord Scylax to officiate."

"Me?" Until now, the Citiumian priest had silently watched the new council go about its business. Now he was on his feet. "You wish me to perform the service?" His face darkened. "Do you know what you did to me? To my life? I was the high priest of Astarte, equal in power to Governor Zinnridi. And then you came, like barbarians. You destroyed my temple and my goddess!"

The council was silent in the face of the accusation. Finally, Elisha said, "But Lord Scylax, our actions were within the codex of your temple. The service of each woman was paid for. Gold was yielded. It was all by the rules."

"Listen to your words. You are no better than that viper Monca, she who remained true to her word while slowly poisoning Hêgêsistratus. You did nothing but distort temple law, to use our order as a lever against Zinnridi. And in that, you cost me Astarte."

"But we did nothing against the goddess."

"*N*'! As if this was the truth. Can you not see? When you twisted the services to the goddess to meet your needs, you challenged her. You threw tradition in our faces. I expected death for such transgressions. In fact, that was partially the reason I left Citium with your exiles. I wished to see Astarte work her will against you. I wanted to be there when your ships sank or some pestilence struck you down. But you have founded your Carthage. You have achieved your goal. The goddess did not act. Such *wrongness* has lodged in my heart. I found doubt in Citium, and the further we journeyed, the more distant my goddess became."

"Faith is a matter of commitment," Tetramnestus pointed out.

"Commitment? I have committed my entire life to the service of Astarte!" The skinny priest's face worked. "In devotion to Her, I cut away my manhood! It is the way of our priests. And after showing me the lie, that my goddess is gone and my life is wasted, you wish me to preside at your wedding?" At the moment of total loss of control, Scylax managed to catch himself. He cast a final glare at Bitias and Elisha before clambering through the hatchway.

There was a long silence following his departure. Finally, Bitias broke it.

"Perhaps this was a bad idea. I did not know of Scylax's resentment."

"Nonsense." Tetramnestus took the admiral by the shoulder with his meaty hand. "You and your woman should be married. Here and now. Astarte might not be present, but Melqart most certainly is. We shall proceed immediately."

Elisha wondered about the holy lord's sudden drive. He knew about her desire for the admiral. His marriage would make things far safer.

"A final issue remains on this matter," Bitias admitted. "I have nothing to offer for the *kusata,* the wedding gift. I have not a single shekel of metal to my name."

"You do have something you can give," the holy lord noted. "You can promise to give Carthage your skills, your blood, and your life. You can give our city your soul."

"I have," the admiral noted. "And I shall."

"Someone fetch the bride," Hêgêsistratus yawned. "It grows late."

TWO

Three days passed. Bitias did not return.

Elisha sat on the beach beneath the noon sun, picking at her fish-paste. Behind her, huts were coming into being. Smoke curled up from the forest where the fields were being cleared. And high on the hill, a cleared site marked the location of Melqart's newest temple. Tetramnestus drove his men like slaves. Already, foundation stones had been cut and placed, followed by the first of the walls.

With all the activity, it was only at rest when their weary minds could mull over their emissary's fate. Could Bitias have met with disaster at the hands of the Uticans? Could pirates inhabit this coastline? The natives?

Os'sh trudged from the stream, twin buckets yoked across her shoulders, water for the infirm in the nearby tents. The brown woman paused, looking past Elisha towards the sea. Looking for her man.

Elisha felt something deep within her, something dark. It was as if Bitias' fate could be countered by the Scythian's distress. Elisha found surprise in this. Until now, she'd not held any grudge towards Os'sh. Or so she'd thought.

How, in the midst of foundation, can I find time for such base jealousy? How can I wish ill-fortune on Bitias and Os'sh? I am beyond that.

But the inner-voice could not overcome her inner-doubt.

Os'sh continued up to the tents. Out on the bay, the fishermen tacked about after elusive schools. Wood smoke drifted down from the slope. The fields would be ready for seeding within the next few days. Men would have to be detailed to safeguard the plantings, to keep the birds and animals away. So much was at stake with the first harvest.

A distant cry rode over the waves.

From a punt's bow, a fisherman gestured north.

A blunt trader swung around the headland. Elisha squinted. It *was* their missing vessel!

The cry was taken up along the shoreline. From the stone cutters on the hillside temple, from the laborers dragging wood to the fire, from the women working on the huts, a welcoming jubilation arose. Os'sh swept past, eyes on the distant ship. She turned and flashed Elisha a smile of innocent happiness. Elisha did her best to return it.

Eventually the craft maneuvered onto the beach. Bitias leapt down into Os'sh's arms, giving her a fierce hug, only to blanch at the perceived risk he'd placed upon his child. She laughed at his overdeveloped fatherhood and play-cuffed him. Elisha waited until the merriment had subsided before speaking.

"You are late."

"Er. Yes," the admiral agreed. "The people of Utica were most enthusiastic to be neighbors to a new colony. It is a pretty hard lot for their station. They can only see things improving if Canaanite presence on this coast is solidified."

"And you were late because..."

"Oh, yes. Well, they were quite impressed with your gifts and felt the need to repay us. There was a celebration in our honor. Much wine, food, entertainment..."

"...and women?" Os'sh inquired.

"Not for me. I've already sown all my seed. Anyway, they gave us a gift in return, something we should find very useful." He shouted to the boat behind him. "Afsan!"

A young man appeared on the deck. At first Elisha attributed the brown of his skin to the glare of the sun. Then he slipped down to the sands to stand beside Bitias, and she saw that his skin was, indeed, dark. Not as dark as the Kush slaves she'd seen, but darker than hers.

His tunic was worn yet maintained with meticulous care. His eyes were like twin almonds, studying her with quiet intent. Most strange was his hair—his long beard and hair had been curled in the manner of a Canaanite man, regardless of its kinky stiffness. It simply was not suited to the styles of her people but yet he wore it thus.

"This is Afsan," Bitias nodded. "He is a native of these parts."

Elisha blinked. So here was a Libyan! She redoubled her study of him.

"He was a gift to the Utican settlement. As a child, he was sent to live with them, to be an interpreter. But trade has permitted Utica and Libyans to understand one another well enough, so they gave him to us."

"I are Afsan," the dark young man bowed to Elisha.

"I am Queen Elisha of Carthage. These people are mine. One day, we shall become great. And your people will achieve greatness at our side."

"I am of Canaan," Afsan said with conviction. "I not Libii. I am of Canaan."

"It is humorous," the admiral explained. "He has lived at the settlement so long, he patterns himself as one of us."

"He *is* one of us," Elisha replied. "He is now a Carthaginian."

"I is..." Afsan paused. "I are..."

"Am," she prompted.

"I am Carthaginian." Afsan's conviction was solid.

Someone snickered. At Elisha's glare, someone found silence.

"I have done as you bid, my lady," Bitias noted. "I have made relations with our neighbors and gained an interpreter. Now, may I be with my wife, to whom I have been long absent?"

"You may be with her," Elisha granted, "in the tent of the infirm. She has work to do."

"Then her work is mine."

Elisha nodded her permission, knowing that he might not have agreed had he known of the diarrhea that was sweeping the ranks of the sick. Still, Os'sh needed the assistance.

"My lady, your generosity was appreciated," Afsan's smile was both earnest and yellow. "I find it wondrous. You had my thanks."

She looked critically at the young man. "Your road will be hard,

Afsan. My people are closed and clannish, not welcoming of foreigners."

"But you is the foreigners in Libii."

"You know well what I mean. You may feel alone and apart. But prove yourself to us and you will become one of us."

"But I is one," Afsan protested. A pause, then a nod. "But I understand. I will prove myself. I shall became true Carthaginian." He thought hard for a moment. "Tell your servant, my lady, what knows you of Libii?"

Elisha began walking along the shore, running a hand along the prow of each of her boats. "What do we know of this place we have come to call our home?" A laugh. "Nothing."

"Then you shall know of *Gld* Hiarbas. To knew him is to knew Libii."

"*Gld*? I know not this word."

"*Gld* is Libii. It is similar to your *r'sh*."

"So Hiarbas is a chieftain?"

Afsan halted to gain her attention. "Yes *and* no. You are a *mlk*, a queen. Your power be absolute. But you are only a *mlk* of this." His brown hand waved towards make-shift Carthage.

"On my other hand, *Gld* Hiarbas. His power is not absolute. But it is not absolute over many villages."

Elisha paused. Her interpreter was more than a rebuilder of words. He could recognize the different ways power was wielded. Bitias had not brought her nearly so much after three days of carousing.

"How many villages is Hiarbas not absolute over," she asked. "Ten? Fifteen?"

Discomfort appeared in Afsan's eyes. Elisha realized he could not count. His Utican masters had clearly not seen any need.

"This many?" She opened both hands, showing all ten fingers.

The sea breeze ruffled his beard as he considered. He opened both hands. Then again. A pause. A third time.

Thirty villages. Elisha felt wavering doubt. Assuming that central villages would be far larger than the peripheral one at the marsh's far bank, this Hiarbas might have a thousand or more warriors at his beck and call.

Elisha probed deeper. "You said *Gld* Hiarbas did not have absolute control over his villages. What control does he have?"

"Each village has a lord. Lords support *gld*. *Gld* commands lords."

"*Gld* commands lords?"

"Aiya, Lady." Afsan now had a teacher's air to him. "*Gld* commands lords, but not like Queen Elisha commands the Carthaginians."

"Exactly how is this different?"

Afsan rummaged through his imperfect vocabulary. Finally, his eyes fell on the fishing craft that worked the bay. He smiled and pointed.

"*Gld* Hiarbas is as the sails. He moves the people of Libii where the wind will take them. But Queen Elisha is the rudder. Her people go where steers she."

She nodded at his summation. "And what of his armies? What of his weapons of war?"

"*Oglh*."

She was not sure she'd heard correctly. "Chariots?"

At her incredulous look, he pantomimed with both hands. One hand a horse, the other, a horizontal platform. "*Oglh*. But only for chieftain and lords. Armies; spears, shields."

"His weapons; are they stone? Or are they bronze? Iron?"

"Aiya," he muttered, trying to remember such details.

A voice called her name. She looked up to see Hêgêsistratus striding across the beach towards them. He looked winded, as if he'd covered distance in haste.

The Greek's eyes fell on the small dark man at her side. "What is this, a little pet Canaanite someone trained? How clever."

"General, this is Afsan, our Libyan interpreter. Bitias gained him from the Uticans."

"Keep it out of my way." He tossed his chin over his shoulder. "I just came up from the marsh. You remember that village across the way from us?" She gave him a nod. "Well, a small road column just entered. Tents are going up, natives running around pointing in our direction." His aged face broke into a wry smile. "It appears Carthage's fame is spreading."

A trumpet call mournfully rose from the marshes.

Work stopped. The Carthaginians froze, tools motionless, every head cocked southwards. A single note would tell of Libyans moving in force from the neighboring village.

A second note echoed into the sky.

All but Elisha relaxed. Two blasts denoted the approach of a diplomatic party. Had it been war, every man and woman of the settlement would have formed behind the hoplites to fight to the death. Now that the result lay with words, she alone would determine their fate.

Men rushed past her, making for the armor arrayed on the beach. Hêgêsistratus berated his warriors towards greater speed. She caught a glimpse of Bitias among them. A moment later, his bronze helmet slid down and he was just another hoplite.

Tetramnestus wandered past them, calling her name. Apprentices followed, shouldering urns filled with ornate jewelry and crafted curios.

"I am here, Holy Lord!"

"We have brought the gifts and offerings we agreed to. Again, I advise you to follow Lord Kotilus' advice and let him negotiate with the Libyans. We have no idea how they might view dealing with a queen rather than a king."

"They shall have to get used to it," she tutted. "Where is Afsan?"

"He comes. He has been assisting Os'sh with the infirm."

The little Libyan scrabbled up, adjusting his robes and hair to match Canaanite standards. Before he could say anything, Hêgêsistratus shoved past him to report.

"All are ready. As agreed, ten men will come with us as an honor guard. The others will remain here on alert."

"Move them back into the trees," Elisha instructed, "lest they roast in their armor."

The general nodded and called an order. Forty hoplites retired into the shadows. The remaining ten formed on Elisha's party. She took a moment to critically study them.

"Let us meet our hosts."

It had been three days since the first activity at the nearby village. An observation post had been established on the north bank of the marsh, the observers keeping a careful watch. The movement between colony and post had worn a path.

Someday, mused Elisha, *this might be the main road into our capital city.*

Forty minutes across broken countryside brought them to a crude campsite within a small wood. At the foliage's terminus, three men looked out over the marshes. One glanced back and nodded to the arrivals.

The air was heavy with the smell of brine. The marsh reeds hissed and creaked, bending before a breeze off the Upper Sea. Pink flamingos clustered on the muddy flats.

She looked further. Yes, there were the Libyans.

"*Oglh.*" Afsan sounded smug.

"Yes, I see," Elisha noted, dark eyes upon the small column. In the van, three chariots bounced through the high grass. The first two were drawn by twin horses, the larger one following harnessed four. Twenty men followed in their ruts.

"Only ten of the footmen are armed," echoed Hêgêsistratus' opinion from the dark recess of his helm. "The rest must be priests or officials." His tone dismissed them as inconsequential.

At his shoulder, another hoplite shook his head slowly. "Beautiful. Simply beautiful." The voice was that of Lord Kotilus. "Look at how wonderfully those steeds are proportioned. I do not think I have seen their equal anywhere. Oh, the brisk authority of their step."

"Perhaps you can bargain for some," Elisha noted, "should we survive. Afsan, who are these people?"

"I know not personally those princes in the forward chariots. They are no doubt local lords of high standing. The large chariot, that be Chieftain Hiarbas."

Elisha's dark eyes narrowed. They were still too distant to make out details.

"Let us not startle them," she decided. "We should step clear of cover so they see us."

It took but a moment for Hêgêsistratus to dress his men into two ranks. With Elisha in the lead, flanked by her translator and gift bearers, they stepped into the sunlight.

A Libyan lord spotted them and called out, gesturing with an ornate wand. The column shifted to follow the marshline. The rumble of the wheels rose.

"Should those chariots charge," Hêgêsistratus' voice spoke authoritatively behind her, "we fall back into the trees."

At twice the distance of a javelin throw, the native column ground to a halt. The two Libyan nobles rolled outward to permit their chieftain to come forth. Silently, he studied the bronze men.

And Elisha studied back. He was tall and broad, his ruddy skin marked by ritualistic tattoos. His protruding brow and cheekbones cast his eyes in shadows. A short beard forked from his rounded chin, and from a crude scalp lock, three colorful ostrich feathers hung.

Hiarbas casually turned and said something to the men behind him. A moment later, a spearman dashed from the ranks, running forward. There came a slight rasp as the hoplites stiffened. Elisha held out a hand to steady them, her eyes on the solitary runner.

Reaching an old driftwood log midway between the two bodies, the man set aside his shield and spear. From his belt, he pulled a strip of white linen which he bound around a branch. With that, he collected his armaments and retired.

From the branch, the white cloth stirred in the uncertain breeze.

The Libyans watched with imperial calm.

"By Melqart's steaming piles," came Aleyn's voice. "I do not believe it."

"Second," Elisha hissed without turning her head. "If you know what this means, speak of it."

"They have marked the log. They wish to trade."

"Trade," she frowned. "What do you mean?"

"It is how things are done along this coast," the penteconter's second officer replied from the ranks. "The natives see a Canaanite trade ship, they leave such a mark and hide. The merchants approach the marked spot and leave the goods they wish to trade away, then retire to their ship. Then the natives cautiously approach, and without touching the offered goods, lay out their own goods, which they hold as an appropriate exchange. They return to hiding and the Canaanites approach again. If the exchange meets their expectations, they take the native goods. Otherwise, they alter their own offerings. They back away, and now it is the native's turn. When either side determines that a suitable exchange has been forwarded, they take the other's goods and depart."

"How long can this go on?"

The armored man shrugged. "Days, sometimes."

"And neither side is ever tempted to take both sets of goods?"

Aleyn's helmet shifted slightly; she sensed he was looking at her oddly. "Highness, to violate the sanctity of the exchange would be to invalidate *all* trade. Who would consider such a thing?"

"I am not here to quibble for native baubles," Elisha grated. "I am here to establish our homeland. I am here to negotiate our existence." She paused, looking back to the Libyans. Hiarbas could have been carved from stone. Realization grew within her.

"They wish us to trade for the land we've claimed." Her thoughts rose unbidden from her lips. "They seek compensation." To Afsan: "What did the men of Utica offer for their land?"

"That were many years ago; a different chieftain, different dirt. Even should I know..." A shrug.

Elisha motioned for bearers. Frowning, she rummaged through their urns, pulling out pieces of jewelry. Some were treasures, some were trash. She had no basis for her choices, having scant idea of the natives' perception of value. In Tyre, such could purchase a ship like *RearEnd*. The trouble was, this wasn't Tyre. This wasn't like anything.

The grass whispered as she started forward, offerings glimmering in her hands. Hiarbas' eyebrow rose at her approach, clearly surprised by the outlanders' representative.

With care, she settled each piece on the weathered log, placing them to best effect. They represented the range of her people, from stunning works of originality to cheap imitations of Egyptian goods. She cast the natives a level gaze before withdrawing.

Hiarbas waited well after she'd cleared. He looked into the sky as if judging it, then whisked at some flies that hovered about. Finally, he started his chariot forward with all the speed of an oxcart. He drew abreast of the log, casually viewing the Carthaginian offerings.

And then he laughed.

His laugh was rich and deep, rolling over the reeds to the small body of hoplites. It boomed on and on.

There was no humor in it.

Like lightning from a sunny sky, his whisk slapped at the offerings, scattering them like a beggar's baubles. The words were hard, his eyes flashing at Elisha.

"What does he say?"

"I cannot repeat such vile things," Afsan replied.

Meanwhile, one of the lesser nobles in the two-horsed chariots lunged forward, rolling up aside his chieftain, a brownish cylinder clutched in his hand. After a final scathing insult, Hiarbas thrust a hand blindly to the noble at his side. The man gave him the item which he unrolled with a disdainful flick. It was an oxhide, dried and treated. He flung it into the scattered jewelry and rolled back to his men, his lieutenant following. From there, he turned and barked some last coarse words.

Elisha looked to Afsan.

"He say," the native replied, "that for those trinkets, you can have the land encompassed by the hide."

Elisha took a moment to study the oxhide as well as the men beyond it.

"Too quick," Kotilus noted. Elisha twisted a questioning look back at him. The horse trader nodded to the exchanges. "He hardly looked at our offerings. And his assistant had that oxhide ready. They were set to reject any offer we made."

"Why?"

"A very basic opening move. They wish to pry more wealth out of us, so they offer us their lowest possible position from the very start knowing full well we cannot build a city within an oxhide." The armored helm shrugged. "The question is, how much will it take to shift them to a realistic offer?"

She looked at Kotilus without seeing, deep in thought. Then she turned to the diminutive interpreter.

"Afsan, you must recall Chieftain Hiarbas' exact words. The Canaanite words you give to us must be correct." She paused for effect. "A single wrongly-translated word could result in war. I ask you one final time; what exactly did he say?"

Afsan scratched at his wiry beard, eyes pinched shut, thinking hard. When his eyes opened, they held a measured calm.

"'For these trinkets, you miserly whoresons may claim the land encompassed by this oxhide.'"

Elisha studied him a moment longer. She gestured for an urn and selected a large exquisite chain of gold worth more than a commoner might earn over his entire lifetime. She draped it over her arm and started forward.

Insects buzzed from the nearby swamp, and gnats rose in clouds from the grass disturbed by her passage. On the log, the scattered jewelry glimmered against the buff animal skin. Hiarbas watched from his chariot, his eyes on the adornment she carried.

Elisha stopped before the log and looked at the settlement's offerings and the single skin. She stooped as if to include the new piece. When she came up, her hands contained the gold chain. And the skin.

Hiarbas' mouth dropped open. A moment later, his lords were gesturing at her while yammering at him. She smiled sweetly before turning.

Kotilus broke ranks at her approach. He'd yanked his helmet off in consternation.

"*Y*, Highness, what have you done? You have accepted his offer!"

"Of course," she replied, tossing the jewelry back into the urn, the hide bunched under her arm. "I am a Canaanite, a member of a race of traders. The exchange is to our favor."

Hiarbas' own yell boomed over any possible reply from the horse trader. Afsan waited for the chieftain to finish before converting the words for his mistress.

"He wish to see you place your tiny city."

Moving past the small man, she replied, "Tell him that we will choose our land tomorrow when the sun reaches its zenith. Tell him to come, so he can acknowledge what belongs to Carthage. What belongs to us."

THREE

"**I** do not like this, Little Priestess." Bitias' scowl was total. "*Lys*, I do not like this at all."

"What is there not to appreciate?" Elisha checked the fall of her robes. In the rear of the tent, Os'sh rooted through jewelry, picking pieces that would enhance the queen's regalness. The shadows outside were vertical; midday had come.

Selecting her favorite headband more for luck than decorum, she added, "I explained how this will work. Two ox were sacrificed and the tinkers have worked through the night. Has anything been neglected?"

"All is as you specified. My men are in place, the fires going. It is only..."

"Yes?" Her eyes were cool.

The admiral gathered himself. "It is only that once again, you are engaging in trickery on a grand scale. Hiarbas might not appreciate the game you play with words. What if he objects? What if he should attack? Our men are scattered through the woods, playing their part of your little amusement."

"His own men are back in the village. By the time he could assemble his forces, our men would be armored and ready." She checked herself a final time in the mirror Os'sh held. "I am willing to risk battle on this."

"We could simply pay Hiarbas a suitable price for the land of Carthage."

"We offered him a suitable sum and he tried to pry more from us. I will not throw away our wealth."

"What else can we buy with it, Elisha? We exist on a desolate coast. Those rubies around your neck are nothing more than pretty stones!"

"I have plans for our wealth. Plans that do not involve Hiarbas."

"Speaking of the chieftain," Os'sh noted, "he has arrived."

True to her words, the trio of chariots broke from the southern woods. Five warriors loped through the dust of their noble's wheels.

Without a word, Elisha left the tent, striding towards a small body of men collected around a bench on the open beach. As if magically summoned, Afsan appeared at her side. From the tent's opening, Bitias watched the trim girl wave to the distant chieftain. Frowning, he set a gentle hand on Os'sh's slight belly. "Should something happen, you are to flee into the woods."

"Fleeing into the woods will simply delay the inevitable. Should something happen, I will stand with the hoplites and share their fate."

"*N*'! I thought fleeing was what Scythians do best."

"I am no longer Scythian, Bitias. I am Carthaginian."

"*Y*, now even *you* share Elisha's foolishness." He ran a calloused palm along her smooth cheek before stepping from the tent.

Elisha took a place before a large bench, the oxhide carefully spread across it. Second Officer Aleyn stood silently behind her, as did the head tinker. Several young men, Moloch and Barcas among them, stood nearby in casual readiness. Bitias joined them.

The four horse team thundered to a stop in a burst of sand. From his chariot's platform, Hiarbas paused to look down upon them before dismounting. The ostrich feathers in his scalp lock fluttered in the sea breeze. He waited until his escort had formed up behind him before speaking.

"I be Hiarbas," Afsan translated. "I rule over people, dwellings, sheep, and cattle beyond measure. My lands stretch from the northern waters to the southern deserts. My armies are great. My powers limitless." The chief tipped his head back. "You will fear me."

"I am Elisha," she replied, the translator's articulations echoing her. "I rule these people of the sea. My city, Carthage, shall rise from this spot."

The headman studied her for a long moment, his expression dubious. Finally he spoke again.

"He wishes to see your magic," Afsan translated. "He wishes to see how you site your town within the oxhide."

"Tell him he shall. But first, there is something we must do. His patience is appreciated." Turning to the tinker, she asked, "Do you have it?"

"Aye," the old man replied. He carefully produced a knife whose ivory handle flashed in the sun. It was the gift that had gone from Arherbas to Qurdi-Aššur-lamur to Zinnridi to herself. Holding it butt-first, he added, "Be wary—its blade is sharper than the truth, more cutting than a lie. My son spent all night honing it."

"Will this suffice, Aleyn? Bitias said you were the best canvas worker aboard *RearEnd*."

The second took the blade, touching it against his thumb. A line of scarlet appeared. He gave a nod of acceptance.

"Begin," she instructed.

The gangly man hunched over the hide. With great concentration, he moved the knife, tracing the edge of the skin. But not quite tracing. The thinnest sliver of leather peeled back, little more than a thread. Barcas stepped forward without a word, collecting it. Aleyn seemed not to notice, so focused was he on pealing away another ribbon.

Barcas remained until ten of the threads were draped between his hands. Without a word, he turned and ran south along the beech. The Libyans watched him go.

"Hiarbas ask if this is a service to some god of yours."

Elisha smiled. "Tell him that this is part of a service to gain our new homeland."

More strips peeled away. Another boy with ten threads pounded off, this time north. The hide was slightly diminished.

The sun flickered off the knife in Aleyn's hand, making the chieftain squint. The nobles flanking him murmured quietly. Another lad pounded off south.

Hiarbas gestured and gobbled. From Afsan came his words.

"What is this service you conduct? I have visited the Canaanites of the Utica settlement many times. I been in their temple to Melqart. I see your worships. This is like nothing done there."

Elisha watched the blade's steady slice. "Ask the Chieftain if he has been across the Upper Sea."

Afsan jabbered. Hiarbas frowned.

"Ask him if he has been to Sicily," she continued. "Or to the splinter islands of Greece? Or distant Cyprus? Ask him if he has seen the lands from which the sun rises." She looked back, meeting the chieftain's eye. "I have come from these places. I bring with me their ways. These things we do might seem strange but soon they will make perfect sense."

Hiarbas listened, then smiled.

Afsan: "Warriors with skins of bronze made no sense. Women rulers make no sense. A city on a skin makes no sense. I await the wisdom of distant lands." A gut-launched laugh.

"All shall become clear," she smiled. More young men dashed away. A third of the hide was gone. A drip from Aleyn's forehead patted onto the leather, instantly absorbed.

The wind shifted slightly. The chief sniffed the air, a scowl playing across his face.

"Cooking," Afsan translated. "You cook us a feast."

"Not for him," Elisha replied. "Animal fat from our oxen. Part of our preparation."

The translator shifted to the Libyan tongue, but already Hiarbas was staring at the half-gone hide. An unpleasant realization formed his face. Just then, another strip-bearer dashed away. Hiarbas watched him run, then barked over his shoulder. A warrior dropped his shield and weapon and ran after the departing youth. The Libyan did not attempt to gain; he merely followed. A second warrior was sent south, to the woods where so many threads had gone.

"He suspects." Bitias' voice monotoned into her ear. "It is too late, of course. But I think he senses your scheme."

Another fifth of the hide was whittled away. Two more lads ran off, their headings more westerly than their predecessors.

Hiarbas' dark scowl alternated between Elisha and the skin.

Aleyn cursed as a strip tore at mid-point. "The knife grows dull."

"Of no matter," Elisha told him, eyes on one of the distant Libyan warriors racing back to his chieftain.

"The blade betrays me. My cuts grow uneven."

"Bitias claimed you were the best. Shall I summon Os'sh to complete the task?"

"*B'sh*," the second officer spat. Gritting his yellowed teeth, he refocused on his cut. The strip came away in razor-thin fineness.

The warrior panted up. His words were incomprehensible. His pantomime involved many horizontal gestures.

"Aye, he knows," Bitias muttered.

Hiarbas stepped directly up to Elisha, yammering indignantly. To the side, Afsan attempted to keep up. "...was not our bargain...you twist me words.... simmering pots of evil magic...black webs within the trees..."

Beneath the blade, the remainder of the hide was rapidly disappearing. Runners pressed up, collecting their share before bolting away.

Elisha waved the chieftain into angry silence. To Afsan; "Tell him to follow me." She crossed the beach towards the hill.

The Libyans followed with Hiarbas barking after her, Afsan's censured translation so much noise. The trees broke the light into uncertain shadows, the canopy trapping the pungent odor of boiled animal fat. Distantly came the sound of small mallets tapping.

Midway up the hill stood the partially-constructed temple of Melqart. Standing before the waist-high stone walls, Holy Lord Tetramnestus prepared a pyre. The remains of two gutted oxen lay draped across the bone-dry kindling.

"Majesty," he called out. "Shall we begin the prayers of thanksgiving?"

"Proceed at once," she replied as she passed. "But pray for success. Immediate success."

Tetramnestus watched the mixed party of Libyans and Carthaginians hurry past the temple. Then he motioned an aide to bring forth the flaming brand.

They broke out across the bald summit. Below and behind them shimmered the bay. A hundred yards north up the beech, a small figure stood, braced feet awash in the warm waters. Another figure stood a short distance up the beech from him; another just before the trees, forming a loose line. A similar group appeared an equal distance to the south.

A young oarsmen ran past her, leather strips flapping over his shoulder. The stink of fat and the tapping of mallets rose from the woods on the far slope of the hill. The Libyans toiled behind her, their voices dangerously harsh. Following them, Afsan looked worried. Bitias brought up the rear.

Elisha turned, her hard gaze locked on the chieftain. "Remind him of his words, Afsan. Repeat them to him. Exactly as you told them to me."

The little man swallowed, then began speaking in low guttural tones. Even through she could not understand the sounds, the words formed in her head.

For these trinkets, you miserly whoresons may claim the land encompassed by this oxhide.

Hiarbas stood, mute. Elisha's own expression was frank. Afsan looked from one to the other, useless in the silence.

Gracefully, Elisha turned on her heel, robes parting the high grass. A moment later, she was passing through the scattered trees of the reverse slope. Hiarbas and his party followed, strung out in a line.

A small band of Carthaginians stepped from some trees to the north. One carefully carried a pot which emitted pungent odors. Another, a tinker, stood with a hammer in one hand, a flat stone in the other. His pouch jingled. A half dozen men watched expectantly as another runner approached. The leather threads were quickly distributed among the onlookers. The tinker moved among them, positioning the ends of the threads on his flat rock before fetching small bronze clips from his pouch. The clips were tapped closed, joining the ends of the thread. Carefully, the men moved apart, bringing the fragile string horizontal. The man with the pot moved between them, wiping the line with warm animal fat. With care, they moved farther apart.

The thread stretched, vibrated, yet held.

Another team moved around a tumble of rocks to the south, calling greetings to their counterparts. Thread was distributed to them. Their line grew.

A runner topped the hill: Barcas.

"This is the last," he shouted. "There is no more!"

Elisha gestured him over. With Bitias, she moved between the two endpoints. They were still one hundred feet apart.

Hiarbas crossed his large arms, his face split with a dark frown.

"Quickly, quickly," she called. A tinker came up. With light taps, he clipped the pieces together.

A reek washed over her from the pot-bearer. While he massaged his gruel into the leather, she, Bitias, and Barcas carried the new line south, the tinker tethering them to that strand. From his lead position, Bitias began easing north. Beneath Elisha's fingers, the thin cord stretched, the grease beading up as the leather grew taunt. Bitias twisted around and looked. The northern line was still fifty feet distant.

He stared into the gap, then looked back to Elisha.

"We could move inward," he suggested. "That would close the gap."

She glanced to the sneering chief, then shook her head. "I shall not surrender any of this land."

"*N'*. You make this difficult." He looked north and south, gathering the attention of those within sight. He took a deep breath before calling out, "Listen to my words, whoresons! When I call, we stretch the line and close the gap. Careful and firm, as if you were pulling on your '*yr*. Pass the command to those beyond."

The order echoed from throat to throat, sounding over the trees. Bitias waited, listening to the voices echo around the ring until silence returned. He cast a glance north and south.

"*Ns'*!"

The command to pull rippled from man to man. The ring contracted around its final gap. The thread in Elisha's hands danced.

Barely perceptible, a leathery creak sounded around the hill.

Bitias and his counterpart closed. The creaking continued.

The admiral thrust out his hand, clasping his comrade's. Carefully, they pulled themselves together. Their threads touched.

The men erupted into cheers, the joyous cry washing back along the perimeter line. Along the new border of their land, men steadied the thrumming thread, shouting like madmen into the African sky. Once again, Queen Elisha had delivered a victory.

"Drive the stakes in," she commanded. The tinkers stooped to obey. Over the sounds of mallets and jubilation, she smiled at Hiarbas.

"We have encompassed our land. It is now ours. For this, we thank you."

There was a pause while Afsan passed her words. The chieftain listened, his eyes transversing the line. The pegs went in. The soil beneath his feet was no longer his.

His eyes came back to the small Phoenician girl. A small tight smile graced his lips, the smile of a reluctant loser. His words were slow, considered. Afsan collected them before passing them on.

"He says you are clever. He says you people from the east have shown him that the lightest of words and thinnest of threads may accomplish great things. He says that he will be far more cautious in any future dealings."

Before she could reply, Hiarbas spoke again. At the conclusion, he turned and departed, his nobles close and silent.

"He says that you are to be respected. For that, you should have a new name, a Libii name. You have traveled far, and have brought your ways to his shores. For that, you will be known as 'Dido'."

"Dido," she echoed, trying the name as one tried a new scarf or sash.

"It means 'the Wandering One'." Afsan paused, then added. "In Libii legends, the wandering one, the Dido, usually be a crafty traveler, one who gains shelter and substance by the twisting of words. I do not think this be entirely complimentary."

Bitias looked over from where he stood, greasy line in his hands. "How utterly fitting."

The fields were visible from the bay. The rows of grain swayed in the wind off the Upper Sea. Even with the late planting, the harvest would be plentiful.

The forward face of the hill was largely denuded of trees. The original tents had been repositioned, lining the road that ran from the beach to Melqart's temple. Other houses had been assembled, with walls of branches and roofs of palm fronds. A few huts were constructed from wood wrenched from two of the transports. Other plank huts served as warehouses, holding everything from *RearEnd*'s benches to the queen's treasure urns.

Their hill had been named *Bursa*. Oxhide. Never had so common a name been spoken with such pride.

Bitias stood on the foreign merchantman's deck, taking it all in. Both homecomings had been the same. He'd gone out on short patrols, returning to find Carthage springing up along Bursa's flank like a weed. With crops in the ground, the people had turned their attentions to their community. The admiral shook his head. He would have never thought she could have accomplished so much.

"It is truly amazing what Elisha has done," he admitted.

"Dido," Tetramnestus corrected, not taking his eyes from the Greek manifest. "She goes by her Libyan name now. Hiarbas decreed it, her people take pride in it, and she prefers it. Are you ready to continue the offloading?"

"Do you need me here? I would rather take *RearEnd* out again."

"Patience," the holy lord proscribed. "Give your men a chance to go ashore and enjoy their city. Rowing with half-banks wears them out."

"Half-banks is all Eli...*Dido* will permit. She says that the men are needed here."

"She is probably right. Chieftain Hiarbas has retired inland, and none can predict how badly his pride has suffered. Some defense must be at the ready. You have done well. A prize taken on each patrol."

"Aye," Bitias admitted. "But both of them were long chases. It would be easier with full banks."

He kicked at the decking beneath his feet, decking that had been assembled twelve years before in the Greek port of Patrae. The hull had criss-crossed the Aegean before greed had lured her master to chance the western waters, waters Canaan considered its own. The master had assumed that there would be little risk. After all, it would be almost impossible for the penteconter to operate so far from the Levant.

When he'd sighted *RearEnd*, his surprise had been total, as was his penalty. There was no place in a penteconter for prisoners.

Bitias watched as his men stevedored the Greek goods ashore. Much of it was metal; the boy-lovers had been homeward bound when taken.

The port of Carthage was not much to look at. Some day, a protected anchorage would be dug. Yet even though the port was only a beach, the typical harbor bustle added vibrancy to the scene. The captured goods were piled across the sands, undergoing inspection and inventory. Nearby, men worked on the skeletal remains of the second transport, its wood more valuable as building materials. Further up the line, another crew worked to ready a ship for sea. Bitias mentally inventoried the goods arrayed near its bow. Urns of salt, rolled skins, ivory tusks, and bundles of exotic plumage, all gained through trade with the Libyans.

"Is Dido planning to send out a trading expedition so late in the season? Even running to Iberia or Víteliú would be difficult if they desire to return before the storms come."

"You *have* been away," Tetramnestus chided. "She plans a mission of diplomacy. When she first raised the idea before the council, you could have heard their anguished cries in Utica. Since then, the *shpt*s have come to see the wisdom of her ways."

"What peoples are worth the effort of diplomacy? This far out from civilization, there are nothing but scattered settlements, Carthage included."

"You should ask her directly. She is right over there."

Bitias followed the priest's nod. Sure enough, Elisha stood on the sands before the grounded diplomatic vessel, seeing to its final details. With her was the ship's commander, Second Officer Aleyn, and young Barcas.

Bitias leaned against the bow post and studied her. At sixteen, she was now a woman. The sea breezes flattened her robes, showing off her breasts to best effect. Her raven hair rippled back, revealing the fine line of her jaw, the graceful plunge of her neck. She spoke to the others with animated gestures and a flashing smile.

He thought of that magical night in the temple gardens, making love atop the ramparts. He could recall her musk mixing with that of stale beer in the small room above the alehouse. He could remember the flash in her eyes, lightning in a night sky, and the way she would buck when the *'drtnt* took her.

He considered Os'sh, clumsy and cranky with her extended belly. The Scythian was good for him. She checked his mad impulses with level-headedness. She made him a better man. But her simple practicality paled before Dido's passion.

Had he taken the wrong path?

Bitias knew his thoughts were wrong. He knew they could never have lasted. Their independent natures burned brightly when thrust together, but eventually repulsed. Her drive would always be at odds against his nature. Together, they personified Tyre, *rzn* versus *'bny*, the doer against the dreamer.

He realized that Barcas was pointing him out to the others. As the young prince lead Aleyn and Dido over, Bitias thought of the child that grew in his wife's belly, of the responsibilities facing him. He did his best to push thoughts of Elisha into the past.

"Commander Bitias, I greet you," Dido smiled. She nodded to the plunder about them. "I see that you still possess the skills that made you an admiral."

He shrugged it off. "Tradesmen are easy pickings. Eventually the Greeks will wonder about their missing vessels and come looking."

"Greeks," scoffed Aleyn.

"Is it the Greeks who we plan to send an emissary to?" Bitias surprised himself with his own intuitive leap. It would be, he reflected, just like her; sink their merchantmen while securing their goodwill.

"Bitias, I was going to present the details with you. As an elder of the council, you have a right to know."

He waved off her assurances. "No matter. But the Greeks are not Hiarbas..."

"It is not the Greeks we send tribute to." She paused to tuck an errant ribbon of hair behind a small brown ear. "It is Tyre with whom we will converse. With King Pumayyaton."

"Pumayyaton?" He shook his head, then gestured to the growing town. "I thought that is what *this* was all about. I thought that we had gone into exile to escape Pumayyaton's wrath."

"We had. But we have secured ourselves against Pumayyaton's vengeance. We are distant enough to safeguard against any assault. Yet we are also Canaanites. We should reestablish relations with Tyre."

"Do you think that a couple of bundles of skins and a strange feather or two is going to win your brother's sympathies?"

"I am not forwarding local curiosities to him," Dido corrected. "I am sending him ten percent of this colony's wealth. Ten percent of its trade, ten percent of its profits." She met his eyes. "And ten percent of the treasure we took with us."

Bitias shook his head in disbelief. "Ten percent of our starting capital *and* our profits? That must add up to thirty or forty talents of gold!"

"Forty-three," Tetramnestus corrected from the decking above.

"What goes through your mind, *Qtn'khn*? You could have purchased Hiarbas's good will with a fraction of that amount. Instead, you alienate him to gain favor from your distant brother."

Dido waited until he'd finished. "As you stated, we are now safe. But we are alone. We are orphaned. Yet we know in our hearts that we are true Canaanites. We worship Melqart. We share language and culture. We should be a colony, an official Canaanite colony. And to do this, we must send our ten percent back. It is our due."

"Our due? Pumayyaton does not have to accept it. He could simply keep the offerings and maintain our status as exiles."

"Of course. Yet he gains little by refusal and much by acceptance. Access to the Levant will strengthen our trade. Official ties to Tyre will make the Greeks think twice before attacking us." She crossed her arms and gave him a frank look. "You yourself said that amid this desolation, our rubies were little more than pretty stones. With them, I seek to purchase trade, goodwill, and a restoration of our heritage."

He frowned and tried to formalize counter arguments, but each toppled like a mast before a gale. She was right; realignment with Tyre, distant as it was, yielded economic, military, and cultural advantages. He could only give an accepting nod.

"One thing, though," he added, "I would hate to be the fool who appears before Pumayyaton."

"I faced a lion on Bursa's summit, the day of the landing," Barcas noted. "I can stand before Dido's brother and show no fear."

"You? Dido, you would entrust all that wealth to someone who had to be dragged into exile? Someone who cannot even march in a straight line? *Lys*, he is little older than yourself."

Barcas' handsome faced winced at Bitias' slight. "I have proven myself to Lord Hêgêsistratus. I have proven myself to Queen Dido. And I have proven myself to me. To no one else must I answer."

Dido nodded. "The council considered long on this matter before selecting Barcas as envoy. He is familiar with the ways of court, and the etiquette of the nobles. And he was Pumayyaton's childhood friend."

Bitias felt his position once again eroding. "Fine. Might as well be him as anyone. Good luck, little fool. You will need it."

"Luck is not all I will need," Barcas noted. "For the journey, I will require someone familiar with the waters between here and Canaan. I would like to take Second Officer Aleyn with me on my mission."

"Aleyn? But I need him here over the winter. We need to see to *RearEnd*. And I was going to try to train those clod-farmers and tinkers into a second crew, in case we manage to build another penteconter."

"You will have to get by without him," Dido ruled. "His presence will give the mission its greatest chance of success. He will return after the storms, mid-spring next year. Then you both can go plundering again."

Bitias rubbed his chin. "You wish me to give up my second during refit season, just so he can chaperone this child? Very well, but we are Canaanites, and Canaanites trade. I wish something in return."

Dido was immediately on guard. "What do you wish?"

"Bronze," Bitias replied. "I took several hide-plates of bronze from that last Greek. I want seven, no, eight pieces."

"Eight hide-plates?" Tetramnestus scowled down from the captured freighter. "That is enough to forge armor for five more hoplites. The bronze belongs to Carthage."

"And so it shall benefit Carthage. But in a new way. I have this idea..."

Dido saw Bitias' eyes travel to his beached penteconter. Besides love, there was something else in his expression. A hunter's hunger, perhaps. Whatever his mad scheme, it might well benefit their city.

"As rubies are pretty stones," she allowed, "Bronze is only pretty metal. I agree to the exchange."

FOUR

Even with the braziers and partial stone walls, the temple was chilly. The late-year winds whistled through gaps in the crude doors. Occasionally, a shower would swirl past, bringing another cascade of drips from the temporary planking constituting the upper walls and roof. A coating of pitch offset some of the difficulties. Completion of the temple would alleviate the remainder.

The seasonal chill was offset by the men who circulated about, conversing in low tones. Many of them were former merchant princes of Tyre. While they had lost their villas, their privileges, and their wealth, they had not lost their hunger.

In sharp contrast, a number of Libyans were also in attendance. They had dealt with Utica in the past; many of them could speak Canaanite. They talked haltingly, listened carefully, and shared the same hunger as their counterparts. Where the Uticans had been content to trade in small amounts for simple necessities, the Carthaginians were different. They spoke of export, and they spoke of bulk. All along the inland trade routes, Libyans were preparing for a surge of commerce.

In the corner, Dido listened carefully, contributing little. She felt like a farmer who has planted a crop, and now need only watch it grow.

Lord Mintho stood closest. His companion was a trader representing an oasis of the southern chotts. The native's gown was a wraparound affair, its decorative fabric joined down his left side. As typical of his people, his arms were marked with ritualistic tattoos, a distinctive scalp lock identifying his tribe.

"No, no, no," Mintho countered, "You do not understand me, my good Safot. *Obdm*, slaves, are no good for us now."

"How can you say you do not need slaves," Safot countered with a sing-song voice which soared like parrots in a jungle. "You said that in your former homeland, countless servants saw to your every bidding."

"That is the issue. A *nor* is a servant. An *obd* is a slave. Yes, in Tyre, we had both. But with all the building and activity, there are no servants to be had. Everyone is making his own life; nobody wishes to make anyone else's. Hence, no servants."

"But then why not import slaves? Use them to build your buildings. Use them to be your servants."

The prince shook his head. "It will not work. Let me ask; do your people hold slaves?"

"No. Not many times. We are a people of small villages. Slaves require too much effort to watch, and it is too easy for them to escape."

Mintho nodded. "There you are, then. A Carthaginian can build his house with his own hands and gain satisfaction and pride in doing so. Or he can stand over a slave to gain lackluster work and poor craftsmanship. No, we have no need for slaves—yet. But give us a generation or two, and once we get farms and workshops in place, perhaps our descendants will speak again of this." He paused to pluck a date from a tray that one of Tetramnestus' assistants circulated. After biting off a portion of it, he gestured with the remainder at the Libyan. "Now these dates; how much silver for a bushel?"

"A single bushel? Or are we speaking of greater amounts?"

At that moment, the door creaked opened and Moloch stuck his head inside. The young oarsmen glanced about before spotting Dido.

"Highness, it occurs."

Without a word, she followed him out.

Gray clouds scudded over Bursa's low summit. The rain had tapered off, but darkness was forming to the west, speaking of more to come. The bay was the color of iron, whitecaps forming further out. Along the beach, the remaining vessels of their fleet had been pulled well above the high-water mark.

A transport was missing, gone to Tyre with Aleyn and Barcas. They should have reached their destination by now. Dido wondered if they were still alive. If so, what must it be like for them, walking through the grand streets of the mother city? She realized that she would give much but for a single day to wander the city of her birth. At night, the pangs of homesickness would return.

RearEnd also lay on the sands. A crude tent, made of its own sails, enfolded her bow. Bitias had been tight-lipped on his plans. The only men privy to them had been a handful of tinkers and sailors. The former worked the bronze, the latter opened up the penteconter's planking, following their captain's instructions. Judging by the expressions she'd seen, they had their doubts.

Of course, the worksite was silent. For Bitias, there would be no work this day.

They proceeded down the muddy lane that dropped from temple to beach. Over the rooftops of canvas and fronds, she could see fields laying in winter idleness. A lone ox lulled across the muddy expanse, grazing at weeds, fertilizing as it went.

The house of Bitias was cruder than any slum in Tyre. Yet here in Carthage, it was envied. Stone blocks had been mortared into posts, forming anchor-points for the plank walls. More boards formed the roof. A cargo ship's deck-hatch served as a door. It was weather-tight and secure, especially compared to the tents and lean-tos that surrounded it. As an admiral and elder, with four Greek prizes to his name, he rated such.

Moloch opened the hatch and gestured her inside, but did not follow.

The interior was simple and sparse. Other than a pallet constructed from the ever-present ship-planking, several urns contained the meager household supplies. Clothing hung from pegs along a wall. A small brazier, borrowed from the temple, provided light and heat.

On the pallet, Os'sh panted, her brow gleaming with sweat. As Dido watched, her belly shifted slightly. The Scythian grunted, exhaling her pain.

The woman Phoenix had been a midwife on Cyprus. Now she attended Os'sh, murmuring a calming drone. One hand stroked the prone woman's hair, the other rested on her belly, monitoring. She shifted slightly, and Dido noticed that she, too, was showing signs of pregnancy. So it was with many of the colony's women.

Bitias, who'd calmly driven his penteconter into the teeth of a gale to escape pursuit off Tyre, paced about the small confines, casting worried glances at his wife.

Off Phoenix's shoulder, High Priest Scylax glowered. As childbirth was the ultimate symbol of the goddess Astarte, he would usually attend such events in Citium. Beneath his arm was a silver bowl for use in his upcoming service.

"This is not the...way it should be..." grunted Os'sh.

Dido felt some alarm. "Is something wrong?"

"Only that she is Scythian," Phoenix noted. "When the birthing time comes, the women of their race slip out of camp, find an isolated spot and deliver their babies. Had Bitias not told us she'd broken water, she might well have slipped away into the brush."

Outside, the wind moaned, spattering rain against the planking. Dido shivered.

"I do not...want anyone here..."

"Bitias is the father," the midwife explained. "It is Canaanite custom that he be present. High Priest Scylax carries out the duties of his temple. And as your child will be the first true Carthaginian, it is fitting that Queen Dido be in attendance."

"Fitting indeed," muttered Scylax.

Something had been eating at Dido for months. Something in the priest's tone gnawed at her. Without thought, words sprang from her own lips.

"Why is it fitting, High Priest? Do not hide your words in dark mutterings. Speak aloud like a man."

Her tone was enough to bring Bitias out of his pacing. Scylax met her scowl with one of his own.

"It is fitting that the child that signifies the birth of your city was conceived in the death of my faith."

"Is that what this is about? Nine months of mutters and curses because you feel Astarte has left you?" To one side, Bitias moved to place a calming hand upon her. She deflected it with a glance.

"Of course the Goddess is no longer in my world," Scylax explained. "She permitted a mockery to be made of her services."

"What mockery? She is serviced by fertility and rebirth." Dido gestured to the two women. "This room is brimming with such. In fact, most of the women who loitered in your cold halls have now been blessed with manseed and will bear fruit." Dido's dark eyes narrowed. "Perhaps that is the root of the matter, High Priest. Your order was stagnant. And with the departure from Cyprus, the women were truly blessed."

The priest recoiled as if slapped; he'd not seen this truth until she'd voiced it. Now the realization burned. He spat his reply with venom.

"Do you believe that Astarte is confirmed by successful consummation? Libyans spawn like fleas, yet they have never heard of Astarte. The countless barbarians that lurk in the world's dark corners proliferate. The issuance of brats does not prove the Goddess's presence."

"Then what does?" she demanded. "What is it we must do to bring the goddess to our shores?"

"We cannot bring her here. She is not a trade good that we can squeeze into an urn and transport. She exists in the hearts of the Canaanites. She exists as an extension of ourselves. And when we reject her services, we reject her. As such, she no longer exists."

"You can make her exist. Tetramnestus oversaw the construction of Melqart's temple while you moped in your vegetable garden. Pick the site for your temple and I will see it built. You can bring Astarte to these shores."

"Can I?" Scylax's dubiousness was obvious. "And you will permit me to call upon the maidens of Carthage to perform their service, to reside in the temple until a man speaks in their behalf?"

"No. We spoke of this before. We will not go back to the old ways. We will not lock women away in the temple. Astarte will be serviced as in Tyre, through priestess-prostitutes; women willing to devote their lives to Her service."

The scrawny priest drew himself up. "Then Astarte is dead. There is no reason for me to remain and conduct the ceremony. The Goddess does not exist. Not for me."

"She exists for Os'sh." A gesture to a corner shelf where a small token of Astarte lay amid tiny offerings.

"So? What concern is that of mine?"

"If it is not your concern, you shall be replaced."

"Replaced?" Scylax roared. "You cannot replace me."

"Of course I can. Os'sh could easily perform your functions."

"Impossible. She does not have what I have."

"And what would that be? Faith? You have lost yours. Knowledge? Such she has. A *'yr*? You sliced yours off to better service your goddess." Dido crossed her arms and purposely blocked the door. "So give me an answer, High Priest. Conduct the service or be cast out."

Trapped, Scylax seemed to collapse in upon himself. When he looked up, it was in defeat. "But She is gone for me."

"For you, perhaps. But not for others."

Bitias had been watching the interplay, ready to step in should Dido provoke Scylax to physical assault. He was still watching carefully when Phoenix nudged him, passing a bundle with the simple words, "Your son, Lord."

The admiral of Tyre and elder of Carthage looked down into the compressed face of his newborn son in shock, disbelief, and wonderment. Legs that had held him on pitching decks threatened to buckle.

"*Rb qbhn olt 'nk*," he breathed. "Great Melqart, wondrous Astarte, fearsome Baal, my thanks to all of you."

Dido stared, thoughts confused.

"Has he a name?" Phoenix inquired.

"Amilcar. He shall be known as Amilcar."

Scylax, too, looked over the baby. Ever practical, Phoenix slipped the silver bowl from beneath his arm. A moment later, she handed it back to him. Contained within was the afterbirth, still warm from its host. The priest looked over it and nodded abstractly.

Dido's tone was firm. "As there is no temple of Astarte, go to Melqart's house and perform the immolation there. Tetramnestus will assist you."

"I shall conduct the service," said the priest dully. "Perhaps Astarte will return to me."

"Perhaps," Dido replied.

O s'sh bundled her baby's swaddling against the air's nip before stepping through the low hatchway of her house. She'd promised Bitias that she would stay home with Amilcar until she grew stronger and he bigger. Two weeks had passed with little intervention or entertainment.

It was time to go out. It was time for Amilcar to see his world.

The sunshine was warm, offsetting the chill. The child in her arms murmured at the glare until she shielded him with her brown hand. *So small*, she thought. *So perfect.*

So taken was she with her child that, at first, the bustle of the growing town was lost to her. Eventually she began to notice the people who passed on minor errands. The crack of mallets filled the air, muffled momentarily as a cart of lumber rumbled past.

A spot had been set aside for the town's market, on the beach at Bursa's base. Dido and the council had carefully considered that spot. But marketplaces, like love, fortune, and death, are rarely so deterministic. For whatever reason, crude stalls had begun to appear in a wide section of the road several houses up from her own. The people had chosen this place to be their market.

Os'sh reflected on how refreshing it was that Dido was not always right.

All manner of things were for sale. Simple items: eggs and grain. Imports: salts and ivory. Even luxury goods: rings and baubles carried in the exodus. All were traded back and forth.

Truly traded. While prices were agreed on in shekel-weights of silver, there was little of the metal to be had. In time, trade with Gadar in the west would supply such needs. But for now, people fell back on more common methods. For smaller items, grain was used as a denominator. For larger purchases, a temple assistant would record the transaction on a clay tablet.

How strange it was for goods to be gained for little more than a *promise* of silver.

She strolled along the stalls, looking without intent. Briefly she paused to watch two men in negotiation over a hut. Whether the proximity of the marketplace enhanced or detracted the crude shelter's worth, she could not tell, but clearly a sale was taking place. The two men argued vehemently, shrieking at each other's dishonesty. Three times, negotiations appeared to be on the verge of breakdown. And then, just as suddenly, the two were shaking hands, summoning an apprentice over to record the transaction.

She walked away, shaking her head at the changes. Seven months ago, this land had been worthless. Now it had a value which shifted about daily like wine in a rocking cup. She smiled at how quickly civilization took hold.

People stopped to admire Amilcar, crooning as if they'd never seen an infant before. He cooed and smiled, bringing sighs and laughter to those who viewed him. *He is a born entertainer*, Os'sh thought, *like his father.*

Small things came to her as she chatted with her fellow citizens. Some of the men had chopped their beards shorter, perhaps unwilling to invest the effort to maintain the elaborate Canaanite curls. The claws and teeth of lions hung on thongs around their necks. Newly sewn clothing was fashioned along more simpler lines than in the cosmopolitan east. The Carthaginians were changing. Their Levant origins were slowly fading. They were becoming a new people.

She noticed two women walking downhill on the opposite side of the street. Excusing herself from Amilcar's admirers, she crossed the dusty lane.

"Phoenix!"

The Cypriot woman, heavy with child, beamed at her call. "Os'sh! You are out of the house already? Did Bitias grant such?"

"My people move with the winds. Women ride the day after birth. Such loitering is foreign to me."

"You are no longer a girl on a pony. You are the wife of an elder. You may loiter all you wish."

"I wish no more, that is certain," she looked to Phoenix's companion, a squat little woman with a weathered face. "Forgive me, my lady. I do not know you."

"Yzebel." A brush broke through the lines of her face. A moment later, she ducked her head.

"She is of the tinker's clan," Phoenix explained. "They spent years traveling the coasts of Cyprus. In that time, she remained mostly on the boat, interacting with few save her family." She gave a reassuring pat to the broad shoulder. "We are trying to get her used to the idea of being a citizen of a larger community."

Os'sh noticed the woman's eyes flickering over Amilcar.

"Would you like to hold my son?" The woman's nod was enthusiastic. Os'sh carefully passed the baby across. Yzebel's arms cradled the bundle.

Turning back to the midwife, Os'sh's eyes took note of something she'd missed before.

"Bows. You have bows on your back."

"'Bl! Are we not like those mythical northern Amazons, so fearful and so deadly? Dido, of course, is behind it."

"How do you mean?" At her gesture, Phoenix unshouldered the weapon and passed it across. Os'sh's fingers closed quite naturally around its shaft.

"On the day of Amilcar's birth, Dido shamed Scylax into reestablishing his order. A new temple is under construction, adjacent to that of Melqart. Yet that was not enough for Dido. A day or so later, she confronted the high priest in a meeting of the council. She pulled him forth like a murex from its shell, saying how he was not doing enough for Carthage. It came forth that he used to teach archery to the women residing in his order. Her thought was that he should instruct our women in the use of the bow."

Phoenix laughed at the memory. "Y! It was as if Dido had suggested they reject their gods. Even with Hêgêsistratus' support, the argument went on all night."

Os'sh tried to imagine the old Greek approving of something so unconventional. Her face showed her disbelief.

"Oh, he was something to see," Phoenix confirmed, slipping into a gruff caricature of the Greek. "'Hoplites might stand against barbarians. But hoplites with archers in support will stand all the better'." With her bluster and extended belly, the sight was ludicrous. Os'sh laughed hard. Even Yzebel peeked a smile.

"Having seen Scylax tutor women in their letters," Os'sh confided, "it is difficult to imagine him drilling them to be archers. 'Bl, he might occasionally take a noble lady into the temple's garden for an afternoon's amusement with a bow, but nothing more."

"Well, he will find no noble ladies here." Phoenix gestured to the huts lining the crude street. "One thing is certain; settling Carthage has made us all commoners. Our good priest will have no discriminations on that account."

Os'sh's eyes went to the bow in her hands. "And these weapons? They seem very light. Were they created especially for women?"

"Those? Nay, they came from *RearEnd*'s stores. They are naval bows."

"Naval bows?" Os'sh drew the weapon experimentally, then let the tension out with a frown. "Hardly a weapon of men. It is like those we give Scythian children to train with."

Phoenix shrugged, taking her weapon back. "Well, do not tell your husband that; you know how prideful men are." She sniggered. "Men hate to be told that their weapons are not big enough."

Os'sh's blush was hidden by her brown skin. Phoenix could be so crude, but it was also what made her interesting. To change the subject, she admitted her own skill with a bow.

"I might be years out of practice, but certainly I should attend the training. I shall accompany you to meet High Priest Scylax."

"Perhaps we can arrange to give little Amilcar a bow. That way he can take his place with the auxiliaries the day Carthage is threatened." Another giggle. "Did I tell you about Holy Lord Tetramnestus' dilemma? Well, here he is, high priest to a new city facing its first winter. The trouble is, he knows not the seasons nor the weather of this coast. He has no idea when the ceremony of Egersis should take place..."

FIVE

Bitias sat on a stack of planks, looking with consideration at the thing that now graced *RearEnd*.

His concentration was broken when the sailcloth tent was thrust open. A moment later, Os'sh pushed her way in, Amilcar bundled under her arm. His son gave a little cranky cry.

He could see that his child was not the only unhappy person in the makeshift tent. Learning to live with a new wife, first aboard a penteconter, then a small hut on a desolate shore, had been no easy task. Further complicating matters was the difference of cultures. But he knew when Os'sh was angry. By Melqart's yellow ear wax, he knew.

Amilcar came to his aid with a petulant little squeal.

"My love, I think our son is hungry."

She looked down, seeming to notice the child for the first time. Bitias saw the tension along her jaw ease. Without a word she parted her robe, exposing a brown breast. Bitias glanced about, thankful for the tent and that he'd dismissed his crew early. With Canaanite sensitivities, he found her casual acts disturbing. Exposing one's self, and especially breast-feeding a child, were activities reserved for privacy.

He watched his son suck contentedly, wondering the morals and ethics their new culture would adapt.

Os'sh stroked the small brown head, focusing herself on her child's need. When she finally looked up, her anger had largely abated.

"That fool!"

"Which fool are you referring to?" Bitias inquired evenly.

"Scylax."

"Ah. Yes, and his bow training." He fingered a suspicious puncture in the tent, holding his tongue. Like Dido, Os'sh possessed rather forward views of a woman's place in society.

"We have watched them practice nearby," he noted noncommittally. "Most of them are improving. Perhaps, with much practice, they might prove their worth."

Her brown eyes locked on his.

"Scylax would not let me practice with the women."

Bitias' eyebrows raised at that. She was, after all, a Scythian. Her people were infamous with bows.

"Tell me what occurred."

"I was taking the sun with Amilcar when I fell in with Phoenix. She told me about Dido coercing Scylax to teach the women bowmanship. I decided I should attend and accompany her. Anyway, we came down on the beach nearby, where Scylax had the women drawn up. He was doing his best, but given the scattering of the shafts across the sands, one could see that his patience was sorely tried. I deemed it best to wait."

"And?"

"And so he trained them. They would shoot away their quivers, collect their shafts, and shoot them all away again. The sun grew long in the sky. Finally, while the women collected their arrows, I ventured down and asked them if I might try my hand."

Bitias nodded.

"To my surprise, he refused. He said that he could not instruct me.

"'May I ask why?'

"'You have a child. A bow requires both hands.'

"'I could place my child on the sands at my feet. If Carthage were threatened, I would do such.'

"'You have a child,' he repeated. 'I balk at teaching women to fight. It would displease Astarte for me to teach mothers to kill.'"

Bitias rubbed his chin. "Truly an odd defense, coming from a man who has claimed to have misplaced his goddess."

"Anyway, I pointed to Phoenix, herself heavy with child. 'She shall be a mother soon. She may drop within the week.'

"'The Libyans might attack tomorrow. We must be ready.' *N'*, such double-talk!"

"And then what happened?"

"I asked him to speak his real reasons to me. He claimed he had. So I told him it was certainly apparent he had cut away his *'yr*. At that, he stormed off the beach."

Bitias sighed, then reached over and took the child. He patted its back gently, raising a milky burp. When he spoke, it was with careful consideration.

"It is not about you, Os'sh. It is about Dido. And myself."

"What do you mean? It is not you he denies."

"But he cannot strike against us. I move in different circles than he, and Dido is, after all, our queen. But you have heard Scylax, bemoaning his lost goddess, blaming us for his troubles. He is not man enough to accept his circumstances and do what is best for his community. He is petty and small."

Os'sh's tired brown eyes were on the sand at her feet. "You are right, my husband. I can sense the displeasure in him. I suppose he still holds me partially to blame for what happened. After all, Zinnridi entrusted me to Scylax. When he failed, he had to accompany us into exile." Her lips pursed. "But it is still wrong. I wish to train, even with those puny bows. My exclusion is not fair."

"No, it is not. So what can you do, my pretty wife? Shall you butt your head into his like a pair of goats?"

The answer to that was obvious, yet she could not think of an alternative. She watched her husband stand, child over his shoulder.

"Dear wife, you must always pursue what you seek. But if you cannot achieve it directly, you must fall back on indirect methods."

"What do you mean?"

"The exact methods are for you to decide. If he will not let you train with him, do something he will not expect. How hard can it be to outfox and outmaneuver that tired little priest?" He swung around to face her, the motion raising a giggle from Amilcar. "Consider your own beloved husband. I have taken four Greek merchants. Eventually those boy-lovers will come looking for me. Now *RearEnd* is a good ship, but she is not that good. Should we go hull to hull with a Greek penteconter, we might lose twenty to thirty men in action. These are men I cannot afford to lose."

"So, what do you do?"

"This!" He gestured to the lower prow of the penteconter. At the point were the bow swept back, something jutted. It was a bronze column, horizontal. Closer inspection revealed it to be cast in the blunt image of an eagle's head.

"I have considered this addition for years," Bitias continued. "We spent all last winter refitting *RearEnd* in order to mount it. And now it is in place. Now it is ready."

Os'sh looked over the low bronze protuberance. "Just what, my husband, is this thing?"

"A ram, forged from Greek bronze, hungry for Greek timbers. No longer shall we swarm aboard our enemy. Now, we will maneuver into position, sprint in, and ram our target. They will sink like stones."

Os'sh stepped past her husband, looking over the strange device. It was cold beneath her fingers. Its craftsmanship was beautiful, almost an honor to those it may someday slay.

"By being unconventional," Bitias smiled, "I am successful."

She nodded, thoughtful. Eventually her eyes fell upon the shim-strips, scattered about after the fitting. An idea came to her.

"My husband, may I have these left-over shims?"

The boy looked from the lean-to at the rain-crazed water.

"*Y!* Will this never stop?"

His father shook his head at the impatience of youth. "Sit. Rest. Soon there will be work, such work as to make your muscles cry out."

The boy eyed the brick molds scattered outside their shelter. "I am not afraid."

This brooked no reply. Instead, his father looked out over the low marsh toward the distant Libyan village. It had been given a name; Tunis. Already the first of the caravans had arrived from the south, their tents dotting the far plains, waiting. For them, proceeding to Carthage would be pointless. Until the time of Egersis had been declared, no ship would sail; no merchant would trade. So here they remained, and like all concerned, watched the late storms roll overhead.

"*Lys*!" The pebble the boy tossed into the marsh was lost amid the rain-patter. "The priests wait. The farmers wait. The sailors wait. The days slip by. Holy Lord Tetramnestus should declare Rebirth and let us get on with our lives."

"The fields are mud. The seas roll. The clay for our bricks lays beneath high water. We can only wait. Remember, the gods determine the fall of Egersis, not the priests."

"But everyone wants this weather to end."

"Not everyone," his father replied, eyes on the play of rainwater over the reeds.

His son waited respectfully for his father's answer.

"Queen Dido would probably wish it would rain forever."

"Dido? What does such weather gain her? Until Egersis, Carthage is nothing but a pile of stones. Without farming and trade, we are nothing."

"*Y*, but consider what Egersis means to she who is our ruler." The smallest of smiles pursed his lips. "She must perform her role in the Rebirth. She must lay with a man. The priests, upon observing, will declare Egersis."

"But, father, her husband is dead. She can have any man of her choosing."

"Tell me, little lord," the elder asked mockingly, "If you were her, who would you pick?"

The boy pulled up a stem of grass, reluctant to speak with his father on such matters. Finally, he noted, "I have heard men talk in the work parties. It is said that Queen Dido has lain with Lord Bitias. Why does she not just choose him?"

"Because he is a husband. And, now, he is a father. And, most importantly, it is known that they were lovers. Dragging him into her bed might be viewed by all as a transgression of her power. It is the sort of thing her brother Pumayyaton might do. Such things she is at pains to avoid."

"Even if they both want to?"

"As you said, everyone knows. Even the lowliest apprentice brickmaker."

The boy thought for a while. "Is she not a lady of the nobility? She represented them in her struggles in Tyre, and her rank as queen makes her one as well. Should she not consent to lay with one of the lords?"

"Such would seem the most logical choice. Lord Kotilus or Lord Mintho springs to mind. After all, twenty-five came into exile with her. Certainly not all of them took wives in Cyprus, and it would hardly stop those who did. But consider the long term; these nobles were powerful in Tyre. He who conducts Egersis gains power and favor. The man chosen might someday call for her to wed him, to legitimatize the act. The last thing Dido wishes is a power-hungry husband to split her rule with."

"To seek power through service to Melqart is blasphemous. Would a man risk the wrath of the gods for gold and position?"

The father smiled. "I see that you still have much to learn of the world."

"Fine," his son replied petulantly. "If not the nobles, then what of the temple? The service is religious. It would be natural for her to call upon them to assist her in this service. Moloch told me Pumayyaton did this years ago in Tyre."

"Again I ask, who could she choose? Holy Lord Tetramnestus? 'Bl, I see your shudder. Beyond the physical, he is a creature made by her. She lifted him from the lowest of ranks and made him holy lord. She is a mother-figure to him. If they lie together, she risks breaking this relationship and losing her hold over the temple of Melqart."

"What of the others? What of High Priest Scylax, or one of the temple apprentices."

"Scylax? Oh, my son, there *is* much of the world you do not understand. As for the apprentices, again, Egersis can be a road to power. A man so chosen might use this to elevate himself in the temple, perhaps eventually challenging those priests she put into place."

The boy threw up his hands in frustration. "You have declined every candidate I have put forth. There are few left. What of General Hêgêsistratus? He exists beyond the orbits of Canaanite power."

"You would suggest a *Greek*? A foreigner? I could hardly consider a worse choice."

"Then the service cannot be conducted. Egersis cannot take place."

"But it must," his father replied with wry grimness. He sighed, content that his troubles were that of a simple brickmaker and not those of a ruler. His son sat with his back to him, angered at his inability of produce a clever answer to the riddle Dido faced.

Some time later, he observed, "It seems to be growing brighter in the west. Perhaps the weather is finally breaking."

Holy Lord Tetramnestus stood at the entrance to his temple. The single road that dropped away among the ramshackle houses was beginning to dry out. The sun glittered off the bay.

"I am considering calling for Egersis in three day's time. Have you any objections to this?"

The queen stood at his side, face unreadable. "Such is for you to determine."

"Have you decided who..."

"No."

A fusillade of arrows hissed. Several struck the figure, two of them killing blows. But many more shafts came to rest amid the sands beyond, clean misses.

"*Lys*!" Scylax's voice was an angry warble. "Perhaps it would be best to simply clout our enemies over the head with our bows."

The women of Carthage largely ignored him, fetching their arrows from around the straw target.

"Who cares what *Bol Okbr* thinks," Phoenix laughed, pulling her shaft from the belly of the figure. "When the time comes, we will be ready."

Dido smiled at the pet name the women had bestowed upon Scylax. Lord Mouse, indeed. It lightened her heart, a counteraction to the dismay she felt at not finding her shaft among those in the target. Dejectedly, she searched beyond, eventually finding it.

"And besides," Phoenix noted with a smile, "What difference does it make how many times we kill this poor straw fellow? His fate is sealed. Tomorrow he goes into the flames, Melqart's effigy at Egersis." She glanced about, her voice conspiratorial. "Have you chosen yet? Do you know with whom you will lie?"

Dido should have been surprised at the blunt question, but not from Phoenix. It was just how the ex-Cypriot farmwoman was.

"I know not," she confessed.

"You can take Straton and be welcome. My husband ruts like a pig."

They drifted back up the beach to where the line reformed.

"Have you seen Os'sh?" Phoenix asked. Dido wondered about the question's linkage. There was only one commonality between Egersis and Os'sh, and that was Bitias.

"No. I suspect little Amilcar takes up much of her time."

"It is strange. Ever since *Bol Okbr* turned her away from practice, she has been recluse. Yet she is not inactive. She makes requests of the hunters and those in charge of the colony's supplies. She collects little things, but Melqart alone knows what. Those she deals with are pledged to secrecy."

The two women rejoined the others in line, bows lowered, arrows secured. Their practice was all-inclusive, from selecting the arrow through releasing it into flight. They stood silently, awaiting Scylax's order.

"High Priest," a woman asked, turning slightly. "Is something the matter?"

Dido cocked her head back. Scylax stood motionless, eyes out to sea. She twisted to follow his gaze.

From around the distant eastern headlands, hulls appeared. Three. Four. Five. Black and low in the morning sun.

She stood as still as the man of straw. A tremor ran along her bow's curve.

Phoenix acted first. "To arms! To arms! Outlanders approach!"

Her voice carried over the community. The sounds of work ceased. Shouts echoed her own.

Further down the beach, Bitias and several men tore the sailcloth from *RearEnd*'s bow. The bronze ram threw a ruddy gleam in the sunlight. More men dashed down from the houses of Carthage. Among them was Lord Kotilus, who had been discussing final matters with several Libyan traders. While he was noble, he also considered himself a member of the penteconter's crew, a position gained through shared hardship. He threw himself in with the others who labored to shift the warship. More men, nobles and commoners alike, joined in. Moments later, *RearEnd* was afloat.

Oars slid out, probing the water. Bitias stood high on the stern, alternating his attentions between town and the distant craft. More men ran down, scrambling aboard. Dido saw him look over his benches and nod to himself. A moment later came his order. The warship slid away, moving outwards, gaining speed.

"You women! Clear off!" Festooned in his armor, Hêgêsistratus pushed past them. Other men followed, their motions clumsy and unpracticed. With the rains, he'd had minimal time for training the farmers and craftsmen of Cyprus. His best men, his true hoplites, were on *RearEnd*'s benches. His displeasure was clear.

"Ladies, form up behind Hêgêsistratus' men." It took a moment for Dido to realize that Scylax had given an order. Numbly she stepped into position, Phoenix to one side, blunt Yzebel on the other. A woman pulled forth an arrow.

"This will take time," Scylax chided. "Stand easy."

Hêgêsistratus felt likewise. The men in bronze stood in their ranks, shields leaning against their thighs, spears jutted into the sands. He moved among them, correcting here, joking there. He reached the line's end and looked back to meet Dido's eye. His expression was both grim and accepting. His armored shoulders cast a small shrug.

Out over the bay, *RearEnd* was almost lost in the glare. It was difficult to see if she was among the enemy fleet yet.

"My man is out there," a woman down the line spoke in numb realization.

"Hush," the priest commanded.

Time stretched endlessly. The hulls were low black shapes, clustered far away. It was impossible to know what occurred.

Her legs should have been aching from standing so long, but tension supported her. No one shifted. No one fidgeted. All looked to the east, watching for signs of resolution.

"I think...." An armored man hesitated, shielding his eyes. "I think they are coming this way."

Dido's eyes were not as sharp. Others around her were muttering in consternation before she, too, could detect the approach of the fleet.

The ships grew as they advanced, black transports riding low in the water. Two penteconters flanked the flotilla.

Without taking his eyes from the ships, Hêgêsistratus shrugged his shield into place. The men along his line nervously followed his example. Scylax, too, called an order. Like the others, Dido threaded an arrow, holding her bow low, ready.

One of the penteconters broke clear, racing towards the beach. As it neared, it turned to run broadside along the sands. Relief broke over her as she made out the ass-raised figurine of Yam on the bow. It was *RearEnd*.

The men at the oars shouted joyfully to the beach as they passed. "They come from Tyre! Barcas returns! His mission was a success!"

The two penteconters, as happy as reunited dolphins, moved clear. The cargo vessels held offshore, a single one moving in to beach. Dido recognized it as the one that had departed late the previous year. Its bow ground into the sand with a noise of weary completion.

Hêgêsistratus held his men back, allowing Dido to approach. Barcas swung down to meet her, tanned from his long journey. He bowed respectfully.

"Lord Barcas. We did not expect you home so soon. Our storms have just broken. Egersis falls tomorrow."

"It is a bit of a long story," her emissary told her. "The storms of Canaan cleared early this year. It was as if Melqart wished us on our way."

"And all these?" She gestured to other craft.

"Colonists. Supplies. All from King Pumayyaton. He has recognized us as a formal colony and wishes us success. He has even sent an emissary to meet with you."

Dido looked up to the transport's deck. In his fine robes, the emissary was easily discernible. The man had his face to Aleyn who was gesturing to the town with pride. It was only when the man turned back that she recognized him. It was Ib, the commander of the palace guard, her brother's closest confidant.

Egersis.

Merriment and confusion flowed through Carthage's single street. The original colonists mixed with the newcomers. A vessel ventured down from nearby Utica, loaded with those seeking an alternative to their trading station's own dreary affair. Even Libyan caravaners, come to see to their transshipments, wandered through the press, eyes round with wonderment.

There was barley beer, brought from Canaan, date wine with its sweet bite, and fermented goat's milk from the interior. Meat roasted on spits, lacing the air with savory aroma. Loaves slid hot from the ovens. After a long year of struggle, the Carthaginians celebrated Melqart's boon, anticipating another blessed year.

And their god would be happy in return; his temple was complete.

Beneath a sail-cloth tent located at the junction between road and beach, Dido watched the festivities. In the center of the sands, the straw man stood among his kindling, a single arrow jutting comically from his head. Dido looked into his empty face and found a disturbing kinship.

Several members of the council sat on nearby cushions, watching the good-natured confusion. Earlier, she'd seen Bitias and Os'sh stroll past, young Amilcar cradled in her arms. She'd nodded greetings to them, and noticed the elders around her fall silent. A flush rose to her cheeks at the thought of the gossip that swept the colony.

Lord Kotilus stooped to enter the tent. The trader had been busy over the winter, refitting a merchantman as a horse transport. While Canaan was too distant to send the remarkable Libyan mounts to, the peninsula of Víteliú was a short run to the north. Her chieftains might squabble like children, but they had both the eye for a good horse and the gold Kotilus sought.

It was then she noticed that Commander Ib was in tow. Over the last year, he'd grown into quite a man. His hair and beard were immaculately curled, his robe cut with expensive purple dyes. His shoulders had broadened from the weight of both weapons and responsibility. While he conveyed a comfortable air of authority, Dido noted the weariness in his eyes.

"Queen Dido," greeted Kotilus formally. "I wish to provide introductions for Envoy Ib, who serves as King Pumayyaton's eyes, heart, and mind. He wishes to convey his respects and speak with you on matters of state."

"Envoy Ib may approach." At her words, Kotilus faded away, his obligation complete. Ib bowed in courtly fashion. In his hands was a small silver urn, which he passed to her.

"Soil from your homeland," Ib explained. "The king thought you might treasure it more than any diplomatic gift. He had the stones of the market pried away in order to secure it for you."

She opened the small lid and ran a finger through the cool dirt, emotions welling within her. It would have been less precious to her had it been filled with gold dust.

"We have great horns of ivory, gained from strange creatures inland. They were meant for trade, but you should have one of them." Ib bowed quite respectfully at that. The tusks were quite a valuable item on the Levant.

"*Y*, Ib, how well you have done. From a young boy guarding the back door of the palace, to commander of the palace guards, and now *ml'k*, emissary."

"Aye, thank you, Highness." A smile flickered. "I see you still have your gold headband. Is it still as sharp as a dagger?"

Dido smiled at the reference to that night at the rear entrance to the palace, where he'd oozed confidence until she'd threatened him with horrible death. *Such children we were then*, she considered. *And have we really changed?*

"And how far you, yourself, have come," he noted. "I still think of you as little Elisha. And here you are, Queen Dido of Carthage. You, too, have done well."

"I have done what I have had to do." She looked past him to the festivities; so many new faces. "I must admit, Envoy, that I find my brother's response surprisingly generous. Considering the events of my departure, we hardly expected such support." Her face darkened. "Governor Zinnridi of Citium attempted to foist his dregs upon us. Nobles we will welcome. Commoners we will welcome. But not idle wastrels who devour our food and yield nothing in return. At my orders, our holy lord shall interview these colonists Tyre has forwarded to us. Should they be cast-offs, they will return with you when you leave. That, or be driven into the Libyan wilderness."

"Exporting our degenerates would serve no one. Of course you would reject them. No, your holy lord shall find them suitable. Thirty families of various crafts, with grain and supplies to compensate until they become productive."

She focused on him with cool dark eyes that pried at his soul.

"Why, Ib? Why does Pumayyaton do this?"

"Since, as you correctly suspect, you were to be killed upon your return from the mainland?" His blunt honesty pulled a gasp from her. "'Bl, a cross waited for you in the marketplace. I, myself, had seen to its erection."

"Your tongue seems rather free. As queen, I could have you on your own cross by nightfall."

"Aye, I am not a very good envoy. As you say, I talk too much." He paused, considering the councilmen lounging nearby. When his voice came again, it came as a whisper. "I must tell you what occurred after you left. It will help you understand Tyre's generous boon."

She studied him. "You wish to speak alone? Should this be some desperate act of treachery on your part, be assured..."

"I understand," Ib noted. "Clearly, our discussion in that dark little hall still stands. You have my word; your safety is assured."

She gave a slow nod before leading him from the tent. They passed between two houses constructed of planks, brick, fronds, and cloth. Beyond lay a vegetable garden, plowed and awaiting its seeds following Egersis. They walked along the furrows until they reached its center, whereupon she turned to face him.

"After our departure, what of Tyre?"

Ib took a moment to look up the slope of Bursa Hill and the temple cropping its summit.

"As you might expect, your brother took your escape in poor graces. There was not a soul in the palace who did not fear for his safety. And while Pumayyaton busied himself with his recriminations, the families of the exiles slipped away, vanishing to Egypt, Babylonia, the ends of the earth. Much of their wealth went with them. The council of elders ceased to exist. Only the trumped-up commoner's committee remained to attend winter court, and much of that consisted of the king's rambling diatribes."

Ib paused for a moment before continuing.

"There were still thoughts of intercepting you before you vanished into the west. I'd argued that the gold you carried would serve to offset the palace's mounting debts. Pumayyaton simply wanted you for a very public execution. But the fleet was unable to sail. It turns out that the newly-assigned Minister of Fleet, Lord Adon, had appropriated its funds. He was taken and confessed. His end was not pleasant."

"Adon had stolen from his original master," Dido remembered. "He turned on my brother in like fashion."

Ib nodded grimly. "So that is how it was with Tyre at the offset of the year. An empty treasury, a unseaworthy fleet, and no princes to direct the trade that would bring in its gold. I assumed it was the end.

"And then, with Melqart's blessing, your brother dropped his mantel of anger.

"He lacks Hiram's vision. Nor has he his father's depth. But he brings something to the throne with him, something special." Ib's smile was sad. "A bad year, *'bl*. But your brother rose to face it like a man. He traded concessions like barley in the marketplace. Instead of gold and silver, he exchanged favors, goodwill, and future considerations. Men of power, angered beyond all hope, would depart his audiences as steadfast supporters. I saw it myself, and simply do not know what I saw."

His charm, she realized. *He had turned his charm upon them. Once he created his convictions, how easy it was for him to pass them to others.*

"The committee followed his lead. Like Adon, the commoners who comprised it saw their opportunity. They rose to form the hdshrznm, the 'new princes'. The abandoned villas they reoccupied. The servants they reemployed. And the trade fleets sailed."

"But holding gold in one's hand does not make a peasant a noble," Dido frowned. "They could not become merchant princes so quickly."

"*Y*, true. But the crews knew their old routes, and the hdshrznm had the sense to seal their own mouths and unstop their ears. There were no brilliant merchant campaigns last year. But grain came in and wood and dyes went out. Tyre's lifeblood, so long stilled, began to flow again. And that leads us to your tribute."

"Our ten percent, as due any official settlement."

"Regardless of promises and cross-offerings, we simply needed more gold. Even the sizable dowery from his marrage to a princess of Sidon wasn't enough. Your tithe came at a critical moment. It gave Pumayyaton the wealth and prestige he needed. After all, what grander announcement to make at year's end than the successful foundation of a new colony."

"One," she added, "he did not even know he had."

Ib nodded. "And this is what it comes down to. He has taken your offering as a sign of victory over you. He boasts how his sister and her exiles are still part of his domain. Your offerings adorn the throne room so he can bask in the sight of them."

"He thinks he has won?" Her eyes flashed. "I escaped his worst. I built a mighty city, a new city, a *Qrthdsht*. He has done nothing. I have done everything!"

Id's smile was conciliatory. "Do not fall back upon your sibling rivalries. You know, I know, everyone knows what happened. In the struggle for the throne, you eluded his grasp. Regardless of my master's bragging, he knows the truth; both of the past and the future. Tyre's position is dire. It will be a long time in recovering from its troubles. Its population swells and must be drained. It also needs new trade routes. Your Carthage serves those functions. And so, regardless of what has passed, your brother supports you."

Ib gave her a final bow, a respectful gesture from a envoy to a queen. With that, he turned to go.

"My brother," she asked his back. "Is he well? Is he happy?"

"He is happy you are away," he replied without turning. "Never come back."

SIX

Carthage's temple of Melqart was a tenth of the size of its counterpart on Tyre. But in a settlement of huts and hovels, it felt vast indeed.

A chair and pallet sat in the middle of the cold room. Dido occupied the former, her legs tucked demurely beneath her. From beyond the walls came the murmur of crowds.

The door creaked open; Holy Lord Tetramnestus's rounded head appeared.

"Highness, we have brought the man you requested." In the darkness, only his words conveyed his dubious expression. "Are you sure this is wise...?"

"Admit him."

Tetramnestus lingered momentarily before ducking outside. A murmured conversation. Then a figure stepped hesitantly into the room.

"Come in," she greeted. "Sit with me."

"My lady, this is not right."

"Of course it is right. I require your service. Carthage requires your service. Come closer."

The figure stepped into the light of the small lamp. *Shnymshtr* Aleyn, Second Officer, who'd stood before storm and arrow flight, looked down upon her with nervousness.

"Queen, there must be a mistake. Certainly you would choose another for Egersis services. Commander Bitias. Lord Kotilus. Even young Prince Barcas; *'Bl*, your ages are comparable..."

"I have chosen," she told him. "I have chosen you."

"Me? But why? I am..."

"Old?"

"Old? Aye, nearly forty summers. But worse, I have had a hard life. I am..." He gestured to the pot belly than ringed his waist, to the bald spot atop his head.

"My beloved husband Arherbas had seen thirty-three years, and I was but ten." She giggled at a thought, adding, "And he had far less hair than you. Now I am seventeen, an adult. My faculties are sound. I stand by my choice."

Still he hesitated. Dido patted the pallet.

"Sit. Rest. You spoke of Bitias. Everyone speaks of Bitias. But Bitias is occupied with his Os'sh and his Amilcar. As for our nobles, not a one do I trust to not seek advantage. I need a true Carthaginian, a man I could trust. You are that man."

He sat, reluctance in his eyes.

"Dear Aleyn, I know that Aëtion, the tanner's girl you brought from Citium, left you shortly after we arrived. That you have been alone over the year." She shifted slightly, the orange lampglow playing along the smooth line of her chin. "Do you not find me attractive?"

"Your choice is unwise." He looked up at her, backlit by the lamp, face unreadable. "Do you know why she left me? Do you know why she chose another?" Dido remained silent, but Aleyn nodded as if she'd answered. "Not because of my age. But because, Little Priestess, I cannot."

"You cannot?"

"My *'yr* fails me. No matter the woman, no matter how much I wish it, it remains flaccid. *Rb qbhn*, but I am as useless as Scylax."

His head dropped. Dido looked down upon him, thoughts whirling. It was critical for Egersis to occur. Over his shoulder, she saw Tetramnestus slip into the room, the official observer. The priests demanded verification. To his questioning expression, she gave a *wait* gesture.

Without Melqart's blessing, the settlement might well fail. This she knew with her heart. She could not allow such to happen.

"Lay back on the pallet, Aleyn." At first he resisted. Then he settled back, fingers laced over his small paunch. He stared at the ceiling, face stony. She studied him for a time before leaning to the side, fetching an urn and cups. The warm smell of hibiscus tea drifted in the air. "Drink, old friend. Be at peace. Speak only when your tongue compels you to." She poured her own cup and sipped demurely. Against the far wall, Tetramnestus settled into the shadows. Time passed.

"You really are beautiful," he said, breaking into her thoughts. He was looking up at her over the lip of his cup. "A fine woman like you should have a man. Not an old man like me; a man like Bitias."

"Bitias was not to be mine."

"Then the gods erred. Everyone knew you were lovers. Everyone knew when you lay together. It was our little secret, the _hrsh b hmshm_, the 'silence of fifty' as the crew called it. A strapping lad like him, and a wondrous girl such as yourself—all were envious. We sailed with the full expectation that you would rule together, king and queen."

"It sounds like a story mothers tell their children. The real world is not like that."

"You speak of the real world to me?" There was an edge to his voice. "You, who lived in palace and temple, daughter of a king, a high lady of the temple? What know you of the world?"

Tetramnestus looked up at this. Dido leaned forward to pour more tea. He drank half a cup and studied the ceiling for some time. Eventually he found his composure.

"Forgive me, my lady. I had no right..."

"Tell me of the world." He looked up into dark eyes that studied him.

So he told her. He told her of a young man's fear in a port brothel. Of women who spit his seed on the floor with contempt. Of women demanding to see his copper first. Women who yawned. Women who laughed. Women who chatted with their comrades through the walls while he pumped them. Years of passion without love, love without passion.

He'd begun to see the world as two worlds. The crisp life aboard _RearEnd_ as it cut the waters of the Upper Sea, and the other world. The one of crude wineshops and brothels, dead rats in cold puddles, crying babies and promising pimps. It was the land of Mot, the underworld, and one's body did not have to die to inhabit it. Only the soul perished.

"A few years back, my *'yr* began to falter, and I no longer sought out whores. I prayed to Astarte for forgiveness. I remained chaste. Every so often, Astarte would visit me in the night, bringing forth my seed. I would take this as a sign and seek out a prostitute, but to no effect.

"When we saw all those women in the temple in Citium, I thought that maybe a good woman would restore me. That Egersis a year past, I took your shekel and gave it to Aëtion. In the darkness of the sacred garden, we tried to honor Astarte. But the noise of lust surrounded us; it was like the brothels I shunned. Yet Aëtion was so desperate to leave with us that she remained silent concerning my failure. We tried once or twice more during the journey, on lonely beaches beyond camp, but with no success. She left me for another after we arrived."

Dido sat silently. There was nothing she could say. Finally, she set her cup upon the floor and leaned forward.

"Speak of your childhood."

"I am the son of a *phntnor*, a warehouse-man. There is nothing to tell."

"All lives can be told. Tell yours to me. And do not stop your words, Aleyn. Do not stop."

He studied her. She looked down at him from the darkness, her expression somber, unquestioning. Setting his cup near hers, he began to speak.

She did not listen to the words. The tapestry of a life was there, the happiness, the sorrow. The words were merely props for the story that unfolded. She closed her eyes and leaned back, letting his voice wash over her. In her ears, her pulse throbbed, in league with his intonations.

His mother. His father. His friends. His toys. Young Aleyn had begun his long journey through life.

His words stopped.

Her foot rested in his lap.

"Continue."

He picked up his tale, faltering, telling of his closest friend. Her foot shifted slightly. She could feel his *'yr*, cupped protectively beneath her instep. She could feel its pulse merge with her own.

More words; the first time he saw penteconters break past the walls of Tyre, when he first knew his life-path. In a momentary pause, she brought her other foot up, cuddling his member. She did not need to command him; he recovered his tale with a faltering voice.

He spoke on, eyes fixed on the ceiling, a pattern of timbers before his eyes, watching his life unfold while sensations radiated.

She worked him like a potter would an urn. Every pulse and every gasp she noted. She built upon what she learned, a musician of sensations.

"Keep talking," she commanded, sliding down. "For Astarte's blessing, keep talking."

She eased up his tunic and settled upon him in easy motion. His words were meaningless in their context. She felt a long-delayed delight at the approach of the *'drtnt* yet paced herself. He must lead, she must follow. It was the way of things.

How clever Tetramnestus is, she found herself thinking. *How thoughtful. Hêgêsistratus would beat him if he knew that our priest had brought* hul gil *here with us. Perhaps even kill him. But it is a valuable extract, one with many uses.*

She smiled a cat's smile as Aleyn built beneath her.

In tea, one can hardly taste it at all.

The second officer bucked, gasping aloud. Dido smiled and blanked her mind, letting loose her own *'drtnt*. She arched her back in the temple lighting, bringing rebirth to Melqart and to the Carthaginians.

Tetramnestus watched silently for a little while more, just to be sure. Then he slipped from the room.

Dido and Aleyn lay tangled in each other's arms. Overhead, a trumpet bellowed from the summit of Bursa. The crowd roared at the effigy's fiery destruction.

Beneath her cheek, Dido could feel the older man's tears.

All of Carthage turned out to watch the departure of the Tyrian fleet.

From the deck of the penteconter, Envoy Ib looked back at the receding settlement.

Holy Lord Tetramnestus respectfully held a small parasol, shielding Dido from the worst of the sun. Around them, people chattered and waved, excited to be a part of the Canaanite trading empire once more. On the beach, other ships were being made ready for their own journeys. Horses whinnied from Kotilus' temporary paddock. Cargoes lay stacked across the sands.

Bitias and Aleyn drifted up the beach, discussing the upcoming sailing season and *RearEnd*'s likely role. They gave casual bows to their queen and holy lord in passing.

Aleyn gave her no undue attention. He respected the role he'd played in Egersis, he respected his duty to Melqart, and he respected her. His silence would be the *ḥrsh b 'ḥd*, the silence of one.

She knew he would stay true to it.

Even before dawn, the day promised heat.

The travelers slipped from the settlement beneath a purpling sky. They followed the road south through fields of young cereals. The delicate stalks hissed in the dawn breeze.

The sun came up as they reached the old observation post. Far over the marshes lay the native village of Tunis.

"Did you have to sell *all* your horses, good Kotilus?" Mintho groaned. The portly noble clearly did not relish the hardships of traveling.

"Could I do otherwise?" his fellow noble chucked. "The first Víteliúy settlement I found, they took them all. Traded quite a weight of gold for that horseflesh. If I am quick enough, I might be able to make a second trip this year."

"As long as you are back before the harvest." Dido glanced back at him from where she stood with the silent Scylax. "Much grain is planted now. Everyone will be needed."

She started down the caravan track that looped around the broad marsh, the translator Afsan at her side. Scylax followed, a pace or two back, followed by the two council members. Following them was their escort; Hêgêsistratus, Barcas, and two others. The dawn flamed their breastplates crimson. Iron shortswords hung from their belts.

There was little conversation. Dido spent her time looking over the landscape spread before her. Low hills rolled, dusted with scattered trees. Small outcroppings jutted, cool beneath the morning dew. Further inland, antelope clustered, watching the distant humans with casual interest.

They passed the brickfields. Boys mixed mud and straw which older brothers shoveled into molds. Fathers placed these molds in orderly lines across a wide shelf of rock, which would sun-bake the bricks hard.

At sight of her, all work stopped. "*Brkhm*, Highness," they said amid bows.

"*Brkhm*, goodmen. Tarry not for me. Carthage cries out for your bricks."

"Aye, my lady," replied an elder. "Mud for gold. Only in Carthage." They parted with smiles.

Mintho watched the exchange. For three hundred steps, he walked silently at Kotilus' side. When he spoke, his voice was low.

"Her rapport with '*bny*, the commoners, is surprising. They sided against her in Tyre."

"They were Pumayyaton's lackeys in Tyre. This is Carthage. This is different."

The heavyset noble looked at the distant Libyan village, the sun highlighting its alien form. "In that you are correct. This is certainly different." Another hundred or so paces, and then, "What think you of this meeting."

"What I think is of little importance. Chieftain Hiarbas summoned the queen to discuss the annual tribute for our land. She goes. We follow."

"*Y*, we follow." Another groan. "You should have kept a few of the horses."

A caravan passed them, bound for Carthage. From the swaying backs of their camels, wizened desert men studied them in passing.

Eventually the party reached Tunis' outermost fields. Dark men looked up from their menial chores, watching the outlanders pass.

Ever watchful, Hêgêsistratus noticed the men leave their labors and follow.

The lane crossed several tiny canals along which water trickled. Dido's eyes tracked the canals back to a nearby rise where a bevy of olive trees ringed a walled enclosure. From the entrance, robed women watched carefully.

"The village fountain," Afsan noted.

"It looks very peaceful," she replied.

"So you would think such. It be the woman's place." The small interpreter gestured forward. "Ahead is Tunis, a *thaddart*; Canaanite word for this: village."

Dido shielded her eyes from the rising sun. "Before the houses is an open space. It is full of men."

"That is the *thajma'th*, the gathering place, the place of men. It is where the council meets. Chieftain Hiarbas awaits you there."

Such was obviously true. The leader's chariot lay beneath a nearby olive tree, the horses no doubt pastured nearby. Ten lean warriors sat under the tree, watching them pass. Hêgêsistratus snorted at their laxness.

Idle chatter rose over the low walls of the enclosed space. Then came Hiarbas' booming laugh, followed by the chitter of sycophants.

"We kept you safe from the hazards of the road, my lady," the general noted. "But should barbarian turn on barbarian, there would be little we could do. If anything, our presence might lead to incident. It would be best if we waited outside the enclosure."

Dido nodded, turning to the two accompanying council members. "Are you ready?" Kotilus' nod was firm, Mintho's less so. Scylax hovered behind them, a nervous shadow.

The queen of the Carthaginians stepped through the *thajma'th*'s entrance.

The space was floored with colored tile. Benches lined the circumference, supporting lounging men. From a carved chair, Hiarbas sat flanked by advisors.

Instantly, an angry silence fell over the plaza.

"**A**fsan," hissed Dido, her face a mask.

"Majesty, the *nif*," her translator sputtered. "I thought, as you a ruler, it would be overlooked."

The silence tore at her like a gale. Those men that did not avert their eyes cast angry glares.

"The *nif*, Queen Dido. The male-ness. This is man's place. To the women; the home and fountain. Then men; the *thajma'th*, the field, and the battle. As it was Chieftain Hiarbas' initiative that you come here, I thought the *nif* would not be."

Dido looked across the hostile faces, eventually centering on the chieftain's. Her jaw worked.

"Speak not," Lord Kotilus's voice rang with authority. "Forgive my tone, my lady; it is for the Libyans' benefit. They hear only the authority, not the words. Clearly, we have entered a diplomatic trap. Hiarbas summoned you to a place where you cannot speak, nor respond, nor defend. He sows duress to harvest acquiescence."

She nodded carefully.

"Mintho and myself are sons of Canaan. We know what your wishes are. We can uphold the negotiations. You *must* be a queen of Canaan. You must uphold your dignity. You cannot remain here."

She dropped her eyes, halfway between the men and the ground, between pointless defiance and servitude. With a flat voice, she asked, "Afsan, who is the lord of the village of Tunis?"

"That be Lord Zumar."

"I seek the comfort and hospitality of his house. I seek the company of his wife. Is such permitted?"

A rapid exchange. Dido glanced up to see a tall Libyan to Hiarbas' left speaking defensively. Clearly they had thought to drive her from the village. They had not considered she would request the shelter of its headman's home. A small victory.

Afsan: "A boy will guide you there."

"I am a queen. I do not follow. Ask for directions."

Afsan paused in confusion, then relayed her words. Silence fell again, but a silence broken by a quiet chortle from men who appreciated her bravado. Zumar's reply was forced; Afsan relayed the directions, adding, "I cannot go with you, my lady. I must assist your envoys. Perhaps Scylax..."

"The home is a woman's place," she reminded him. With eyes

locked forward, she left the plaza in the described direction, silently moving into the heart of Tunis.

She spared not a glance to the low houses whose confusion turned the Libyan village into a maze. She focused on Afsan's instructions. A man on a bench watched her pass in surprise. Two women gossiping in a doorway fell silent as her shadow swept over them.

She had never been so alone. She was beyond the assistance of the Carthaginians. She was beyond the help of Hêgêsistratus' hoplites and Bitias' *RearEnd*. Not a single Canaanite was near. She was isolated in an alien land.

Only once before had she felt such abandonment. The night beneath the rugs in the palace of Tyre, the night her brother's naked sword shimmered in the moonlight.

She stood in the heart of the village where a small stone house opened onto the narrow street. She hesitated before the dark portal. Swallowing her fear, she stepped forward.

"*Brkhm*," she spoke softly. "*Brkhm*, high lady of Tunis."

Her dark eyes adjusted to the single room. It was neat and tidy. In the opposing corner lay a hearth, burning low. Directly opposite was a loom over which a woman worked. She turned at the greeting.

She was taller than Dido, with skin the color of rich clay. Midnight black hair fell from a headband of scarves. Her clothing was both colorful and modest. Her smile broke like the sun through clouds.

"*Brkhm*, Queen Dido of Carthage. Welcome to Tunis and to my humble house. I am Takama."

Dido stood for a moment before replying. "You speak Canaanite?"

"*Y*, such a surprise for you this must be. Years ago, when I was but a little girl, a Canaanite vessel went aground on the eastern peninsula. One man was found alive on the rocks, his legs crushed. The common thought was to let him expire, but my family sheltered him. In caring for him over the years until his strength gave out, he gifted me with the words of the Canaan. This permitted me to tutor Chieftain Hiarbas in Canaan words, ways, and peoples. Such prestige elevated my family, permitting my marriage to Lord Zumar."

"Words? Hiarbas speaks our language?"

"He has a rudimentary understanding of it. As for speaking, merely a few phrases and simple words."

Dido considered this. Hiarbas had given no hint this was so. He was trickier than she'd thought.

The other woman stood. "Such a fine hostess I am; storytelling to a parched traveler."

Dido tried to decline the offer but Takama had already crossed to the hearth. From a heated urn she poured two cups. Unlike the hibiscus tea of her people, the Libyan tea was sharp and sweet.

"Mint," her hostess said at Dido's surprised expression. "It gives the tea its bite." They settled onto a small bench that caught the midmorning sun. After a delicate sip, Takama gave a small smile.

"The men sprang their trap on you, did they not? They invited you to the *thajma'th* and then recoiled in horror at the violation of their precious *nif*, no?"

Dido set her cup down. With reservation, she admitted, "Yes. Yes they did."

"We women knew of this sad ploy. Men are such blabbermouths. We did not agree to such underhandedness, but then, the men ask not our opinions. Their plan was clever but lacked basic honesty."

Dido nodded, silently listening. Takama cocked her head, studying her visitor for a moment.

"Majesty, there are those who are happy of the Canaanite presence and the opportunities it brings. And there are those who see them as a threat to our ways. We women only know that Utica is here and now Carthage is here. The Canaanites have set down their roots. We must negotiate the future with you. And negotiate without tricks."

Dido felt a pang of guilt. "Tricks like those of oxhide?"

The Libyan laughed delightedly. "Concern yourself not with that. Chieftain Hiarbas attempted to out-trade the greatest merchants of the Upper Sea. He tried trickery and bluster, and was rewarded for his pains. The women shared a laugh around the fountain that day, let me assure you.

"Now, let us assist you in your negotiations. Patas!"

The head of a small boy appeared overhead, peeking from a loft Dido had not noticed. At his mother's command, he monkeyed down a corner ladder. His ears were tuned on his mother's instructions, his eyes straying to their foreign guest. When she finished, he scampered out the door.

"He will listen outside the wall of the *thajma'th*. When his little head is full, he will come back and tell us what he has overhead." Takama smiled at Dido's surprised expression. "As I said, Highness, nothing occurs in Tunis without our knowing."

"And you do this for me? A Canaanite?"

"It is what is fair. Now, we have time until Patas returns. Let us do what men expect of us; let us gossip."

"But we share no common acquaintances nor references."

"Good. Fresh gossip is the best gossip."

SEVEN

Dido giggled at Takama's recounting of two boys who had gone separately to the fountain for a clandestine courtship, only to discover each other in the darkness. She'd just begun a story of her own when Patas dashed back in.

Her hostess listened to the boy's recount, then relayed it; "The parties begin in opposition. They argue over the annual tribute due Chieftain Hiarbas. He seeks an annual payment equal to five times the silver-weight of the initial payment. Your men claim that the purchase was outright and no further tribute is forthcoming. Patas says they cockle like roosters."

Dido thought for a moment before replying.

"Tell Patas to seek the little Libyan who looks like a little Canaanite. He will be between both parties, cockling the most. His name is Afsan." Underscoring Dido's words, Takama whispered to the boy. "Afsan is to relay my message to both parties: The land beneath Carthage is dirt and rocks. The only change in the value of the land is in the perceptions of men. The land has not changed, so the value has not increased; the Canaanites should not pay more. But the existence of Carthage deprives the Chieftain of its use; the Canaanites should pay for such use. The amount has been established already; that is the amount the Knony should pay." At her terminating nod, the boy dashed out.

"Your son is a brave little man," she added. His mother smiled at the compliment.

"Zumar and I have been blessed. For the first few years of our marriage, no child formed within me. Zumar considered taking a second wife to bring forth an heir. Eventually we were blessed and my belly swelled, but our happiness was short-lived: the child died at birth. Yet this gave my husband hope. Our second child survived passage into the world: Patas. Someday this house will be his."

"Your husbands take multiple wives?"

"Sometimes. Most of the time, one woman of Tunis is more than enough for them. And what of you, fair Dido? Have you a son or daughter?"

Dido felt the smallest pin-prick of jealous regret. She willed her face to neutrality. "No children yet. Someday, perhaps, I will take a husband. Someday I shall produce my own Carthaginian."

"Aye. You have great beauty and many years. You will find a fine man and together have many children. This is what I feel is right."

"Sometimes the gods see otherwise."

They chatted for a while longer before Patas returned.

"They agreed on the tribute," Takama forwarded. "Now they argue even louder about Carthage's obligations to the Chieftain."

"What obligation can Hiarbas expect beyond silver?"

"Military service."

Directly to the boy, Dido instructed, "*N'*! No. Never!" What words did not convey, her expression made up for. He tore into the street.

"I cannot advise you," Takama noted. "But in paying tribute, Carthage now falls within Hiarbas' domain. It is customary for his subjects to support him with their grain, their gold, and their arms."

"What if he uses us in wars against neighbors we hold no grudge against? They will quickly learn to hate all Canaanites. This would go against the interest of my homeland. Just as Tunis supports Chieftain Hiarbas, Carthage must support King Pumayyaton."

" *'Bl*, I can see your position."

"But will Hiarbas?"

He did not.

"We are Canaanites," Dido's words passed through mother to son. "We are not Libyans. We pay silver for our land. We do not pay in blood and bronze. No Carthaginian will be a tool for the Chieftain's feuds."

The two women awaited the answer in silence. The standoff in the distant *thajma'th* reverberated in the room. The wait was quite short this time.

Patas stood without words, staring at Dido.

"Do not tell this to Afsan," she said slowly, words to the mother, eyes to the son. "Tell this directly to Hiarbas. Tell him the Canaanite warriors are like wasps sealed in an amphorae. If the stopper is removed and they are released, they may well sting all within their range. Tell him it is his hand upon the stopper."

Takama spoke quickly. Patas eyed her with reluctance before departing.

Again, a silent wait, slightly longer than its predecessor.

Takama listened to the words before smiling to Dido. "The place the bricks are made. It is outside of the bounds of Carthage. Hiarbas seeks one brick out of every four produced."

"Done," Dido agreed in relief. The new demand denoted the abandonment of the old. Concession for concession.

Through the afternoon, Patas ran between home and plaza with his burden of words. When the Libyan declared an intent to tax imports, Dido countered with an equal tax against exports. Hiarbas gained back ground by winning access to prize pasturage on Bursa's west slope. In a futile attempt to define fishing rights in the bay, it was eventually agreed that only the fish could decide whose nets they would swim into.

Patas returned again, but this time he was not alone. High Priest Scylax stood in the late afternoon sunlight.

"The negotiations are nearly complete," he explained. "Kotilus and Mintho are performing Libyan oath rituals. I am to bring you back."

"I thought the house was a woman's place."

"That beastly little Afsan," Scylax growled. "He told the barbarians about what I had done to myself in service to my goddess. They laughed and proclaimed that the house was more my place than the *thajma'th*. The fools!"

"Do not take offense, good priest," Takama replied. "It is only the men's simple way. Just as it is their way to send you away without feeding you. Allow me to prepare food for your travels." She began bustling about the hearth, preparing a small wrap of provisions.

Scylax, unbidden, slumped down on a small sleeping bench on the opposite wall. Their hostess stiffened minutely, making Dido realize the violation of Lord Zumar's place. She made discreet gestures which Scylax utterly missed.

"These marks," he eventually asked, tracing figures on the wall. "What are they?"

"Magic," Takama replied. "House magic, to bring blessings to our home."

Scylax squinted. "This one. It looks like a girl."

Dido came across and looked to where he pointed. Indeed, the figure looked like a stylized woman; round head, horizontal stick arms, and a triangle for a dress.

"It is the sign of Tanit," the Libyan replied. "We placed it there to summon Patas to this world."

"Summon him to the world?" The priest's intent gaze swung to her.

"Fertility magic."

"Fertility?" He swung back to the figure, trembling fingers tracing the scratch marks.

"Scylax, are you well?" Dido asked in concern.

"Well? You trumped-up slip of a girl! Do you know what this means?" He whirled to face her. "Astarte is here. Astarte moves among these people!"

Dido carefully studied the pictogram once more. Something nagged at her about it; she'd seen it before. Then it came. The Egyptian Anhk symbol, the sign of life. It, too, was made along simple lines, a cross with a rounded head. Sometimes, it was stylized with a flared lower leg.

"Tanit and Astarte," Scylax continued, "Astarte and Tanit. Gods often travel between nations. The Greeks worship Hercules and Aphrodite, who are clearly Melqart and Astarte. And now I find my Goddess here on this barbaric shore, recognized as Tanit!"

Dido turned and considered Takama, laboring in the light of the cooking fires. The woman's skin and features were not those of the Kush who lived to the south. In fact, she looked very much like the Egyptians who shared this very coastline, a month's sailing east. Could her tribe be a wandering branch of that noble race? Had her people followed the coast west to these fertile lands? If they had, they might well have carried with them such symbols, their meanings lost across the generations but for the faintest of echoes.

She might have voiced such thoughts but Scylax was beyond thinking now. He'd broken into fervent murmuring, an impromptu service to Astarte. He had found his goddess.

Takama placed an aromatic bundle into Dido's hands. "Queen Lady of Carthage, I thank you for honoring my house."

Dido used her free hand to grasp those of her hostess. "High Lady of Tunis, I thank you for your gracious hospitality and your aid to my people."

The Libyan smiled warmly. "Journey safely, my new friend. Be us not strangers."

Dido turned but halted. "Prince Patas," she called. The small boy blinked from the corner he'd watched the foreigners from. Recognizing the summons, he drifted meekly to her.

"You have served the Canaanites this day. For that we thank you." She slipped a hand within her robe. From it she drew the small knife with the wondrous ivory handle. She'd carried it into the village, a small protection should things have gone awry. "This was a royal court gift, passed from Assyrians to Cypriots to the Canaanites. Now it is yours." She placed it into the small brown hands of the beaming boy.

His mother rattled off quick words, most likely the equivalent of *what do you say?*

Patas bowed deeply and spoke words of obvious gratitude. Then he scrambled up the loft ladder with his new treasure like a small monkey.

"Come, Scylax," Dido instructed. "You were to fetch me, remember?"

The priest growled like a dog over his meat but conceded. They passed through the village and met their party before the entrance to the *thajma'th*. Hêgêsistratus eyed the murmuring priest.

"What has occurred to him?"

"He has found his Goddess."

"I see. Well, she had better be able to travel quickly. I want to be home before sunset."

They traveled north in the lengthening light. The tall grasses swayed before the crisp winds off the bay. Dido passed portions of Takama's victuals, meat and vegetables wrapped within an envelope of bread. The men laughed gently among themselves, happily finished with the negotiations.

But most happiest by far was Scylax. He laughed louder than the others, even sharing in a traveling song. Other times, he would speak of Astarte like a young besotted lover. He made references to Melqart as an old god. He laughed that Baal had no true temple in Carthage.

Dido caught the two nobles exchanging glances. Listening to the high priest's boasts, she realized that in finding Tanit, he'd not regained his lost spirituality. Only his confidence.

The line shivered in his callused hand. Twisting, the fisherman shot a glance over his stern.

"It draws closer," his cousin shouted up.

"Stay low," he snapped. Keeping their weight near the hull afforded them the best speed. He darted a glance back. The thing was slowly closing.

He made a decision, life against profit.

"The catch," he ordered. "Overboard with it!"

They looked at him as if he was mad. A Canaanite would die rather than lose his cargo. The fisherman supposed this was a happy myth, carried by those not in his precarious position.

"Overboard! Now!"

His cousin, son, and the apprentice instantly obeyed. Over the side went the catch, net and all. So much silver lost.

A glare over his shoulder. "*Rb qbhn olt 'nth,*" he shouted at the pursuing monster.

From the wet decking where he huddled, his cousin called up, "Is Carthage near?"

Much bay still separated them from home. He gave his small crew a sharp shake of his head.

"Then what shall we do?" quailed the cousin.

"I have a plan," he told them, firming his grip upon rope and tiller. "A desperate one. If you have a favorite among the gods, pray to him now."

His cousin decided that he would just look sick. The apprentice chose to silently pray. His son gave him pride; only ten summers old, and he lay calmly like a man, waiting his father's orders.

There was a crack as if a line had parted. The fisherman snapped his head about. An arrow quivered in the decking.

Behind them, several archers stood over the prow of the Greek penteconter, weapons taunt. Another shaft flew, hissing past to starboard. Fifty oars churned the water, driving the warship's hull at breathtaking speed.

An arrow passed just over his head, holing their sail. Close enough.

"When I call, scramble as far starboard as you can go. Ready?" Three desperate nods. "Melqart have mercy upon us. *Now*!"

The planks of the boat squealed as he threw the tiller over. The blunt little bow went starboard, directly into the wind. Only the men hanging over the side kept it from turning turtle. Still, momentum fell away quickly. The sail flapped overhead like a carrion bird's wing.

And then another sound—the sounds of oars thrusting through water.

They'd caught the penteconter by surprise, that much was certain. It would bear past their stern. But the oars...

The fisherman looked up to see them thrash just behind him in glistening explosions.

Arrows hissed down at them. His cousin shrieked, a shaft driven clean through his arm. He'd no time for such trivialities; their boat was nearly in irons. He heaved the tiller over again, attempting to get the bow to come around starboard. His son, his fine son, was the only one with sense enough to shift weight and aid him.

The little boat hung for a long moment before falling away. The sail boomed open. They now had the weathergauge on the enemy penteconter, and briefly the fisherman considered tacking clear. Then the warship's sail fell like a collapsing dream. With fifty oars, she would overhaul him even faster upwind.

Downwind, then.

A moment to wait for the Greeks to commit. He glanced to where the apprentice fussed with his mewing cousin.

"Break off the shaft and pull it clear," he ordered, not watching to see the outcome. The bastards had decided: the black bow with its knowing eyes swung starboard. He pushed his own bow around, driving down the warship's port side, long arrowshot from its stern. On its deck, archers ran back and forth like ants, unsure of their firing positions in the ever-shifting contest.

"Whoreson boy-lovers!" he shouted at their closest point. Someone shouted something in return, hostile and indecipherable. On the stern, the enemy captain bellowed at the tillerman to reverse his oar. Curling through a wasteful S-turn, the penteconter resumed the pursuit, several hull-lengths lost.

Even without their sail, they still gained, driven on the churning muscles of fifty strong backs and one hundred callused hands.

Hardly time for a glance to gauge the distance to Carthage; he'd made headway but not enough. They were back to their original positions. The penteconter slowly swelled behind them. Turning to port might gain speed, but would carry them from home. They'd turned starboard into the wind once, taking the Greeks by surprise. It was unlikely to work again but there was no other choice.

"Again; starboard on my mark." Arrows plinked into the water like rain. Bastard Greeks. He braced.

"Now!"

Again the bow came around. A shout from the Greek forward lookout—they'd been watching for it. The little boat clawed upwind. He looked over—the bastards were helming starboard, attempting to run him down. But he was clear of their bow. Clear of their...

"Oars! Get down!"

The rowers were peering over their shoulders, bracing themselves, oars horizontal, twenty-five lethal weapons. The sail crackled impotently. He hit the deck, the sound of the water's passage beneath the hull falling to nothing. Shadows flickered overhead, lines parted like lute strings, followed by a splintering crash.

And over it all, a shriek.

He was up just in time to see the mast tumble over the side. A scream from behind; the apprentice had been snatched by an oar like a mouse taken by an owl. He clung to the slippery blade, pleading. Laughter came from the penteconter as men from the nearby benches swatted at the desperate man. There was a crimson flash from an opened scalp and then he slipped off, sinking like a stone.

The mast was gone, the deck a harvest of arrows. His cousin cowered in the bow. His son came to him, passing him one of the gutting knives. While the Greeks would likely stand off and rely on their bowmen, there was always a chance they would attempt to board. Always a chance to die fighting.

The penteconter was turning, leisurely this time. The bow-eyes fell upon him again and he met their fixed gaze with one of resolution. He could see the archers coming forward. The boy-lovers were not going to give him his chance. So it went. Melqart would judge him by the courage in his heart.

They closed like a Nile-barge, casually coming back into range. He could see his enemies grinning over their shafts. Standing shoulder to shoulder, father and son waved their knives, screaming defiant, hopeless threats.

A wall of wood burst between them and the Greeks.

With oars breaking its rush, *RearEnd* twisted between the two ships, nose to nose with the Greeks. The recently jeering archers let off a disconcerted volley that did little save dislodge pitch and score wood.

Admiral Bitias stood high on the stern, assisting the tillerman, keen eyes locked on his foe. With milling oars, the two ships seemed locked in a staring match, the Greek captain confused, Bitias watchful.

"You came seeking us, did you not?" Bitias hailed. "You sought your missing traders? They trespassed into Carthaginian waters. We have taken them, just as we will take you!"

The Greek bowmen had regained their composure. With arrows strung, they stepped on onto the prow railing, seeking clear bowshot into *RearEnd*'s packed oardeck.

From his shelter in the bow, Aleyn sprang to his feet. "Bowmen up!"

A dozen women rose above the gunnels. The Greeks hesitated at the sight.

"*Tpp!*" the *shnymshtr* bellowed.

Arrows lanced between the ships. The northern archers crumpled, some tumbling over the side, the others toppling to the deck.

A sharp call. The Greek penteconter backed oars, moving away from *RearEnd*. The Canaanite warship held station, letting their opponent gain distance. The women sent another flight of arrows after it. One or two oars could be seen dragging uselessly in the water.

From his pitching little boat, the fisherman could hardly credit what he'd seen take place. But there was Lord Bitias standing larger than life in the stern. Casually, the captain called out, "Ladies, you have had your fun. Now please sit. We promised your husbands and lovers we would see you home safe." A series of cat-calls met this request, but the women dropped back below the gunnels.

The Greeks had pulled back far enough and had swung their bow north, perhaps considering fleeing the bay. At Bitias' call, *RearEnd*'s oars began to churn, the tiller banging over. She moved on an intercept course on the enemy, bearing in on their flank.

The Greek starboard oarsmen pulled their shafts inboard. Weapons were drawn for the inevitable grappling and boarding that would shortly take place.

From where he bobbed in his disabled boat, the fisherman watched as *RearEnd* gathered momentum. It made no attempt to swing parallel to its counterpart. Rather, at full speed, it slammed into the enemy vessel's flank.

Across the waves came the crash of timbers giving way before the bronze ram.

Momentarily the two ships lay locked together. Then *RearEnd*'s oars methodically began to back. Slowly she eased clear.

The fisherman could see that the Greek had been critically holed. Already it was listing, its crew dashing about the deck. Fire they could fight. Boarders they could fight. But against the onrushing sea, there was no defense.

It sank slowly, bow down, curved stern covered with struggling men. And then the hull dropped beneath the waves as if pulled below by Yam himself. *RearEnd* remained clear, its women archers shooting anyone clever enough to know how to swim. Carthage had neither the time nor the facilities for prisoners.

Only then did *RearEnd*'s bow come about. Standing in his shattered boat, watching the approach of the penteconter, the fisherman suddenly realized that he would live to see another dawn.

D ido luxuriated in a stolen moment. The council's debates echoed in Melqart's hall, but for her, standing in the temple's doorway, there was only the sun's warmth and the fresh air of summer.

As the mid-year fields required little labor, construction now occupied the citizenry. Bursa summit was getting more than its share. Next to the city god's temple, the new worship house for Astarte/Tanit was slowly rising. Scylax had based his design on a replication of Carthage's founding temple, but with one alteration: a single row of bricks would be added before the timber roof was placed, making it slightly higher.

At the hill's crown, craftsmen were seeing to the foundations of a small palace. Others worked on the royal apartments that would share the site. Having gone through one winter in a plank and canvas shelter, Dido would be more than happy to have a warm suite to call her own.

Carthage changed so very quickly. What had once been a collection of rude tents and scrap-lumber lean-tos was now a street lined with single-story buildings. More streets were forming. Crude shelters sprang along these roads like mushrooms following a night rain, and she suspected that they would soon be rebuilt in brick and stone. The roads would press ever outward. When the walk to the central market became too long, second stories would begin to appear.

To sea, the fishing boats plied about, working up their catches. A transport rounded the point, homebound after a short run to Utica. Shining hoplites drilled on the sand runway. A distant caravan threaded up the road from Tunis with its late-season trade. Her city breathed like a living thing.

"Of course she would agree," Lord Kotilus complained. "She is one of *them*."

"One of what, my friend?" she asked, turning. "Like you, I am an exile. Like you, I am a *rzn*."

"You are a woman," the horse-trader groused.

Leaning back on a crude hideskin cushion, Bitias grinned. "He still complains about using women as naval archers. He finds it *untraditional*."

"Not untraditional," Kotilus corrected. "Unsound. From our women comes our next generation of Carthaginians. From them, our race will issue forth. They are too precious to risk in something as chaotic as combat."

"You had no problem with it when we set out to engage the Greeks," Lord Mintho noted. "You saw them come aboard and raised no complaint. For myself, I will admit that I was happy to see them join us. Facing a Greek warship with its battle-hardened crew was rather frightening. The women proved themselves to be more than capable, a valuable addition to *RearEnd*'s capacities."

"I did not voice concerns at that time because I did not think they were going to be used in the battle."

"Why did you think they came aboard, bows over their shoulders? To trail their delicate hands in the water? To watch the battle in indulgent idleness?" The short noble paused, measuring his counterpart. "Or could it be that it was all right until you saw your darling new wife in their company?"

"Why should I be the only to risk a wife? Dido was not there. Neither was Bitias' Os'sh. That is not fair."

"Nor is your implication," Bitias replied, sitting up sharply. "Dido was at the new palace site, taking part in the consecration sacrifices. By the time she'd reached the beach, *RearEnd* was gone. As for Os'sh, she has been forbidden by High Priest Scylax to join on the grounds that she is a mother."

"The tinker's wife, what is her name? Yzebel. She was there, bow in hand, and she has two children of her own."

"As I said," Bitias replied evenly, "Os'sh's exclusion from the auxiliary archers is *Bol Okbr*'s ruling. You should speak with him. I know that Os'sh plans to, shortly."

Tetramnestus stirred uncomfortably at the admiral's use of his brother priest's uncomplimentary nickname.

"But why not men?" Kotilus demanded. "Why risk women when we have men?"

"We plan to lay a new hull over the winter months," Bitias explained, "a sister ship to *RearEnd*. Once the Greeks learn our trick, it is unlikely they will present their flanks to us again. Two ships can operate like two hands, one to hold, the other to thrust."

"How can the Greeks learn of our secret weapon? In every engagement, you have triumphed. And in every engagement, the entire enemy complement was consigned to the afterlife. How could the Greeks find out?"

"We are traders, Lord Kotilus," Dido forwarded. "This year, our cargo ships lay routes across the Upper Sea. They will sell their cargoes in whatever port profits them the most. While they are there, the crews will visit the harbor wineshops. They will drink, and they will talk."

"Mere conjecture," Kotilus noted, but with a voice that betrayed his confidence.

"Is it?" Dido replied, "It is likely the Greeks already grow suspicious of our presence. Several of their merchants are missing. And Envoy Ib was hardly discreet. Such a flotilla must have raised Greek suspicions. I have no doubt that Greek penteconter we defeated was back-tracking Ib's fleet, trying to find where it had landed and what its business was."

Bitias cut in, his voice wry, "A distant reconnaissance of this nature is usually not conducted by a single ship."

"What is it you are saying?" Kotilus demanded.

"That the fish we caught is not likely the only one out there." Bitias leaned back on his cushion, voice easy but eyes hard. "That there are likely more Greek warships in these waters, nosing about, looking for us. Sinking that one ship did not end this. If anything, it has only begun."

EIGHT

The heat was fading in the glory of late day. The typical activities took place on the beach that served as both drill field and harbor. A line of women bent bows and sent arrows hissing at a straw target bound upright to a post. To the side, Hêgêsistratus dressed a line of disjointed hoplites, attempting to drill another group of new citizens into the techniques of close-formation combat. From his oaths, he had a long journey before him.

On a road equally long, Second Officer Aleyn worked with his own trainees, attempting to turn their new colonists into a second penteconter crew. Today's drill involved boarding *RearEnd* with oars with maximum efficiency and minimum concussions. In the cramped quarters, a long oar in the hands of a novice was a dangerous thing indeed. Aleyn, a combat veteran, excelled at ducking.

"Within the planks, ladies," Scylax's reedy voice commanded. "You must remain within the planks."

"Can we just go back to practicing supporting a hoplite formation?" a bow-woman groused. "I have string burn along my arm, and it came not from my own line."

"Someone pointed out that your training was inadequate when it came to fighting from our penteconter's deck during the recent battle," the priest curtly replied. "That a number of you fouled one another. These planks outline the deckspace you have to work within."

"We dropped most of those boy-lovers in the first volley," another woman observed.

"You should have gotten them all. After we learn to fire forward, we will rotate the boards and practice firing to port and starboard." He ignored their groans, stepping clear. "Draw your weapons." As one, the bows rose, creaking under tension. "*Tpp!*"

The buzz of hornets. The straw figure shuddered beneath the impacts. Three quarters of the shafts had struck home. It was good accuracy, giving the range and the packed quarters. But to Scylax, praise was like gold; he was loath to yield it willingly.

"Fair," he allowed. "Fetch your shafts and we will try again." The women went forward to claim their arrows, good naturedly ribbing those who had to find theirs in the sand.

He looked over to where the penteconter lay on the beach, wavering oar shafts spouting like a sea urchin's spines. Aleyn stood on the bow, berating his charges on their sloppiness. At sight of the second officer, Scylax felt a stab of jealousy. The holy lord had told him of the man's duties the night of Egersis. The thought of this commoner and Dido, proud Dido, cavorting in Melqart's empty hall made his blood churn with something other than *'drtnt*. He forced himself to remember that Tanit (*Astarte*, he corrected) was a goddess of fertility and love. With effort, he buried his resentment.

It was only then that he noticed his women standing near their target, unmoving. He was about to tongue-lash them for their dalliance when he realized they were all looking at something beyond him. He turned.

As far beyond the planks as they were from the target stood Os'sh. Bundles were festooned across her back. Scylax squinted and saw a little arm move in the late sunlight; she had her brat strapped to her back. A barbarian way to carry children, no doubt.

But there was something else. He could not make it out at first. Then she shrugged her shoulder, catching the bow as it fell into her hand. To Scylax, the weapon appeared malformed. Unlike the Canaanite naval bows with their smooth arc and fine lines, this thing was a double-curved crudity. It was thick and utilitarian, hardly the graceful weapon he was comfortable with.

She reached past her child and drew an arrow, notching it on the line. Dispassionate brown eyes focused on the straw target. The women around it drew well clear, knowing that the only way an arrow might cover such a range would be through high elevation, and high elevation shots were largely un-aimed.

She brought her bow up, a touch past level. The weapon gave an oddly harmonic creak beneath tension.

It kicked slightly in her hand. The arrow went past Scylax with a menacing hum.

He turned to see the shaft quivering in the shoulder of the target figure.

"Lucky," the high priest spat.

Os'sh drew a second arrow, threaded it, and sighted. A second low thrum. This one hit the target in the center of its chest, punching into the post with a sharp crack.

Her third shot was off. Even though it missed, it carried far beyond where the other arrows had landed.

Os'sh brushed an errant brown hair from her forehead, lowered her weapon, and crossed the sands. Scylax looked from her to the target and back again, looking for the trick of the thing.

She raised her weapon for his examination.

"This is a bow of my people. It is made with strips of wood, bone, and dried sinew. It is a little smaller than your weapons, but has far greater power."

He would not take the proffered weapon.

"So this is what you were doing," Scylax observed. "If you think I will be swayed..."

"You *will* be swayed," Hêgêsistratus corrected as he came up from behind. "Let me see that weapon, girl." He took the bow, ran a finger along its odd double-curled form, and hefted it. "May I?" Os'sh passed an arrow across. The general drew, aimed, and released in one single practiced motion.

The arrow missed the target by a wide margin, yet flew much further than the naval bows were capable of.

"A bow such as this takes time," Os'sh noted. "Time to construct and time to train. We Scythians have time for such things. It is for the Carthaginians to decide if they do as well."

"We do not," Scylax answered defensively.

"We do," Hêgêsistratus countered.

"General, your responsibilities are your hoplites. Mine are these archers. It is for me to determine how best to employ them."

"You are mistaken, High Priest", the Greek replied sharply. "My responsibility is Carthage's defense. Such a weapon would allow archers backing my men to get two, perhaps three volleys in before the formations close." He raised the ugly missile weapon. "We must have it."

"I chose to put emphasis on training and discipline. To switch to this weapon will require too much time and effort. Better to be accurate at short range than inept at long."

Hêgêsistratus eyes narrowed as if he'd detected a rank odor.

"I do not care what occurred between yourself and these people on Cyprus. Your grudges do not concern me. This weapon is superior. We will have it."

"What occurred in the past has no bearing on my decision," Scylax flared. "I have made up my mind. We will retain our Canaanite bows."

"Consider, priest. I will take this issue up Bursa Hill to the council. I will present my case to the assembled elders. You know Queen Dido as well as I. As soon as she sees this weapon, she will demand we switch to it. So choose your defeat, High Priest. Lose here on the sands or before the assemblage. Either way, you will lose."

Scylax watched as the Greek handed the weapon back to the brown woman, bestowing a respectful nod.

"So we should abandon our bows, Commander? Leave Carthage defenseless while we glue bones together?" He gestured to the mouth of the bay. "Lord Bitias said your countrymen are out there. You wish to leave our city open before them?"

"Of course not," Hêgêsistratus sighed. "You work so hard to be difficult. Our women's accuracy is passable. Drop their training to a quarter of what it is now; this will keep their edge. The balance of the time, build these. Lady Os'sh will instruct you."

Scylax watched silently as the Greek crossed the beach to his hoplites.

"I only wanted to serve Carthage," Os'sh said quietly. "You would not let me, so I had to seek other paths to do so. The past is behind us, High Priest. Let us settle our grievances and move forward."

Scylax kept his back towards her. "Gather the materials you will need. We will begin construction tomorrow." Without dismissing the women, he made for the road that led to his incomplete temple.

On her back, Amilcar began to whine and fidget.

"Hush little one," she told him, watching the receding priest. "Everything will be all right."

"**O**ne, Highness?"

"Two," Dido instructed the baker. He nodded, placing two small loaves on his stall table. It took but a moment for him to locate her entry on his clay tablet and scratch two additional marks near her name. When the balance rose high enough, she would clear it with a shekel of silver.

Tucking the bread against the frond-wrapped baked fish beneath her arm, she continued up Bursa. Tonight was the night she dined with Tetramnestus. They would reminisce over the old times, the good and the bad, long into the evening.

People collected on the stoops of their houses, enjoying the final moments of sunlight. Somewhere nearby a lute added melody to the evening breeze. A baby cried, bringing a smile to Dido's lips; Carthage was growing by the day.

She noted fewer women than usual. Evidently they were at home, working on the new Scythian bows. They had seen its power and were eager to have such for themselves. Building such took time and effort. Materials were scarce; hunters had found they could get more for the bones of their kills than the meat.

Near Bursa's summit stood the temples of Melqart and Astarte, the latter largely complete. Beyond, her own palace was beginning to take shape. There was even talk of raising a wall around the summit, a citadel to fall back upon if the community were threatened. While such would be a valuable addition, she felt it could be years before they could initiate such an undertaking. There was just so much that needed doing.

A strange scent drifted over her. She frowned at it, trying to identify the odor. It was tangy and unpleasant, a metallic smell.

The sun wavered and faded.

She stared into the sunset, confused. Where a moment ago had been a sharply defined orb, now there was only a reddish blur. And the sky, *it wavered.*

She thought of the sandstorms Afsan had spoken of, those that blew off the southern desert. Sometimes they came north. If this were so, they would have to get their goat herds in fairly quickly. Furthermore...

Something struck her chest. It fell to the dirt, spun for a moment and grew still. It looked like a grasshopper but for its motley yellow coloration. The insect used a small rock to pull itself upright. Its wings blurred and it was gone.

Three more thrummed past, sounding like arrows from Os'sh's bow.

The bread and fish tumbled to the packed dirt.

A cloud of insects swarmed past Dido. Some slapped into her. One tangled in her hair. She shook her head madly, flinging it away, before dashing through the living cloud for the temple.

Distantly, from the observation post near the marshes, a warning trumpet rose. It was echoed by the cries and screams that rose over the city.

"Melqart's benevolence," the holy lord exclaimed from the temple's doorway. "What is happening?"

"Locusts," shouted Dido, pushing him inside and shoving the door shut. It crunched. "Father told me stories how such things visited Egypt in times past. I thought they were simply stories to scare little girls."

Tetramnestus looked up to the temple's high windows. Insects whirled through, unchecked. "They are stories that scare grown priests. Queen Dido, what are we to do?"

An insect fluttered down nearby. She paused long enough to crush it beneath her bare heal. "The shield; the one that is to be rung to summon the council. Have your apprentices strike it, and keep striking it. We must gather and decide what is to be done."

The portly priest dashed off. Dido unconsciously moved to place her back into a corner. Thick yellow bugs withered on the floor. One or two bore through a brazier's flame, scarlet arcs against the gloom.

From outside, a desperate clanging rose. Engulfed by winged horrors, the apprentice was putting his fear into his swings.

Mintho was the first to arrive. He shivered uncontrollably while Dido brushed the locusts from him. He then proceeded to stamp any of the nearby creatures. Soon his feet were crusted with yellow paste while tears ran down his cheeks.

"Lord Mintho! Control yourself!" Kotilus stepped through the door, brushing the horrors from him is if they were little more than fallen leaves. "You are an elder and a noble."

It was as if the horse-trader had thrown cold water, not simple words, over his counterpart. The stocky man blinked once, then looked at his stained feet dumbly.

More men of the council pushed through the doors. Outside, the locusts swirled past like driving rain.

"Melqart's clenched anus," Bitias exclaimed as he arrived shortly afterwards. "I have been in all number of storms in my life, but never a storm of bugs." With care, he pulled one creature from his curled beard, taking grim delight in feeding it into the flames of a nearby brazier.

"Was there anyone behind you?" Dido demanded.

The admiral looked at her through a sickly tendril of smoke. "Nay. I was seeing to *RearEnd* when the swarm hit. I ran up Bursa as fast as I could—the streets are empty. If we are missing any elders, they are not coming."

The clang of the summoning shield fell silent. Tetramnestus entered, supporting a weeping apprentice. The large priest took his subordinate by the shoulders and gave him a firm shaking. Insects fell to the ground, buzzing angrily. Only when the boy was clean did he give himself a furious shake, with a shudder as an aftershock.

Dido turned to the assemblage. "What danger do we face?"

"The horses broke from my paddock," Kotilus replied. "The winged evil drove them mad. I can only assume the goats and oxen will likewise scatter."

Mintho followed upon his words. "The well. We have just completed the open cistern near the marketplace, but have yet to cap it. Those things will have fallen into it in the hundreds. They will have to be scooped out, and quickly, before they foul its waters."

"*N*'! Frightened ponies and nasty water are but minor setbacks," Bitias spat from the brazier. He was flicking locusts into it, one after another.

Dido gestured up to the windows where the ruddy light of sunset flickered through the living maelstrom. "You call this a setback? Our livestock and water supply are in danger."

Bitias consigned another insect to the flames. "On the way up the hill, I passed those small trees, just below the marketplace. They were covered with insects. Every leaf. And they were stuffing their little yellow faces like a hungry peasant at a nobleman's banquet."

"Who cares of the fate of some shade trees?" Kotilus shot back.

"You do not see the true danger? They eat trees. They feast upon all things the goddess Arsay provides." He tossed a final bug in. It sizzled and popped. "Including our crops."

Dido felt a chill come over her. "But the harvest is only weeks from being brought in! The granary is nigh empty!"

Bitias replied with a sad shrug.

"We must gather the people," she continued. "We must drive these things from the fields!"

"They are not lions, my lady," Tetramnestus noted. "They cannot be driven. They would flow around us like the waters of the Upper Sea."

She looked from face to face desperately. Her eyes fell on Bitias' brazier with its bittersweet curl of smoke. "Fire. They fall to fire. We can give each man and woman a torch. Perhaps such would drive them from our wheat."

Mintho shook his head. "If you send our people with torches into dark fields, the night alive with those fiends, you will most certainly see the crops alight."

"Better burned than devoured," Kotilus noted.

"The flames might claim Carthage, as well."

"*Lys*," Kotilus exclaimed. He turned and paced away, careful to avoid the withering insects. After a moment's quiet thought, he said, "The Libyans. We trade with them. Horses. Ivory. Skins. Feathers. Anything they bring north, we can sell. Perhaps we can trade for grain."

"Doubtful," another elder replied. "Hiarbas seeks advantage over us. Should we beg for food, what price might he set? He might even withhold it."

Dido's thoughts went to Takama and her village. "Who knows how big this swarm is. Libyan villages might also lay under this horrible cloud. There may be no food to spare."

"There may be food to take," Kotilus countered.

Dido shook her head. "How much could we bring back before the Libyans sieged us on our blighted peninsula? Force might delay the outcome, but make it even more certain."

"We forget; we are traders," Mintho observed. "Could we not sail north and trade with the tribes of Víteliú?"

Bitias thought it over. "There are only two transports on our beach. The rest are off trading, and will likely return just before the end of the sailing season. Even with both boats, we might get two or three loads home before the storms come. Still not enough."

Dido caught Tetramnestus' eye. "What succor can we seek from Melqart? Is there some way we can appease him, to remove this plague?"

"It is not from gods present whom favor must be sought," came a voice from the door. "We must appease the god we have forgotten."

Scylax stood in the doorway, the living night at his back. Locusts crawled across his robes with jerky alien motions.

"Not another anguished cry for your misplaced goddess," Bitias groaned. "Spare us your whinings."

The high priest drew himself erect. "I have my Astarte. I have my Tanit. The Goddess might be petulant with Carthage's shabby respect for Her, but She would hardly summon the Aklm, the devourer demons. This is the work of one mightier than She."

"Baal," breathed Tetramnestus.

"Aye. The last member of Tyre's triad of gods. You have exported Melqart and Astarte to this cursed shore, but no temple exists for Baal. No sacrifice or praise was sent to him."

"We planned to begin his temple next spring," Dido exclaimed, mouth dry. "We hoped to gain a priest from Tyre following our next tithe."

"Clearly that was not soon enough," Scylax noted darkly.

"But it is not customary to build Baal's temple during the initial year. Melqart's temple is the community's hub. Once He has cleared the way, the Others join."

"Clearly this is not Melqart's doing," the thin man gestured through the door at the swirling darkness. "He has been worshipped. As Astarte has been worshipped. But by granting favor to Them, you have neglected Baal's due. Only He is strong enough to summon the Aklm. And only He is strong enough to banish them."

Dido gripped her robes in order that her hands not be seen to tremble. She knew of the world and the gods that ruled it. She had lived her entire life in Their mastery. She'd paid homage to Melqart and his boon had been great; Carthage had thrived. But now these horrors were upon them. As much as she despised the scrawny priest, his words rang true. They *had* angered Baal.

"What must me do?" Dido asked, voice small. "Advise us, High Priest."

"There is only one thing that *can* be done."

In her peripheral vision, she saw Tetramnestus pale.

"A thousand years ago," Scylax continued, "Baal made greater demands upon the Canaanites. Demands for greater sacrifices. Living sacrifices."

"But we sacrifice such things to Melqart. Oxen, goats..."

"Humans," Scylax thundered. "In times of dire need, humans were sacrificed. It is the ultimate symbol of our love and subservience to Baal that we readily offer up life to him."

Kotilus stared at the small man before him. And then he bowed in respect. Mintho shadowed his motion. The other elders did likewise.

Tetramnestus shook his head silently, sweat beading across his shaven head. It was not fear that flickered in his eyes.

"Who," Dido asked, "Who is sacrificed?"

"Children," Scylax replied. "Children are our most precious possession. In those times, a child of the nobility was sent to Him. As it must be now, if we are to save Carthage." His finger came up like a hoplite's spear. To Bitias it pointed. "The first child of our city must be slain. No greater offering exists."

Bitias's face went gray. Before Dido's eyes, he aged years. He might be a man prone to flippancy and nonsense, but he knew the gods. He'd lived his life by Their graces. For a simple sailor, they *were* life itself.

"My son," he croaked. "Certainly Baal would take another. I am an admiral. I am an elder. I would give my life, and do so gladly."

"Your child, Lord Bitias," Scylax decreed. "The first born of Carthage, so it must be."

Bitias turned slowly to Dido and fell bonelessly to his knees.

"My Queen. My Holy Lady. My love. Carthage faces doom. I realize such. But my Amilcar, he is my..." A sob welled up from him. He swallowed. "You are queen of this city. Your power is nigh that of the gods themselves."

She felt hot tears. "Bitias..."

His words poured out. "But you are also the trickster. You tricked King Pumayyaton. You tricked Commander Qurdi-Aššur-lamur. You tricked Governor Zinnridi. You tricked Chieftain Hiarbas." Desperation flared in his eyes. "If any human can fool a god, it would be you. A ruse, a twist, a misdirection. They are your weapons. Use them for me, *Qtn'khn*, Little Priestess. Save my son. Save my Amilcar."

She looked down at him, her mind flooded with emotions. She felt him in her arms again, on the temple's parapet that first night. The love stolen while Tyre convulsed in open revolt. Every glance, every smile, every kiss he'd ever bestowed upon her, sharper than memories. So their lives had twisted together, flesh and sweat and seed and *'drtnt*.

And in those images, other moments. Bitias and Os'sh....

Something deep within her opened, a dark little pit she'd never suspected. And within that pit was a thing too loathsome to consider, too horrible to face.

She crushed it as fiercely as she would a grain-bloated locust. But it had been there. And she had glimpsed it.

In the end, there was only one path available to her. But the pit-dweller had touched her; the words were fractionally easier to say.

"You must serve Carthage, Lord Bitias. Baal demands it."

He closed his eyes. Like a dead man, he stood. An elder attempted to steady him; he shook it off, his growl bestial. The elders moved back. Alone, the admiral of Tyre walked from the temple, to fetch that which the gods demanded.

NINE

She stood outside, the ground alive beneath her.

Locusts withered and stirred. Occasionally one would buzz through the night air. She was beyond it now.

When the wind shifted from the south, a rustle would carry to her. A million mandibles, ripping away the priceless crop a tiny fraction at a time.

The nearby temple of Melqart was largely empty. The council had slipped into the darkness, business done. Only the holy lord remained, his large form silhouetted in the doorway by the fires within. In his hand, a ceremonial knife reflected the flames.

Down Bursa's slope, from the darkened hovels of Carthage, a voice wailed. Occasionally words were howled, northern words, barbarian words. But mostly, it was a river of anguish that flowed into a sky of flickering insects and incomprehensible gods.

Things crawled across Dido's feet. Horrible things clambered up her clothing on tiny grasping legs. But none were as horrible as the thing she had glanced within herself. The pit-dweller.

A dark shape ascended Bursa. Bitias. Each step ground locusts into the dirt. Hundreds had perished in the course of his errand. But their army was beyond number.

As he crossed to the temple, Elisha heard the faintest cry come from the bundle in his arms.

Bitias paused before Tetramnestus, the smallest moment to grant the greatest farewell. Then he handed the child across and turned away, descending into Carthage's darkness.

Bearing the child, the priest turned and entered. High Priest

Scylax had outlined the ceremony. Without a priest of Baal present, Melqart's holy lord would have to perform the ceremony. Tetramnestus had glimpsed this possibility earlier and now lived with the horrible reality.

The shield rang forth again, strike after strike. A military trumpet joined it, their cacophony filling the night. They were not to signal nor summon. As in times a thousand years past, they served to overlay any sounds that might escape the temple's stout walls.

Dido felt the insects move over her and wondered if death felt thus. She could no longer hear the clamor. She could only look into the stars that shimmered in the cold night sky, seek out her gods, and ask *Why?*

In the light of dawn, Straton examined the stalk of wheat. He knew much about such simple things, having raised twenty harvests in Cyprus. He rolled the grained head between his callused fingers, his mind full of simple wonder.

The wheat was intact. The fields lay largely untouched.

And the ground was littered with the bodies of dead locusts.

They lay like a yellow-brown sheet, silent and still. Against houses and trees, they clustered in low drifts. The night prior had been filled with motion and noise and destruction; daybreak had fallen on a scene of disquieting serenity.

Straton knew that things had occurred last night at the summit of Bursa, dark offerings to the gods. And They had been appeased. The proof lay scattered at his feet. He looked across wheat that stirred before the day's first breeze and offered his own private thanks.

Carthage was slowly recovering from the tiny invaders. Women and children moved through the streets, collecting the small corpses in sacks. After threatening the food supplies, they would add to it. Fried, they were delicious.

On the beach, the lapping waves had carried the dead insects out, which would bring the fish in to feed. With haste, the fishermen readied their two boats, anticipating the boon. None of them commented on the disturbed sand nearby.

Living near their boats and the beach, the fisherfolk had all witnessed it. In the light of the rising moon, Bitias had come down and pulled at his penteconter, struggling to launch it himself. His second had stood by, observing for a while, before joining in the hopeless task. More men had come, a combination of old crew and new, drawn by instinct or the will of a god. With locusts fluttering around their feet, they had all put their backs into it, shifting the heavy warship into the cold waters. Without a word, the oars had slid out and the penteconter had moved away, lost to the night.

The sun crossed the sky. Those insects not claimed for the hearth were buried in pits. Near the marketplace, men allowed themselves to be lowered into the well. When they were drawn forth, they would drop their brimming baskets of pasty remains before retching. It was a grim task, one that was shared by all. Even Lord Mintho allowed himself to be lowered into the hellhole; nobles could not expect to be excluded.

Os'sh lay in her little home, staring at the ceiling with bloodshot eyes. The screaming was over. Tetramnestus had sent a priest to her, bearing some of the *hul gil.* Just as the Scythian knew how to overcome the drug, she knew how to prepare it. Her bow, such a source of recent pride, leaned forgotten in a corner.

In the late afternoon, Phoenix and Yzebel sought out Dido. The queen had not been seen all day. While the men worried, it was not their place to enter the woman's tent and see to her.

Like Os'sh, they found her laying on her small cot, eyes fixed on the canvas overhead. Her robes were stained with crushed bugs, the fabric stiff and pungent. The women eased her from her clothing, bathed her, and slipped a light tunic in its place.

The blunt tinker's wife paused in the doorway, looking at the prone girl. Concern twisted in her wrinkled face.

"She reviews her life and actions," Phoenix replied to the unspoken question. "Now that she has made that decision, she must determine how best to live with it."

The red sun lay on the wild horizon. High Priest Scylax watched its fall before stepping inside his temple. The doors he carefully barred. Then he lay before the Astarte's alter, his prayers deep and silent.

When his face came up, it could barely contain his glee.

How perfect it had been, he considered. How perfect his revenge. He'd hated them all, Elisha or Dido, whatever her name might be. Heroic Bitias. Exotic Os'sh. Corpulent Tetramnestus. He'd been comfortable in his position in Citium, second only to Governor Zinnridi. And then *they* had come, with their gold and tricks and urgent voyages. He'd been all too happy to anticipate Egersis, the rebirth signifying their departure. His life would have been his once again.

But they had stripped his temple, little different from the Sea People centuries before. They had stripped him of his female charges and of the trust he'd built with Zinnridi. They had dragged him into their exile. And because of them, he had nearly lost the goddess.

He'd found her again. Tanit. How wondrous the moment she'd made herself clear to him. The memory drove him to further devotions.

And then the locusts. A perfect foil to gain the perfect revenge upon them all. Dido; a horrible decision against her ex-lover. Bitias and Os'sh, with their perfect little life and perfect little Amilcar. And Tetramnestus, who'd leapt from temple aide to holy lord, toadying his way into a position that had cost Scylax twenty years to achieve. How the knife had trembled in his pudgy hand.

So very perfect. So very satisfying.

A small buzzing rose from one of the high windows. A moment later, an insect spun down, alighting on Astarte's alter. Scylax looked up in shock at the trespass. The locust regarded him with black unreadable eyes.

He crossed to the alter, raising a hand, preparing to sweep the creature away. The insect remained motionless, staring.

What if the swarm was not just a natural phenomena? Scylax's hand hung in the air. *What if the Aklm had truly been sent by Baal, a sign of his displeasure?*

Scylax fell to his bony knees, eyes locked on the creature before him.

If Baal felt such displeasure at a colony that did not pay homage, what would he feel towards a priest who took a god's weapon and made it his own?

Dido had known she could not fool a god.

How could he have presumed otherwise?

A trickle of sweat beaded on his forehead. He'd twisted Baal's vengeance to be his own. From His palace atop Mt. Zephon, Baal must now be glaring down, considering ant-like Scylax and his petty little schemes. The gods missed nothing. And their vengeance upon humans who dared cross them was swift and certain.

Hot urine stained Scylax's robes. He trembled before his alter, bowing to Astarte again and again, begging the Goddess to intercede. She had restrained Baal when He sought to attack Yam's messengers. She had ordered him to scatter Yam. Baal had listened then. Would He now?

His desperate pleads went on into the night. From the altar, the locust watched.

"Boy-lovers!" Bitias hung from the bow mastline, gesturing like a wildman.

On the endless beach, two penteconters lay at rest. Tiny men milled around them. As Aleyn watched, they grouped around their boats, shoving. A moment later and one, then both, were away.

From the stern, the second looked to his commander, his expression questioning.

Bitias thrust his hand forward. Of his intentions, there was no doubt.

"Two," the tillerman observed. "Two Greeks."

"Aye." It was all Aleyn could say. His mouth was quite dry.

Like the locusts of three days before, the two warships drove towards them, oars churning the waters. The vessel's eyes were rounder then those of *RearEnd*. To Aleyn, they seemed to cast an expression of expectation, as if the Greek vessels knew what had befallen their sister ship and hungered for revenge.

Bitias remained in the bow, watching the pair swing apart. The admiral gestured again; between them.

The Greeks closed in parallel, jaws through which *RearEnd* could throw itself. As Aleyn expected, when they came nigh abreast to either side, they swung in like twin temple doors. Their goal was obvious—they would foul *RearEnd* between them. With twice the weight in men, the Carthaginian vessel could not hope to win.

Bitias' attention traveled from one to the other, gauging. His hand came up, pointing abstractly forward. The Greeks piled in from either quarter.

A gesture from the admiral, low and casual. *Wait*, it said. *Almost.*

Aleyn had served Bitias for years. He knew his way of thinking. The rowers looked up to him, confirming the silent order. All knew what was expected.

The enemy penteconters bore in, close enough to see the bow foam that marked them like rabid dogs. They were so close that...

"Now," Bitias bellowed.

The men came up from their benches, leaning into their oars. Fifty shafts creaked. So sudden was the stop that Aleyn grabbed the nearby steering oar, lest he be thrown to the deck. *RearEnd*'s stern rode up on its own wake.

"*Sd*! *Sd*!"

The men shoved against their shafts, pushing like men possessed. In a repeat of the maneuver that had gained the craft its original fame, *RearEnd* backed out of danger. There came a splintering crash of oars as the jaws of the Greek trap slammed shut, sans victim.

Bitias looked over the bow as casually as a man might look out the window at a commotion in the marketplace. The Greeks had locked onto each other's oars. Men had leapt from their benches and found nothing to board. It would take time to sort it out.

No counter order came from the admiral. Foam licked around *RearEnd*'s stern as she backed further. The entangled vessels rotated slowly before the uncertain desert wind. One was now hidden, the other, broadside.

"Forward," Bitias commanded. Instantly the men reversed their strokes. Water churned around the oars. Spray lanced around the bow again. Under the acceleration, the bronze ram rose from the water like a stinger deploying.

The one penteconter was still shielded. From the nearer, desperate arrows sailed out. Bitias disregarding them like summer rain. The black flank loomed. Aleyn noticed a couple of the Greek rowers shift their oars aside as if to preserve them from the impending collision. *Just as a woman about to be raped reluctantly spreads her legs*, he found himself thinking.

This time, Aleyn found himself thrown to the deck. The crash of failing timbers came almost as an afterthought. Then came the roar of water unchecked.

"_Sd_. Back." Bitias sounded like a craftsman completing a task. A shudder ran through _RearEnd_ as she eased clear. Already her victim was settling. The men swarmed across the slanting deck, seeking sanctuary from the smothering waters.

Their plight did not register on Bitias. Instead, he looked over the doomed men to the sister ship. Like Bitias, her commander stood in the bow. Likely he'd gone forward to direct efforts to unfoul. Now he looked over the destruction, to _RearEnd_ with her eagle-head ram visible in the clear water. His eyes rose to Bitias, taking his measure. Then he turned and called an order in his foreign tongue. His ship completed its rotation. Clear, it pulled away, rowers wrenching at their shafts.

"The boy-lovers run," Bitias called out. "I will not have it! Aleyn, pursue them!"

The water before _RearEnd_ was filled with floating oars, planks, and choking, struggling men. Aleyn pushed on the steering arm, guiding the tillerman to go around.

"Through them," Bitias screamed back, composure gone. "Have I a woman for a second? Through them!"

Flushing, Aleyn corrected their course. Fearing their commander's wrath, the men hauled their oars. Dying men screamed, clawing desperately at the black hull that rode over them. Something briefly fouled the steering arm, dragging it. Without looking back, the tillerman gave it a hard shake. A doomed cry fell away but the helm was restored.

The Greeks fled east along the desert coast, _RearEnd_ grimly following. In their wake, the wreckage fell away, forgotten.

The Carthaginians had been at their oars since sun-up. But the Greeks had been at sea for more than a month. Days of brackish water, reduced rations, and sleeping in the open had taken their toll. Stroke for stroke, the pursuers gained.

Aleyn gained the true measure of the enemy captain the moment the ship came about. He'd let _RearEnd_ gain until it was too close to gather itself in a good sprint, but not so close as to catch him broadside. Clearly, the man was every bit as talented as Bitias.

The ships closed, the Greek wandering off to *RearEnd*'s port side, feinting and shifting like a knife fighter. Bitias stood in the bow, studying the approach, watching to see if the enemy would attempt to deflect their ram with their heavy prow or sheer off. Aleyn and the tillerman watched both enemy and their own captain, hoping for indications.

At the last possible moment, the Greek dropped his port oars and wrenched its bow over, twisting to run down *RearEnd*'s starboard side. Bitias stared at his swelling target as if judging the value of head-on impact. At the last second, he flung out his left arm. Aleyn threw himself against the steering oar, attempting to break away clean to port.

The Greek commander knew that his only chance was to board. As *RearEnd*'s ram turned away, he reversed his coarse, doing his best to foul oars. There was a moment of uncertainty as if the gods could not determine which ship they should bless.

Oars shattered as the opposing banks came together. Some rowers managed to haul theirs inboard. Others ducked as the impact slammed the shafts forward. A few were simply too slow.

Leaning into the tiller, Aleyn saw Moloch's oar catch the young man beneath his chin. His head snapped back, throwing the boy into the man behind him. With little ceremony, the rower shoved the corpse to the decking.

The enemy penteconter ran down their length. Momentarily, bows paralleled sterns. The enemy commander, still on the prow, passed within spitting distance of Aleyn. The man twisted, shouting to three archers in his stern, gesturing to Bitias. The men nodded, bows flexing.

Bitias turned and faced them, unflinching.

He seeks death, Aleyn realized.

The range was close but the ships were pitching, driving in opposite directions. Two arrows flew, missing. The third man held for a second, half-rising, tracking. The arrow vanished; Bitias staggered. Aleyn had no time for him; *RearEnd* was like a fish—it had to move forward to live. He called the stroke, the surviving oarsmen quickly falling into the cadence. The two ships pulled away from each other.

Time for a glance; Bitias stood, a red line grazing his upper arm. Aleyn had known that the gods blessed madmen. A moment later, the admiral signaled a hard turn. Shoving at the tillerman's side, the second officer glanced back.

The Greek was coming about. Like an unarmed man facing a blade, he had to get close. He could not give *RearEnd* the room it needed for a killing sprint.

There was a mad moment where the horizon spun, the Greek spun; everything was confused motion.

"*Ns'*! *Ns'*! *Ns'*!" Bitias shouted the stroke from the bow, leaning into the wind. The Greek drove towards them, its bow furrowing the waves.

As the speed increased, *RearEnd*'s handling changed. Wind gusted against her flank, confusing the handling even more. And it was easy to lose sight of the Greek behind the raised prow. In the last moment, Aleyn had no idea if they were on target or off enough to splinter oars and lock hulls.

Only his grip on the steering oar allowed him to keep his feet.

He looked up to see the Greek ship close to theirs, slightly bow-off. A swell picked up *RearEnd*, then the Greek. Aleyn realized the ships were linked through the ram.

The Greek commander stood opposite Bitias, scarcely a spear-length away. With sad eyes, he looked down to where the bronze ram jutted through his hull. *RearEnd*'s ram had struck, at low speed, against the heavier timbers just off the bow. The wound was mortal.

He was a tall, thin man, chin shaven. He returned his attention to Bitias. He spoke with a twisted northern accent, loudly enough for all to hear.

"Men of Canaan. We have fought hard and you have beaten us. We acknowledge your superior seamanship and equipment." He looked to the tan ribbon of the distant shore. "Our hull is breached. When we pull free, the sea will rush in. Permit us to make for the shore. In the unlikely event we reach it, we face the desert, its beasts, and its natives. Our deaths are certain. Permit us the attempt."

"*Sd*," Bitias said calmly. The oarsmen backed a stroke, pulling

RearEnd clear of the Greek timbers. Meanwhile, Bitias stooped, fetching up a small clay pot on a rope. He nodded to Barcas on a nearby bench. Aleyn watched the young noble pull forth a flint, sending a spark into the pot's maw. A moment later, its contents ignited.

Standing, the admiral whirled the pot three times around his head before letting it go. It traced a smoky trail through the air, dropping onto the Greek's amidships decking. When it struck, it exploded in flame.

"I send you to Baal!" Bitias shouted in damnation.

Men screamed as oil and pitch splashed fire through the packed benches. Any thought of making for land was lost. The dry wood of the vessel began to catch.

The Greek commander turned sadly, in time to take an arrow in the chest. Bitias, the bow quivering in his hands, watched him fall. Methodically he notched arrows and shot into the struggling ranks. The smoke of the sacrifice rose into the sky.

The ship was burning quicker than it was settling, driving some of the men into the water. Blade-like fins coursed back and forth. It was a scene Aleyn knew he would never forget; men burning, men screaming, men drowning, and men being devoured by monsters of the deep. And over all, Bitias drove arrows into the damned while shouting sanctifications to the god of lightning and thunder, He who had demanded his son.

"As if this were Miry," observed the tillerman sadly, "Mot's domain in the underworld."

The ship sank, its fires hissing into extinction. Charred flotsam lulled in the waves. The sharks feasted; the men of *RearEnd* raised their oars in after toothy jaws nibbled one or two. Bitias stood on the prow, watching the activity until it was complete. Then he crossed to Moloch's empty bench, settled in, and dropped into a death-like sleep.

The tillerman looked to the second officer for direction.

"West for home," Aleyn told him. "Quarter strokes."

T he final leg was into the teeth of a stiff wind. The rowers pulled at their oars, their homeward creep frustrating.

Home, thought Bitias from the bow as he looked over the tiny buildings sprawled over distant Bursa. He'd sworn that Carthage was not his home; it was simply a town into whose service he was sworn. But deep down, he knew such was untrue. Regardless of his intentions, he was a Carthaginian.

As they drew nearer, he sensed Aleyn behind him. The man took a place along the gunnel, looking towards the approaching buildings.

"The harvest is coming in," the second noted. He gave the air a seaman's sniff, nodding to himself. "The year grows old, the winds grow harder. The storms will be on us soon."

Bitias listened to the words of his trusted officer, looked at the city he both loved and hated, and felt innumerable conflicts rise within him. The horrors of the last few days lay within his consciousness like a jagged reef.

"I may have said things, done things..."

"Words and actions drop into the past. They are forgotten." The man studied the distant peaks. "Your sacrifice was for us. *That* will not be forgotten."

"But the blood of the Greeks was not enough. The anger burns within me. Such anger is an abomination against Baal, but..."

"*N'!*" Aleyn waved it away. "Worry not. There are plenty more Greeks in the world."

Bitias looked as if he wished to say more, but *RearEnd* was now approaching the beach.

People had spotted the penteconter's slow advance and had gathered to welcome it home. A somber mood hung in the air; all knew what had taken place the night of Bitias' departure.

The crowd stepped back as the bow ground into the sands. Bitias slipped over the gunnel, eyes scanning the crowd. He spotted Os'sh at a tent above the high-water mark. Women stood at her back, half completed bone bows in their hands. His wife had found her way back into the world.

He noted that High Priest Scylax was not to be seen. For some reason, this relieved him. Something about the man...

The admiral passed through the citizens, not noticing the respectful bows that waked his passage. His eyes were on his wife, who watched his approach with an unreadable expression. His heart broke at the sight of her.

Without a word, he gently took her in his arms. She leaned against him, arms to her sides, returning nothing.

He held her even tighter, crushing her into his chest. Tears soaked into his shoulder. They stood thus for an eternity before she pulled away, returning to her women, returning to the bows.

Aleyn watched his commander standing mute and alone. The gods were capricious in their dealings with men. Had not Bitias given enough? He checked his thoughts before they could go further.

"Second Officer," came a sharp voice. Aleyn turned to find Lord Kotilus striding up, concern written across his face. "Where did *RearEnd* go?"

"Patrol," he replied evenly.

"The council approves any such ventures. Why did not Lord Bitias seek such?"

"You should ask the lord his reasons." Aleyn's expression spoke on how he wished the noble truly would.

"What if the Greeks had come? Fifty of our best men, absent. We would have been helpless."

"The Greeks will not come, not now, and probably not next year." The officer shrugged twin oars from his shoulders. "There are trophies, taken in combat against them. Commander Bitias engaged two penteconters; *'bl*, he sank them both." Aleyn fixed the horsetrader a hard stare. "If unauthorized patrols are so effective, the council should approve more of them. Now, if it pleases my lord, I am to present these trophies to Queen Dido and the council. They are to be offered to Melqart, a sign of thanks for His blessings."

"Bring them to the temple," Kotilus looked across the crowd to where Bitias still stood. "The council will accept them. The queen will not be in attendance."

Aleyn frowned at this. "Is her Majesty unwell?"

"Something of that nature," the lord replied dismissive.

TEN

The queen of Carthage ascended Bursa with slow steps. The winter air was as cold as iron. Even her wrap could not keep it at bay.

Just past the twin temples lay the newly constructed palace. It was functional and simplistic, devoid of any ornamentation. The craftsmen of future generations could enhance its prestige.

She looked it over and felt a little sad. No more would the council meet in Melqart's temple. Like a living thing, the functions of the city were branching out.

The heavy door groaned on its new brass hinges, arresting the attentions of the gathered elders. Lords Mintho and Kotilus were among the membership, while Bitias, to her relief, was not present. Their attention was focused on High Priest Scylax, who had been speaking when she arrived.

A handful of citizens ringed the walls, interested in the day's court. Young Barcas lounged in the corner. She was amazed at how mature he appeared these days, quite the handsome young man. She felt a small surprise at the realization that they were contemporaries; that she, herself, was now eighteen. She felt far older.

Beyond the standing elders, against the far wall, was a crude stone chair. Over the winter, craftsmen would add decorative inlays, turning it into the true throne of a queen.

She chose to stand.

"Ah, Queen Dido," Kotilus greeted. "I am so happy you are well enough to join us. Long has it been since you have attended court.

Currently, our good priest was just outlining the colony's divinacle needs."

The scrawny man nodded carefully. "Aye. It is as I said. The night of the locusts serves as clear indication of our danger. We *must* assemble a temple to Baal, as quickly as possible. If necessary, we should delay work on all other projects until it is complete."

The noble looked to her, yielding the floor to their ruler, as was customary in meetings of the council.

"I have no comment," she replied quietly. She felt tired, her stomach clenched. Her own issue occupied her thoughts.

"Well, let me put forth my own concerns," Mintho launched. "I do not see why a priest of Astarte should be so driven to see Baal served. The God has received his due that night a month ago. His thirst should be sated. Besides, your own temple requires your attention. You have new priestesses who must be directed in their duties, as well as the auxiliary archers."

"Os'sh sees to that now. That task is hers alone. I am done with it."

Scylax argued on, repeating himself. Often, he blended Astarte and Tanit, claiming their support for Baal's needs. Dido remained on the sidelines, her heart not in the debate. Still, she noticed that Scylax seemed nervous. It was as if he had a personal stake in founding Baal's house in Carthage.

Her observations blew apart like chaff before the winter wind; Bitias had pushed through the doors. His beard and hair were curled as an afterthought, his tunic worn and stained with pitch. It was as if he held his work on his new penteconter and his role as elder as of equal importance.

She studied his profile, her heart heavy. He did not appear to notice her at all. It was as if she was not there.

Melqart, he is so beautiful.

Something within her spoke.

Is that why you acted as you did?

"No," she hissed, drawing the attention of those around her. She hugged herself, willing her thoughts to stillness.

"Let us vote," Mintho's voice rose to her as if from the bottom of his well. "Let us vote on the matter of the new temple..."

She watched Bitias' eyes travel from man to man as the vote was taken. His turn came and he nodded. Scylax rotated, following the tally. His expression grew harder.

"...next year," Kotilus opted. "My vote carries the majority. We shall reconsider erecting another temple one year hence. Should we gain a priest in the meanwhile, he can use our other temples on a temporary basis."

"May Tanit forgive you," the slight man muttered. He stalked from the chamber room, giving Bitias wide berth.

"I would like to raise a matter of my own," Kotilus continued. "I would like a month's leave from my duties on the council. I must travel inland to procure horses..."

"I must speak."

Dido blinked. The voice had been hers. She turned ever so slightly, to move Bitias from her perception.

"Yes, Highness," Kotilus prompted, his annoyance barely masked.

Her mouth was dry. Her heart pounded within her ribs like an Assyrian siege ram. She pulled at the memories of her father and of Arherbas, seeking their balance and strength.

"My lady?"

"I have an issue of my own." It was as if her breath would not draw. "I have been long absent from the court. I have struggled with my thoughts." She braced, then forced out the words. "I wish to abdicate my duties as queen. I no longer wish to rule."

Tension made her rock on her feet. She darted a glance about the room. Tetramnestus nodded quietly as if understanding her motives. Mintho and Kotilus exchanged quick glances. And Bitias, when she dared look his way, stared back with fierce intensity.

It was Mintho who cautiously broke the silence.

"Highness, we know you have been unhappy. You have hardly left your hut over the last month."

"I admit my unhappiness. But what I do, I do for Carthage."

"But you are exactly what Carthage needs. You founded her, you made her grow..."

"She grows without me. As you pointed out, a month has passed without me and still she stands. Carthage no longer requires a queen."

Again silence fell as the men considered. This time, it was Kotilus who spoke, his words unsympathetic.

"You cannot abdicate. You are not ill as was your father. You are whole and hale. Under your rule, we have survived every crisis. The locusts. The Greeks. You have bested them all."

"Still," Mintho permitted, "I suppose we could consider her wishes. Relations between ourselves and Tyre are ever improving. Their envoy met with us. They have forwarded priestesses of Astarte, and soon, a priest of Baal. Even though we are technically a colony of exiles, we could always work to make our relationship...more traditional."

"We could have Tyre appoint a governor," someone pointed out, "as was done in Citium."

"That is not the point," Dido burst out. "Kings, queens and governors are bad. They permit power to be concentrated, and concentrated power can be used unwisely. Carthage is a new city; perhaps it can develop new ideas."

"What nature of ideas?" Mintho carefully asked.

"The Greeks rely far more on their councils. When they vote, often they consider the wishes of the citizens. Occasionally, the vote is even extended to them. Hêgêsistratus told me of such things."

"He is a Greek," an elder growled.

"Councils advise rulers," Kotilus hammered out. "They steer their rulers to correct decisions."

"Such is the power of consensus, in which I agree and for which I argue," Dido replied. "Assemblies of men can make bad decisions, but only a ruler can promote evil ones. Councils are far more likely to be wise, and wise government is what is best for Carthage and her people."

The elders of the council considered her words while regarding one other. Mintho looked from man to man as if looking for a solution. Kotilus, on the other hand, studied the ground while thoughtfully rubbing his chin.

"So *Qtn'khn* no longer wishes to be queen."

Bitias's carriage was as disrespectful as his tone. He crossed his arms over his stained tunic.

"The 'Little Priestess' no longer believes in rulers at all," he smirked. "Perhaps even the servants and slaves will get to vote in her utopia."

"Do not be ludicrous," Kotilus snapped. "Perhaps the woman is right. Perhaps it is time for a change."

"Perhaps it is what we wish, or what we prefer," Bitias' glare frosted into place. "But it is not to what we agreed." He stepped into the center of the assembly, eyeing each man. "Perchance you recall that cold morning aboard my pitching boat. All of you, afraid, alone, exiled. And then she stood and spoke, every bit as eloquently as she did today. She told us of a city, one of riches and glory. A city she would found and rule. This city! Carthage!"

A moment to consider them all.

"We agreed to her vision. We gave her our word and our bond. She would rule. We would follow."

He glared at them, in defiance to their years, their wealth, and their power.

"In bequeathing ourselves to her, we formed a pact. An agreement as solid as that of any Canaanite trader. She would lead. We would follow. She would command. We would obey. Such has it been; Carthage has prospered. No man can deny such.

"But now the road becomes hard. Our mighty queen suddenly changes back to a little girl. She speaks charmingly of Greeks and their strange democracies. She tempts you with greater power. Yet it is nothing more than a weak appeal to help her break her oath to us, as ruler to subjects. She seeks permission to abandon us."

"*Lys*, such is not true," Dido flared. "I founded the city. I guided it through its initial crises. But now I feel I should step away, in the manner of a parent freeing a child."

"Many are the ways a parent can give up a child," he snarled.

"Lord Bitias," Kotilus warned, stepping forward. A broad man with muscular shoulders, he had the advantage over his younger counterpart. Yet Bitias' flaming glare checked him like an invisible wall. His finger shot in Dido's direction.

"You wanted to rule. You hungered for it. It made you move against your own brother. The battle between you and he, *rzn* verses *'bny*, nearly toppled Tyre and its empire. Failing there, you used every trick you could think of to get us to this shore, to build this city around you."

Dido felt his flaming hatred curl around her. She accepted it silently.

"It mattered not what lives you destroyed in pursing your goal. Lord Mintho left his family behind. Lord Kotilus lost his position and wealth. Young Barcas, there in the corner, was heir to his family's fleet. And I, too, had a great many things which I gave up for you and your Carthage. But now your *'drtnt*, your passion for the throne cools. Now you wish to back away from what you sought, abandoning us, breaking your word.

"No. We will not accept it."

She looked at him, desperately seeking a trace of the carefree man he'd once been.

"Bitias," she managed.

With set jaw, he advanced on her. The others stood mute, motionless. He grabbed her hand, dragging her across the floor to the far wall with its vast stone seat. He halted short, waving at it dismissively.

"Soon it will be covered with ivory. Soon it will be inlayed with precious stones. Soon men will grovel before it. It is what you sought. And it is what you deserve."

With wiry strength, he shoved her into the throne. Its cold surface leached the warmth from her body. Placing a hand on the great armrests, he leaned forward, trapping her. His voice was low; only she could hear his words.

"You purchased this seat with my son's blood. It shall be yours until your death."

With a swirl he was gone, sweeping across the room and out the door. Silence fell with his passage.

Queen Dido hunched in the great seat for some time, eyes downcast. Finally she found the will to look up. The council had slowly and subtly reformed into a loose half-circle about the throne, as was proper in the court of Tyre.

"Highness," Elder Kotilus began, "I would like a month's leave from my duties on the council. I must travel inland to procure horses..."

The morning was chill. Kotilus lay beneath the throws, his eyes on the tent-cloth overhead. Today he would meet with the Libyan horse traders. His mind spun with details.

"Lord Kotilus," hissed a voice beyond the flap.

"*Y*, what is it, Afsan?" he sighed.

"The men, the warriors and guide." The translator hesitated. "They go."

Kotilus frowned, then rolled out of bed. It was but a moment's work to toss on his tunic before emerging into the pale sunlight.

The tent stood on the slope of a bald ridge. To the north, the chain of mountains dropped eastward to mark distant Carthage. The rising sun played across the plain, shimmering its dusting of frost. His sigh hung visibly in the air.

"Afsan, your words twist like snakes. The men do not go. They have gone." He looked at the matted grass where the party had encamped. "When did this happen?" His eyes narrowed. "Why did I not hear it?"

He saw the wineskin hanging from a tent pole. *Drugged, no doubt.* He rummaged through his baggage. Oddly, all his gold was intact.

His weapons were missing.

He stepped back, shaking his head as he looked over the desolation. Lord Zumar of Tunis had sworn to the loyalty of the men. And now they were gone. He would speak with Queen Dido of this. The Libyans would regret this transgression.

At first he did not notice it, so consumed was he with his thoughts. He felt it before he heard it, a low rumbled that shook the ground like an urn rolling across a ship's deck. He squinted south.

A line crossed the plane, dust trailing in its wake.

"Ah, our trader friends. *'Bl*, I still have gold and wits. We shall ride back to Carthage, Afsan."

The diminutive interpreter remained silent.

As the mass moved closer, it came to Kotilus that these were not horses being herded to trade. The low sun shown across lines of swinging shields. It was a dense formation of men arrayed in tight order. He looked to the native for clarification.

"It is Chieftain Hiarbas," Afsan noted. "During the winter, he summons the men of the villages to train. Each new moon, they meet for three days." Kotilus, distracted by the distant army, overlooked his interpreter's growing nervousness.

As they neared, Kotilus could make out four chariots at the head of the square formation. Distant voices sang through the cold air. As neatly as could be, the rear ranks folded out to form winglike flanks. What had been a tight body of men was now a distance-spanning line. Without breaking step, the army continued forward.

Kotilus respected the handy display of formation shift. It spoke well of Hiarbas' abilities. He reflected upon this pattern and what it might mean. The various races formed their armies as best suited their demeanor. The Assyrians relied on columns of chariots backed by thick formations of foot soldiers. The Scythians with whom he'd traded were more free-form, their army a collection of howling horsemen whirling like the wind. The dour Greeks, all brass and balls, with their thick ranks of armored hoplites. And the Canaanites: Kotilus smiled at this. Canaan's formations were stacks of gold. They paid others to do their fighting.

But this formation was nothing like he'd ever seen. It appeared to be no more than two or three ranks thick; very fragile, from Kotilus' viewpoint. But perhaps that was how Libyans did things. Perhaps when Hiarbas went to war against one of his neighbors, the armies flung their wings out in a peacock's display, as if to awe their opponents with their frontage. It was a curious possibility. Kotilus resolved to ask the chieftain about it the next time they met.

The sun was now up from the horizon, the day burning away as uselessly as a lamp in an empty room. Where were the horse traders? There was much business to see to before nightfall.

Afsan appeared to be on the verge of saying something, yet remained silent.

Now Kotilus frowned. The formation was nearing the foot of their slope. Certainly they would have to wheel soon. He did not wish to think what would happen if the formation rolled right over their tent. He'd suffered indignities enough, and it was not even midday.

The formation began its ascent. The long crane-skinned shields were dazzling in the sun, the spear-tips uniform and erect. The horses hauling Hiarbas' chariot pawed and pranced, his lieutenants rumbling at his side. They seemed to be aimed right for the camp. Right for Kotilus. The ground shook with their approach. The Canaanite trader fought the urge to turn and run.

At a short stone's throw, one of the charioteer's released an undulating cry. The men bellowed its echo, crashing to a halt. Dust swirled uphill, settling across Kotilus.

The silence was deafening.

Chieftain Hiarbas' stirred, the creak of his war platform carrying across the body of silent men. He looked at Kotilus as if not fully seeing him. Finally, he spoke, his voice booming over the rock outcrops and the dry river courses.

Afsan listened carefully. When Hiarbas' words echoed into nothingness, he spoke.

"The Chieftain. There is something you have. You will yield it to him."

Kotilus' frown deepened. He was quite familiar with the bluff and bluster of primitive peoples. Making sure displeasure was clearly visible on his face, he called out, "Canaanites do not yield. Canaanites trade. I will not yield."

Afsan looked at him, as if to confirm his defiance before translating it. His reedy voice drifted across the raised spearpoints.

A long silence met this. Hiarbas never stirred. One of his lieutenants barked out a single word. Four men broke from the ranks, rushing forward. Kotilus was too surprised to move, though Afsan slipped aside.

Two of the men grabbed his arms; their grips were like shackles of iron. The other two studied him for a moment. Together, they dropped their shields and reversed their spears. Then they thrust.

A fire-hardened spear butt took the noble trader in the center of the forehead. As he rocked back, the second butt slammed into his gut, driving him forward. The hardwood rods lashed in, again and again. His beaters worked in perfect harmony. Every blow set him up for the next. A strike to his thigh caved in his legs; he hung from unyielding grips. A moment later, a shaft slapped the side of his face. Now his mouth filled with blood and tooth fragments. It drooled down his front, a crimson splash across his linens.

The beating had stopped. Kotilus did not immediately notice. Pain echoed through his body. He looked up with his good eye, his other puffed shut.

Hiarbas watched dispassionately. Again he spoke. Kotilus knew what he'd said, having heard it once before.

"You must yield this thing to him," Afsan confirmed with a whimper.

Kotilus shook his head, then slowly spat blood.

"Tell that whoreson...Canaanites trade."

There was an old fallen tree nearby. It had stood for long years before age had toppled it. Some of its limbs had fed last night's campfire.

Before he knew what was happening, its rough bark was tearing at his tunic front. He was pinned face down across it. Ruddy hands held him tight.

A moment later, his tunic was flicked up. Cold air played across his exposed ass.

"Melqart...*Bl znh*! Not that!"

One of his tormentors drew phlegm and spat. A moment later, a wet spearbutt pressed against him, a perverted parody of *'yr* and *'bn*. The pressure mounted. Kotilus howled curses but to no avail. With firm resolve, the wood shaft pressed inward, filling him. The pressure grew.

"Be still," Afsan hissed into his ear. "They will cease when you acquiesce."

Kotilus lay motionless, eyes screwed shut, tears burning down his cheeks. Part of him wanted to scream defiantly, to provoke his own death. A greater portion wanted to live.

He became aware of an oscillating creak. Through his lopsided vision, he saw a chariot wheel roll to a stop before him. Almost tenderly, a dark hand cupped his chin, raising his head. He shuddered as his spine bent slightly, bringing renewed awareness to the shaft.

Hiarbas glared down at him like a barbaric god.

"My mother. She is not whore."

Kotilus' eyes widened at his words. The chieftain could understand the language of Canaan. Not fluently, but well enough.

The trader's thoughts went back to the meeting in the *thajma'th*. To himself and Mintho and the endless deadlocks with Hiarbas. Waiting for the boy to bring Elisha's thoughts from the headman's house. Joking with his counterpart. Casually insulting the chieftain, protected by the barrier of language.

Kotilus realized death was near. His pride and tongue had damned him. Should he live to see the sunset, he would be surprised indeed.

Hiarbas nodded gravely, knowing Kotilus was now fully aware of how things stood. His words, when they came, were low and hard. Conqueror's words.

Afsan knelt down into Kotilus' vision, as if to be sure he understood.

"The chieftain wishes Dido. He wishes to marry her. You will make this happen."

Heedless of the pain, Kotilus twisted to look directly at Hiarbas. The chieftain's expression was blank. Kotilus' took a sharp breath of air, words forming.

The wood within him twisted. His lungs emptied in a small shriek.

Afsan looked horrified. "Lord prince! If they break your insides, you will die. You will fill with poison and expire, over many days, in horrible pain. Be still!"

Hiarbas grunted something.

"He asks if you still wish to trade." More heavy murmurs. "He offers you a trade. He trades your Dido for your Carthage. He will come for her a month following the planting festivals. Three months from now. Dido will be his wife. Otherwise he will destroy your city and all within it."

The wheel rolled away. The hand cupping his chin let go. A moment later, the shaft was yanked clear. With care, it was wiped across his back, removing his essence. Only then did the iron hands open. He slid from the log to the ground.

With geometric precision, the army reversed itself. One moment it was facing him, the next, their backs were to him. The ground beneath him shuddered as they descended the hill. Kotilus watched their withdrawal, his body aching from the abuse.

A thousand men swung back into their box formation, not a single step lost.

Kotilus thought of Hêgêsistratus and his seventy-five hoplites. Farmers and sailors, wrapped in bronze. Backed by women who played at being archers.

Pain throbbed through him, slowly overcome by an unsettling fear.

ELEVEN

Three days on the road to Carthage.

They'd left tent and gold. Over Afsan's shoulder was a blanket. Kotilus carried their only knife. Their travel was slow and painful, Afsan supporting the noble as they limped north.

Each evening, Afsan would make his master as comfortable as possible before entering the nearest village in search of food. He would claim to be Chieftain Hiarbas' envoy, bearing directives for the Carthaginians. In that, he was technically truthful. He would bring whatever fare the villagers would provide back to Kotilus. The two would cut their portions with their single knife before huddling beneath the blanket. In the dry air, the cold was biting.

Afsan would chatter encouragement on the way. With ratty beard curled in Canaanite fashion and travel-worn robes, he looked more like a son of the Levant than did Kotilus. The noble limped along, tunic torn and bloody, hair matted, face hazed with pain.

Most of the time, the interpreter would babble about inconsequential things. Often he would speak of someday visiting the great Canaanite cities of Tyre, Sidon, and Byblos. His requests for details of these far-away places were met with grunts but still he persisted.

But other times, his mood would darken.

"What will we tell Queen Dido, Lord? The lady will never willingly marry Chieftain Hiarbas."

"Silence," Kotilus muttered, his mind on his own thoughts.

It was late afternoon on the third day.

"Tunis, Lord! See it there, beyond the fields? The last Libii village! Carthage lays just beyond!"

Kotilus did not look up from his dusty feet.

The village dropped behind them. To the right, the marsh grew closer. Beyond lay the rough forested hills, and then the orderly fields of the settlement.

"We are at the brickworks, Bol. *Lys*, the workers are all in town. Otherwise, we would make a litter and bear you that final short distance."

"I think I bleed, Afsan. Help me to sit for a moment."

Concern in his eyes, the Libyan helped the noble settle on a pile of broken bricks. The older man's head hung down, his breathing heavy.

"Lord, are you unwell?" He laid a comforting hand on the trader's shoulder, leaning forward.

The knife caught him under the chin, driving through his bilingual tongue, through his sinuses, into his brain. In the instant of his death, Afsan regretted that he would never see Tyre.

Kotilus used the knife hilt as a handle to push the crumpling body clear. Wearily he stood, looking down at the small dead man.

"You wished for things of Canaan. Such is what other races call 'Punic Faith'. Fitting that it was your final experience."

With careful movements, Kotilus pulled the little body into a muddy pool. Broken bricks pinned it into the silt's embrace. By the time he was finished, the sun was nearing the western horizon.

He crossed the road and eased into the brush. As much as his body pained him, he would have to go cross-country from this point on. He could not let his presence be known in Carthage.

Not just yet.

The small house was filled with silence.

Os'sh sat in one corner, a bow in her lap. With care, she wrapped its graceful arcs with warm, wet sinew. It creaked softly at the pressure she placed upon it.

Opposite, Bitias threaded cordage, his fingers automatically going through the motions, his mind distant. There were a million things to attend to before his new penteconter was ready.

From the door came a gentle rap.

The couple exchanged glances. Bitias crossed to the door, giving it a wary look. "Who is there?"

"Mintho."

Bitias frowned, yet opened the door. The portly noble stood in the cold darkness.

"You must come with me, Lord Bitias. It is urgent business." He glanced to Os'sh. "Your discretion, please, my lady."

Over her bow, she studied the man before giving a small nod.

Bitias fetched a lion-hide cloak from a peg before slipping into the night.

Mintho did not traverse the main avenue up Bursa. Rather, he cut down an alley before ascending one of the lesser streets. Given the late hour and the hard chill, no one else was about.

Still, Bitias could only smile wryly to himself as they picked their way through the darkness. Carthage was just shy of two years old and already politics formed. He had no desires to become mired in the games of the council. Come Egersis, *RearEnd* would sail.

Atop the summit, the palace thrust its blocky form against the stars. Mintho now left the road, cutting over a wall and through a small garden. There was a long, low building with a series of small doors, cribs for Astarte's new priestesses. Bitias' sharp sense picked up the lingering hint of female musk. He thought of Os'sh and their relationship. Should things not improve, he might consider bestowing a shekel of silver for Astarte's blessing.

Mintho crossed to the rear of the temple of Astarte, gestured to him, and slipped through a small portal. Shaking his head at his own foolishness, Bitias entered.

A good portion of the council was in silent attendance. Bitias nodded his greetings about. Then he realized that Kotilus was sprawled on a bench, bruised and battered. High Priest Scylax bent over him, seeing to his many wounds.

"We are all here," Mintho noted. "Extinguish the lamp."

A Necropolisian darkness fell over them.

"Speak low, my Lord," cautioned Scylax. "The temple of Melqart is next door. We must take pains the holy lord does not overhear. After all, Tetramnestus is little more than Dido's pet."

"I thought you were south, Kotilus," Bitias spoke into the darkness, feeling vaguely foolish. "Buying ponies."

A dry cough. "My trip was...interrupted. Chieftain Hiarbas approached me with the following demand: Either Dido weds him in three month's time, or he pushes us into the sea."

There was a long silence and then hissing, whispering confusion. Every elder tried to speak at once. Bitias slapped blindly at those within reach. Finally order was restored.

"We have no time for debate on this," Kotilus grated. "The chieftain made it clear."

"She will not marry that barbarian," Bitias observed.

Kotilus growled. "We must devise a plan lest we fall to the Libyans."

Silence fell as each man thought long and hard.

It was Scylax's thin voice that eventually broke the spell.

"If I might propose an idea..."

"**I** do not think it is right."

Os'sh's voice was hard in the darkness.

"There is nothing to be done," Bitias replied from his side of the pallet. "It is our only course."

"You could approach Dido like true men. You could inform her of Hiarbas' demands."

"And what would that bring us?"

"She is clever," Os'sh allowed. "She could devise some trickery to safeguard her honor and Carthage."

"No trickery will alter this. Hiarbas will have her in three month's time. It is as certain as the rise of the sun and moon."

A drawn silence came from Os'sh. Finally:

"The idea; was it *Bol Okbr*'s?"

"Scylax? Aye."

"There is something about him." Os'sh's scowl was obvious in the darkness. "Something evil."

Bitias felt his fists clinch. "Do not start. It was Baal's will." A calming pause. "Perhaps we shall have another son someday."

He heard her roll away to face the far wall.

Anger trickled through him, pooling in his belly, keeping sleep at bay. He looked at the unseen roof and thought of the day to follow, and the part he would play in it.

Os'sh was correct. It *was* not right. But it was all that could be done.

The face reflected in the bronze was not the one she remembered.

She ran a finger along her chin. Dark rings underscored her eyes. Her cheekbones were pronounced. Lips that had once smiled at life now pursed.

It came as a shock. She'd looked at her reflection over the years, seeing hair and skin, but never the whole person. In her mind, she was still a carefree nine-year old girl, child of Tyre, darling of King Mattan.

She did not want to enter court today. Taking her throne became harder each time. The issues raised were more and more obtuse, the squabbles more petty. For the first time, she could understand her father's weariness at the end of that day. Yes, part of it had been due to his sickness, but not all.

There was nothing for it. Wishes and regrets were nothing more. She picked up her favorite golden headband, the only constant across her life, and slipped it into place. It shimmered across her forehead like sunset.

From her small royal apartment, the palace was a short distance away, across the grounds. A gardener worked his winter crops, turning the weeds. At sight of her, he bowed respectfully. She did not see him.

She stepped through the rear portal of the royal chamber, blinking at the noise. The room was filled, the council reclining on their cushions and rugs, citizens ringing the walls. Holy Lord Tetramnestus stood near her throne; he gave a respectful nod as she approached.

"What is this all about, old friend?" she asked, nervousness stirring within her. "A sizable portion of Carthage must be here today."

"Lord Kotilus returned early this morning. He brings ill news."

"Why was I not told of this?"

"I only just found out myself. Yet rumors have raced through the community like wildfire."

Dido felt anger flush across her features. Had Kotilus had information, his first stop should have been the palace. The fact that the commoners were more informed than she was galling.

She'd only taken her seat, the chamber bowing respectfully, when a commotion rose at the door. A litter containing Kotilus was carried in. With care, his assistants placed him at the head of the council. Dido could see the bruises, the stiffness of his motions.

She waited until the litter bearers had withdrawn.

"We welcome you back to court, Elder Kotilus. You appear to have suffered great tribulations."

"Aye, Majesty, much has occurred over the past few days."

"Please, recount."

He nodded. "As you wish. As you know, I was on an inland trading mission. I was to meet with representatives of several of the southern tribes to trade gold for horses. I was accompanied by guides and guards supplied by Tunis. Interpreter Afsan was also in attendance.

"We were two days south when disaster struck. Hill tribe raiders fell upon us. With surprise and numbers, they quickly gained advantage. Our fate was sealed when the Tunisians fled, leaving Afsan and myself at their mercy."

An angry murmur swelled through the chamber. Acting as courtier, Tetramnestus stepped forward, shouting for silence. With the return of order, the trader continued.

"I fought ferociously but was soon clubbed down. I can only guess that the raiders, upon seeing my injuries, assumed my demise. When I awoke, my weapons, gold, and supplies were gone."

"And Afsan?" Dido inquired.

"Missing. I have no idea what became of him. Likely the tribesmen mistook him for a Canaanite and took him prisoner. Perhaps a demand for ransom will be forthcoming. If so, I would be honored to pay it myself."

More murmurs, this time in approval. They stilled before the holy lord intervened. Dido waited an appropriate time before speaking.

"We are glad you survived to return to us. I understood you carried dire news from inland. If it concerns these hill tribes, they are a known danger."

"Nay, it does not involve them at all. While the raid was bad, what followed was worse.

"I was bloody, dazed, and alone. So battered was I that I could barely walk. I knew I would never reach Carthage. Hence, I made for Tunis."

"That den of thieves," Lord Bitias snarled. "One hopes those cowardly deserters returned to their roost. We should descend on them and teach them the wages of deceit."

"This is a council meeting, Lord Bitias," Tetramnestus shouted. "Not a committee of war."

"Perhaps it should be," he responded, rousing the onlookers.

"Shall I fetch Hêgêsistratus?" the priest asked Dido quietly.

Dido ignored him. She was Mattan's daughter. She did not stand nor did she shout. She simply waited for the bravado to drain away. Her dark eyes fixed on her ex-lover.

"The council were once offered greater powers," she observed. "They would no longer have offered advice; they would have ruled. But that power was turned down. The rule of monarchs was continued. In that vein, should I desire your opinion, I shall ask for it." Bitias glared hotly but her eyes had moved on. "Elder Kotilus, if you would continue?"

"'Bl, as I said, I limped to Tunis. I did not see those who had abandoned me. They could have been harbored in secret, or simply had quit the area all together. What surprised me was that Chieftain Hiarbas was encamped there."

"Hiarbas? I did not expect him in Tunis until after Egersis and planting. That is when we meet to discuss matters of state."

"It was hunting, not governance, that brought him north. He and his entourage were tracking game in the area and were taking advantage of Lord Zumar's hospitably. The meeting was fortuitous in that it occurred. The outcome was anything but."

"Certainly they treated you well."

"They most certainly did not." Kotilus's dispassion broke to reveal deep anger. "I was treated little better than a travel-worn horse. I was given only the food their servants and slaves rejected. My wounds were left untreated."

Outrage broke across the room. Tetramnestus bellowed until his face purpled. Through it all, Dido sat in disbelief. It seemed to fly in the face of all she'd experienced. The Libyans were primitive, well beneath the Canaanites. But blatant disregard to a neighboring noble in need?

When she could be heard, she asked, "Certainly Lady Takama would come to your aid. She has assisted distressed Canaanites before."

Kotilus cast a dismissive laugh. "She said that men who suffer defeat deserve their lot. That if I wished food and shelter, I should not have given mine to the hill people."

Mintho, ordinarily so moderate, added his thoughts: "They are a wretched, dirty people. They scrabble for stunted crops and feud amongst themselves. It is not that they have no true gods. It is that no god would have them."

"Certainly this is truthful," Bitias noted. "When their caravans call, small items come up missing. We lose all manner of goods from our stores; cordage, pitch, tools, even an oar. Melqart alone knows what those primitives do with such things."

"And the stench," another elder recalled.

"I cannot abide their cooking," Scylax sputtered. "I have heard they often eat meat uncooked, a throwback to their feral natures."

"Enough," Dido cut in, stilling the room. She turned her attention to Kotilus. "You spoke of ill news. What was said?"

"Chieftain Hiarbas is envious of our ways. He sees the growing riches of Carthage, and wishes to curry favor through his own nobles by sharing such with them. Disdainfully, he told me what he intends to forward at our spring meeting.

"He will demand that a number of our nobles venture forth and live with the Libyans. They will reside in grubby little villages for several years each. A like number of their headmen will reside in Carthage."

The body of councilmen leapt to their feet, angry questions filling the air. Like bees, the citizens also became agitated, shouting from their peripheral vantage points. Tetramnestus bellowed ox-like into the chaos.

Dido watched the breakdown from her throne. On the ivory armrests, her fingers trembled.

From the doorway, the shouts suddenly became cries of pain. Hêgêsistratus strode into the room, swinging his spear butt-first, paying little regard to who he struck. He waded to the room's center, casually poking at those who would not still. Soon no one remained who wished to earn a taste of his staff.

"You barbarians," he chided the glowering multitude. "Cannot a weary old man rest his bones in the sun without all hell breaking loose? If you cannot hold your own tongue, perhaps I will be forced to hold it." Nodding into the silence, he turned and bowed to Dido. "My lady?"

"Thank you, general." She turned once more to Kotilus. "No more opinions and conjecture. How many nobles did Chieftain Hiarbas say he would wish quartered inland?"

"Three. Perhaps as many as five."

"Five? That is all?" Kotilus began to sputter but she cut him off. "And what did he say the consequences would be if we did not abide with his wishes?"

"He would gather his army of several thousand trained warriors and drive us into the Upper Sea."

Only Hêgêsistratus' presence prevented another uproar. But even the general showed signs of concern.

She placed a hand to her head, thoughts racing. The gold band felt so cool beneath her fingers.

"If there is one truth," she observed, "it is that Carthage is small. While we might hold off occasional Greek warships and bandit raiders, an all-out assault by the Libyans would tax us greatly. I have done all that I can to avoid ill bargains, but occasionally, ground must be given."

"Do you realize what you say?" Kotilus blurted. "You will send men of Canaan, great men of leaning and culture, to live among the fleas and filth of those savages? You would exile them into that hell?"

"I know full well of what I speak, Lord. They do not ask for the entire council; only four or five nobles."

"That is easy for you to say," Bitias groused. "You are a woman, not among those to be considered."

"Nothing I say from this chair is easy," Dido spat back. "I do not wish to exile good men against their will. However, the balance falls between the goodwill of five and total war, I must chose for the well-being of Carthage."

"Majesty, if I might speak," Mintho asked, pulling himself to his feet. Pudgy and soft, he represented the soft side of cultured living.

"Life in Carthage is difficult. I will admit that. But now, after two years, goods and comforts are finding their way to us. We are on the verge of becoming a true city. And suddenly this mad plan arises. Please do not force me from that which I have worked for. Do not drive me to live among the savages, with their dirt and pain and discomfort. I beg of you, please do not yield."

Dido frowned. "You think of yourself as a man, as a Carthaginian? In the face of discomfort, you quail like a child. *N'*, where is your spine? Canaan did not become great by herding sheep and living in the coastal caves. It beget greatness by hardship and effort. By men taking their ships farther west than any civilized man dared. They willingly faced hardships.

"Now we are faced with a crisis. Five men will be asked to surrender their welfare for the good of their people. A true Carthaginian would not fret over discomfort. A true Carthaginian would not shirk his duty for the larger community. He would sacrifice home, health, and life for his city and his people. The individual is nothing. Carthage is everything."

Silence met her words. There was a moment where she thought she had carried them.

The council exchanged glances. Bitias gave a sad nod.

Something occurs. Sweat broke across her brow. *It was a trap.*

Kotilus stood painfully, his stare hard.

"My Queen, the truth is otherwise. It is not our presence Chieftain Hiarbas desires. It is yours. He demands you join him as his wife in the spring. Otherwise, he will drive us into the sea."

Her breath would not come. The blood pounded in her ears.

"Remember your words," the lord continued, "spoken moments ago. Words as to how a true Carthaginian serves by sacrifice. That the individual is nothing when balanced against Carthage? Can you break your words now? Can you show yourself to be so untrue?"

The throne was ice-cold against her back. A shiver ran through her.

"You must wed Hiarbas. You must leave Carthage and become his wife. Without your sacrifice, all will be lost."

For a moment, she felt faint. Her eyes traveled from one council member to another. In an instant, she could see all truths as they were. Kotilus with his eye on future ascendancy. Bitias, tasting the revenge for his son and finding it sour. Mintho, doing whatever was needed to preserve his position. And Scylax, hovering in the crowd. He was the rotworm of the colony, a creature that lived within it and worked towards its destruction.

Their treachery had been perfect. They had filled the hall with as many citizens as possible. Against the council alone, she might have argued. But the people of Carthage had heard her words. It made little difference that Kotilus had altered his tale. Her very words damned her.

Nothing more could be done. Nothing more could be endured. She left throne and court, striding out the back portal in a swirl of robes. She made it as far as the center of the garden before she sank to the cold soil, face in her hands, sobbing.

TWELVE

Wind wrapped night rain around the royal apartment. Dido lay on her pallet, listening to its moan.

Her horizons were defined by the walls of her dwelling. She'd not returned to court. She'd hardly eaten a thing. The treachery had cut deep.

She thought of the world outside, the place she'd thought she'd known. The streets and structures of her city had taken on an alien quality. The veneer of the commonplace had been stripped away, revealing a land and people she hardly knew.

Over sleepless nights, she thought back to her comfortable apartment in Tyre's palace. She could recall every crack in its walls, every item to its exact placement. In the dark, her hand would reach out for the cup that had always been nearby. Each time her fingers closed on emptiness, her present turmoil would rush in to fill her consciousness again.

She would spend hours remembering, in the greatest details, the two men of her life. Arherbas, with his rumbling power and brushing touch. Her body could recall the most minute details of his caresses.

And Bitias, lost through pride to another woman. His whimsy and passion had made her complete. She could only compare him to the single occasion she had lain with another; Aleyn. And in that, there had been no comparison. Bitias drove his passions like he drove his warship, recklessly headlong.

Thoughts of Bitias added to her torment. Beyond the love, there was also the pit-dweller. Had she agreed to Amilcar's sacrifice only to drive a wedge between Bitias and Os'sh? Or had it been to punish

Bitias for daring to have a life beyond her? Such answers were beyond her; humans are not equipped to judge themselves with absolute honesty. In her state, she could only assume the worst and hate herself all the more.

As the cold days passed, she slowly dropped into the void.

Tetramnestus' dark bulk filled the sunlit portal.

"My lady? Someone requests an audience with you."

Dido stirred on her pallet within the darkened corner.

"Direct them to the court."

"You never attend court." His customary huff. "Chieftain Hiarbas' envoy wishes an audience with you. Specifically."

A sigh. "Usher him in."

"It is not a him." The priest stepped aside. The opening silhouetted a tall woman, a child clinging to her hand.

"Queen Dido? Are you in here?"

"Lady Takama?"

"Aye. I come bearing the wishes of my chieftain. I am the only Libii readily available who speaks Canaanite."

"There was another. *'Bl*, little Afsan. I am afraid we have misplaced him somewhere." Dido stirred as if waking. "I see that you have brought young Patas with you. Are you well, young prince?"

The boy nodded at the woman shrouded in gloom.

"Tetramnestus, is Commander Bitias not testing his new toy this day?"

"The *Shnyshrsh*?"

Dido frowned at the new penteconter's name. Bitias claimed that *SecondOffspring* referred to its place as the second Carthaginian warhull. She thought it might denote Bitias' own personal hopes. The gods smiled upon brashness.

"Aye. Please ensure Patas is permitted aboard for the maiden voyage."

The small boy's face lit up at the thought of sailing on a warship. The holy lord was far less enthusiastic.

"Lord Bitias will not be pleased."

"Remind him that I am still queen. My word is law."

Tetramnestus reluctantly bowed, collected the boy, and departed. Takama watched them go.

"That was a wonderful thing you did. For my son, this will be a golden day."

"I am pleasured to give such a gift to a friend's child."

Takama stepped inside. Dido had thought to call for a chair but the Libyan squatted against the far wall. Somehow, she made the demeaning position appear graceful.

"I would like to talk to you as sister might talk to sister, but the words of my lord take precedence."

"Rid yourself of them," Dido told her.

"I am to tell you that the time of your wedding grows near. When the seas still and the winds cease, Chieftain Hiarbas will come to claim you. He shall come to the beach before Carthage. When he arrives, the wedding will immediately take place. You will then accompany him inland to your new abode."

"I see. Is there anything more?"

"He bids you take heed: he will come at the head of his army to claim you. He will brook no delays." Takama cocked her head slightly, the words now her own. "He knows firsthand of your trickery. He is afraid your wits will be your wings, lifting you clear of his grasp."

"If only it were true. I cannot avoid it. Between your chieftain and my council, I am trapped."

"Are you certain?" asked Takama softly. "There must be a way."

"There is no way," Dido said sharply. Then, more softly, "There is no way."

"This is a bad thing."

The women sat on opposite ends of the room, staring at nothing for a time.

"I am surprised that you agreed to yield Carthage," the Libyan noted.

"I have not yielded my city," Dido corrected. "Merely my freedom."

Takama looked to her in some confusion. "But then you do not know...? You did not realize...?" A sad shake of her head. "Men. The world owes all its hatreds and heartaches to men."

"What do you mean? How does my wedding affect my city?"

"In our culture," the emissary noted, "often diplomacy is sealed with a political wedding. It is used to tie outer regions more closely to the kingdom."

A thought stirred. "How many wives does the Chieftain possess?"

"Five at present. All were diplomatic weddings, binding their villages to his rule. It serves as an oath of fealty."

"But I will still be queen of Carthage. You once told me how women retain the property they bring into marriage. How does this differ?"

"The woman retains rights to it. But in reality, the man generally manages it. Imagine that a woman owns a pasture with a dozen sheep. It is hers to retain and profit from. But who will visit it daily, seeing to the creatures? Who will keep the wolves at bay? The women? Nay, we are tied to our village. Men control our external properties. Just as Chieftain Hiarbas will control Carthage."

"But the council will still rule in my place. I could abdicate, permitting them to select a new ruler."

"The shepherd does not concern himself with the politics of his sheep."

Dido felt her guts knot. "What will become of Carthage?"

"You provide him with ties of legitimacy. He will likely never rule Carthage, not directly. But one of his sons might. The marriage certainly binds your city more closely to Libya. Eventually it may become a Libyan capital, linking the inland with the Canaanite sea routes. Whether this is good or bad, I cannot say. I just can see it happening."

"Then the elders have doomed us. Rather than risk a mortal blow in combat, they have elected to be bled to death slowly. Hiarbas tricked the council, who in turn tricked me. And in the end, brick by brick, life by life, Carthage passes to the Libyans."

Sorrow etched Takama's face. "It is not how I would have wished it, my lady. It is not how things should be done."

Dido did not answer. Lost in the darkness, she mourned her lost city. Tears trickled down her face, her sobs were private. Opposite, Takama could only wait in silence.

Sunlight from the portal moved across the floor, marking the time.

Eventually Dido snuffled, regaining control.

"What of me? What sort of a life shall I live?"

"I suspect you will be taken to the city of Thugga. I hear it is a pleasant place, perched on a hill overlooking a fertile valley. Here the chieftain keeps his wives. They have their own collection of dwellings, one to each. You will maintain your household, just as any wife does for her husband. You will be in charge of its larders, its cleanliness, and its magic."

"And my wifely duties?"

"As I understand it, Hiarbas is rarely in Thugga. Matters of state and the hunt keep him moving across his lands. His needs are often attended by concubines. Once a year, he will spend an evening beneath your roof, reestablishing the bond of matrimony. Such duty he performs with all his wives."

"I see," Dido responded levelly.

Again, time was consumed by the silence. Takama watched the shadows lengthen across the floor.

"What am I to do with myself?"

"Queen Dido, as a wife, there is much that you must see to. There are the amphorae in the loft containing the foodstuffs of the household. The contents and quantities must be carefully monitored. Not a grain can be lost to rodents or to offspring. There is the weaving. There is the household law and household magic, both of which to be established and maintained. Children must be raised and tutored. In very fact, it will be much like ruling Carthage, but smaller."

Dido sat in the darkness, saying nothing.

"And then there is your place in the pecking order of the chieftain's wives. The village fountain will become your council. You will have to make allegiances and ward off your enemies. You will have to seek favor for any offspring the chieftain may bless you with. But you are a strong woman; I am certain that, in time, you will prevail."

No answer came from Dido's gloomy corner. She remained motionless, alone with her thoughts. Time passed.

Eventually Takama stood. "I sense the return of Patas. My time here is nearly over." She looked across to the woman who did not stir. "Queen Dido, you stand above all others, men and women both. I know that you will be a powerful influence over my ruler. But you must come to terms with the world. You *will* wed Hiarbas. And Carthage will be assimilated by the Libii. These are facts you must live with."

At that moment, Tetramnestus returned with Patas. The boy was flushed with excitement. He had felt the power of the gods within the *SecondOffspring*'s planking. He quivered to tell his mother of his adventure. But he had been raised well; he remained deferential in the company of the ruler.

"Patas, you should offer thanks to Queen Dido for the gift she has given you. Such gifts forge great bonds between people."

The boy nodded at his mother's words. With careful grace, he stepped to the center of the room. Takama translated his words.

"Queen Dido of the Carthaginians, I thank you for the kindness you have done me. I thank you for gift you bestowed." He settled to his knees, bowing to the floor before her. "Please accept this gift in return. It is an item I have treasured most. I present it to you in gratitude."

When he stood, a small object remained in the floor, his offering. He returned to his mother, who gave Dido her own respectful bow. The two departed.

The holy lord, uncomfortable with Dido's prolonged silence, drifted away.

She remained on her pallet, looking at the boy's token of gratitude. The light of the setting sun played along the knife's edge, bringing out the luster of its carved ivory handle.

The moon rose, filling the apartment with blue light.

Holding perfectly still, concentrating, Dido could still detect Takama's earthy scent, lingering long after her departure. In her friend, she saw power she could respect and a peace she could never obtain.

Something drew her attention to the opposite wall. Curiosity overcame lethargic momentum; she climbed from her pallet and drifted across the room. There, scratched into the wall, was the sign of Tanit. The sign of fertility magic, peace and prosperity. Clearly her guest had placed the symbol while Dido had drifted in depression. She had sought to bring positive magic into Dido's life, casting this small spell to help her friend.

Dido looked at the symbol. In it was acceptance. A reward for surrender before a world that had to be.

Her eyes were black pits in the darkness.

"You *will* wed Hiarbas." Takama's words echoed in her mind. "Carthage will be assimilated by the Libii. These are facts you must live with."

And understanding came to her. She nodded to herself in acceptance.

With care, she brought the gift knife forth, carefully scraping at the symbol until no trace of it remained.

"My Queen," Lord Kotilus exclaimed in surprise. "It is an honor that you attend the council. It was our understanding that you were still unwell."

She took no heed of the noble's words. With a regal grace, she stepped to her throne and settled within.

Holy Lord Tetramnestus knew her best, so the change was most striking to him. Her cheekbones were still pronounced, her frame gaunt. Such were the ravages of angst. But her eyes. Beneath the golden headband, the eyes shimmered with wisdom. It was the vision of a true ruler.

"The seas calm, my lady," Kotilus prattled on. "The world warms. I believe the time of storms is ended."

Dido did not respond. It was not her duty to acknowledge the obvious. Lord Kotilus came to this same conclusion. He shut up.

She looked to Tetramnestus. "Holy Lord?"

He gave a slight bow. "With the Lady's grace, I deem Egersis to be upon us. The ceremony should take place in three days."

She signaled acceptance. Looking to the gathered elders, she asked, "What business faces the court this day?"

Tetramnestus replied, loudly for all. "General Hêgêsistratus brings forth a critical matter." In the back of the hall, the old Greek stood.

"My lady, our forward post has observed activity around the Tunis. Shelters have been erected. Men drill. Hiarbas' wedding army assembles."

"I see," Dido replied. "Is the Chieftain present?"

"As of yet, we think not. Lesser chariots have been observed, but none with four chargers. However, a great tent has been raised. His arrival seems imminent."

The ruler nodded. "Have a runner dispatched to Tunis. Seek out Lord Zumar. His wife can translate. Tell him that should Chieftain Hiarbas arrive in time, it would be fitting for our wedding to coincide with Egersis."

"So the wedding shall take place?" Kotilus inquired casually.

"Of course it shall," Dido responded. "I have agreed to yield. But there are a number of details that must be seen to." Her eyes went to the old Greek. "General Hêgêsistratus, my wedding day will require a fitting display of honor and dignity. For that, I will require an honor guard to be drawn up, a fitting backdrop to the festivities. How many men can you put into service?"

The mercenary general scratched his chin. "We have armor enough for seventy-five men. There are a scattering of shields and leather armors available as well. For combat, I would press them into service as secondary ranks. But for a wedding ceremony..."

"I want every suit used, including the partials. Place them in the background where they can lend numbers while concealing their haphazard nature. And as this day is so important, I want only your best men in the ranks to represent me. I cannot afford to have some farm boy drop a shield or trip over his spear. Such would be a bad omen."

"Certainly my crews will be exempt from this order," Bitias observed. "I want to have my warships out as soon as the service concludes. We need to be in the straits north of Sicily before the Greek transports run west."

"*RearEnd* and *SecondOffspring* will be arrayed on the beach," Dido decreed. "Unmanned and on display."

"Good," Hêgêsistratus noted. "Bitias and his men have trained the longest. They were my primary candidates for the honor guard."

"But I have my duties," the admiral blustered. "Many prizes will slip by if we do not gain our position."

"You were paramount in seeing that this day came," Dido replied coolly. "It is only fitting you be here to witness it."

A flush came to Bitias' face. Without a word, he settled amid the elders.

"And Holy Lord Tetramnestus; a day this critical requires a sacrifice. I shall wish to make a burnt-offering of an ox. I shall wish it done as Hiarbas approaches, to gain the blessings of the gods."

"I will need assistance with this service. Probably two apprentices. As per the law of sacrifice, that would be ten silver shekels per man."

"You may claim such from my accounts. But I wish a large bonfire, so as better to gain the gods' attention."

"For an ox, tricky." The holy lord scratched his shaven head in professional calculation. "It is difficult to get heavier animals into the center of large pyres. A ramp will have to be constructed."

"We can build it," a shipwright cut in from the back of the hall. "We have much leftover materials from constructing *SecondOffspring*. It would be easy to assemble such, and is small repayment for the new lives you have given us all."

Dido bestowed a regal smile. "Thank you, my friend. The holy lord will give you needed details." Her lips pursed momentarily. "High Priest Scylax?"

The hall grew silent. Tetramnestus frowned, then repeated her summons with a booming voice.

"Aye," the wizened priest stood reluctantly. He flinched before her gaze, a dog expecting punishment.

"After Chieftain Hiarbas arrives, the wedding will immediately take place. Following that, there will be much time before evening falls and the main festivities of Egersis begin. There must be games and merriment provided during the day. Holy Lord Tetramnestus will arrange for the more minor amusements. But to you, I place the organization of an archery contest between the women."

"But Lady Os'sh now trains the women. It would be her place..."

"The lady has shown her own skill with the new Scythian bows. She cannot compete if she also judges. Further, the women of

ROBERT RAYMOND

Carthage will require a great prize to motivate them. As they all seek the blessing of Astarte, you shall reward she who has the keenest eye and sharpest skill a special blessing."

A murmur went through the court at this. Astarte's blessing would be a wondrous thing for a household to gain. There was no doubt that practice on the bows would immediately commence, and that the competition would be well attended.

Lord Kotilus half-rose off the carpet. "There is an issue that needs to be raised."

The queen gave sign for him to continue.

"With your wedding, you will become Chieftain Hiarbas' woman, living far away. While Carthage exists from your efforts alone, it must continue. Your rule from a distance will not benefit us."

"What would you replace me with? The representative rule of the council alone?"

"Such is not in our interests. The Canaanites have been ruled by monarchs over long centuries. We are not Greeks, to rely on voting and consensus. We rely on counseling a strong leader. In that, we are desirous to maintain the old ways."

"Meaning...?"

"Meaning that your wedding will signify your abdication. The council will select a new ruler. A new line of rulers shall be established."

In the ring of onlookers, young Barcas gave the slightest of nods. Dido smiled to herself. How clear Kotilus' ploy was. The elder was a powerful member of the council. He could gain much support for elevating Barcas to king. Clearly the youth was the ideal candidate. He'd been schooled with her and Pumayyaton. He attended Tyre's court regularly. He had served as envoy. His lineage was pure. And he was handsome and charming, a natural king if ever there was.

But she could see beyond this. Kotilus might have influence over the council, but there was a natural instinct among its members to check any elder who became too powerful. Yet if he supported Barcas and won him the throne, he would gain the king's favor and influence. Indirectly, he would rule Carthage.

Dido chose her words carefully.

"We thank you, Lord, for your concerns for your city. Indeed, I will not be able to rule from my distant new home. Let us agree, queen to council, that a new ruler will be selected upon the moment my marriage is finalized. No replacement may be assigned before then."

The elders looked to each other and voiced affirmation. The pact was agreed to.

"Is there any further business that requires my attention?"

"Nothing significant, Majesty," Tetramnestus replied. "There is a discussion scheduled concerning the construction of an additional granary. The matter is hardly ready for any decision at this point."

"Then I shall retire. There is much for me to do in preparation for my wedding."

She stood, as did the council, who bowed with courtly courtesy.

THIRTEEN

"**M**y Lady Dido," Tetramnestus greeted, bustling though the temple hubbub. "How good it is to see you. Forgive the confusion. With Egersis falling tomorrow and Hiarbas close at hand, there is just so much to do."

"I understand, my friend. I came to you with two wishes. I was hoping you could assist me."

"But of course!" Tetramnestus' attention focused upon her. "You are my queen. You raised me from a simple aide and bestowed all this to me. I would give you my life."

"Nothing so drastic. My first request—may I have Melqart's house cleared for a short while? I wish to pray to the god of our city in seclusion."

"I trust you will not take after that fool Scylax. You must recognize that Melqart will be with you, where ever you may go."

"That I know. I wish to be with Him in the sanctity of His house one final time."

"I will clear the temple at once. And your second request?"

"I find myself in great anxiety over my coming marriage. I fear it might have a negative impact. Some *hul gil* would help settle my nerves for what I shall be called upon to do."

"Of course. I shall have Os'sh prepare several portions for you. One for tomorrow, if you feel the need. The others for events in the days to follow."

"Thank you, dear Tetramnestus. You have given me all that I need."

He bowed before turning to shoo the apprentices out.

Bitias stood on the beach, facing into the bay's breeze. It carried the heavy smell of oil soaking the wood of the nearby pyre. All was in readiness.

Observers had dashed into town at dawn, reporting that Hiarbas' army was on the move.

The main avenue down Bursa thronged with citizens. Temple attendants moved up and down the center of the street, keeping a passageway open for Dido's use. Their staffs were quick to correct those who trespassed.

Vendors moved about, selling water, fruits, and sweets. Trained monkeys performed tricks for tin shekels. Music trilled and trumpets blared. The excitement of the marriage and Egersis was sweeping the crowds.

"Aye, there they are," Hêgêsistratus noted.

Bitias looked down the coastal road. There, just clearing the marsh trees, came the Libyans in road order. In the van rolled Hiarbas' chariot, its four-horse team prancing in their harnesses. Immediately behind him marched his lieutenants, festooned in all manner of colorful wraps. And then his infantry, their shields and spears swinging with their pace.

The general sighed. "All right, you barbarians. Let us give these savages their eye-full. Helms up."

Bitias hated the closeness of his narrow helmet. It closed off the breeze and made his breath resonate in his ears. Give him an open deck any day.

Hêgêsistratus dressed their lines. Given the weight of their shields and the potential length of the ceremony, they were permitted to lean them against their left thighs. In their right hands were their twin spears. The salty breeze raised a subtle whistle off their iron tips.

There came an expectant sigh from the crowd. Turning his head slightly, Bitias could make out Tetramnestus, flanked by his apprentices, descending the hill. An ox docilely followed on a line. The holy lord's garment was stained with old blood.

Was that the clothing you wore when you took Amilcar? Bitias' grip tightened on his spears. Yet just as quickly came a calmer reflection: *Baal demanded the sacrifice. The priest was simply his tool.*

His gaze went over to his twin penteconters. *The sooner we put out, the better. The open sea is simple and honest. And it will bring welcome distance between Os'sh and myself.*

His attention returned at the rush of flames. An apprentice had lit the pyre with a torch. He rushed back to help Tetramnestus and the other force the ox up the ramp. It shied from the edge where the flames licked. The apprentices calmed the beast while their holy lord called down the gods' favor. From his linens, he drew forth a hooked knife; a quick slash and the beast collapsed at ramp-edge. It was the work of a moment to butcher the animal, withdrawing 300 shekel-weight of meat for the temple's larder as was his due. The steaming red flesh was placed in the silver bowls of the apprentices. This done, a final prayer was sent skyward. Taking the fallen animal by the hooves, they tipped it over the edge. Fueled by the fats, the flames leapt and crackled. The smell of burning meat washed over the armored men.

"Melqart's bile, but that makes me hungry," someone muttered from the ranks. Hêgêsistratus glared back at his charges but the helmets concealed the speaker's identity.

The Libyans were now closer. A small boy had detached from their ranks, his arms laden with a carved ivory box. Exotic pelts lay draped across his arms. He was their giftbearer. With a smile, he advanced before the army.

It was not a sound, but rather the lack of one, that gained Bitias' attention. The crowd had fallen silent. Heedless of Hêgêsistratus' ire, he turned towards Bursa. Many of the honor guard did likewise.

Queen Dido descended the avenue, flanked by Phoenix and Yzebel. The people of Carthage fell back in respect at their ruler's passage.

She was radiant.

Simple white linens fell like mist along the curves of her breasts. Her hands, almost lost in the voluminous sleeves, were clasped demurely before her. Her cheekbones and jawline were hardened by the weeks of self-denial, making her appear mature beyond her years. Beneath the golden headband, the midnight eyes were calm.

Bitias gawked. Here, in physical manifestation, he saw the true Dido, the Elisha he had loved. Her power, her convictions, and her truths all combined within her austere beauty. It was as if her very soul walked the earth.

Where the avenue met the sands, her two companions stepped away, letting her proceed alone.

Bitias glanced south. At the sight of Dido, the army had stopped on its own accord. Hiarbas' smile was predatory. In contrast, the gift bearer's expression was simple wonder.

She passed down the line of the honor guard, eyes fixed on her husband-to-be. The men fell into perfect order in her presence. Bitias watched her pass, taking in every detail of her beauty. Her slight stumble was discordant.

She is drugged. She has ingested hul gil.

At that, he felt a pang of guilt for his role in the deception.

Dido continued onward. For a moment, Bitias thought the drug had caused her to sway off course. Her small foot came down on the pyre's ramp. Carefully balancing, she ascended.

"She is mistaken," Bitias blurted.

"Hold," Hêgêsistratus commanded, watching the girl.

She reached the top of the ramp. The superheated updraft rippled her linens. Her hair swirled about her head, checked only by the headband. Her hands came up, parted. Something flashed in her right fist; the knife with the delicate ivory handle.

"Elisha," Bitias called, stepping from the ranks. Without looking, Hêgêsistratus thrust his spear horizontal. The blade tip slid between helm and corslet, pricking Bitias' throat.

"Advance and die, Lord," came the simple threat. "She has picked her path."

Cold iron to his throat, the admiral could but watch. She shouted something into the sky, something lost in the roar of the flames. Then the knife ripped down. Again. And again.

Her linens were scarlet. She slowly hunched forward over the clenched hilt. The updraft rippled her hair like a pendant. Bitias caught a final glimpse of the perfect jawline and delicate cheek. An instant later, she toppled over the lip. The flames roiled.

FIRE AND BRONZE

Silence fell over Carthage. It was broken only by the crackle of the pyre and the bellows of the berserk chieftain.

The Epilogue

It ended as quickly as it began.

One moment, Bitias' struggled against an endless river of Libyan warriors. The next, the broken remnants were streaming south, discarded shields and spears littering the ground. Before the hoplites lay a wall of corpses, waist high.

Bitias let his crimson spearpoint jab into the ground. His battered hoplon slipped from his numb fingers. He was spattered with gore but ignored its crusting embrace, content just to fill his lungs with sweet air. A moment later, the bronze helmet was off.

Y! he thought. *To be alive.*

Around him, the others returned to their senses, no longer a line of warriors. Just men. One or two joked. Another stood in mute shock, examining a bloody gash down the length of his arm.

Now women were among the men, bows tucked over shoulders, passing out festival wineskins that were voraciously emptied. Bitias squinted along the line, counting only five comrades laying amid the piles of dead. Clearly the armor had made the difference.

He began wandering along the ridgeline of carnage. Every so often, he would pat a fellow warrior on the shoulder, marveling at the life beneath his touch.

Aleyn stood with a wineskin, peering in awe at the smoking pyre. "Did you see what she did," he murmured. "Into the flames. Just like that. Into the flames."

"Does wine remain," Bitias inquired, "or are you just going to gesture with it all day?"

"Bitias...Bitias!" His second blinked as if waking. "'*Bl*, some remains." He passed the skin across. It cut through the grit in Bitias' throat like nectar.

Aleyn looked across the battlefield, seeing it as if for the first time.

"Y, look there. Is that not amazing?"

A wrecked chariot lay where the bodies where thickest. Standing at the summit, a single hoplite rammed his spear again and again into the body of the dead chieftain.

"Is that not Lord Kotilus?"

Bitias squinted. "Aye, I think you are right. See, here comes Mintho. He leads him away."

"I thought nobles were beyond such things."

"Nobles are men. And men are men."

"Men. The Libyans fielded so many. Do you...," a haunted glance, "do you think they might return?"

"No. Chieftain Hiarbas has several sons. Here, rule does not go to the eldest. Rather, it is split among the male offspring. His kingdom will fragment. It will be a long time before they can mass against us again."

"That is good," his officer replied. "I would rather not go through that a second time."

A commotion drew Bitias' attention. "Something occurs near the bay. Come."

The Libyans who had attempted to outflank the hoplites had come under withering fire from the women archers. A large number of them had taken shelter behind the hull of *SecondOffspring*. When the main Libyan host had broken, they found themselves trapped by the Carthaginians. Mortally afraid of the bronze men, they groveled against the planks of the penteconter. The defenders smiled to one another, hefting their spears. Women formed up behind them, bows tensing.

"Enough," Bitias shouted, pushing through the ranks. Placing himself between the two groups, he looked over the natives. He almost failed to recognize Lord Zumar of Tunis. Shivering in fright, clutching his arm where a shaft protruded, he was a long way from the proud headsman who had given nothing to the Canaanites save impudence.

"I grant you your life," Bitias declared. "I give you to your wife and your son. Return to your village. But never forget this day."

The man did not understand the words but he knew the gift he'd been given. Kneeling full upon the bloody sands, he paid homage to his savior.

Some of the Carthaginians grumbled angrily at this. Bitias was well-versed in controlling men.

"You three—escort these men to our border. Do not harass them. Providing safe passage will show our compassion. And the five of you—fetch a cart. Take twenty of their dead to our border as well. Array their bodies high in the branches of trees for the carrion birds to feast upon. This will show our resolve."

There were some mutters but his orders were carried out. He was a noble, they the common people. Such was the way of it.

To the rest, he issued a final command. "Drag the remaining Libyans north along the beach. Build a mound of their dead. The priests will be along shortly, bearing oil and torches. The gods reward those who leave bodies to rot with plague."

As the men around him fell to work, a voice sounded to his rear.

"You are wasted on that boat, Bitias. You should consider becoming my second."

"Thank you, but no, Hêgêsistratus," he replied without turning. "My battlefields are cleaner. The bodies sink."

"*Y*, you barbarians. You do not grasp civilized concepts. Warfare is a craft. And this is how a craftsman puts away his tools."

"You are mad, old man."

"*'Bl*. Mad or sane, I bring you information. Carthage lost six men today."

"Six? But I only counted five among the fallen."

"Not all the dead were on the line. High Priest Scylax fell, struck through the throat by an arrow. As nice a bit of bowmanship as you might ever see."

"But the Libyans did not have missile weapons on the field..."

"Other matters of more importance. The council meets."

"I am certain that they will. There will be much discussion concerning these events."

"Not will. Are." Hêgêsistratus' hard eyes held Bitias. "Right now.

They stand upwind of the fallen, so as not to smell the blood. But meet they do." A pause. "As an elder, you should be there."

Bitias nodded at the man's urgency. As directed, he found them upwind of the carnage and flies. A assemblage of elders, their cultured ways a contrast to their blood-streaked armor. Their ring was exclusive.

Not all the men were elders. Barcas was in attendance, Kotilus' hand upon his shoulder.

Coming as he was from the corpses, the words carried downwind to him.

"...we represent a majority of the council. By logic, anything we agree upon becomes law. We need not bother the others. And so I would like you to consider young Barcas..."

"Consider him for what?" Bitias asked with false naiveté. To his credit, Kotilus maintained his innocent air. Mintho started as if goosed.

"Nothing more than a municipal matter," Kotilus assured him. When it became clear that Bitias wasn't leaving, he added, "Dido cast herself into the flames. Carthage requires a new ruler. It should be clear to all that Barcas would make an excellent choice."

"It is so certain that you do not wish it debated against the full council? Is this how it is to be done? Gather a majority of elders under some rock and pass new laws?"

"That is not it at all, Bitias," Kotilus countered. "The other elders are exhausted. There is no need to concern them on a largely automatic issue."

"Largely automatic? Exclusionary, more the like. As for Barcas, he can hardly pull an oar or hold a shield. Has he some hidden attribute I know not of?"

"I can wield a spear," Barcas replied hotly. "I did so on Cyprus when I chopped your second officer to pieces."

"I understand that he had it coming," Bitias kept his voice level. "Just as I understand that you had help. Did the old Greek hold him still while you stuck him?"

"I struck him down on my own," the young man rebutted, angered at how close Bitias had landed to the mark. His hands shifted dangerously on his spear shaft. "And if I can strike down one sailor whoreson, it stands I could strike down another!"

"Stand fast, Barcas," Kotilus ordered. His attention went over to the admiral. "Lord Bitias, why do you stand in opposition? Our city needs a ruler. The throne will be filled. But if you feel otherwise, go ahead. Run screaming down the beach. Gather the remaining elders. In will matter not. The majority has decided."

Bitias looked over the blood-splashed men. Kotilus' words were correct; they held a majority. There was no way around it.

Dido would know what to do.

Bitias found himself already feeling her loss. Then another thought struck him.

Perhaps Dido did know what to do. Perhaps she had already done it.

"I shall not address you as King Barcas," Bitias grinned. "I never will."

"Well, who shall be king, if not me?" the young noble sneered. "You honestly think I will address *you* as King Bitias?"

"No," Bitias replied, his confidence growing. "No man among us shall be called king." He laughed into their grimy faces.

"Bitias," Kotilus warned, "Your petulance grows tiring."

"Does it? Do you not see, my plotting friend? Queen Dido has beaten you at your own game. Recall the words to which you agreed, the words for her abdication."

"A new ruler would be selected upon the moment her marriage was finalized," Mintho dully recounted. "No replacement may be assigned before then."

"So?" Barcas demanded.

"So," Bitias calmly nodded to the smoldering pyre. "She never married. She threw herself into the fire before any service could be conducted." His smile was hard. "She'd grown to dislike the power a ruler wields. She wanted to try something different; rule by council, perhaps. You would not agree, so she tricked you into it."

"That was not her meaning," Kotilus growled. To this, Mintho shook his head sadly.

"Those were her words. Words to which we agreed." He stepped back from the circle. "Lord Bitias is right. There cannot be a new ruler selected. There never will be. In our haste to see her gone, we made it so."

Kotilus argued the matter, but the elders were edging from the ring, distancing themselves. They knew when a battle was lost.

In the end, Kotilus had little more than a dark glare for Bitias. He stalked away, Barcas in tow.

Bitias watched them go. Hard looks mattered not. As soon as he could wash the blood from his skin and assemble his crews, *RearEnd* and *SecondOffspring* would be away.

He crossed the beach but drew up short.

Os'sh stood on a sand dune, watching him. In her right hand hung her stocky Scythian bow.

He approached carefully. Her large brown eyes followed him, offering nothing. Finally he stood close, seeing her as if for the first time.

His arms brought her gently to him. He felt her lungs expand, her heart beat. He waited for an eternity.

The bow dropped to the sands. Her strong arms wrapping around him, hugging him fiercely.

In that moment, he found hope.

Elisha's Life and Times

Shared among those who read earlier drafts of this effort was the question: "How much of this really happened?"

Like all good questions, this one is difficult to answer. The legends of Elisha and the founding of Carthage (or *Qrthdsht*) are based, largely, on the recorded histories of races that held the Phoenicians in less-than-admirable esteem. True, they were bold traders and extraordinary sailors that reached Briton and circumnavigated Africa. On the other side of the coin, they were sharp wheeler-dealers who could become slavers at the drop of a hat. In *The Histories*, Herodotus places the origins of the Greek/Persian wars squarely upon them: a Phoenician ship calls upon Argos, the merchants conducting orderly trade with the locals. But then, "...there came down to the beach a number of women, and among them the daughter of the king, who was, they say, agreeing in this with the Greeks, Io, the child of Inachus. The women were standing by the stern of the ship intent upon their purchases, when the Phoenicians, with a general shout, rushed upon them. The greater part made their escape, but some were seized and carried off. Io herself was among these captives..."

History is indeed written by the victors. Tyre was destroyed by Alexander in 332 BC; Carthage by the Romans in 146 BC. Whatever truth might have existed concerning Elisha was likely lost with those cities. All that remains are the legends.

We do know of King Mattan II of Tyre, whose short rule lasted from 829-821 BC. His son Pumayyaton took the throne at age eleven, ruling until 774 BC. Early in his reign, a feud erupted between himself and his sister, Elisha, who was now the wife of Arherbas, high priest of the temple of Melqart. The nobles aligned themselves behind her, while Pumayyaton gained the support of the commoners. It is generally held that Pumayyaton murdered Arherbas inside the temple, at which point Elisha's coup failed. And here, the uncertainty begins.

One story has Elisha fleeing Tyre in a small colonizing fleet. In looking at that version, questions crop up. It seems like a rather extensive fall-back plan. Something of this scale would be impossible to conceal and easy to prevent. One can suppose an alternative to this story, perhaps where her merchant princes seize the port and quickly ready their evacuation fleet. Perhaps.

The more popular story has Elisha and her nobles forced to sail to the mainland to recover the wealth of her dead husband (after his ghost tells her where it has been hidden). Returning across the narrow straits, she tosses the gold into the sea, blackmailing the crew to join her. The gold, of course, is hidden. And here crops up another headache—if there is enough wealth to drive Pumayyaton to have it fetched, it seems like rather a lot for one girl (or even a number of men) to toss overboard. Frankly, gold is heavy. Further, on the small open ships of the time, concealing such wealth would be difficult. Still, this scenario had a certain panache I found redeemable, and so I did my best to work it into the plot.

But one begins to see the pattern. Phoenicians bickering among themselves, disrespectful of blood ties and the sanctity of the temple, relying on "tricks" to win. They are the villains you love to hate.

Incidentally, among the exiles was one "Bitias", an admiral, and one "Barcas". The later is particularly important as his decedents would include Hamilcar and Hannibal Barca, generals who would devil the Romans six hundred years later.

It is fairly certain the exiles landed in Cyprus. Given the routes of the time, that island was a good haven to pause at before continuing west. Curiously, it was an early exporter of opium (*hul gil*) which eventually spread to the far east (rather than the reverse, as is commonly supposed). The practices of its temple of Astarte come to us from Herodotus. And it is here, according to legend, that Elisha somehow stole away eighty women from the temple. Exactly how this took place, again, is lost. In looking at the requirements of colonization (and given my earlier choice), I had her get away with far more than that; the farmers and craftsmen her colony would need.

Which brings us to Carthage and the most famous Elisha myth; the oxhide. To modern-day Tunisians, this is their equivalent to the Dutch purchasing the island of New York for a handful of trinkets. Again, it is the "myth with the moral", a warning that when you deal with Phoenicians, you had better read the fine print.

The final foundation myth centers around her death, that of stabbing herself and plunging into the fire. Of this event, little is known save the occasional reference to the Berber chieftain demanding the Carthaginian nobles produce Dido (as she is now called) to be his wife. They trick her with their supposed reluctance of a cultural-exchange with the natives, all the while spooling her enough rope to hang herself. She talks herself into a corner and, with honor to her late husband, dies on the pyre.

There are variations, of course. In Virgil's *Aeneid*, a wandering Aeneas wins the heart of Queen Dido, but the gods force him to continue on his quest to found Rome. Broken-hearted, she stabs herself and plunges into the flames. For the Romans, it serves as an explanation as to why the Carthaginians hate them so much. Hollywood rewrites are nothing new.

But within all the myth, there must be a grain of truth. Death by self-immolation became a cultural thread of the Carthaginians. Losing generals killed themselves thus. When Carthage fell to the Romans, Hasdrubal's wife threw herself into the flames. Clearly, something had set that pattern into motion.

Moving beyond the Elisha/Dido myths, it is curious to examine the manner Carthaginian culture deviates from its Phoenician ancestry. The most noticeable of these is the reemergence of child sacrifice. It was practiced very rarely by the Phoenicians. In fact, by Elisha's time, it had been largely abolished. Yet something caused the colonists, on their alien coast, to bring it forth once again in times of great need. Sometimes, hundreds of children would be put to death. Often, when nobles were commanded to produce their offspring, they would purchase children from the slums to take the place of their own. From the summit of Byrsa Hill, trumpets would bellow and drums beat, to mask the sounds of industrious infanticide.

Something caused this grim cultural idiosyncrasy to emerge. In my fiction, I tied it to the sacrifice of Amilcar and the death of the locusts.

Other foundations of the Carthaginians were laid. They differed from the ancestors in governance. While tyrants might occasionally rule, there were no lines of kings. Rather, the council of elders governed, often with rather mixed results. Occasionally, outspoken members of the opposition might be beaten to death with chamber benches. Very few would object to such occurrences in our own congress. It would certainly liven up C-Span.

Lastly, there is the emergence of Tanit. Her growth is tied to Carthage, but her origins are unclear. She appears to be a replacement of Astarte. The link between her symbol and that of the Egyptian Anhk is purely speculation, but interesting, given that the native Berbers are held to have migrated west from Egypt. In this story, one assumes that Scylax's associates continue their awareness of Tanit until she rises to popularity some hundred years later.

Hoplites, with their round shields and tight formations, would rule battlefields for centuries. Ship rams would revolutionize sea warfare in the Mediterranean and light off an arms-race (in a literal sense, as designers attempted to pack more and more oar banks into their hulls). Both weapons were just coming into play at the time of this story. My right as a storyteller permits me to attribute them to Hêgêsistratus and Bitias. Something had to give the early Carthaginians the edge.

Special thanks goes to Dr. Mark McMenamin's wonderful *Concise Phoenician-English English-Phoenician Dictionary*, as well as his *Introduction to Phoenician Grammar*. Any twisted misuse of the language is my fault entirely. Also helpful was the fabulous Phoenician website hosted by Salim Khalaf (currently at http://phoenicia.org). He was most kind in answering my questions, and his site was a godsend at 2am when some obscure Canaanite factoid was needed. And deepest thanks must be given to Hammi Hassen, who guided us across the length and breadth of Tunisia.

To stand on the summit of Byrsa Hill, looking out over the bay at the distant headlands, was something that will stay with me forever.

Also earning laurels are my agent, Jake Elwell, who supported this project from the start. And appreciation is also due to Dwight Zimmerman, my editor, who forced me to take out 95 percent of the Phoenician words I'd used. As much as it pains me to admit it, it's a far smoother read this way.

All in all, very few hard facts are known about Elisha/Dido. She was a woman who confronted the authority of a male-dominated world, who founded a "new city" on an inhospitable coast, one which would eventually challenge the Romans for world domination. She relied on her wits and clung to her honor. While the details of her life are lost, her story comes to us in the echoes of history.

ROBERT RAYMOND's first book, *Don't Jettison Medicine*, was aimed at the health care professional in crisis. *Fire and Bronze* is his first historical fiction, inspired in part by his journeys across Tunisia. He is currently working on a second novel, also a historical fiction, centered in Egypt. When not visualizing the ancient world, he lives in Central Florida with his wife, Jane, and cat, Princeton.